Summer Love Puppy

Have a Hart Romance #6

The Hart Family

Rachelle Ayala
Amiga Brook Press

>>><<<

Copyright © 2017 by Rachelle Ayala
All rights reserved.

ISBN-13: 978-1977685315
ISBN-10: 1977685315

No part of this book may be used or reproduced in any manner without written permission from the author except in the case of brief quotations embodied in critical articles or reviews.

The characters and events portrayed in this book are fictitious. Any similarity to real events or real persons, living or dead, is coincidental and not intended by the author.

All trademarks belong to their respective holders and are used without permission under trademark fair use.

Contact Rachelle at:
http://rachelleayala.me/author-bio/contact/

Have a Hart Sweet Romance Series

Christmas Lovebirds, Rob and Melisa, Book #1

Valentine Hound Dog, Larry and Jenna, Book #2

Spring Fling Kitty, Connor and Nadine, Book #3

Blue Chow Christmas, Brian and Cait, Book #4

Valentine Wedding Hound, Larry and Jenna, Book #5

Summer Love Puppy, Grady and Linx, Book #6

Dog Days of Love, Dale and Vanessa, Book #7

To my sister, Constance, who always loved dogs, and to Sasha and Ginger, two of her wonderful companions

Chapter One

Four years ago

Flames shot up outside the tiny cabin. Sasha's aggressive barks fell silent. Her ears flattened, and fur raised on her hackles as she darted through the kitchen toward the doggy door.

A rush of fire flashed through the doorway and blocked her, licking her nose. She squealed, backing up as smoke rushed into the cabin.

Gasping for breath against the thickening smoke, Sasha raced around and around the wooden cabin. The acrid smell stung her nose, and she whipped her head wildly, not knowing where to turn.

Blindly, she threw herself against the walls and doors. She dug with her paws, scratching, begging, hoping her man would come, but there was no sound other than the crackling of burning wood.

She had to get out. Had to escape. Her fur spiked on its ends, and the mewling cries whistling from her throat sounded too distant to be hers.

Where was her man? Where was the large, steady hand that held her tight and made her feel safe?

A loud boom shocked her to the bone, and all was strangely silent. A maelstrom of flames rushed at her. Horror gripped her. She reared herself up onto the sofa and pounced at the window with all of her eighty pounds.

The glass shattered, and she plunged through it onto the burning porch, surrounded by dancing flames: red, yellow, and orange.

What happened to the man she loved? Why wasn't he calling her?

There was no way out except through the fire, and Sasha wanted her man. He had to be out there.

Her eyes and lungs burning, she dived into the wall of fire, heading for the small patch of sky she could barely glimpse.

She ran, and ran, and ran, rolling in the grass to cool her burns, until she came to a creek.

With her tongue and throat parched, her paws bleeding and raw, she plunged into the water and let the current carry her away.

Chapter Two

Grady Hart couldn't remember the last time he celebrated his birthday—especially with his twin sister, Jenna.

He sat in front of a long dining table at his parents' newly rebuilt home in the Sunset District of San Francisco. A year ago, an arsonist had burned their house to the ground, and they had lost all of their possessions, including photographs and videos of bygone birthday parties.

A large sheet cake, with twenty-nine candles burning bright, sat on the table in front of Grady and Jenna with the slogan, "Our Twins, Twenty-Nine Forever."

"For they're jolly good people, for they're jolly good people ..." the large family sang as they wore party hats and blew noisemakers.

"Get ready to blow when I count to three." Cait, their oldest sister, aimed the camera.

Jenna nudged Grady. "They're betting we can't blow out all the candles."

"Piece of cake for a smokejumper." Grady gave his twin a wink.

Obviously, they weren't identical, being boy-girl twins, and their coloring and appearances were so opposite, it was hard to believe they were brother and sister.

Grady was dark, with dark-brown hair and eyes, and a year-round tan, thanks to his outdoor job, whereas Jenna was pale and blond. She was also a happy newlywed, unlike Grady, who was a no-commitment type of guy.

Underneath the table, Jenna's glutton of a hound dog, Harley, sang along with his baying voice, "Aaahhrrooh."

He was obviously waiting for a piece of cake to accidentally drop onto the floor. Other family members also had pets, including a Dalmatian, a gray tabby cat, and two little lovebirds chirping in their cage.

The family segued to the birthday song, and Grady eyed the flaming candles. The heat from twenty-nine candles could melt the cake and ignite their parents' house anew.

"Don't worry." Jenna elbowed him. "Every man in here, except for Dale, is a firefighter."

Dale was their baby brother and the current concern of his well-meaning parents. He hadn't told anyone other than Grady that he'd dropped out of college, because he didn't want to be pressured into fire-fighting school.

Grady eyed the twenty-nine dancing candles. His thoughts flickered briefly to the cabin he'd once had in a remote location in the Sierra Nevada mountain range—and his precious Sasha, the bravest, smartest, and most loyal dog a man could ever love.

All of it had gone up in smoke while he was out fighting another fire.

Cait counted down. "Three, two, one, ready, blow!"

Grady inhaled deeply and whoosh, he blew along with Jenna, sometimes at cross purposes, with her blowing one way and he the other. Eventually, they pushed the flames into tiny whiffs of black smoke.

"Yay!" his family cheered, and his older brother, Connor, slapped his back. "You finally put out a fire this year."

Grady closed his eyes briefly, beating back the image of the last forest fire he was in—the one where the wind whipped itself into a fire tornado, catching him and his jump partner off-guard.

He'd managed to land on the face of a rock, bruising his entire body, but his partner hadn't been as lucky.

Grady shuddered when Cait tapped him and shouted, "Smile!"

Jenna hooked her arm around him and tilted her head toward his. "You've got this. Don't let Connor upset you."

"I'm not upset," he grumbled. His older brother, now a fire chief of his own station, had always overshadowed him.

"I said to smile, not talk." Cait waved her hand. "We can't cut the cake until we get pictures of you two."

Grady pasted on a grin. His mother bent between them, kissing both the twins, followed by his father with his hands on their shoulders. Various combinations included a self-timed, wide-angled family photo with every pet on every arm, and in the center of all, Connor and Nadine's three-month-old daughter, Amelia, the world's prettiest and most adorable baby.

The birds sang, the cat meowed, and the dogs barked up a storm, while Amelia cooed and babbled. His mother laughed, Cait yapped, and his father boomed.

"Did you make a wish?" Jenna whispered close to him.

"I was too busy blowing to wish. How about you?"

"I want a baby," Jenna said, eyeing Amelia and their sisters. Both Cait and their youngest sister, Melisa, were expecting. "You still have time to make a wish."

Grady pressed his lips into a grim line and exhaled through his nose. "I'm too old for wishes."

"And I'm too young to quit wishing," Jenna said. "How about another dog?"

"No dogs." Grady felt a rumble of anger ignite in his gut. "No dogs, and no women."

"No one said anything about women," Jenna said with a huff. "Is there a particular one you're avoiding?"

* * *

Linx Colson frowned as she brushed her dog, Cedar. "What were you doing running through the creek?"

Cedar gave her a baleful look and laid her head down, allowing Linx to pick the burrs and twigs from her long reddish coat.

Linx found Cedar four years ago after a forest fire worked its way to the edge of her hometown.

Cedar had been burned and suffered smoke inhalation. Her paws were blistered and parts of her fur were charred, but the dog had bravely traveled down the creek and found her way to safety.

Her owner hadn't cared to post in any of the lost dog forums, nor did he show up in town looking for her. Linx didn't feel too guilty keeping the dog, who obviously needed a stable, loving home.

Tenderly, Linx brushed Cedar's lush reddish fur marked with a white crest on her chest. As far as Linx could determine, Cedar was a chow chow and collie mix with a touch of Akita.

She was intelligent, loyal, and very loving, keeping Linx company and providing her with a listening ear through the lonely nights up in these parts of the woods.

"There you go, little girl." Linx detangled the last of Cedar's fringe. "All pretty and sassy again. Don't you go running off up that creek. You hear? There's nothing up there for you. Your home is here, with me. Forever."

Chapter Three

Grady was technically homeless—not that it mattered when he lived at various firefighting base camps year-round. The northern and southern hemispheres alternated fire seasons. While other smokejumpers went home during the off-season, Grady had kept himself on the move, fighting wilderness fires in California, Montana, and Idaho half of the year and decamping to Australia, New Zealand, and South Africa for the other half of the year.

For almost ten years, he was like a migratory bird, moving like clockwork across the globe.

The clock stopped this fall during a wicked late season fire, causing him to retreat home to his family. He'd been squatting at his twin sister's apartment since Christmas, the longest time he'd stayed in one place since he left home after high school.

"Since you're living with me, you might as well make yourself useful," Jenna said to Grady the next morning at the breakfast table.

"You telling me to move out?" Grady flicked through the messages on his cell phone.

"No, of course not, brother dearest." Jenna ruffled his hair. "I need help with the fall collection, and you smokejumpers are good with the sewing machine."

Jenna was a talented fashion designer, and while she, too, had sown plenty of wild oats, she'd surprised him by falling in love with a stalwart and loyal firefighter—the last kind of man his sister had been attracted to growing up.

"Repairing our parachutes and stitching up jumpsuits don't exactly qualify for high fashion," Grady said. "For one thing, our stitches don't have to be neat."

"True, but you've been moping around here half a year already. What really happened out there? I know there was a death in your crew."

"If you're saying it was my fault, you're wrong." Grady pushed from the kitchen table.

Jenna's brows turned down, and her mouth opened into a circle. "That's not what I'm saying. I only want to know how you feel about it."

"There are risks in everything we do—some more than others. Besides, it's not like I'm doing nothing. I'm busy running my Dogs for Vets charity."

"True." Jenna walked to the refrigerator and pulled out eggs, bacon, and cheese. Before she was married, she never cooked, but now that she was determined to become a mother, she'd been practicing on her husband, Larry, and by extension, Grady. "I wonder why you're doing all of this work with dogs when you don't want one yourself."

"No conflict of interest. I have a list of veterans and the types and characteristics of dogs they need, and my job is to be on the lookout for them—preferably rescuing them from shelters. If I were looking for a dog for myself, I would want to keep every one of them."

"You only need one," Jenna said, looking toward the side of the refrigerator where Harley, her and Larry's male basset hound, inhaled his breakfast.

He was one ugly mug of a dog with saggy skin, ears so long they trailed on the ground, and a bulging tummy from his constant gluttony.

"Good morning," Larry stepped into the kitchen and greeted them. He bent down and patted his dog, clearly adoring the messy hound. Still wearing the shorts and T he slept in, he wore the satiated smile of a happily married man. After acknowledging Grady with a curt nod, he made a beeline for Jenna and kissed her long and hard on the lips.

Grady turned away. He was definitely crimping their lifestyle by staying here. Here they were, hot newlyweds, and they had to share a small two-bedroom apartment with a grouch who'd given up on women—and dogs.

"Nothing against you, Harley, but you fart too much," Grady said as he walked toward the kitchen door.

The dog gave him a droopy-eyed look and slurped his drink, splashing and flapping water with his long, hanging ears.

So sloppy, unlike Grady's long-lost Sasha, who was beautiful in grace and form with sleek, light-red fur, tufts of pristine white accents on her chest and muzzle, and ears that stood erect and alert.

Missing and presumed dead.

Grady hadn't had a chance to look for her after his cabin burned down because he was hospitalized for smoke inhalation. When he was released, he'd been immediately assigned to an out-of-state crew where a fire burned out of control.

He'd kept his eye on the dog "lost and found" pages online, but after several false leads, he gave up.

The fire that had consumed his cabin had started right outside the kitchen door, trapping Sasha away from her doggie door. If she had died, Grady could only hope she had passed out from smoke inhalation before the flames burned her to a crisp.

Blinking from an eye irritation, Grady shut the door of the bedroom he was staying at. He traveled light. In less than half an hour, he had his clothes packed. It was time for him to head back up the mountain and rebuild the dregs of his useless life.

Dogless and womanless.

Only one big problem. The dog might be gone, but the woman was definitely not gone, not by a long shot.

She was a long-legged, lusciously curved, brown-haired Gypsy-looking spitfire who occupied permanent residency in both his dreams and nightmares.

Linx Colson.

She lived near his property, as owner and director of the Mountain Dog Rescue Center.

And he couldn't trust her as far as he could spit.

The woman was a liar, a manipulator, and the worst type of tease—as unpredictable as a wildfire snapping itself into a frenzy, egged on by a snarling wind.

Hot as a towering fire tornado.

And just as dangerous.

But still, she had what he needed—dogs needing homes. Even if he had to sacrifice his own sanity, he'd find the best dogs for the veterans he served, and that meant working with Mountain Dog Rescue.

He brought up his email app and sent Linx Colson a request for an appointment to scout out her available dogs.

* * *

The Mountain Dog Rescue Center sat on four acres of land, bordered by Sandman's Creek on the south and a large track of forest on the east. It was on the outskirts of her hometown, Colson's Corner, far enough so that the dogs' barking didn't disturb any neighbors, but close enough to walk to the town square. The plot of land was too small to be a working farm, but large enough to house twenty dogs in a renovated wooden barn.

Linx lived in a box-shaped cabin that served as both the office and adoption center. Chain-link fence surrounded the rescue center, and she had constructed several fenced-off areas large enough for dogs to run free in the meadow behind the barn.

Running a rescue center was a constant struggle between outreach, financing, pet care and rehabilitation. Right now, because of Linx's big splurge at buying a designer wedding gown she'd never need or use, the center was running in the red and in danger of being foreclosed.

She'd already laid off staff and was at the mercy of volunteers, and every day, when the bills came, she endured nail biting stress as she borrowed from her credit cards to pay for electricity, water, and dog food.

Still, Linx loved rescuing dogs, mainly because she'd failed at every other endeavor she had tried.

Dogs weren't judgmental.

Dogs didn't gossip.

Dogs didn't hold grudges.

Even the meanest, most maladjusted and abused dog could be won over by loads of patience and a smidgen of love. Unlike men—especially a certain smokejumping instructor she'd had the misfortune to train under.

She almost blushed at the "under" part of her training, but she slapped back the naughty thoughts. She'd reached too high when it came to Grady Hart, and he'd disavowed her in her greatest time of need.

Nope, dogs were way better than men, and after her experience with Grady and the horrible thing his lack of responsibility made her do, she'd decided it would be dogs over men for her, forever.

Morning came early at the rescue center as the dogs woke up and barked at every disturbance. Cedar, who slept in bed with her, rushed to the window and barked toward the direction of the barn, ready to go out and play with her friends.

Linx stumbled down the stairs of the loft and answered the insistently clanging old-fashioned phone. It was standard issue black with a rotary dial. These phones still worked in her town, and the town council's biggest accomplishment this year was fighting the phone company to keep the payphones outside of the diner and general store.

"Hello," she answered before the call kicked over to the tape-recording answering machine she inherited from her grandmother. "Mountain Dog Rescue. What can I do for you?"

A breathless female's voice huffed and puffed. "I was jogging near the river bend trail, and I heard high-pitched squeals. I think it's a newborn puppy, but I'm afraid to look. It's stuck under a tangle of grass."

"Is the mother dog around?"

"No, I don't see her," the jogger said. "We saw a couple of stray dogs at the Wildman campground, but a mother dog wouldn't just leave her puppy, would she?"

"Most likely not," Linx said, grabbing a pencil and paper. "Can you let me know exactly where you're at?"

"Sure, but I can't wait around. My family's packing to leave in half an hour, and my mother told me to be back quick."

Linx took down the location as best as the jogger could describe. The puppy had been abandoned about half a mile from the campground, and Linx would bet her eyeteeth the mother dog was already packed up and gone with her family.

Tourist season meant a spike in lost and abandoned dogs, and the upcoming Fourth of July fireworks show was pure torture for dogs and cats, causing them to run for cover and oftentimes becoming separated from their families—especially if they were camping or visiting from out of town.

"Come on, Cedar," Linx said as she put on her boots and grabbed a small baby carrier she'd picked up at the thrift shop. Newborn puppies were born blind and toothless, and they couldn't regulate their body temperature. She wondered about the condition of the puppy, its size and breed, but the most important thing was to bring it back and hope it wasn't too late.

While she and Cedar hiked the mile or so up the mountainside to the campground, Linx went through the available space in the kennel. The puppy, of course, would sleep at her bedside with a hot water bottle, but the kennel was at full capacity. She even had a few dogs doubling up.

She needed to run a big promotion in the days leading up to the Gold Rush Festival ending with a Fourth of July Rescue Auction, and that meant spending money she didn't have on advertising and social media.

She checked her cell phone for emails and frowned.

The devil always had perfect timing.

Grady Hart emailed her with his list of dog requests. He ran a charity matching dogs with veterans, and it was the perfect place for some of her more elderly guests to find homes.

But to do that meant getting reacquainted with Grady, and an acquaintance with him meant one thing only.

Bed first.

Talking later.

She'd kept him at bay by pretending she didn't know him from before. She'd even had his family fooled. She'd flirted with him at his sister's wedding, and she'd used up the last of her inheritance as seed money to start his charity—yep, the proceeds of that ill-fated wedding dress went to Dogs for Vets. Very reckless, but at least she'd gotten a reaction out of him.

He still hated her, of course.

And he obviously didn't trust her.

But he'd hinted at hooking up, and she'd teased him to the hilt. They both knew what came next should they ever meet up.

Cedar let out a sharp bark as she stopped in front a giant sequoia stump. Her nose twitched, and she looked back at Linx, wagging her tail.

"You found it?" Linx stuffed her phone back in her pocket and knelt in front of the hollow in the tree.

She removed the tangle of grass and weeds and gasped at the reddish ball of wet fur. The puppy, a female, squealed and wiggled when she picked her up. Her mouth suckled on air and her eyes were closed. Her umbilical cord was still protruding from her belly button.

"Oh, you sweet little thing." Linx tucked the cold and wet puppy into the baby carrier while Cedar sniffed and licked her. "You're going to have a good life. You'll see."

The puppy snuggled close to Linx's heart, and even though she already had a dog, and she had a rescue center full of dogs, Linx fell in love again.

"Should I call you Sasha? Or would that confuse Cedar?"

Cedar barked and gave her a quizzical look, as if saying those were both *her* names.

"Not Sasha." Linx stroked the puppy's back, cuddling it as she walked. "How about Ginger? Cedar, you like Ginger?"

"Woof. Woof." Cedar bounced happily and headed toward home.

Chapter Four

Grady said goodbye to his family at the end of their weekly Saturday night dinner.

"I'm headed out." He held his hand up to wave.

His father and younger brother, Dale, barely looked up from the TV while his mother and two pregnant sisters waved him off with no interruption to their heated discussion on natural versus medicated childbirth.

Connor, the devoted father and husband, was in his own little cocoon of syrupy, sweet love with one arm around his wife and the other one cradling his baby.

Only Jenna dashed toward him, realizing this was different from an ordinary goodbye.

"Are you feeling okay?" she asked, touching his arm. "You looked preoccupied."

"Making plans. I've troubled you and Larry long enough."

"I didn't mean for you to leave. You know you're welcome to stay as long as you like."

"It's time," he said. "You were right about me moping around."

"Where are you going?" She wrapped her arms around him and hugged him tight. "You'll keep in touch, won't you?"

"I will." He tried to extricate himself and make an escape, but Jenna's actions drew the attention of Cait, who felt it was her duty as eldest child to meddle with all of her younger siblings' lives.

She waddled over with her pregnant belly leading the way. "Grady Hart. No sneaking out before the card games."

"Sorry, but I have to get going," Grady mumbled with his hand on the doorknob.

Cait narrowed her eyes and assessed his body language. "You're as twitchy as a long-tailed weasel in a room full of rocking chairs."

Grady rocked from foot to foot, as Cait's loud voice drew the attention of his mother.

"Leaving so early?" Mom asked. "Do you want to take some food?"

"No, it's not necessary." Grady's palms started to sweat. He should have simply snuck off without attending the family dinner and game night.

"You're running away, aren't you?" Cait concluded, picking up on his nervousness.

"Oh? Running away?" Mom inquired, tilting her head. "You can stay with us as long as you want."

Now that Cait spilled the beans, Grady opened the door and said. "I can't stay. I have to keep moving or I'll rust."

This opened the flood gates as everyone dropped what they were doing and charged toward him.

Dad wanted him to go back to firefighting, while Mom thought he should settle down and get a permanent job, preferably close by.

Connor wished him luck with his wanderlust. "Gotta get it out of your system before you start a family."

Meanwhile, Jenna made him promise to text pictures and updates of his travels. Melisa wanted postcards for her classroom, and Nadine wanted him to kiss his niece and to be back for Melisa and Cait's joint baby shower.

"Where are you going?" Mom asked. "I'm concerned you're not putting down roots."

Roots were the last thing he needed, and he could never imagine himself sharing the same type of warm, gooey love his parents, and now most of his siblings, were wrapped up in. Cozy, too cozy, and so stifling. Of all his siblings, only happy-go-lucky Dale was a free man, but for opposite reasons.

Dale always thought there was someone better out there. He was an eternal optimist, flitting from one pretty girl to the next.

Grady knew better. He was realistic. Love wasn't for him, and even if it were—it always ended unhappily.

The only sure thing in life was death, and if it wasn't death, it was deception.

He hugged his mother and kissed her on the cheek. "Thanks, Mom, I won't be far. Just have to get some fresh air."

"Don't stay away too long," Mom said, tearing up. "We enjoyed having you here since Christmas. I knew you'd eventually go back to the fire lines. It's in your blood."

"Yeah, well, I'm sitting the year out. Trying something new."

"You need to get back on that horse," Dad said, coming up to him and roping him into a man-hug. "The sooner you're back fighting fires, the better. Don't put it off too long."

Larry clapped a hand on his shoulder. "If you ever need to talk, I'm a good listener, and I'm not a Hart."

"So am I. You have any questions about women, you come to me," Cait offered, even though she was technically a Hart—although she'd belatedly taken her husband's surname, Wonder.

"Grady's given up on women," Jenna said to Cait. "He doesn't even want a dog."

"You'll need companionship." His mother patted his arm. "If you stay with us, you can even get a dog. I'm taking allergy shots now. I don't want there to be any excuse why we can't have our entire family, including our fur and feather babies here."

"I know that, and thanks." He gave his mother a kiss and turned toward the door.

"Here's a list of fire chiefs I know." Dad shoved a piece of paper into his hand right before he stepped out. "In case you want to apply for a position."

"Don't worry, everyone." Grady waved to his large and utterly adorable family. "I'm taking a time-out, but I'll be back. No need to act like I'm going off the end of the earth."

"If you happen to go by Colson's Corner because of a certain female, tell her 'hi' from all of us," Cait, the most nosy of all his sisters, said as a parting shot.

Last December, Cait and Brian had spent time in the mountains renewing their marriage and had gotten to know Linx Colson when they found two lost chow chow dogs.

"Come back here." His youngest brother, Dale, finally realized he was leaving. "We're setting up the poker table. At least stay until you lose all your money."

Dale was the prankster and joker of the family, and all he cared about was having fun. Nothing ruffled his feathers, and Grady doubted he had a serious bone in his entire body.

"Don't you ever feel like jumping on a motorcycle and riding off to parts unknown?" Grady asked. "You should try it sometime. Let's you know the real you."

"Sounds fun. I might join you if they don't stop trying to push me into firefighting," Dale said, laughing.

"Actually, it's more fun if it's just you and the open road," Grady grumbled, but allowed himself to be steered back to the Hart household.

He had considered taking his brother along, but they were opposites, and Grady could only take so much of his brother's jolly bonhomie.

Nope. Grady was a loner and there was nothing more remote and undisturbed than the site of his burned down cabin.

Hours later, after playing Texas Hold'Em, Spades, Hearts, and Hand and Foot as well as two rounds of Clue, Grady made his final escape and checked into a motel in Sacramento for the night.

The next morning, after renting a used fifth-wheel trailer, he pulled it up the mountain and found his plot of land. Weeds had grown rampant over the burned-out foundation of his cabin, and the forest had taken back the clearing.

Grady unhitched the fifth wheel and set it up under a spreading pine tree for shade. He spent the rest of the day clearing brush and whacking weeds. Instinctively, he put up a firebreak between the forest and the foundation of his cabin. He dug a trench and planned to fill it with gravel. It was hard work, and it took the edge off of his restlessness—a little.

Would he put down roots in this remote mountain cabin? He'd been happy here once, long ago. During the weekends he had off while training smokejumping rookies, he'd come here under the canopy of tall trees to enjoy the solitude.

One day, a tiny puppy had crawled out from behind the woodpile, and Grady was no longer alone. He'd named her Sasha, after his crazy red-headed jump partner in Siberia who washed everything down with vodka. His Sasha went with him everywhere: to the creek, on long hikes, and even skiing where she eagerly pulled him at fast speeds down cross-country trails.

It had all ended with a fire.

Grady stared at the place where the woodpile had been. If he had ever had a desire to put down roots, this small piece of mountain would do. It was as if Sasha had sprung out of the earth and then gone right back to it, ashes to ashes, dust to dust.

A warm settled feeling came over him, and he felt her presence. Everywhere he looked, he saw her. Her favorite spot next to the fireplace, the way she ran around the yard, and the place where she once treed a bobcat.

Closing his eyes, his mind took him back to another female who still haunted this very location. A wild and tempestuous woman who'd trained to fight fires, who'd shared his passion for preserving the forest, who'd climbed peaks with him—and who'd kept his bed ablaze and his heart on tether hooks.

He'd been running from her long enough. She'd been haunting him for way too long.

It was time to exorcise her hold on him, and for that, he would have to make her tell him the truth.

Was there a baby, or was it all blackmail?

* * *

"How many online applications did we get for the adoption event?" Linx sat in her sister's diner across from her best friend and most loyal volunteer, Tami King.

The two of them went back to elementary school, and had only lost touch when Tami went to college.

"I'm still going through them to remove the flakes and trolls," Tami said, checking her notepad. "But I'd say we have a good seven or eight. We also have that guy who's running Dogs for Vets ..."

Tami's voice trailed as her eyes quirked with mischievous interest.

Linx shrugged and stared at her reflection in her black coffee. "He's asking for older dogs, and God knows how hard it is to place them."

"Why would he want geriatric dogs when they don't last as long?" Tami asked as she picked up a breadstick and munched on it.

"They're calmer, if they don't have personality issues," Linx replied. "Most of the vets want companionship. An older one is already housebroken, hopefully, and has been through sorrow and grief—kindred spirits."

"Then we should give him as many as he wants," Tami concurred.

"There's a problem, though," Linx said. "Our policy is that whoever adopts our rescue dogs is the final owner—not a pass through. We are the ones who should vet the eventual homes of our guests."

"Ideally so," Tami said. "But we're overcrowded, and some of the old guys have been here forever. Plus, we're running low on funds, and we need to enlarge the kennels."

"I don't trust the guy."

Tami let out a snort. "With your heart, sure, but you've got to admit it's interesting he's turning up now."

Tami didn't know the details on Linx's long-ago relationship with Grady, only the fallout—which was bad enough.

"What's so interesting?" Linx swirled a breadstick in the dip and looked for her sister, Joey. Why was it taking so long for her to take their order?

Her gaze froze.

"Speak of the devil." She clenched her jaw. "There he is."

Six-foot-two inches of rough and tough man took off his aviator sunglasses and glared at her from the entrance of the diner.

That man was too arrogant for his own good. What gave him the right to walk around like a modern-day James Dean, complete with black leather jacket, black boots, and skin so tan he could be mistaken for a pirate?

Heck, he even smoothed his thick hair back like he was a twenty-first century reincarnation of a rebel without a cause.

"You'd think he owned this town." Tami eyed him with eager curiosity as he wove his way toward them.

Linx fought to keep her face from heating up as she reached for her phone and commanded it to call her brother, Todd, the town sheriff.

Grady put his hand on the back of the booth. "Why, Miss Linx, I thought you fought your own battles."

Linx tapped the end-call button and slid her phone into her pocket. She'd clue her brother in later, and yes, she did fight her own battles, and she wasn't going to let the likes of Grady Hart worm his way back into her good graces with some tall tale of doing good for veterans.

Bed was a different story, maybe, but a woman had to keep up appearances, especially in front of her family.

Except doing battle with Grady Hart was always a losing proposition. The man had an advantage—the smoldering gaze, work roughened hands, the grizzly stubble on his strong jaw—and he took it—early, often, and with much relish.

Linx tore her gaze from the mouth which would so easily and knowingly ignite her most sensitive zones. She grabbed a breadstick and shoved it into the creamy dip, in and out. Slowly, she twisted it between her succulent lips and gave him a sweet, innocent smile. "Jumped any fires lately?"

Fire season in the Sierra Nevada region, Gold Country California, started in May, and with the weather as dry as tinder, fires broke out all over the state, keeping crews of smokejumpers and wildfire firefighters busy, sooty, and exhausted—too busy and exhausted to cause trouble in her hometown of Colson's Corner—a tiny village too high up and remote to garner much traffic.

"Only spitfire I'm jumping this year is you." Grady bent down and scooted into the booth facing her, with Tami traitorously making room for him.

"You've never missed a fire season in, what, ten years?"

"Sitting this one out." Grady took a breadstick and crunched it nonchalantly, as if she'd invited him to join them.

"But why?" Linx made her voice smooth with a dab of flirtation. "Big man like you always did two fire seasons a year. You injured?"

"Nope." Grady looked over his shoulder at Joey, Linx's younger sister who owned Joe's Diner. "Figured I'd try something new. Something along your line of business."

Linx expected him to wince, to dodge her jab, but Grady had faced down flames armed with only a shovel and a saw.

A little snark from a woman wouldn't faze the tough guy at all.

"Coffee?" Joey put down a menu and turned over an unused coffee mug.

"Don't mind if I have some." Grady gave Joey a flirtatious wink. "Can I ask you a question?"

"You just did." Joey's eyelashes fluttered as she refilled Linx and Tami's mugs.

"Then I'll ask another. Why is the diner called Joe's Diner and you're a girl named Joey?"

"That's three questions." Joey's cheeks flushed pink under Grady's friendly gaze. "I think you owe me a big tip."

Tami almost choked on her coffee as she stared at the tip of her breadstick which was soggy and limp. Linx kicked her bestie under the table, not at all happy with Grady flirting with her baby sister.

"We'd like to order, if you don't mind?" she said. "And in answer to Grady's impertinent questions, the 'Y' fell off the sign and Joey doesn't like her real name."

It was Josephine, of course, but what young woman wanted to sport an old aunt name?

"Breakfast is on me," Grady said. "I'm here to discuss business. I'll take a lumberjack special."

Linx ordered her usual blueberry waffle with a side of eggs sunny side up, and Tami ordered fruit compote over yogurt.

After Joey departed, Grady hooked a glance at Tami who was President of the Chamber of Commerce and the town's only realtor. "Looking for office space. Might I bother you for a showing?"

"Definitely. I'm sure we have quite a range to suit your needs," Tami purred. She was already pressed against him, since she was an almost-plus-size who was perpetually dieting.

Linx didn't want to feel possessive, but she'd draw the line between her and her sister and best friend.

"Something must have happened." She zeroed her gaze in on Grady. "You missed Australia in December, and now you're missing all the action here."

This time, she detected a slight wince between his eyebrows. "The dogs and veterans need me more. Besides, isn't your shelter overfull?"

"True, but we have a policy that only the final adopter can take the dog from our center," Linx said.

"You got my list, didn't you?"

"Yes, but I don't handle third-party adoptions."

He didn't know how desperate she was to place the elderly dogs, but then, he didn't have to. She would uphold the standards of her policy to let him know he wasn't God's gift to rescue centers—no matter how many good deeds he was prepared to do.

"Your dogs need homes, I presume?" He lifted an eyebrow, letting her know he wasn't buying her resistance.

"How do I know they're good homes? How do I know they can handle a dog? Just because they're veterans doesn't mean they're exempt from the application process. What if they have PTSD? Or they're mentally ill? There was a veteran not too far back who tied her therapy dog to a tree and shot him."

"Suspicious, much?" Grady narrowed his eyes. "What's this really about? You afraid of me?"

"You, no way." Linx puffed her chest, drawing his heated gaze.

"Then let me go over and scout out the dogs. I can take pictures and do a preliminary evaluation of personality and temperament. I'm also working with a trainer and therapist to make the match."

On the surface, he seemed reasonable, without a hidden agenda, but Grady Hart was angling for something, and it wasn't a quick, no-strings roll in the hay.

Still, he was a master at making her look crazy and unreasonable.

"Fair enough," Linx said. "Meet me there when we open."

Next to Grady, Tami made faces to remind Linx why Grady should not go over to the rescue center.

Linx used her foot to nudge Tami's leg, letting her know she was well aware of the danger. She'd lock Cedar up in the bathroom. No problem.

Chapter Five

Grady Hart frowned as he drove his truck down the rutted dirt lane to the Mountain Dog Rescue Center. He hadn't expected Linx to be quite so hostile about him adopting the dogs on behalf of the veterans.

Wasn't she the one who had donated the seed money for his charity by buying Jenna's sexy see-through high-concept wedding dress for a reality show fundraiser?

True, she'd told him to stay away from her place because her dog supposedly hated him.

Last Christmas, he'd come to Colson's Corner when his sister Cait was kidnapped by a deranged psychopath. He'd met some of Linx's family, and she'd pretended she hadn't known him, by allowing Cait, who she'd befriended, to introduce him.

He'd returned the favor and didn't let his family know about her—or their past—either. It was better that way—given the heavy accusations she'd thrown his way—threatening to blackmail him for sexual harassment if he didn't do as she demanded.

True, he'd been her smokejumping instructor, but she was over eighteen and she was the aggressor, chasing him all over the camp and cornering him when he'd least expected.

He slammed the door of his truck and walked up the path to the wooden cabin which served as the office. A chorus of barks ranging from deep bass bellows to the sharp yips of smaller dogs competed to welcome him.

He stepped onto the porch and spied the sign. It said, "Closed."

What game was she playing? She'd agreed to meet him, but now she was playing hard to get?

As if he'd have anything to do with any woman, including her. All they wanted was a man's money and having him whipped to the size of a kitty cat at their beck and call.

Nope, because of Linx Colson and others like her, he would never allow himself to be caught up in their drama and games. He simply needed the dogs, nothing more, nothing less.

Grady pressed the buzzer, and a dog barked and whined behind the door. It wasn't a warning bark, or an aggressive "get off my property" bark, but a playful and demanding bark.

The sound was almost familiar. It was a big dog, that much he could tell. Maybe female and very affectionate—begging for a tummy rub.

How could a dog expert like Linx interpret these noises as hate?

He heard sounds of her scolding the dog named Cedar who she dragged away from the door. Another door slammed and footsteps returned.

Linx opened the door, looked around, and grabbed him by the lapels.

"Get in here before anyone sees you." She slammed the door, then shoved him against the log walls of her cabin. Still clutching his jacket, she attacked his lips.

Her hot tongue drilled into his surprised mouth—not that he was shocked, and her breath came fast and panting. She devoured him, kissing and nipping his lips and rubbing her cheek against the two-day growth of beard he sported.

He quickly took control of the kiss and grabbed her tight, turning her so she was pressed against the wall, and he was the one plunging his tongue into her mouth.

What was going on here?

But then, this was vintage Linx through and through. She used to jump him behind the mess hall, entice him to follow her to the far side of the hangar, or find him on "mop up" duty and tumble him onto the still smoldering ashes, trusting their flame retardant clothes would take care of any lingering embers.

Then there was the skinny dipping. How could he forget?

But he needed answers, and as long as her lips ravished his, he'd get nothing useful from her—not even the reason she shut her friendly-sounding dog in the bathroom.

Taking a breath of her spicy and seductive scent, he pulled back from her swollen lips enough to mutter, "What's wrong with your dog? Aren't you going to put her out before she hurts herself?"

"How do you know it's a her?" Linx's head snapped back. "Have you been snooping around? You know my dog hates you."

"I think she wants to play."

"You don't know my dog." She pushed back from him, and he wanted her lips back on his. Kissing was better than arguing. "We shouldn't be meeting here. Too dangerous."

He changed the subject instead. "Let's go to the barn out back so you can show me the dogs."

"No, you're not supposed to be here—"

A loud pounding cut off her reply. "Open up. Sheriff."

Linx patted her hair down and tugged her shirt, smoothing her jeans before opening the door.

"Oh, hi, Todd!" she chirped. "Grady was just leaving."

The big man, who had once seemed so friendly when he was rescuing Cait, put his hands on his hips, his right hand near his holstered gun. "Grady Hart. You know damn well you need to leave my sister alone. Leave peacefully, or I'll be forced to take you to court."

"To court? What for?" Grady wiped his lips with the back of his hand to remove any traces of telltale lipstick.

"A restraining order. My sister filed a complaint and you're not supposed to come within fifty feet of her residence."

Linx shrank from Grady's side, appearing to hide behind her brother.

What the heck? This woman was no shrinking lily. She was a hellcat on wheels. Why was she acting like she needed her big brother to rescue her?

"The only person who needs restraining is her." Grady jabbed a finger her direction. He brushed by the lawman and stomped down the steps of the porch.

Linx Colson had just pushed his last button.

* * *

Linx stared out the window at the dust left by Grady's departing truck, followed by Todd's patrol car. Apparently, Todd had gotten a missed call from her, so being the protective brother he was, he'd headed for her cabin once he was finished with another call he was on.

She wiped a stray strand of hair from her forehead and opened the bathroom door, letting Cedar out. The dog rushed to the front door, sniffing all the spots where that hot man had taken all the oxygen from her lungs.

Her stomach twisted. Should she have kept Cedar from Grady all these years?

Definitely.

Leaving her alone in a remote cabin where fire broke out was pure negligence.

She reached over and gave Cedar a firm rubbing of her reddish mane. The poor thing had practically been abandoned. She'd needed Linx.

Just like the puppy she'd rescued a few days ago.

"Let's see if Ginger's up. Come on." Linx patted her leg for Cedar to follow her up to her loft where Ginger slept in a box with a hot water bottle next to Linx's bed.

The little puppy was awake. Her head swayed from side to side, and she squealed, looking for the bottle.

"You adorable little sweetie," Linx said as she cradled the tiny pooch to her chest. Actually, as newborn puppies went, Ginger was quite large, already the size of a Yorkie. Her fluffy fur was dry and soft, and she'd stopped shivering after putting on weight.

Cedar sniffed the puppy and licked her, but when the puppy tried to latch onto her nose, she jumped back like an alien worm had attacked her.

"You're not jealous, are you?" Linx patted her dog's back. "She looks so much like you, that if I didn't know you're spayed, I would have thought you'd given birth and kept it a secret from me."

Cedar groaned and gave a half-hearted bark.

Linx jogged down the stairs and into the kitchen. Poor Ginger was so hungry she squirmed and wiggled between Linx's breasts. Not that there was anything there for her.

After warming up a bottle of prepared formula, Linx settled on the couch near the front door to feed her little puppy.

Correction, the Center's newest guest.

She couldn't afford to adopt every dog she rescued, and puppies like Ginger could bring in donations and a higher adoption fee—money she desperately needed to keep all of her guests housed, fed, and comfortable.

She should get Ginger's story out on the internet. Any attention and publicity would help with fundraising and attract adoptions for all the dogs.

Cedar's ears perked up, and she jumped toward the front door as footsteps clambered onto the porch.

It couldn't be Grady, could it?

The front door opened. By reflex, Linx caught Cedar by the collar. Her heart threatened to jump to her throat, but settled down at the familiar voice hailing through the doorway.

Tami bustled into the cabin like a thunderstorm without the rain. Her platform heels clip-clopped over the heart-pine floor and her large and lethal purse knocked down a plastic vase, spilling a bouquet of dried flowers onto the coffee table.

"Looks like I missed Todd. Passed by him on the way over here." Tami's eyelashes fluttered as she propped her hand on her hip. "Next time you sic him on Grady, make sure to clue me in."

"It wasn't intentional," Linx explained, hoping her lips weren't tell-tale swollen from beard burn.

"Good thing, too, or he would have been clued in about Cedar." Tami took out a compact and checked her lipstick. "You live dangerously."

"That man is dangerous, not me," Linx grumbled as she put the nipple of the bottle into Ginger's mouth. "Did he come up here just to stick it to me?"

"He can stick it my way anytime," Tami said, slapping a stack of file folders onto her desk. "Got several people looking at commercial property and offices."

"Oh, really? Who?" Linx paced around the desk, still bottle feeding the puppy.

"Your man's sister, Cait Wonder, called. She's looking for a central retail location for her wedding store."

"A wedding store? Here?"

"Seeing that the town's full of singles," Tami primped her hair, "it would make a lot of sense. Maybe she should run a dating service, too."

Linx had made friends with Cait and her husband, Brian, last Christmas when the couple found two lost chow chow dogs. Their family owned a cabin in a remote area up the mountain, and Linx had taken the dogs in when Cait and Brian had to return to San Francisco.

"Right, a dating service." Linx's mind wasn't on dating—not with her dismal track record. She and men were like oil and water—full of piss and vinegar with a dollop of gunpowder. Explosive chemistry with no safety valve.

"And then there's your man, Grady Hart." Tami glanced at her to see if she'd get a reaction.

"He's not my man," Linx grumbled, still boiling inside with unspent lust and anger.

Grady Hart had more on his mind than simply getting a dog or two from her. Judging from the way his cock had prodded her, she could easily suss out his secrets—like why, of all places, was he looking for office space here, and more to the point, why wasn't he out fighting fires?

"If I'm a betting woman, and I am," Tami said, "I'm thinking he has unfinished business with you."

"Well, duh." Linx glanced at Cedar who was busily inhaling every bit of Grady's scent at the doorway where they had so violently groped each other.

"You poor darling," Tami teased Cedar. "Bet you still remember him, don't you?"

"He doesn't remember *her*," Linx retorted. "Abandoned her like he abandons anything female and inconvenient."

"What do you think he'll do if he finds out you kept his dog?"

"Finders keepers, losers weepers. Although I don't think that man's wept for anyone." Linx kissed the top of little Ginger's head. "I don't want any complications."

"Then you shouldn't invite him over here." Tami turned on her computer. "Keep him at arm's length."

"What about the office space he's looking for? You should tell him there's nothing available in the entire town."

"Don't worry, I'll keep him away from you," Tami said, wiggling her eyebrows. "Somewhere far off, remote, and private."

Linx burned inside, knowing Tami found Grady attractive. But what could she say? Grady was fair game for all the single women of the world.

His type never lacked women willing to throw themselves at him, as if he were a lottery jackpot. Ironic, wasn't it, that the biggest assholes and the most commitment-phobic men were the most highly prized.

"You do whatever you want," Linx said. "I don't care. I have to feed the rest of the dogs."

She set Ginger's empty bottle on the table and put the puppy over her shoulder. Pacing around the small room, she rubbed the puppy's back. Instead of a burp, wetness seeped and dripped down the front of her blouse.

"Oh, Ginger, you had an accident." Linx nuzzled the little bundle of sweetness.

"About Grady's list," Tami called out as she scrolled through the center's email. "I think it's okay if the dog trainer he's working with approves of the adoption."

"I don't agree." Linx wet a paper towel and wiped off Ginger's fur. "What happens if we give a dog to the trainer, and it turns out the veteran doesn't want him?"

"There are no guarantees even with all the screening we do." Tami sounded exasperated. "You could have someone who's perfect on paper. Has great references from his neighbors and says all the right things, and then something goes wrong and the dog is surrendered again."

"Or abused, or worse ..."

"I think we should give Grady's program a chance," Tami said—or rather Tami's hormones spoke. "Let's give him one of our hardest-to-place dogs and see how he does."

"They're not experiments." Even though Linx grumbled about it, she had to look at the realistic situation. The more dogs she placed in their forever homes, the more she could rescue from kill shelters.

"Here's a good one," Tami said, staring at the screen. "Grady has a veteran who needs a mean-looking dog. One who's calm and collected, but scary to look at."

"Men with small balls always want a mean-looking dog, and then when they can't handle it, they dump the dog at the pound." Linx set Ginger into a box lined with a towel and heated a hot water bottle in the microwave.

"You need to take a chance," Tami said. "Besides, I'm betting there's nothing small on your man, Grady."

And Linx was betting Tami was dying to find out—firsthand. She kept needling her with the "your man" thing, hoping Linx would flat out deny it and give her the green light.

"Fine, I'll take a look and see what we have. Watch over Ginger." Linx strode across the small box-like cabin through the kitchen to the back door.

Dogs barked and bayed at her as she dragged the bag of food from kennel to kennel, exchanging dirty bowls with clean ones. She stopped to pat and chat with each guest, from the old bulldog that had been with her since she'd started the center to the newest arrival, a majestic-looking German shepherd pitbull mix who stood quietly at her side while she filled his bowl.

He didn't dig in until she gave the command, and he didn't join in the incessant barking that the other dogs did to pass the time.

"Still getting used to us, aren't you?" She rubbed his neck. He was one of the dogs who had been surrendered by his owner. The usual excuses were death in the family, loss of living space, or move across the country. This one was a soldier deploying to a warzone.

She sighed as she surveyed the rows and rows of kennels, each housing a shell-shocked former pet who had either been abandoned or had been abused to the point of running away. Finding new homes for them was a priority. Her shelter was no-kill, and she relied on donations and adoption fees to keep the operation going.

Which reminded her. She needed to get the center spruced up for the Fourth of July festivities. Hang up the flag, red, white, and blue banners, and make sure everything was clean and spiffy.

Every year, in the week running up to July 4, Colson's Corner had a Gold Rush Festival which attracted tourists and locals alike. She would have a booth plastered with photographs of the available rescue dogs, as well as incentives for people to visit the shelter where she could pre-qualify potential adopters for the pet auction held after the Fourth of July parade.

There was no time to worry about whether Grady found an office or not. The only thing that mattered was keeping him and Cedar apart.

Oh, sure, he hadn't looked for her much after that fire four years ago, but then again, she hadn't posted anything either.

Cedar was hers, and she had a much better life with Linx than with a traveling smokejumper who didn't understand the first thing about responsibility.

Chapter Six

Grady was revved up with nowhere to go. He needed a dog for a female veteran who had been sexually abused in Afghanistan—one who could be trained to clear rooms, to stand guard, and to sleep by the doorway and look mean and unapproachable.

Darn that Linx for calling the police on him. What was wrong with that woman?

What was wrong with him?

The woman taunted him about not smokejumping this season. The woman grated on his nerves and crawled under his skin. She was a rule-breaker, and there wasn't a sweet bone in her body.

He didn't need her, but he did need a supply of dogs to match with his veterans needing companionship.

Since he wasn't sure he was welcome at the diner, Grady headed to the Sixty Miners Saloon—an establishment not owned by a member of Linx's family.

It wasn't open, but he leaned on a buzzer at the service door until a grizzly voice yelled, "Where's the fire?"

"It's Death Wish," Grady replied with his nickname.

He heard grumbling before the door cracked open. His jump buddy, Paul "Blue Bunyan" McCall rubbed his bleary eyes and shielded them from the sunlight. "Get in here before I burn up."

"You hungover again?" Grady stepped into the dark, dank corridor reeking of stale beer and sweat.

"Not on the fire line anymore. Can drink morning, noon, and night."

"Better keep up with the PT," Grady said, referring to the physical training necessary to stay in shape for the rigors of both jumping into a fire and manning the fire line.

"Look, you want to go back, don't let me hold you," Paul slurred, groaning as he slouched on a couch in his office.

"That's not what I'm here for," Grady said. "Just coming by to see how you're doing."

"I'm good." Paul shrugged. "I'm frying up some bacon. Want any?"

"No, but how are you doing?" Grady peered at his buddy who was unshaven and reeked of cigarette smoke. If he didn't shape up, he wouldn't be physically or mentally fit to go back to the firefight.

"How do you expect?" Paul clenched his jaw. "If you had dropped the streamers down the right way, she wouldn't have been blown into the fire."

"It was a rough jump for all of us. Was bad luck."

He was well aware that Paul blamed him for his fiancée's death when she was blown off course and landed in the middle of a raging forest fire.

"Salem was damn good with the chute." Paul's voice was drained and rough. "She always landed on two feet and she could thread a needle through the forest."

Paul was referring to Salem Pryde's expert steering of her chute by toggling the right or left steering line. In practice, she had hit the bull's eye. Problem was, she wasn't good at reading the streamers, and with tricky crosscurrents and turbulent wind gusts, there was no guarantee that the direction the streamers flew would be replicated by the parachute.

Grady let Paul whine and complain while he woke his phone to check his email. The truth was, Salem didn't deserve Paul's extensive mourning. She'd only latched onto Paul because his father was a venture capitalist, and he could buy his son any toy he wanted: fancy cars, houses, and even this bar in the middle of nowhere.

Besides, Salem had a side to her she hid from Paul, but far be it from Grady to speak ill of the dead.

An email popped up from Linx in reply to his request for a calm, but mean-looking dog.

From: Mountain Dog Rescue
To: Dogs for Vets

I have the perfect dog for you. A youngish male German shepherd pitbull mix. Name's Sam. He was surrendered a few days ago. Quiet, but observant. Doesn't bark for the heck of it. He's well-trained, and less than three years old.

Meet me at the Roadside Inn off the Gold Chain Highway. Text me for time and room number.

It was unsigned, but Grady's lips curled into a grin.

He was about to jump a wildcat.

* * *

Linx wiped the sweat from her forehead as she took a break from cleaning the dog runs. The majestic peaks of the Sierra Nevada rose above the treeline, still white-capped at the top.

She let the cool morning breeze sweep over her face and took a deep breath of the resin-scented air. This mountain community was her heritage, and she knew every inch of the backroads and trails coming off the mountain range. Her family was as old as the dirt in the hills and the rocks in the rivers.

Colson's Corner was founded by her great-great-great grandfather at the height of the Gold Rush, when nuggets of gold could be found ripe for the picking. He'd built the first series of sluices and owned the general store where he sold supplies to the miners. Once gold fever died down, her family stayed in the area, expanding into farming and ranching.

The town was too far off the beaten track to attract the strip malls and chain stores that blighted other towns close by. The lack of cell phone signal in the remote cabins outside of town kept Colson's Corner the gathering place where people came to check messages or find out about the news.

Although lately, the phone company had been putting up towers designed to look like the giant sequoia trees native to the region. Just the other day, she'd been stopped behind a large utility truck blocking half of the road to put up a tower. There was no stopping progress, despite the old-timers who wanted to remain out of touch.

Linx wasn't sure what she thought about it. On the one hand, development could bring more people into the mountains and grow the economy, but with more people came more traffic and other nuisances.

Linx received a text from Grady. *Sure thing. Let me know when.*

Bingo. He'd taken the bait.

She tucked the phone back into her pocket without replying. No matter what. She had to be in full control.

If he thought he could put stakes down in her town and run her out, he had another thing coming. Arrogant Grady Hart was not going to waltz into Colson's Corner under the pretext of adopting dogs for veterans and drive her into hiding.

She was no longer in awe of the hotshot firefighter—the man with the death wish who would jump headfirst into a blazing forest fire and fill her nights with heat and smoke. Once, she'd crushed on him, believed in him, and counted on him.

But he'd rejected her when she'd needed him most, and for that, he deserved to be burned and burned badly.

Oh, the heat and attraction still sizzled, and desire still held a torch between them.

But this time would be different.

This time, she would have control.

She would twist and turn him inside and out, have him begging for more, and then she'd pulverize his heart the same way he'd destroyed her innocence.

Linx finished hosing off the walkway and swept the debris over the redwood chips. It was time to let the dogs out of the barn and into the meadow for their daily exercise.

After securing the front gate, she opened another gate leading to the fenced-in field of green grass and wildflowers.

The dogs were excited, yapping and barking, jumping up and down as she channeled them from their pens through a series of parallel fences to the exercise yard.

Linx patted Bob, the old bulldog, who waddled after the younger dogs. "I bet your idea of a good day is to sleep under a desk or beside an armchair."

The elderly dog panted as she petted him, enjoying the little bit of love she bestowed on him.

Truthfully, she loved all of her rescues, and she spent a lot of time taking them on wilderness walks. She groomed them, did first aid on them, and sang to them.

Linx looked after the dogs. Most of them ran in groups, herding into packs, with Cedar front and center, leading the game of chase. But that new one, the German shepherd pitbull stood off by himself. He sniffed around the fence posts, marking them. He'd been neutered late in life, maybe after siring a litter of puppies.

"I wonder what your story is?" Linx muttered after the silent but strong male dog. She couldn't help comparing him to Grady Hart—a loner who had trouble connecting to people, despite being a middle child in a large family—just like her.

Linx wandered back into the cabin to do the dreaded paperwork which came with running a charity.

"I hear the doorbell," Tami said from her desk as soon as Linx stepped through the backdoor.

The problem with Tami was she hated getting off the chair. She'd gone to college and was an English major, and she was as smart as a whip. Her dream was to revive Colson's Corner's Gold Rush past as well as bring in new business.

"I'll get it." Linx answered the door. It was Jessie Patterson, the five-year-old daughter of the town's pastor. "Did you come to see the puppy?"

"No." The little girl wiped her teary eyes. "I lost Betsy. We came home from church, and the door was wide open."

Betsy was an old gray Labradoodle and just about the friendliest dog in town.

"Oh, sweetie, that's awful." Linx held out her arms and Jessie folded herself into her embrace.

"Can you help me find her?" Jessie waved a picture of the sweet dog with curly gray hair. Her family had had Betsy since before Jessie was born, and the two were inseparable.

"Of course I will. Do you have anything of Betsy's you can give to me? Anything with her scent?"

Jessie nodded and produced a blue and white gingham-checked dog bandana. Betsy's name was embroidered on one edge of it. "Can you use your Wonder Woman powers to find Betsy?"

Linx stroked the little girl's silky hair. "I will do everything I can to find Betsy."

When Linx was a little girl, she'd lost her dog, or the family dog, for longer than a week. Every day had been torture—imagining the worst. She couldn't sleep at night and had no appetite until the day Dolly was found.

"I really miss her," Jessie said. Two large tears tracked down her face.

"Let's make some posters," Linx said, taking the photo of the dog and putting it on the scanner. "Then we can put them up and pass them around."

It would give the girl something to do, and hopefully help bring Betsy back. It was strange that someone would break into their house, but a lot of people in town didn't bother locking their doors.

The only problem was summer vacation season had started, and now that the kids were out of school, some families had rented their houses to outsiders while they took vacations elsewhere.

Linx scanned the picture and brought the image up on her computer. She typed in the basic information about Betsy and contact information.

"I'll put a reward on this," Linx promised, not that she had any money. She must have been drunk on sex hormones or simply out of her mind when she'd splurged the last of her grandmother's money on a wedding dress to fund Grady's charity.

That man would never use her for anything other than a quick lay, and she should have more self-respect.

But then, after what he'd made her do, she had no self-respect left, and the only way she could justify herself would be to make him feel as horrible as he'd made her feel.

As to how effing his brains out would do that? She didn't know. A guy without a conscience wasn't easy to hurt.

As the printer printed out the posters, Linx entered Betsy's information to the online networks for lost dogs. She also checked the "Found" listings in case anyone had already located Betsy.

Unfortunately, there hadn't been any sightings for an eight-year-old gray Labradoodle.

While Jessie wasn't exactly happy when her mother came to pick her up, she was hopeful that the posters and "Wonder Woman" would do the trick.

After they left, Linx called Cedar into the cabin and let her sniff Betsy's bandana. Cedar wasn't a bloodhound, but she'd once been a lost dog herself.

"I don't know what I'd do if I lost you, baby." She kissed Cedar and attached her leash to take her out on a walk. "You're the only way for me to have a little bit of him—the only link."

It wasn't as if Cedar's owner had looked all that hard for her. He'd given up way too easily—treated it too cavalierly, the same way he'd stomped over her heart and brushed her off like ashes off his helmet.

Chapter Seven

Grady spent the rest of the week on his patch of mountain high above the town where his cabin had burned down. He rented a small Bobcat for grading, digging, and backfilling. The first step was to level the ground and compact the soil so he could rebuild the foundation.

This time, he would build a bigger cabin, one that would give him more space—three bedrooms and two bathrooms on the ground floor and a loft with two sleeping areas up top.

He would fell logs from his property as well as purchase them from his neighbors. Both the exterior walls and interior ones would be made of logs, and he would make the foundation from mortared stone.

He spent two days grading and digging the trenches for the foundation, then returned to town.

Two days of fresh air and hard work had cleared his mind—especially since he'd left his phone turned off.

Silence was golden, especially when he was about to go to battle and possibly bed with Linx Colson. He needed the respite from all chatter and talk.

He parked in the center of the town across from the square and founder's statue—one of Linx's ancestors—and checked his cell phone.

His sister, Cait, had called, saying she was en route to his parents' cabin a few miles away on the other side of town. His mother and Jenna had called to check how he was doing, and the therapist who worked with him had left a message asking about the dog for the female veteran.

Linx said she had one. Should he go to her? Or find the dog at another rescue center? It depended on how many times Linx had texted him—how much she needed him.

Licking his lips, he checked his text messages and grinned.

She'd left him three in a row.

The first text said, *Friday, two in the afternoon. Park under the large oak. Room five.*

Since he hadn't answered, she texted him a few hours later. *Don't tell me you have no signal.*

A day later, she got more demanding. *Are you ignoring me? You want the dog or not?*

He shut off his phone. He'd be there, but she didn't have to know.

* * *

Friday afternoon, Linx checked her text messages before loading Sam into the tailgate area of her Dodge Durango SUV.

Nothing from Grady.

Did he or didn't he want this dog?

Oh, sure, he'd emailed Tami and had sent in his application. The therapist he worked with from the Veteran's Administration was above board, and she was also a certified dog trainer for therapy and service dogs.

The veteran who needed Sam had grown up with dogs when she was a child, but after her experience in Afghanistan, she became agoraphobic—afraid of leaving her house. She habitually needed to clear every room she entered, look in all the closets, under the bed and behind the drapes, and she would only sleep with furniture barred across her doors.

Linx didn't like it, but Tami convinced her to try it, at least this one time, and if it worked out, they could expand the network of forever homes for their guests.

"Let's hope he shows up," Linx said to Sam as he jumped into the SUV. The dog gave her a doleful look, circled around the tailgate area three times, then lay down with his head on his paws.

Poor thing was still reeling from being given up, and now, he was in for another change. But a German Shepherd pitbull would be hard to place, so this was his best bet.

She got into the driver's seat and bounced her Durango over the rutted country lane until it merged onto the asphalt road.

She wasn't exactly sure what she wanted from Grady Hart—an apology would be nice, but probably not forthcoming.

Maybe it was an acknowledgment that he'd crossed paths with her before, instead of acting like she was a complete stranger.

"He knows what he did to me," she muttered as she sped down the hairpin turns of the mountain road.

Their paths had more than crossed before, more like tangled in a mess of arms and legs crossed. She'd fought fires since she was sixteen, working her way up the ladder until she'd earned a spot to train for smokejumping.

Grady was her instructor.

The spark was immediate, and they'd held out for a week. By the second week, they were actively flirting, stole kisses and touches the third week, and were sleeping together the fourth.

No one had known, because Grady was harder on her than he was on any of the other rookies. He ragged on her, rode on her, picked on her, and made her do all the worst drills under the worst conditions.

But behind closed doors, he'd made her body hum and trill like the whip and snap of a raging wildfire. And silly her, at age nineteen, she'd thought she'd snagged herself a real winner—a man she could bring home and play house with.

She passed a slow-moving Prius and let herself indulge—just while she drove, of Grady's dark masculinity, the tough alpha covered in soot and blood, charging toward blistering firestorms armed with a chainsaw. He'd been hard on her, on all of the rookies, but he'd also been fiercely protective, and surprisingly gentle. Like that time her roommate, Salem, had caught a flying firebrand in her leg. Grady had dropped everything to tend to her. He'd held her still while another crew member yanked the burning stick, then padded up the wound and cared for her until the Medevac appeared.

And then there were the more intimate moments, when Linx imagined she'd gotten behind that big, tough-guy wall, and he'd let down his guard and made love to her—so tender and yet raging, like a man possessed.

Wrapped in those big arms of his, she'd felt desirable and special for the first time in her pathetic life, and she'd let the entire torrent of his power, his wildness, and his basic goodness flood into her naïve heart.

Stupid of her, wasn't it?

Now, he was here—back in her hometown of all places. And he was tantalizing her, hiding their past from both of their families. And she couldn't let it go—not until she'd gotten the answers she needed.

Navigating the mountain roads with ease, Linx stroked an idle hand through her straight, silky hair. He used to wake her by petting her, smoothing his rough fingers through her hair, twirling it around and reeling her in for kisses and caresses. He'd whisper in her ear, hot breath fanning embers into sparks, and she'd turn to him, sleepy-eyed, and gaze into those deep brown eyes, certain that she was cherished, nurtured, and loved.

Mornings had always been the most vulnerable of all times, and it was in those dimly lit moments that she'd glimpsed forever—until it was over.

Linx swallowed at the devastation of unanswered calls, ignored texts, returned letters, and the weeks and months of waiting as her mornings turned into nausea and the baby in her belly grew.

She'd needed to make a decision—needed an indication from him, anything, that he'd take responsibility, or in her wildest fantasies, swoop into town and take her away to a mountain lodge where they'd live happily ever after.

When he finally contacted her, he'd told her he didn't believe it was his, and not to contact him again.

He'd left her no choice.

Linx swiped a stray tear and fortified herself for the meeting with her nemesis as she swung her SUV onto the interstate and jammed her foot on the accelerator.

She made good time and checked into the Roadside Inn fifteen minutes before two. Her room faced away from the office, so it was easy to sneak Sam in. She set a bowl of dogfood for him in the bathroom, and he sniffed around the room, but didn't jump on the bed.

After a bit of exploring, he made himself comfortable on the bath mat, watching Linx fix her makeup and dab perfume behind her ears.

At exactly two on the dot, a knock sounded at her door. Linx preened her hair and eyed the peephole. A smile crept to her face as she shut Sam in the bathroom before opening the door to Grady Hart.

"You came." She tried to sound bored, but utterly failed. The spark that had always burned between them popped like a nest of burning pinecones, fanning flames up her face.

"Are you surprised?" He barged into the room and shut the door, then cupped her head with both of his hands, drilling a deep, tongue-tangling kiss that made her knees turn to jelly.

Moaning, she sucked on his lips and wound her hands around his strong neck, over his shoulders roped with muscles, hard and hot.

Did she want to talk? To get her answers, or should she let him spear her through and through?

But what about the answers she owed him? Was he even curious or the least bit interested in what had happened to her after he dropped off the scene?

She bit back a moan when his grizzled beard shadow trailed down from her lips to her neck, lighting every greedy nerve in its path. Oh, Grady. So unfair. He knew all the pathways to pleasure on her body, and she was helpless as she let the tangles of emotion ignite through her hot, needy body.

Closing her eyes, she harkened back to the base camp, to the utter exhaustion after a firefight, the sticky soot, the searing heat, and choking smoke, soothed by cascades of cool clear water, as they soaped each other and celebrated the aftermath of a successful fight.

She might not want to talk, but she wanted an apology before he picked her up and smashed her on the mattress and pounded that desperately empty place inside of her, a void only he, Grady Hart, could ever hope to fill.

As he bent lower and looped one arm behind her thighs, she drew in a harsh breath and willed her arms to push back.

He lifted a puzzled eyebrow, his deep mesmerizing gaze weakening her resolve and melting the last bit of ice from her veins.

"Tell me to stop, and I will," he muttered with that low, growly voice of his.

"No, don't stop, but ..." Her heart banged against her ribcage. "Do you have anything to say to me?"

"Nope. Do you?"

His expression challenged her and irritated her, and his narrowed eyes accused her of being the liar.

She jutted out her lower lip and crossed her arms over her heaving chest. "Nothing."

"If you aren't asking me to stop ..." He dived for her lips, and she couldn't smother the moan of anticipated pleasure as her body thrilled at his attack.

Fine. She'd dodged the bullet, for now. He didn't seem to want answers from her, at least not yet, and she wasn't going to offer unless he came prepared to acknowledge his role in her misery.

He turned up the heat, lifting her from her feet and laying her down on the bed with such excruciating sweetness that it brought tears to her eyes.

The man was a living contradiction.

"You okay?" His eyes held a concentration of desire as he lighted his lips to her cheek.

She managed to nod, knowing he still harbored accusations against her, but not willing to explain until he was ready to eat crow.

"Hold me, Grady, the way you used to."

He wrapped her in warmth, trailing his fingers through her hair, and smoothing his palm on her back, calming her, but at the same time stoking the flames.

She opened her mouth and let out a sigh, of desire, and heartache, then welcomed him in, drinking of that essential male touch, the branding of his tongue, the taste of his strength, the grasp of his protectiveness.

He was trouble—big trouble, but she'd hungered for him all these years, wondering if she'd ever have the chance to set things straight—to make him pay.

She hated that she was all warm and soft and aching for him, but at the same time, the firestorm inside of her broiled over, as she grazed her fingers over his rock hard body.

He rose and dragged her tank top over her head, exposing her bare chest, and in a single motion, shrugged off his shirt.

Hooded eyes filled with lust gazed down on her, and he licked his lips.

"It's always been you." He shook his head, almost regretfully. "Always been you."

What did he expect her to say when he got all hot and romantic like that—so unlike his usual demeanor?

It was better not to talk, better to get naked and press skin against skin.

Linx pounced at Grady, knocking him onto his back. Snarling, she whipped her head around to get her long hair off her face as she yanked his jeans, along with his boxers to his ankles.

Their gazes locked, and fury swirled deep inside of her as she gave herself over to her wicked desires.

Chapter Eight

Grady was helpless at the pleasure surging through his veins and the hot, fiery woman taking him into her hands.

What the heck was he doing? More like she was doing him, and he hadn't gotten a single, cotton-picking answer from her.

When she'd asked if he wanted to talk, he'd said no. She, not he, was the one who should be begging to talk. She was the one who'd level those false accusations on him—tried to get him fired and ruin his reputation. He should be the one demanding answers.

But then again, she'd only lie. No, much better to get her while she was vulnerable, and then she'd admit she'd lied and maybe beg for forgiveness. Not that he had any to offer.

"Is this all you want?" he asked, gritting his teeth to keep from falling apart—way too soon.

"Does it matter?" She bore down on him, gripping him tight.

"No, guess not."

He wasn't going to admit any need to her. No way. If all she wanted was his body, then he'd give it to her. He'd had other women, but the only one who left him raw and disturbed was this brown-haired, brown-eyed hellcat occupying every nook and cranny of his mind and sucking the oxygen out like a river of flames devouring the wilderness.

Problem was, after meeting her again last Christmas, he hadn't wanted any other woman—actually wanted nothing to do with the entire female sex.

What the heck was he doing here?

She was lovely. Lovely and forbidding like a vengeful goddess. Bent on seeking her own pleasure first. Selfish and so freaking spiteful, but he wouldn't have her any other way.

This pillar of womanhood, this inferno of feminine guile was right where he wanted her.

If he could break through to her—break her stubborn will—if only to admit her feelings and faults ...

"Grady, oh, Grady, why? Why?" she cried out as she neared completion, carrying him over the top with her.

He wasn't done with her, so he flipped her onto her back and stared into her gorgeous, but usually shielded eyes.

For a split second, he thought he glimpsed a crack in her face—a small shadow of regret or was it sorrow?

And then it was gone.

She shoved him from the bed. "Time's up."

What the eff? She was harder than nails and just as mean.

What had he expected? A cuddle and a warm shower with an ice cold glass of sweet tea after?

"Don't worry, I'm out of here," he grumbled, grabbing his boxers, but not before tying off the used condom and putting it into his pocket.

He'd learned long ago to be careful with his DNA, and the minx who was pushing him out of bed was one of the worst offenders when it came to false pregnancy scares.

"How about we do this again next week? That is, if you want another dog." She pulled the sheets primly over her body, the one he'd thoroughly mounted only a few moments ago.

"There are other rescue centers," Grady said, zipping up his jeans. "You're not the only one."

He wasn't about to let Linx put a spell on him, especially after what had just gone down.

"Your loss." She leaned back on the motel's plush pillows, looking as if she was having a smoke without a cigarette.

Sure, he'd put that smug, satisfied expression on her face.

He had to be careful with her, as he was with all women. They couldn't be trusted as far as he could shoot his wad. He'd had his fair share of fake paternity suits before, all because he was a traveling smokejumper, fighting forest fires worldwide, and too busy to show up in court—an easy mark.

Thank goodness for DNA testing.

Grady gave Linx a middle-fingered salute and grabbed his shirt and shoes. "The dog?"

He'd heard him scratching the bathroom door while they had been engaged in their bout of sin.

"He's all yours. Paperwork's in order." Her face hardened into a frown. "Better treat him right."

"Better than you locking him in the bathroom while you get your jollies." He shot a glare back at her still tempting body.

Gritting his teeth, he slipped on his shirt and shoes, took the large dog by the collar, and sauntered out the motel door without looking back. He should go and keep on going. Forget about her.

The problem was all him, and he couldn't even blame his misbehaving body part—although Mr. Perfect was only too happy to play along.

Nope, the effing thing was his brain and the endless erotic movie it played in his mind, over and over, again and again—a twenty-four hour nonstop channel of the Linx Colson Peep Show. Then there was the Linx Colson

News Hour where her voice would loop over everything she told him about her business, her likes and her dislikes, her opinions and her peeves—she had a lot of them. Followed by the Linx Colson Weather Channel, as she went from angry gust, to howling tornado, to torrential downpour in a blink of an eye. No Linx Colson Comedy Hour, though. That woman had no funny bone anywhere in her body. Not anymore.

Her scent hung heavy on his body, and he briefly closed his eyes as he stepped into the heat of the afternoon.

When had she become so hard?

She no longer smiled or joked around, and definitely didn't want after-sex cuddling and teasing like she did seven long years ago.

That was when she still liked him.

That was when he still trusted her.

Grady marched to his truck, taking care not to glance back over his shoulder at her window.

* * *

Linx slid into the cabin of her dog rescue center through the back door, hoping to sneak up to the loft and take a shower.

No such luck. Cedar ran to greet her while Tami turned around from the kitchen table which was directly across from the back door.

Her dog sniffed curiously all over her clothes, and Tami opened her yap, giving Linx a sidelong glance and a barely suppressed smirk. "Well, well, well. Cedar, honey, tell me what smells so delicious and sexy. Might there be more special deliveries?"

"I'm going upstairs," Linx said lamely.

"Good idea." Tami pointed to her own head to signal how messed up Linx's hair was from her mid-afternoon tryst. "Maybe you should have taken a shower with him while you were at it."

"Maybe I didn't see him at all," Linx lied to deflect her nosy friend.

"You were always a bad liar."

"None of your business." Linx snarled and made a mean face to cover up the warm and gooey feeling swarming her lower body.

"Oh, but you're always my business, and there's only one reason you have that glow on your face." Tami thrust her index finger in and out of a tunnel made with her other hand. "Did I tell you he shares office space with me, and he not so coincidentally told me he'd be away at the same time you left?"

"He shares an office with you?" Linx sputtered, while finger-combing her mussed up hair.

"Oh, yeah, I keep him in my closet and let him out for phone and internet." Tami licked her lips exaggeratedly. "Since you won't 'call him,' there's no bestie code I have to honor."

"You're not ... doing him, are you?" Linx's jaw slammed to the floor, but she quickly recovered. "I mean, fine, enjoy yourself. But a man like Grady needs to come with warnings. Large, red warning signs."

"Warning heeded." Tami primped her fluffy mop of hair while snorting like she thought the entire deal too funny.

Cedar stuck her nose over Linx's crotch, sniffing with interest, causing Tami to lose the battle against laughter.

"Girl, get your nose out of my privates." Linx put Cedar out the backdoor and watched her join the other dogs in their free playtime.

When she returned to the den where she and Tami had their desks, Tami was still chuckling. "You're going to get caught. His sister Cait's not going to like you toying with him."

"I bet you'll want front row seats when the crap hits the fan, don't you?"

"Definitely, with popcorn, hot and bothered, er, I mean buttered." Tami pantomimed stuffing popcorn in her mouth.

Linx couldn't help smiling as she mock swatted her bestie. They'd gone to school together, from Brownies to high school. Always the smart one, Tami went away for college, while Linx joined the fire crew.

"You keep being entertained," Linx said as she headed for the shower.

"Wait, I hear the mailman," Tami shouted. "Can you dump the mail on my desk? I ordered something for Ginger."

"Urgh!" Linx heaved a sigh. "You need to get up more. You know sitting is the new smoking?"

"My feet hurt." Tami tapped the keyboard and stared at the monitor intently.

She always had a dozen excuses why she couldn't walk the dogs or lift a finger, and then she wondered why she couldn't lose weight.

Linx grabbed the mail and sorted through them, handing Tami her package. A crumpled postcard slipped onto the floor, and Tami picked it up.

She flipped it over and her eyes grew wide. "I don't believe this."

"What is it?" Linx stared at a past due bill and added it to the growing pile on her desk. "Does it say I won money?"

"No." Tami handed the card to Linx. "It's for you."

It was a generic picture postcard showing a snowcapped mountain peak above a forest.

The other side, however, was the shocker.

Dear Linx,
I hope you're doing good with your dogs.

Guess who my jump partner is?
Grady Hart!
I'm a lucky girl.
Your friend, Salem

Linx blinked and gaped at the words. "I don't believe this."

"When's it postmarked?" Tami peered over her shoulder.

"There is no postmark," Linx said. "See? The stamp's clean."

"Sometimes the post office forgets to postmark stuff," Tami said. "I'm always peeling off stamps and reusing them."

"It must have been sent early last season," Linx said. Her gut clenched and a weight pressed down on her shoulders as she sank onto the couch. "She sounded so happy, and now she's gone."

"I'm sorry." Tami sat beside her and rubbed her shoulder. "Were you two close?"

"She took care of me when I was pregnant. I would have lost the baby if she hadn't checked up on me."

"Oh, Linx." Tami hugged her. "I wish I could have been here for you, but I'm glad she was."

"Me too," Linx said. "I feel bad that we lost touch."

Linx stared at the words on the card and shook her head. Salem had decorated the card with hearts, as if she'd been in love.

Salem had always had a crush on Grady—but then, what woman hadn't? She used to tag along with them that first summer until she got injured and had to drop out. But she'd kept in touch with both Grady and Linx, and after Grady took off for Australia, Salem had been able to track him down.

Maybe they had always been closer than Linx had imagined. Just like that, her post-Grady bliss shattered, and rivulets of cold poured over her.

Linx pointed to the hearts next to Grady's name. "You think they dated?"

"Hey, don't go buying trouble," Tami said. "She's dead now. What does it matter if she and Grady dated?"

"It shouldn't matter, except if they were involved, and she died on a jump, and he was her jump partner—"

"Are you saying he caused her death?" Tami's eyes widened.

"No, but if Grady was her jump partner, why didn't he show her the way? What really happened up there?"

"There's only one person who knows," Tami said. "And you'll have to ask him."

Chapter Nine

"I'm telling you, this is the kind of dog you should get," Grady said to his eldest sister, Cait. He brought Sam into the Hart family cabin where she was staying. It wasn't quite as far from Colson's Corner as his plot of land, but remote enough so that they weren't bothered by neighbors.

The dog sniffed everything carefully before tentatively wagging his tail.

"He's definitely a man's dog," Cait said. "I'm looking for something a little smaller and sweeter."

"You mean a powder puff dog?" Grady scratched behind Sam's ears. "You want to live in the backwoods, you need a guard dog."

"He looks mean and ugly." Cait said, sitting as far back on the sofa as she could away from the large dog. "Mixing a German shepherd with a pitbull is asking for trouble."

The dog did look like a scrappy fighter, with a flatter snout than a German shepherd, ears that partially folded down, and a barrel chest over stout and powerful legs.

"Oh, come on, give him a chance." Grady rubbed Sam's short-haired coat which was brown underneath with black-tipped hair. The dog sat at attention and wagged the tip of his tail but didn't make any submissive moves such as lying down and exposing his underbelly.

Nope, a German pit was not cuddly or cute, but the veteran who requested one needed a dog like that to help her gain the confidence to live on her own and venture out of her apartment.

"You should keep him," Cait said, nursing a glass of ice tea.

How did she know he'd been entertaining exactly those thoughts? Then again, she knew her younger brothers and sisters better than they knew themselves. And she was also good at finding out things.

"Can't do that," Grady said, steeling himself. "The best dogs go to the vets. This guy is healthy, has a great disposition, and is tough at the same time."

"Then keep one that has issues, maybe an elderly one who has a hard time getting adopted," Cait said.

"I don't want another dog." Grady swiped his hand over his sweaty forehead.

"Man's best friend," she teased in a sing-song voice. "Really, you need to give it another shot."

"No, I don't. All dogs do is die on you, or get lost, or you have to put them down. No, thank you."

"Pretty much sums up your story with women, too." Cait set her glass down on the coffee table and curled her legs onto the couch sideways. "You want to tell me why you've given up?"

"Nope." Grady rose from the sofa. "Think I'll take Sam for a walk."

"I'll come with you." Cait pushed herself off the comfortable sofa and waddled to the front door. "Brian and I are in the market for a house in town. If I'm going to put up a wedding business and gift shop next door to the diner and across from the general store, then I need to know whether I'm welcome or not."

"You have no problem." Grady snapped the leash onto Sam's collar. "You're Linx's best buddy."

"Not quite," Cait said. "Tami King, the head of the Chamber of Commerce, goes back to grade school with her. I haven't been able to buddy up to her."

"I can help you with Tami." Grady grinned as they walked out the door and down the porch. "She and I share office space. Come by on Monday, and I'll make the introduction."

The summer heat permeated the evening air, even at this altitude. Grady's boots crunched over fallen pine needles as he and Cait strolled under a stand of old sequoia trees along a babbling creek.

Sam did a great job of heeling, walking precisely one foot behind him, while Cait kept darting curious glances between him and the dog.

"You thinking of keeping him?" she asked again.

"Thought I told you I can't." Grady dragged his voice. "You know why."

"It's been years," Cait said. "Even Connor got a new dog after Bear died."

"Yeah, well, Bear lived a good long life with him, and he got to say goodbye."

"I think you and Sam are a good match," Cait said. "Look how he follows you. It's like he's in the Marines or something."

"No more dogs," Grady said.

"Getting another dog would be a good start."

"To what?"

"Love, that's what." Cait blinked and flashed him a know-it-all smile. "It's in the air."

"Not for me." He turned his back on her and looked down at Sam, whose sad eyes told him he understood.

Every love story ended in tragedy. Either dumped or dead.

"Seems strange of you to run a dog matching service for veterans without having a dog yourself," Cait persisted as only a persistent and absolutely annoying eldest sister would do.

"Will you quit bugging me?" Grady hunched his shoulders. Hopefully, once his sister became a mother, she'd have her own brood to nag and pester.

They walked on in an uncomfortable silence while Sam sniffed tree trunks and fence posts. Unfortunately, with Cait, silence was never golden for long.

"Instead of staying up in that trailer, you should stay here with us," Cait said. "This cabin is as much yours as it is ours."

The cabin belonged to their parents, so what she said was true, but Grady coveted his privacy, and he wouldn't get any—even within his thoughts—with Cait yapping all the time.

"I have to be there to guard the building materials, take delivery, and do the construction," Grady said.

"At least catch your meals here," Cait offered.

"I'll think about it, but don't you two need your privacy?"

"Brian's already volunteering with the local fire department, and I'm out all day house-hunting," Cait said. "It might be fun to live above our store."

"I don't know if this town is such a great location for business," Grady said. "It's too remote, and the locals aren't friendly."

"Unless it's you who's causing all the trouble." Cait's nose wiggled like a bloodhound scenting a particularly intriguing trail.

"What's that supposed to mean?" Grady's stomach pinched at her implication. "Are you asking me to leave?"

"Should I?" Her eyebrow cocked as she tilted her head. "Somehow, you've turned the entire Colson clan against you. I heard Linx was the instigator. I thought you two had this flirtation thing going."

"We don't even know each other," Grady said, kicking a stone from the path.

"Don't tell me you tried to hook up with her and got turned down." Cait's eyes gaped in mock horror. "That would be a first—a woman actually turning you down."

"Oh, you don't know the half of it," Grady said. "I'm done with women. I thought I made that clear. No. More. Women."

"You got shot down." She smirked triumphantly. "I'm not stupid. You and Linx were flirting your asses off over Christmas. But since her dog hates you, she shut you out."

Grady ran his hand through his thick pompadour hair. "What's the big obsession about Linx? I don't give a rat's tail about her."

"Of course you don't," Cait said. "You're a man of the world, leaving a trail of broken hearts from Alaska to New Zealand. But if you're thinking of settling here, I'll put you on notice, brother or no brother—take your 'hate them and leave them' stunt somewhere else. I'm starting a wedding business here, and I don't want you scaring off potential customers."

"You might want to reevaluate the wisdom of a wedding business in California. Home of the no-fault divorce with the divorce rate over sixty percent." Grady wasn't a fan of romance and love—two of the fakest and most insincere concepts ever to plague mankind.

There was nothing more disgusting than a simpering woman whose only hope in life was to marry a man—as if he'd solve all her problems and whisk her away to a life of luxury. No, thank you.

He needed someone with a backbone.

Actually, scratch that, he just needed to get his rocks off and a woman who hated him was perfect for those purposes.

"To get divorced, they have to be married first." Cait turned up her nose and shielded her eyes from the slanted rays of sunlight streaming through the forest. "I only care about the beginning, not the end."

Sam sniffed around a fencepost and marked his territory, but he was well-behaved, not pulling or tugging. What a calm dog with such presence.

"Cynical, much?" he grumbled at his sister, who until last Christmas, had merely existed in a loveless marriage.

"Nope, not at all." She beamed at him, tugging his sleeve. "This place is a fresh start for me and Brian. So far above the pollution of the big city. The scent of mountain pine, the natural beauty, and a community of good people. It'll be refreshing to put down roots in a place where we can make a difference."

"For you, but not for me," Grady said. "A rolling stone gathers no moss."

"If you're really a rolling stone, then why did you quit smokejumping?" Cait angled her all-seeing face and cornered Grady in front of the stepping stones crossing the stream.

Sam lapped at the water while squirrels in the trees above them sounded the alarm. The dog's ears perked, but he didn't lunge or bark.

"I didn't quit smokejumping," Grady said. He brushed by her and took long lanky steps across the stream. "I'm skipping this season, that's all."

Yeah, yeah, yeah, that was what he told himself. He was good at what he did, and nothing could beat the excitement and exhilaration of parachuting into a firestorm, prepared to do battle with an angry Mother Nature.

Nothing except for that last jump where things had gone horribly wrong.

"Wow, you're really going to leave me on this side of the creek?" Cait called, unable to decide on a path for her pregnant body to take across the slippery rocks.

For a moment, smoke and flames clouded his vision. Worse than the images were the sounds—the loud cracks, pops, and greedy snap of red, orange, and gold, consuming everything in its path. And the smells—thick, acrid smoke digging into the nostrils, gagging soot and choking ashes.

He blinked at the sound of her voice, and then his eyes widened. A plume of smoke rose over the treetops from the direction of his parents' cabin.

"Smoke." He bounded over the creek back the way they came. "Stay back."

"What's happening?" Cait's voice shrieked from behind him. "Is there a fire?"

"Call 9-1-1 if you can get a signal," he shouted, hoping that the new cell towers were operational.

Without waiting for her to answer, he dashed toward the cabin. This couldn't be happening. Shouldn't be happening.

His parents already lost their house in a fire and had only recently finished rebuilding. How was it fair for them to lose their mountain cabin?

All because he'd distracted Cait who had probably been cooking dinner.

Sam bounded beside him and when they reached the cabin, it was engulfed in crackling flames and thick with smoke.

"No!" Grady shouted as he ran toward the fire.

Chapter Ten

After her shower, Linx plucked Ginger from her doggy bed and changed the sheets and towels. She warmed up a wipe under the faucet and wiped the puppy's bottom to stimulate her bladder and bowel movement. Normally, a mother dog would lick them and consume the results, but poor little Ginger was orphaned and had to sleep with a hot water bottle.

Linx fed her every two hours, making sure to smother her with plenty of attention, but she wasn't a good enough substitute mom for the puppy, who cried and whined when uncomfortable.

"I shouldn't have left you alone." Guilt swarmed Linx that she'd gone to satisfy her own physical desires while leaving little Ginger without comfort.

The puppy had already gained weight and her front feet were strong, pawing at Linx for affection. The little girl's eyes were still closed, but she appeared to be peeking out of one eye.

Linx rubbed her face in the puppy's downy fur, and the tip of the puppy's tail wiggled.

"You love me, don't you?" she crooned to the little red ball of fluff. "I don't want to give you up, but you'll have a better life with a little boy or little girl."

After cleaning Ginger and drying her, Linx tucked her under her arm and fed her a bottle of puppy formula.

Tami had gone home already, and it was time for Linx to traipse up to the family ranch for their weekly Friday night fish fry.

Her cousin, Kevin, was a social media whiz and a photographer and videographer, working to set up a dude ranch with her brother, Chad. He'd promised to help her publicize the rescue center using Ginger as the star.

Linx tied a pretty pink bow around Ginger's neck and tucked her into a small, padded carrier with a hot water bottle wrapped in a cloth diaper.

The little puppy squealed and snuggled up to the water bottle, her tummy full, for now.

On the way, Linx stopped by the town square and picked up Joey and Vivi, her younger twin sisters.

"Oh, she's so precious," Joey squealed as she got into the back seat. "May I hold her?"

"Go ahead. She loves to snuggle." Linx pulled back the puppy's blanket.

"I want her," Vivi said, bouncing on her seat. "I could use a watchdog at the store."

"I could have a diner dog," Joey said. "We can share her."

"Do you think there are other puppies like her?" Vivi asked. "Don't they have larger litters?"

"Maybe this one was a runt, and they abandoned her." Joey held the puppy close to her face. "I'm in love already."

"Okay, you two, duke it out." Linx laughed as she let Cedar lay her head on her thigh and started the ignition.

Linx drove down the switchbacks into the Sierra Valley, a high-altitude valley full of pasture-land and marshes. Her father had a hay farm where he bred horses and raised range-fed cattle and pasture-fed pigs.

Her mother, meanwhile, had run away twenty years ago when Linx was five years old, but all of her siblings, except for Becca who'd gone away to law school, still lived in the county.

Dear old Dad had miraculously held the family together, along with her grandmother who'd passed away six years ago.

Linx had grown up pretty much on her own on that ranch, hiding out in the wilderness and exploring all the back trails. While her older brothers helped their father, and Becca did the cooking and mothering, she had been left alone since Gran was busy tending to the twins.

She lowered the windows, letting the crisp breeze rattle into the SUV. Cedar left her lap and stuck her head out as they joggled down a country road, past antique barns and miles of grassland. The sun was setting over the majestic mountain peaks behind them, brushing the sky with grand purple and orange hues.

Like the gold still hidden in the hills, she was here to stay, and no city boy would ever drive her away.

* * *

"How are my girls?" Linx's father took off his hat and clambered through the farmhouse door. He was as rugged and handsome as ever, even though his hair was gray all the way through and his blue eyes crinkled from working outside in the sun.

"Look at Linx's puppy," Vivi said, holding up Ginger who squealed and pawed at the air.

"Your mom would have loved her." Dad cupped his big hands to receive the puppy. "She had a thing for red hair—thought it brought good luck."

Mom had been gone twenty years, and Dad still spoke about her as if she were right around the corner. While other men would have gotten angry and forgotten about a runaway wife, good old Joe Colson would only look at the positive—how their mother, Minx, was a free spirit, and how she had to follow her muse, and how talented and creative she was.

Oh, she was beautiful enough in her day to wrap their father, good old Joe Colson, around her pinkie, and enchant him to the extent that he gave her free rein to express herself: erecting large metallic sculptures made of railway spikes, rusted cast iron skillets, nuts, bolts, and whatever pieces of metal she could scavenge from the junkyard, combine it with animal bones, skin, leather, and feathers, and call it art.

But taking care of and disciplining children? Cooking and cleaning? No, thank you. If it weren't for their dear departed grandmother, the Colson kids would all have been delinquents—with Linx the worst one of all.

"Let me see that little runt." Kevin, who was the mayor's son, pointed his phone camera at the sisters. Behind him, her brother Chad grinned and asked, "Think that dog's part Australian shepherd? I want me a red one, for good luck."

"You and your red for good luck superstitions." Linx shook her head. Why was everyone so hung up on what their mom believed? Was Linx the only one who hated their mother for abandoning them?

Linx had been five when it happened, and the only thing she could remember was her mother's flaming dyed red hair and the colorful tie-dyed sunburst shirts she used to wear. There had been no hugs, no cookie bakes, no kissing owies, or any of the other motherly things she saw on TV.

Nope, Tami's mother had been more doting on Linx than her own, and as the years went by and she saw how other mothers sacrificed their time and energy for their children, she began to understand why her mother, the free and artistic spirit, had to run away from seven demanding children.

She, too, would have been a horrible mother.

"Are Todd and Scott going to make it tonight?" Dad asked after Kevin finished taking pictures and videos of Ginger from all angles.

"Todd's on his way, but Scott's on duty," Joey replied. "Becca's on a case in San Francisco, and Uncle Chip has a meeting at the Sixty Miners."

Her position at the diner made her the central switchboard when it came to information around town, with Vivi not far behind at the general store selling everything from groceries and hardware to flowers and craft supplies.

"Chad and Kevin took a bunch of tourists out fishing and caught a whole load of trout," Dad said. "We got them all dipped and fried up already."

Since Becca was absent, Linx took the seat opposite her father at the end of the table where a mother traditionally sat. Tonight, she was the eldest female of the bunch.

After Dad said grace, everyone passed the fish and salad around the table. Dad asked Joey how business was and went over kitchen safety with her, while Vivi was all over Chad and Kevin about the tourist activities and what items she should stock for the summer

Todd rushed in halfway through dinner, looking harried and overworked. He slung his jacket across the empty chair next to Linx and served himself a large portion of fish and chips.

"Busy day?" Linx asked. "What happened? A rash of lockouts? Or did you catch Tami speeding through the town again?"

Todd grunted and chewed his food slowly, his cheeks reddening at the mention of Tami.

"Come on, spit it out," Linx teased. "Tami was on her way to the Sixty Miners Saloon. Did you meet her there for Happy Hour? Is that why you're late?"

"No, as a matter of fact, I caught Grady Hart speeding around Dead Man's curve. Gave him a big fat ticket."

"And that made you late? Couldn't have been more than a few minutes." Linx studied her brother's flushed face. A light sheen of sweat dampened his forehead as he chewed his food.

"That man's a menace." Todd thumped his water glass on the tabletop. "I don't want that playboy within fifty feet of any of my sisters."

"He doesn't bother me," Linx said, wondering what crawled up her brother's craw.

"Have you forgotten the pain he put you through?"

"I'm a big girl," Linx said. "It's over and done with, and I want to move on."

"How the heck are you going to move on when he's a walking reminder?" Todd set his fork down with a thump. "I heard he was flirting with Joey at the diner. Does that not concern you?"

"Then keep him out of the diner," Linx retorted. "And while you're at it, he should stay away from Vivi, too."

She hadn't told her family the identity of the man who'd gotten her pregnant, but somehow, in the past few months, they all seemed to have figured it out—with Todd being the most belligerent. Could Tami have slipped up?

"I'll let him know the general store is off limits too, all except Friday evening when Vivi and Joey are here," Todd plowed on, oblivious to her sarcasm. "Him being around town has started the gossip mill going. You know what they're saying about him and your friend, Salem?"

"They were jump partners. No big deal." Linx kept her voice steady as she stirred dressing into her salad.

"Is that all you think it was?" Todd said, leaning forward and lowering his voice. "Paul thinks Grady caused her death. Apparently, he whispered something in her ear right before her fatal jump. He says Salem was pregnant and he suspects Grady was the father."

"That man must have holes in his condoms," Linx said, before a cold sliver of fear slithered down her spine. "What do you think he said to her?"

Todd's eyes darkened. "Maybe he accused her of lying. Maybe he said he wasn't taking responsibility. In any case, it messed up Salem's concentration and she ended up drifting into the fire."

Linx crumpled a napkin in her fist. "That's horrible. Poor Salem."

"Right. He has to be stopped," Todd said. "I don't care if he knocks up all the women in California, he's not touching my town and my sisters. You call me anytime if he gives you any trouble. You hear?"

"He's not giving me trouble," Linx said. "Besides, he'll roll his stone out of here soon. The less attention we pay him, the sooner he'll be gone."

"I'm not so sure." Todd scratched his five o'clock stubble. "I did some patrolling and he's cleared the mess from his plot of land. Ordered building materials."

"He's rebuilding?" Linx felt a mixture of hope and despair war inside of her.

"Maybe he's flipping it to sell, you know, increase the value and sell it to one of those San Francisco millionaires." Todd shrugged as he stuffed another filet in his wide mouth. "Yesterday he called Scott and had him inspect the burnt foundation. Claims the fire started on the back porch."

"Back porch? How? It usually starts on the roof—you know where a burning ember lands." Linx's mouth went dry. "Are you saying it was arson?"

"Scott thinks it was. It's been years and many rainstorms have gone by, but he remembers inspecting the ruins and thinking it could have been arson."

"Why didn't you do anything about it?"

"Grady was out of the country, and no one filed a complaint." Todd shrugged. "We had a rash of fires back then, so it kind of got lost in the shuffle."

"It's happening again." Joey looked up from her phone, her face ashen. "Scott just texted. The Hart cabin up near the creek is on fire."

Chapter Eleven

Grady shielded his eyes and cursed. A huge cloud of smoke billowed over the property. Flames shot all around the cabin and there was no way he could get close. Instinct made him glance up in the sky, even though there would be no package dropped from an airplane: no chainsaw, Pulaski, and water pump.

His truck was parked on the gravel, not yet engulfed from the fire. He could still save it if he was fast.

"Stay back," he commanded Sam, who was thankfully not considering going into the fire.

Grady charged into the hot smoky wind whipped up by the fire, tucking his head down and clawed his way into his truck, hardly able to see. The roaring of the fire was deafening as he started the ignition.

Smoke stung his eyes and rubbed his lungs raw, but he gunned the engine and barreled his truck from the parking shed, throwing hot gravel from his tires.

The sound of fire engines wailed up the road, and Grady pulled to the side. Brian was the first man off the pumper truck. A second tanker truck pulled up, carrying its own water. Thank God.

"Where's Cait?" Brian charged toward Grady's truck.

"She's safe. We were walking and she called it in." Grady grabbed a jacket from inside the truck and helped himself to a chainsaw from the toolbox. "There's a creek back there we can run the lines. I have to keep the fire from spreading."

The guys at the tanker truck stretched barrel strainers over the hard suction hoses to tap water from the creek, while other men unfurled hoses from the tanker truck.

Grady motioned a group of hotshots with chainsaws and shovels to the backside of the cabin to clear the dried brush and trees.

June in California was prime fire season, and with fires burning out of control all over the west, they had to nip this one in the bud. If it spread down the hillside, it could threaten the town and all the surrounding areas.

His adrenaline pumped high, he shouted his throat raw, guiding and commanding the volunteer hotshots. They fought hard, chopping, sawing, shoveling dirt to deprive the fire of fuel, while the guys with water worked on saving the structure.

Little by little, they beat the fire back. Grady's muscles screamed with exhaustion and his mouth was parched as he threw dirt over the last drifting ember.

He found Cait huddled under a blanket, surrounded by the Colson sisters: Linx, Joey, and Vivi.

"Grady!" Cait rushed toward him. "It's all my fault. Did I leave a pot on? Mom and Dad are going to kill me."

"Are you okay?" He caught her as she stumbled, one hand clutched over her pregnant belly. "It's not your fault. I distracted you. You're not in pain, are you?"

"I'm okay, I am." She fanned herself and panted.

"She needs to go to the hospital to get checked out," Linx cut in. "She won't listen to us, but I think she might be going into labor."

"It's too early," Cait wailed. "I'm okay. I'm okay. Where's Brian? Brian's missing. Where is he? I can't see him."

She strained at Grady's arms, but he held her tight. "Get into the truck. Brian will see you at the hospital."

Without further argument, he lifted his trembling sister and carried her to the cab of his truck.

"I've got your dog," Linx said from behind him while he put his sister in the passenger seat. "He was at Cait's side when we found her wandering around."

"Thanks for taking care of them." He swiveled around after shutting the passenger door. "It means a lot to me."

Before he knew what he was doing, his arms were around Linx, and his dipped his thirsty lips over hers.

Goodness, she tasted like the morning dew, sweet and refreshing, and it was all Grady could do not to let himself sink into the soothing sensations. He didn't need her, didn't want to need her.

With a deep groan, he pulled away and gazed into those deep-brown eyes. "Can you hold onto Sam for me? I'll pick him up tomorrow morning."

Time stood still—for a moment, and his simple question felt normal, a glimpse beyond the lies and games, a tantalizing vision of what could be.

"Sure." She touched his sooty, hot face. Swallowing hard, she blinked. "I'm so sorry about your parents' cabin."

"Yeah, well, cabins can be rebuilt, but not lives."

She nodded, then leaned in and kissed him again, contradicting him and unravelling that last string of resistance.

Could he rebuild? Could they?

* * *

Why did he have to be so utterly hot?

That smoky kiss, the tang of his tongue, the rasp of his beard shadow, and most of all, the intense focus, the grit and godawful sexiness of a man stretching himself to the limit fighting for his family, his home, fighting an evil greater than himself.

How could she fight against it? And yet, he was the cause of the greatest pain in her life, her most abject failure, her deepest regret.

She shouldn't be kissing him, comforting him, and baring her soul to him. But she couldn't help it.

She was the hapless moth banging herself against Grady Hart's fiery but impenetrable light. He didn't need her, didn't even want her, but she'd make him feel her pain, acknowledge it, and then, maybe she could finally move on.

The wallop of a siren shutting off jolted Grady's lips from hers, and she stepped back in time to spot Todd and his deputy exit the police cruiser and head down the driveway to the smoldering remains of the fire.

"See ya," Grady grunt and jumped into the cab of his pickup to take Cait to the hospital, while Linx's twin sisters sidled up to her.

"That must have been some kiss," Joey said, putting an arm around her. "Best be glad Todd's working the crime scene and not throwing Grady out of town."

"Cr-crime scene?" Linx snapped her gaze to her sister. "What happened? Is someone hurt?"

"Scott says the fire spread way too fast to be a cooking fire. Cait's husband, Brian, has experience investigating arson, and he says someone doused gasoline over the porch."

"But who? Why?" Linx's hand flew to her mouth.

"We Colsons are the only ones who want to run Grady out of town," Joey said. "But we all have alibis. Especially you. If this was a mystery novel, I'd be asking who's been trying to keep Grady away from her dog."

"Oh, stop it." Linx gave her sister a light shove. Joey was always the one who spouted insane theories—an attention getting tactic in her large family. "This isn't a joke. Besides, this isn't Grady's cabin. It belongs to his parents."

"Maybe someone doesn't want competition for the wedding business." Joey poked Vivi. "Weren't you thinking of having a bridal shop at the general store?"

"I could say it was you, Joey," Vivi retorted. "Cait bakes a mean cupcake and you want to add a bakery to that diner of yours."

"Come off it." Linx swiped her forehead. "We all love Cait and Brian, and no one would want to hurt them. This has to do with Grady Hart. Whoever burned down the cabin thinks it'll hurt Grady and drive him from the town."

Both twins trained their eyes onto her. "That would lead right back to you."

"Or Todd." An icy shiver spread its web over Linx's shoulders.

Todd had been late to the family fish fry, and he'd been especially vehement in denouncing Grady.

But no, Todd was a lawman. He would never break the law, would he?

Which meant it was down to her again. Except her idea of burning Grady was burning up the sheets with him.

Chapter Twelve

Linx woke early the next morning after staying up late the night before. Cait had called to let her know that she was okay and staying at The Over Easy Bed & Breakfast near Joe's Diner. Her contractions had subsided and had been caused by exhaustion and dehydration.

She hadn't heard from Grady, so she put Sam back in the kennel out back. She should get him ready and deliver him back to Grady before he came over to claim him.

The phone was ringing downstairs, so Linx pulled a robe over her naked body and bounded down the stairs, followed by Cedar.

Linx rushed to pick up the phone, but whoever was calling hung up without speaking. Who bothered with landlines these days?

Oh, right. She still had one with a vintage nineteen-eighties answering machine. Maybe the person had only wanted to check if she was in.

Cedar barked and jumped near the door, wanting to go outside for her morning bathroom break.

Linx opened the door and almost tripped over her own feet as she skidded to a stop in front of a monstrous pile of metallic art sprawled on her porch.

Rusty patches of scrap metal were welded in a rough shape of a grinning skull. A railroad spike pierced one of the eye sockets, and a beckoning hand protruded from the other eye. In the hand was a heart made of rusty wires and scrap twisted together complete with arteries and veins made from ridged toilet connector tubes.

Her absentee mother had left another calling card.

"Minx!" Linx swirled around and shouted at the empty space in front of the center. "Get this crap off my property."

No wonder the dogs had been restless in the wee hours before dawn.

"Belongs in a junkyard!" Linx shook her fist and yelled, in case Minx lurked to see her reaction.

Beside her, Cedar sniffed at the heap of scrap and emitted a low growl, as if she also found it offensive.

"You're darn right." Linx petted her dog, glaring at the skull which was embellished by a ring of flame-like shapes. "What's this thing supposed to mean anyway?"

Cedar's ears perked up at the sound of tires on the gravel driveway. Linx grabbed her before she bolted toward the approaching vehicle.

"Sorry, girl, can't let you bite her." Linx yanked Cedar back into the cabin and slammed the door. Her heart pounded and sweat erupted over her forehead. Whatever words they'd have would be bad and nasty—hurtful, and right now, with the fire and Grady in town, she couldn't deal with another all-out emotional assault.

Minx Colson was the polar opposite of Grady and Cait's mother. Where Mrs. Hart was warm and cuddly, like an overeager golden retriever, her mother had the demeanor of a Rottweiler ready to attack.

And she sure knew how to bare her fangs.

Linx lowered the shades and peeked out the corner of the window while Cedar barked.

The person getting out of the truck wasn't her mother.

It was Grady, and Grady and Cedar didn't mix, at least without fallout raining all over Linx.

"Oh, crap!" Linx dragged Cedar back. "I need to get Sam ready. You're going to have to stay out of sight in the bathroom."

She shoved her dog, whining and complaining, into the bathroom.

Before Grady could knock, Linx bounded onto the porch and slammed the door behind her.

"Hi! Sam's out back. How's Cait? Is she going back to San Francisco?"

Grady raised one eyebrow sky-high. "What's gotten into you? A squirrel crawl up your ass?"

What kind of greeting was that after the hot, searing kiss they'd shared last night?

"I, uh, well, let me get Sam for you." The wind picked up the edge of her robe.

"Dressed in nothing but a flimsy robe?" Grady's leer spread across his wide mouth. "And what the heck is that?"

He tilted his too-sexy chin at the pile of metal on her porch.

"Nothing. A skull. Art."

"Nice." He advanced on her, smooth and knowing, as he lowered the shoulders of her robe. His heated gaze drew sparks up and down her body.

Linx swallowed hard, as he lowered his slick wet lips onto her neck, melting all the panic from her body and replacing it with dreaded desire.

"I can't, I mean, the dog, Sam." Her words were useless against the press of his hard, hot body, and the suckling of his mouth as he trailed kisses down the column of her neck to her bare shoulders.

All he had to do was drop the robe, and she'd be exposed to the entire world—including her mother, if she were lurking around with a pair of binoculars.

"We can't." She summoned all her strength and pushed from his embrace. "Someone might see. I wasn't expecting you."

"Then let's move inside." Grady's low voice electrified every sensual nerve on her body.

Woof. Woof. Thud.

Linx froze. Cedar had gotten out of the bathroom and was lunging against the front door.

"Oh no! My dog got loose." Linx scrambled to tie her robe and turned to the door.

"Then let her out." Grady laughed and reached for the doorknob.

"No, you can't!" Linx grabbed his hand, but he was too quick.

He jiggled the doorknob.

Locked.

Whatever relief she felt quickly fanned into a firestorm of panic. She was locked out in nothing but her light summer robe, buck naked underneath, and Cedar was on the other side of the door.

"Hey little doggy," Grady said. "Your mommy's locked out with big bad me."

"Stop teasing her. Can't you tell she's scared?" Linx yanked Grady by his arm. "Let's go get Sam, and you can be on your way. I know that veteran really wants him, and we can't keep her waiting. How's Cait, by the way?"

"You're popping like a busted sack of popcorn in a microwave." Grady tapped his fingers on the door, eliciting heavier barking and whining from Cedar. "Hey, little doggy. I bet you want to play."

"Let's go." Linx gritted her teeth, but he wouldn't move from the door.

The barking grew more frantic.

Linx's pulse panicked when the curtains moved against the window and Cedar's paws showed underneath, digging at the window sill.

"Look, she's trying to get out," Grady hooted. "Maybe she has to pee. You do have a key somewhere out here, don't you?"

She did—under a potted plant, which was thankfully hidden by her mother's huge metallic spike in the eye.

She couldn't expose Cedar to Grady—not right now. She wasn't ready. Not yet.

There was only one thing to do. She had to get Grady's attention off the dog and onto her and get him away from the window.

Slowly, she untied her robe and pulled it aside, flashing her boob. Giving him a come-hither wink, she wiggled her behind and sashayed around the wraparound porch to the back of the property where the rest of the dogs stayed.

* * *

Linx was acting strange, but after the last twenty-four hours, who wouldn't?

Grady turned away from her hysterical dog who would hurt herself if she broke through the window and chased Linx around the cabin.

The fire at his parents' cabin hadn't left it completely in ruins, but there was still substantial damage to the porch and front entrance. Fortunately, they had caught it in time and the propane tank hadn't blown, but for now, his sister and brother-in-law were holed up at a bed and breakfast.

Grady caught up with Linx in the barn housing kennels of dogs. The barking was deafening and drove every bit of lust from his bloodstream. Oh, she'd cast a sexy image, and he could undress her and have his way with her in a minute flat—but in front of all these canine witnesses?

No way.

Grady tucked his shirt in and met up with Linx in front of Sam's pen. "How's he doing?"

"He's a good boy. Kept Cait safe."

Grady tugged Linx into his arms and kissed the top of her head. "Hey, I'd like to play, but I have to deliver this guy to the therapist and pick up clothes for Cait and Brian. Knowing my parents, they're going to swarm into town, so I'll be busy the next few days. Raincheck?"

"We can't meet here anyway." She backed away from him. "And we're not in a relationship, in case you're getting any ideas."

The pupils of her eyes tightened, and she now looked decidedly hostile.

What was it with this woman?

Oh, right, she was hard as nails, and he hated her. All this sweet gooey stuff was hormonal—the aftereffects of fighting a witch of a fire.

Nothing more, nothing less.

"Thanks for the dog. We have some new requests come in. The therapist I work with mentioned a husband and a wife who want a pair of retrievers for companionship." He craned his neck at the other kennels. "Can I have a look around?"

The din of barking hadn't let up the entire time they were in the barn, and he was really getting a headache, but he'd promised he'd look.

"No." Linx clamped her arms over her breasts. "I can't let you have them without an application. Please, don't come to the center again. If you want a dog, I'll bring him to you."

So, she was back to game playing again—her version of pump and dump.

He took Sam by the leash and left her standing there.

Chapter Thirteen

"I heard all about it, so you better spill." Tami dropped by the center later that day. "You kissing Grady in front of the fire. Everyone's talking about it."

"So? He's single and available, I'm single and available." Linx sat on the couch feeding little Ginger. The puppy was starting to open her eyes, peering out of the right one more than the left, as she batted the bottle with her front paws, trying to hold on.

"Are you two dating now?" Tami's eyes widened.

"Hardly. I told him to get lost." Linx tucked a strand of her messy hair behind her ear. "He came over to get Sam and almost found Cedar. Thank God I'd locked myself out, and he didn't know where the spare key was."

"Why don't you just tell him? What's he going to do to you anyway?"

"Hate me forever." Linx knew she sounded grumpy, but the rollercoaster ride her hormones had just endured was pissing her off.

She was supposed to remain in control—not him.

If she wanted to make him feel the hurt and pain she'd gone through, she couldn't be letting down her guard.

He was the one invading her hometown.

He was the one who had to pay.

"Men don't hate women who give them favors," Tami said in a sing-song voice.

"They don't respect them, either." A niggling feeling prickled the back of Linx's neck. "By the way, did you tell anyone that Grady was the guy who knocked me up?"

"No, I didn't even tell my mom." Tami said, sitting down at her desk. "Why are you blaming me? Seems like everyone already knows."

"Someone leaked it." Linx adjusted the bottle so the last bit of formula went to the nipple. "Last Christmas, no one was talking about it."

"Right, but if you think hot, studly guys coming to town isn't worth talking about, it's because you hide here with your dogs all the time. Someone got wind of him and Paul, and now, everyone knows everything."

The puppy squirmed as she finished the last drop of formula, so Linx put her over her shoulder to burp her. "Everyone knows what?"

"Oh, just everything." Tami waved her hand and booted up her computer. "You and Grady, Salem and Grady, Paul and Salem. Now that Paul's here, some of his buddies have been coming by the saloon."

"Stop. I already heard." Linx let herself sink deeper into the plush couch. "Which is why I'm done with Grady."

"You keep saying it, and maybe even you'll believe it." Tami's eyes focused on her computer screen. "What's that thing sitting on your porch?"

"My mother left me her calling card," Linx said. "Apparently, she's been wanting to talk to all of us. Something about making amends."

"That's good, isn't it?"

Linx shrugged as she stroked the puppy's soft down. "I've got nothing but bad things to say to her, so it's better to say nothing at all."

"Aren't you curious why she wants to get in touch after all these years?" Tami clicked through her email.

"Not as long as she keeps leaving trash on my porch." Linx didn't want to admit the tiny spark that ignited in her chest or the thought that at least her mother had sent her a gift—so to speak. "There must be strings attached to it."

"Hey, look," Tami said, pointing to her screen. "Kevin's already posted Ginger's videos and we're getting lots of hits and people filling out applications. We even have some outright donations."

"That's great." Linx perked up and got up off the sofa with Ginger. "How much?"

"Someone donated a thousand bucks, and the little ones add up to about three hundred. Can we build more kennels?"

"Once I pay off the debts." Linx tamped down Tami's unbridled enthusiasm. "But it's good news."

"Just got an email. Grady is looking for two more dogs. He wants to come by and pick them up before he returns to San Francisco. He wants to make an appointment with me." Tami talked as fast as she read.

Linx needed to hold her ground—hold firm, especially after what her traitorous body almost made her do on the porch this morning.

"Oh no, he's not coming around here."

"But didn't he come by to pick up Sam?" Tami gave her a sidelong look. "Did something happen?"

Linx gulped and walked back and forth, petting the puppy over her shoulder. "He made fun of my mother's sculpture."

"Oh, you nasty little liar." Tami snickered. "You don't give two flying figs about that sculpture. Stop deflecting."

"It's pretty basic. Grady plays by my rules, or he doesn't play. You know the reason."

"Sure, you love giving him personal deliveries with wagging tails and happy endings." Tami did that copulating motion with her fingers. "The good thing is he's rebuilding on that piece of land he has, and you won't have to drive as far."

That was another reason she couldn't sleep.

Linx closed her eyes, willing Tami to stop bothering her about Grady. The man was a menace, and yet she couldn't leave him alone. It was one of those damned if you do and damned if you don't situations. Life without Grady was unbearably bleak and empty, but having Grady around grated on every nerve fiber in her body.

He disrespected her. He was rude and snide with her.

But when he was in bed with her, he made her feel like a goddess. How could something so wrong feel so right?

"I'm not going near him or to his place," Linx said. "Unless it's to plop that skull onto his property."

"Ohhh ... giving love gifts already." Tami's finger copulation sped up, making a sandpapery sound. "He calls the cops on you, you call the cops on him, just let me know to bring the popcorn—especially if Todd's the responding officer."

Linx threw a wet wipe at Tami. "I'll give Todd a nudge your way."

"You better." Tami picked up her purse. "I'd rather he use his hot breath for something other than giving me lectures on driving too fast. Well, I'm off to my real job. Got to scout down listings for Cait and her husband. Such a wonderful couple, and now, they're homeless."

She whooshed out the door, wiggling her ample behind like a category four hurricane.

Linx chuckled to herself. Tami and Todd. They'd never work. Todd was a stickler for rules and preserving the town in the old way, whereas Tami was a rule-breaker and bent on modernization and redevelopment.

They'd sparred frequently at the city council meetings and were always at loggerheads. But apparently fighting led to chemistry, at least on Tami's side.

Linx cleaned Ginger up and tucked her into her doggy bed. She had a whole list of chores to do out back, and she had no time to play matchmaker or wonder what Grady was up to.

So, he was rebuilding his cabin—the one he and Cedar had once lived in—the one Linx had spent what little time off they got splayed in his bed.

Memories she didn't want to indulge invaded her along with the feel of the soft rug in front of the fireplace, the scent of cedar and pine, the clean crisp linens on his bed, and the warm musk of the fireman himself.

Cedar had been a part of those memories.

"Come here, girl. I'm so sorry." Linx wiggled her fingers at her dog. Cedar ambled toward her, her head down and crestfallen. "You're not feeling good, are you?"

Grabbing Cedar's brush, she had her lie down for a thorough brushing. Usually, running her fingers through Cedar's fur calmed her racing heart and gave her peace.

But not today—not when Cedar moped around like an abandoned dog—lifeless and dejected.

Guilt crawled up Linx's throat as she brushed out sections of Cedar's luxurious fur. It was wrong for her to keep Cedar from Grady, now that he was back in town.

It was one thing to keep her while Grady was out fighting the fires of the world, but now? What excuse did she really have?

Grady rejecting her had nothing to do with keeping Cedar from him.

She couldn't even say he'd taken advantage of her, although he'd been her superior when they'd slept together. He was the drill instructor, and she was a rookie.

She'd wanted him the minute she laid eyes on him, and she'd worked hard to get into his bed—tempting him at every turn.

But in the end, he'd done the dishonorable thing and turned his back on her. He'd ground his heel into her heart.

He'd ruined her life.

Linx buried her face into Cedar's furry mane. She hugged her and stroked her, and Cedar returned her affection with soft, warm licks.

Her dog always knew how to comfort her, but her selfishness had denied Grady the same canine companionship he craved.

There was only one thing to do. She had to fess up. Would he let her keep Cedar? Or would he devastate her yet again, by ripping another chunk out of her heart?

Before she could stop herself, she texted Grady. *I have the two retrievers. Meet me at the All Roads Motel.*

Chapter Fourteen

"I should think not," Grady drawled to himself as he stared at Linx's text message commanding him to meet her at another roadside inn.

Since she told him to get lost, he'd gone back to San Francisco to hand Sam off to the dog trainer. Placing dogs with veterans wasn't as easy as he thought.

Some of them had night frights, and others were liable to snap in anger at the drop of a pin. Some had disabilities, partial paralysis, traumatic brain injuries, or were wheelchair bound. Others suffered from addiction or had abusive tendencies.

He made his best guess on rescuing a dog, and then he worked with the trainer to assess the dog as well as the veteran they were trying to match.

He typed a quick message back.

No go. Meet me in SF and we'll talk.

Before she could text back, he silenced his phone and rang Vanessa Ransom's doorbell.

Two dogs were already barking from behind the door, excitedly yipping and scratching. Sam stayed calm. He stood at attention, ready for anything, but completely silent.

"Okay, okay, you two," Nessa scolded her mutts, Randi and Ronni. She opened the door and grabbed her two little rascals by the collars to keep them inside.

Randi was black and white, had an upright tail and wiry fur, a rat terrier sheltie mix, and Ronni had short, but soft brown hair with black tips, floppy ears and a bushier tail—a shepherd terrier mix.

"Got another dog for me?" Nessa stepped back to let Grady in. "Let me put these two in the bedroom. Be right back."

She half-dragged, half-carried the two yappers down the hallway while Grady crossed the threshold.

Vanessa was a psychotherapist specializing in post traumatic stress disorder, suicide prevention, and sexual abuse recovery. In addition to seeing patients, she trained dogs for the Dogs for Vets program on a volunteer basis.

She came back from her bedroom with a big smile breaking over her pretty face. She was tall and slim, a black woman with long straight hair, large expressive eyes, and a wide, friendly mouth—and she was too much of a goody-two-shoes for him to mess with in his "hate them and leave them" state of mind.

Without coming too close, since she didn't want to appear threatening to the dog, she stood still until Sam approached and sniffed her.

"He's a very calm one. Unruffled," Grady said. "I think he'll be perfect for Zulu."

Zulu was a former Army officer who'd been held as a sex slave by terrorists before coming back to the United States. She was living at a residential rehab center for female veterans suffering from PTSD, but had recently gotten a small apartment with her sister, a victim of human trafficking.

Both of them were Vanessa's patients, and she worked with them during the day, learning and practicing coping strategies. At the moment, a male friend of theirs stayed with them on "guard" duty, but conditions were strained since he wanted a relationship with Zulu and she was not ready to go down that road.

"He's a beautiful dog." Nessa reached out and rubbed the dog's back. "Strong too. How old do you think he is?"

"Younger than three," Grady replied. "He was surrendered because his owner had to deploy to the Middle East."

"Ah, so he had a soldier train him," Nessa said. "Still, I'll keep him separated from Ronni and Randi for the first few days, not that I think he'll tear them up, but they can be annoying."

"That's because they're so playful." Grady cracked a grin. "By the way, the lady at the rescue says she has two retrievers for the husband and wife veterans."

"Will she let them go without an interview?" Nessa asked.

Grady rubbed his chin. "Let's see how it goes with Sam. She's bending the rules, letting me bring him here."

"Hope it goes well with Sam," Nessa said. "Oh, where are my manners? Would you like to stay for coffee or tea?"

"Actually, I have to get going." He patted his pocket where his cell phone had been vibrating. "Bye, Sam. Be a good boy."

The dog gave Grady a doleful look and walked away, not caring who he went with.

"He knows we're all temporary people," Vanessa said. "And this is not his forever home."

"Hopefully Zulu will take a liking to him."

"Yep. I'll train him to search out a room first when entering, and to sleep beside the door, blocking the entrance, that sort of stuff. But the dealing with night terrors will take longer," Vanessa said, almost to herself.

"I trust you." Grady waved goodbye. "Keep me posted on how he's doing."

"No prob." She flashed him a smile. "Drop by any time. I make a mean jambalaya."

"Maybe I will." He gave her a mock salute and backed out of the door. When he got into his truck, he looked back and she was at her window, waving at him.

She was a nice woman—stable and level-headed, professional, smart, good at what she did, and not for a jerk like him.

He got into the cab and fished out his cell phone.

Sure enough, Linx had texted several times.

The woman was crazy about him—or maybe plain nuts.

I can't just up and go to San Francisco. Who's going to take care of the dogs?

Meet me halfway, or else.

"Eff you, Linx," he muttered as he scrolled to the next text.

Fine, ignore me. The dogs will be gone.

Yep, she was positively certifiable, so he ignored her, giving her what she wanted.

That kiss in front of his parents' cabin had been the eye in a monster hurricane—a quiet moment where he'd glimpsed into a life that wasn't theirs—before the raging winds of the turmoil belonging to them returned.

He looked back at Vanessa's neatly trimmed apartment, complete with potted geraniums on the window sill.

What would peace look like between him and Linx?

* * *

Linx sat in the corner booth at Joe's Diner, trying not to boil over. She found the perfect pair of dogs for Grady, two dogs who'd been surrendered together, Molly and Rex, but he'd been ignoring her.

She'd heard around town that he'd been helping his parents with their insurance claim, clearing their property, and also driving Cait around.

And now, after several days of no text messages, he finally texted that he was in San Francisco and wanted her to meet him there, knowing she didn't have the time to make the drive.

Why was he being so difficult?

Gritting her teeth, she dashed off a load of nastygram text messages and shut off her phone. This was all about control and punishing her for not letting him come and go at the rescue center.

So she was being bitchy about this, but couldn't he at least cater to her wishes just this once? Now that he'd been around Tami, infecting her with his charm, even her best friend was advocating for him—wanting to make exceptions.

Did no one understand her?

Linx groaned and fanned herself with the plastic laminated menu. She wished she had a twin—someone who would automatically take her side. She put the menu down and watched her sisters hanging out at the lunch counter.

They'd always had that twin connection going—finishing each other's sentences, mirroring body language, and prolonged eye contact.

They weren't identical twins, however. Joey was a brunette with hazel eyes and a tall, lanky frame, while Vivi was petite and curvy with light brown hair and sky-blue eyes. But other than looking different, they were the best of companions and they both loved to ride horses, sing in the choir, and volunteer to teach children useful skills in the 4-H club.

Vivi waved her hands excitedly, describing an adventure, as Joey laughed and gave her a rapt audience. The next minute, Joey rolled her eyes and tapped Vivi's shoulder, and Vivi nodded eagerly, showing her support for whatever scheme Joey conjured up.

They had been too young to remember their mother—too young to wonder if Minx leaving was their fault. Too young to replay their mother's cruel words over and over again.

No one wants you for a friend.
You're just like me, a bitch.
You can't outmad me.
Jealous, spiteful girl.
You're ugly when you cry.
That's too pretty for you to wear.

Linx remembered that last Christmas with her mom, when she'd received a bright red satin dress and matching ribbons. She'd been so excited to put it on, wanted her mother to do her hair up and tie the pretty ribbon around her locks.

"That's too pretty for you to wear," her mother had said. "Let's save it for Joey or Vivi. A pretty dress on an ugly girl looks all wrong."

Linx had flown into a fury, like Krakatoa blowing its top. She'd thrown herself at the Christmas tree, toppling it, then broke the ornaments against the stone fireplace.

When Dad took the rest of the family outside to play in the snow, Linx was left behind to clean up the mess. Instead, she received a spanking to end all spankings, with her mother breathing in her ear. "You're ugly on the inside, and no amount of window dressing will make you pretty. You have a black heart. Don't pretend you're anything better. You make me sick. Sick. Sick."

She'd fought back, scratching and biting, until her father heard the commotion and stopped the beating. He'd said harsh words to her mother, and the very next day, the witch took off.

The dress still hung in Linx's closet. She'd never worn it, and the ribbons were still tied to the clothes hanger.

And no one had ever explained to her why her mother thought she was ugly, when she was the one who looked the most like her.

"More coffee?" Joey's musical voice caused Linx to startle.

She looked up, almost not seeing her sister, her mind still fractured by the ugly memory. Their mother had left because of her.

"You okay?" Vivi slid into the booth across the table from her. "You look like you saw a ghost."

"Just thinking about the past." Linx pushed the coffee cup at Joey so she could fill it.

"About Gran?" Joey asked. "I miss her, too."

"Actually, I was thinking about our mother." Linx noticed both her sisters stiffen. "Do you ever think about her?"

"Not really, we have no memory of her," Vivi said, looking at Joey to bolster her.

"Right, we were only two," Joey said.

"I remember her." Linx blinked, her lips tight. "I don't think she liked being a mother."

"Probably got tired of changing diapers." Vivi laughed. "I don't blame her. That's why I never volunteered for the church nursery."

"We did just fine without her," Joey said. "Why are you thinking about her?

"She dumped off one of her prize sculptures on my porch." Linx stared into the black coffee as if it were a mirror. "I wonder why?"

Joey shot Vivi a puzzled look and Vivi gave a shrug.

Todd stepped through the doorway, wearing his uniform.

Linx waved him over, and everyone in the diner grew quiet. The town had been buzzing about the fire and possible arson, and everyone had their speculations.

Todd hefted his weight into the booth, making the vinyl squeak. His eyes were red and rimmed with dark circles, and he blew out a tired breath.

"How's the investigation going?" Linx asked as Joey filled Todd's coffee cup.

"You know I couldn't talk about it eve if I knew," Todd said, hunching his shoulders. "Scott's handling the coordination with Cal Fire. They sent in a big city investigator."

"So, it's definitely arson?" Linx asked.

Todd grunted and ordered his usual cholesterol special, while Linx went for oatmeal and raisins.

"Heard Cait and Brian are staying at the Over Easy," Linx said. "Is she doing okay?"

Todd shrugged. "Haven't gotten any calls about them. Brian's a shoo-in for the Pumper Driver position, so it looks like they're staying put."

"You okay with that?" Linx stirred sugar into her coffee. "Just yesterday, you wanted to run the Harts out of town."

"The Hart family are our friends," Todd said, slapping his coffee cup on the table. "It's Grady who's the problem, but if you're okay with him rubbing your face in his beard, then I've got nothing against him."

"I'm okay with him." Linx stiffened her back.

Her brother lifted an eyebrow and grunted. "Then why did you want a restraining order? You two have something sick going on if you ask me."

"No, it's quite simple. All I want is for him to acknowledge what a jerk he was, but he has a head as hard as mine. Maybe harder."

"Is that so?" Todd leaned back as Joey placed a large heaping plate of bacon, sausages, eggs, and hash browns in front of him. "When you told me you wanted a restraining order, I thought you felt threatened. Has he ever been violent?"

Only during consensual sex, Linx thought, then quickly squelched the randy images and memories that went with it. She bit her lip. "No, he's never been violent.

Never hurt me physically. It's just that I hurt all over when I see him swaggering around like he hasn't a care in the world."

"Meanwhile, you're carrying around all the shame and heartache." Todd dug into his food, his brows drawn together in thought.

"He thinks I lied about it." Linx stirred the fruit into her steel-cut oats flavored with coconut oil instead of butter.

What could she do? Grady refused to believe she'd been pregnant, and she no longer had the baby to lay claim to him.

"There's got to be a way to knock it through his thick head," Todd said. "You have medical records, right? Maybe drag him to your doctor's office."

"It's no use." Linx lost her appetite. The last person she wanted to see was the doctor. "All I want is an apology."

Right, keep telling that lie. When she first saw Grady after so many years of absence, her silly heart had believed he'd come back to town to tell her he finally believed her. She'd even imagined him groveling—a little, because alpha guys like him didn't grovel. But even a small acknowledgment that he'd been wrong about her would have helped pave the way for her to tell him about his dog.

"Tell you what." Todd clenched his fists so that the muscles on his forearms bulged. "I'll have a man to man talk with him and tell him he knocked you up."

Todd's voice boomed so that several people around the diner turned their heads.

"Shhhh!" She wanted to sink into a hole as she gave her former classmates, her father's beer buddies, and several tourists a sheepish grin.

A sense of urgency grabbed the bottom of her stomach and squeezed low in her gut. "It's only a matter of time before Cait finds out everything—the baby and the dog. She's so nosy and now she's living in the center of the town, surrounded by gossip."

"Too bad we can't run them out of town like in the old days." Todd drawled like an old-time sheriff. He chuckled to himself and added, "Besides, I like the Harts. They're good people."

"Maybe it's time I faced the music." Linx covered her head with her hands. "I suck. I'm just like Minx. A black-hearted bitch. Ugly on the inside."

Reaching under the table to her phone, she texted Grady. *We need to talk.*

Chapter Fifteen

"Miss Linx, Miss Linx!" a small voice shouted at Linx as she wheeled her grocery cart out of the general store.

Jessie ran up to her with her mother, Jean Patterson, in tow. "I told Mama you have superpowers, but she says we have to pray to God. God has bigger powers than you."

Linx knelt down to Jessie's level and hugged her. "Your mother's right. God has superpowers."

"But I did pray to God, and Betsy's still lost." Jessie's eyes brimmed with tears.

"We're trying our best to find her." Linx stroked the little girl's silky hair. "I put up a reward, and Betsy's on our website."

"Right next to the puppy!" Jessie's eyes brightened. "Mama says we can get a puppy."

"Only if we don't find Betsy," Mrs. Patterson cut in, giving Jessie an indulgent look.

"We'll find Betsy," Linx reassured. "We have posters everywhere. I'm sure some nice person will find her and bring her back."

The odds were against Betsy ever being found, but Linx had to keep the child hoping. There was nothing worse than the "not knowing." At least no one had reported a dog hit by a car who looked like Betsy.

"If I get the puppy, then will Betsy be lost forever?" Jessie's eyebrows twisted and she looked like she was trying to solve a difficult puzzle.

Linx glanced at the girl's mother for guidance. She didn't want to set any expectations, and besides, she didn't think getting a puppy should be tied to whether Betsy was lost or found.

"Let's not bother Miss Linx," Mrs. Patterson said to her daughter. "She has to go home and feed her dogs. See that big bag of dog food she has?"

"Okay, bye, Miss Linx." Jessie dutifully waved her hand the way small children did by wiggling her fingers.

"Bye, Jessie," Linx said. "I'll send out another search party for Betsy today—ask around the campsite. Maybe someone saw her."

After Jessie turned toward the store, Mrs. Patterson whispered to Linx. "Don't get her hopes up. Betsy's been missing over a week. I'm trying to get her to accept another puppy."

"It's too soon," Linx said. "She needs closure for Betsy."

"I understand, but I'm wondering if Jessie can come by the rescue center and get acquainted with the other dogs. I heard your brother found a basset hound with puppies."

"Sure, I'd love to have her volunteer." Linx's heart leaped and a smile broke on her face. "I can teach her how to take care of a dog."

"Great. I have to prepare for Vacation Bible School, and you know how it is at her age. Jessie's always asking me questions, and I can't get my work done. How about twice a week to start with?"

"Bring her by any time."

Linx drove back to the center in high spirits, but when she opened the door, the uneasiness she'd woken up with returned.

"Cedar, Ginger," she called. "I'm home."

Instead of coming to the door and greeting her, Cedar lay on the sofa and looked out the window. Her nose parted the curtain as if she were a woman pacing on a widow's walk watching and waiting for her seafaring husband to return.

She wagged her tail weakly as Ginger made small noises from a playpen Linx got from the thrift shop.

"You miss him, don't you?" Linx rubbed her dog's back. "So do I, but at least he loves you—if he remembers you."

Cedar had been moping around the cabin ever since the morning Grady had shown up and teased her, tapping on the door.

What kind of unfeeling monster would take a beloved pet away from its owner?

Someone like her, obviously.

Keeping a lost dog was all kinds of wrong when the owner still held out hope for it. It was only a step away from kidnapping.

Linx wanted to punch herself for being that kind of unforgivable person. Story of her life. She acted out of anger and never considered the other person's point of view. Except Grady hadn't truly looked for his dog.

That was the only shred of an excuse she had, so she clung to it. He was so eager to disappear from her life that he'd never visited her rescue center or emailed her about Cedar.

Now that he was putting roots in this town, her excuses had run out.

Why was she holding onto Cedar?

It wasn't as if she could bring the past back—the times when she and Grady would snuggle in his cabin with Sasha lying on the rug in front of the fire. Times she'd imagined were happy. Only, she'd built a lie around herself, feathered it with childish stories about charming knights and white picket fences. Swing sets and playpens, playing baseball and hopscotch. Summer barbecues and winter snowmen.

Both she and Grady thrived on adrenaline and the rush of firefighting, but what they had that fire season wasn't based on anything other than lust and thrills.

He was over her as soon as the season ended, but she couldn't deal with rejection. She never dealt well with rejection. Who did?

She hadn't even realized she was pregnant—at first, because she continued her harsh physical workout during the off season. Her body adjusted to working out hard and her periods became irregular, so she'd lost track until the pressure inside of her was too big to ignore.

It was Salem who'd first suspected Linx was pregnant, and she'd made her buy a pregnancy test. Salem had been injured during rookie training. After she recovered, she'd rented a room in town and was Linx's training partner. They worked out together and she pumped Linx for information about every detail of her season and was determined to try again.

Now, Salem was dead. It had to have been a freak accident. The wind could change on a dime and the fire itself created its own weather. One errant gust was all it took to push the parachute the wrong way.

As for Grady and Salem.

Saying their names together was like licking the bitter dregs on the bottom of a moldy cup of coffee.

She had no claim to Grady, and if it were true that Salem's baby was Grady's, it could explain why Grady gave up smokejumping.

Linx never wanted to pity Grady, and he would be upset if he ever detected a whiff of pity from her, but truly, Grady had sorrows she knew nothing about.

Keeping Cedar was the least of it.

"I'm so, so sorry I kept you from him." She buried her face in Cedar's mane to hide her suddenly wet eyes. "Even though it'll break my heart, I have to let you go."

* * *

Grady woke with a start and shot up from his trailer bed perched over the fifth wheel. He was back at his property and an unsettled feeling ate at his gut.

The night was pitch black and quiet—too quiet.

He fought a chill from jiggling down his back and pushed aside the curtain on the side toward the building site. He'd taken delivery of the rocks for the foundation and the logs for the walls of the cabin.

The digging had been hard work, but he had nothing else to do. There had been no leads to the arson at his parents' property, and he'd spent the last few days helping with the cleanup.

Grady pulled the curtain shut and turned onto his side, closing his eyes. He could still see his small cabin the way it was. It was the last place he'd seen Sasha, the last place he'd felt like a whole man, the last place he'd made love—with Linx Colson, before she'd turned into a raging lunatic.

How had it gone so wrong?

Sure, she was a temptress, and she'd hoped to use his influence as drill instructor to go easy on her. She'd been disappointed when he gave her the hardest time, but she'd surprised him by passing—despite the rope burns, the tangled chutes, and the hard landings.

Then she went nuts.

She'd expected him to change his plans after that first fire season—assumed too much. She'd followed him to the airport, begging him to let her either come along or to stay home with him for the winter.

Five whole freaking months later, she pulled the pregnancy stunt.

Like she had to wait that long before figuring it out?

That was when he'd blown up—screamed at her over the phone and told her in no uncertain terms that she was not to contact him again.

She'd gone stoic on him and promised he would never hear from her—and she'd done exactly that.

Around her supposed due date, he'd called her once to check up on her. Asked her about the baby, and she'd denied everything—accused him of getting her confused with some other woman.

I was never pregnant. You must have dreamed it up. I never threatened to sue you. You're nuts, Grady. It wasn't me you knocked up.

And that was that. Except for the telltale quaver in her voice, she'd played her innocent role well.

So, why was it *now* so important for him to stay away from the Mountain Dog Rescue?

She wasn't hiding a baby there, was she?

He groaned as the pieces snapped together.

Big brother Todd turning overprotective meant there might have been smoke.

Where there was smoke, there was fire—the possibility she'd actually been pregnant and her family believed it was his.

Heck, she must have believed the baby was his, because otherwise, why all the drama? There was no baby now. No lawsuit. No threat of harassment, especially since he was no longer on a fire crew this season.

He sat up too fast, hitting his head on the canopy above him.

Damn. That was the only thing that made sense.

If she was pregnant, then she'd gotten rid of the baby—a late term abortion. His baby. Killed.

Unless she hid him or her at the dog rescue center.

With the noise of dogs barking, no one would hear a baby cry.

Crap. Was he dumb? His kid would be almost six by now. It wasn't a baby he should look for, but a little boy or girl.

Grady flicked on the flashlight he kept near his bed and pulled on his clothes. He couldn't sleep anyway, so he got dressed and got into his truck.

As his truck bumped its way down the dark, rutted dirt road, Grady couldn't help the guilt swarming through his gut.

If he'd listened to her and came home, if he'd gone with her to the doctor and verified her pregnancy, then waited for a DNA test, she wouldn't have killed the baby—or hopefully, hidden it.

His eyes blurred, and he yanked his steering wheel hard, barely avoiding a tree.

And if it had all been a fake, he would have known also and been able to rest easy. Why hadn't he followed up?

Dawn broke over the eastern sky as Grady pulled into town. The little town of Colson's Corner was nestled in a small river valley between two parallel ridges of granite. A river ran through the center of the town, forded by a steel bridge.

Grady pulled out his cell phone and stared at Linx's last text message.

We need to talk.

Four words from Linx that could mean everything and nothing.

His heart thudded like the thunder following dry lightning strikes—the kind that ignited forest fires. Was Linx going to finally fess up, and if she did, would he believe her?

His gut twisted and he wondered if he'd been too hard on her. She had been a nineteen-year-old who acted a whole lot older. She'd worked her way up the fire crews until she nabbed a smokejumping training spot.

The woman was fearless and wild, and she carried her load without complaint. She'd wielded the saw, swung her Pulaski, and did her fair share of mop-up duty. Other than her bad temper, "Short Fuse" was an asset to the team, and she never cut corners—unlike Salem who was careless with her equipment and depended on her jump partners to double-check her chute and rigging.

Grady turned the corner and barreled up the dirt road leading to the Mountain Dog Rescue Center. The only reason Linx wouldn't allow him inside her cabin, despite being so turned on she could have combusted on the spot, was because she was hiding something—most likely his child.

This time, he wasn't leaving until he got what he came for.

He slid to a stop in front of the cabin, and his heart threaded into his throat.

Linx's SUV was gone.

Chapter Sixteen

Grady wasn't going to slink away. Not even if the sheriff himself were to point a howitzer at him. He stepped out of the truck and wandered around the Mountain Dog Rescue Center.

The dogs out back barked up a storm, but there was no sound from inside the cabin. Had Linx somehow gotten wind of him coming down the hill toward her and slipped away?

But then, she claimed she wanted to talk.

Her text message, *We need to talk,* was front and center in his mind.

She was holding a secret, maybe more than one, and it was time for her to fess up. Or maybe she was still playing a game, setting him up for not coming at her beck and call for the two retrievers she suddenly decided to lure him with.

He should have met her at the motel for another dog transfer. Casual sex was no problem for a hotshot firefighter—make-up sex, even better, although there was, according to her, no relationship between them.

What did he know?

Linx was so prickly and short-tempered that most of the time, he couldn't tell if she was coming or going. But then, that was what made her interesting, and so very addicting.

He was never sure where he stood with her, and that appealed to the adrenaline junkie in him. She was fiery and one hot, determined woman.

When he was her drill instructor, he wanted to see how much pain she could take. He'd pushed her harder than any of the other rookies and exposed her to danger to test her mettle.

She never once complained—never whined and never shirked her duty. She'd grit her teeth and her eyes would focus with laser intensity as she charged forward. There'd been days and nights when he was sure she would collapse. He'd tell her to quit, and she'd refuse, insisting on completing his orders, no matter how extreme.

And then, she'd get a second wind after he carried her into the shower and cooled her down only to heat her up in bed.

His cell phone rang and his heart jumped, until he saw it was only Nessa.

"Hello," he mumbled, getting back into his truck. "What's up?"

"It's Sam. He's bitten someone, and the city is serving notice to you, the registered owner, for a hearing to determine whether he's dangerous or vicious."

Grady's pulse shot up to attention. "Wait. What exactly happened?"

"Zulu has a male friend who's been sleeping on her couch. This guy's former military—big man. He didn't like Sam right off the bat, and Sam didn't like him either. It's almost like they're in competition."

"How serious is the bite?"

"Not too bad. A superficial bite on the hand." Nessa said. "But the guy filed a complaint."

"Was it provoked?"

"Zulu says Sawyer, that's the Army guy, was upset that Sam wouldn't let him into her bedroom. I think he tried to grab Sam's collar and Sam nailed him. I believe that's provocation, don't you?"

"I agree, so what do we have to do?"

"I've got Sam here at my house now. If we can get Sawyer to drop the complaint, or admit he provoked him, then we're golden. Otherwise, there's a hearing and determination of whether he's dangerous and vicious, and if he is, they could impound him."

"Would they have him destroyed?" Grady gritted his teeth, unwilling to picture that quiet and sullen dog put down.

"Not if we can show he was doing his job protecting Zulu," Nessa replied. "The easiest would be to get Sawyer to withdraw his complaint. I think he's more upset because his pride was hurt. Zulu isn't interested in him as anything more than a friend, and he's been protecting her for months without getting to first base."

"You want me to speak to him?"

"Yes, if you can, man to man. I've already tried, but he's resistant. I told him a woman with her traumatic background is not open to a relationship, and he denies it—says he's only being a friend."

"I'm not a trained counselor like you are," Grady said. "But I'll give it a try. How do I get in touch with him?"

"It might be easier if you came by," Nessa said. "You're Sam's legal owner, and you'll have to attend the hearing."

Grady ran a hand over the back of his neck. "Let me follow up on the retrievers and then I'll be over in a few days."

As he hung up the phone, he noticed a car turning up the dirt road and recognized Tami King behind the wheel.

Tami waved at him, then parked her car in front of the rescue center and opened the door.

"What can I do for you?" She bumped her way through the door. "Linx said okay on the two retrievers, but you never got back to her."

"Well, I'm here now, is Linx around?"

Tami wrinkled her nose and shrugged. "She said she had to take care of some personal business. I thought she was with you."

"Me? Why would you think that?"

"Because you're not at the office this morning, by coincidence." Tami winked. "Don't worry, your secret's safe with me. I know you and Linx have the hots for each other, and I'm sure it'll all work out."

"Not if she's keeping secrets from me." Grady lowered his voice and noticed Tami's facial features freeze.

"Secrets? What secrets?" Tami fanned herself and crossed over to her desk. "If you're trying to find out if she's in love with you or not, sorry, I'm not going to give you a hint."

"I want to know why she won't let me step into this cabin." Grady glanced around at the décor. A comfy sofa sat against the front window and a large, plush doggie bed lay next to it.

A child's playpen filled with towels and chew toys held a tiny puppy, the one that was on the center's website and social media page.

Could this have been used for a baby before?

"You're in here right now," Tami said, shrugging as if there was no issue. "I hope you find what you're looking for."

There was no evidence of toys or children's books, if that was what she was referring to.

"Mind if I have a glass of milk?"

"Uh, I'm sure it's okay," Tami said. She glanced at the clock. "I have to be going soon."

Grady wandered over to the kitchen and opened the refrigerator. Orange juice. Milk. Chocolate milk—the kind kids liked to drink.

But no cookies and no ice cream.

He opened the pantry to grab a glass. The only cereal Linx had was muesli and granola. Didn't children eat sugary cereals with marshmallows and leprechauns?

"What are you looking for?" Tami's voice closed in on him. "Linx isn't here. I'll let you know when she gets back."

"I'll wait. Got all day." He flashed her a charming smile. "She texted me that she wanted to talk, so I'm giving her the opportunity."

"Fine, but when I have to leave, you'll have to wait outside." Tami huffed and stomped back to her desk.

Was it Grady's imagination, or was Tami trying to hurry him from the office? In that case, she didn't know him at all.

The more someone tried to push him, the slower he got. He poured himself a glass of milk and sipped it as he wandered around the living room. The mantel over the fireplace was made of a quarter hewn log, and held family pictures.

"You really don't want to be caught snooping around," Tami yelled from across the room. "She could be back any minute. Believe me, you wouldn't want to get on her bad side."

"As if I haven't seen every side of her," Grady mumbled and scanned the family pictures. No children of any age, not one, appeared in any of the pictures. He stopped at the end of the row and picked up a picture of Linx and her dog.

"She's not going to be happy," Tami warned as she stalked to his side.

"What's this?" Grady brought the picture close and narrowed his eyes. Her dog looked exactly like Sasha—down to the white crest on her chest and the orange-red patches over her eyes—one more pronounced than the other.

"I'm sorry, but I have to leave," Tami said, grabbing him by the arm. "We'll be open later once Linx returns."

"Where did she get this dog?" Grady shook the picture. "Is this what she's been keeping from me? Is this the big reason why she has her brother throwing me out of the town?"

"You'll have to talk to her about it." Tami yanked the picture frame from him.

"Where is she? Why isn't she answering my text messages?" Grady asked, even though he was the one who hadn't answered her. "This is inexcusable. She kept my dog. Why would she do this to me?"

"I'm sure she's busy. Look, I have to let the volunteers in to feed the dogs and clean the kennels, and—" Tami pushed him toward the door.

Grady dug in his heels. "I'm not leaving without my dog."

"Well, genius, in case you haven't noticed, your dog isn't here."

"Right, she's taken off. Don't tell me she's playing another game with me, because I'm sick of it."

"She doesn't play games." Tami opened the door and pointed the way out. "But you hurt her long ago, and she can't get over it."

"I hurt her?" Grady's hackles rose. "What about the lies she told me? Like now. She's stolen my dog. I bet she skipped out of town and she's not coming back."

"Then you'll have to find her. I'm telling you, she's not here." Tami gave him another shove. "You know, you're not much of a saint either. She's trying to make amends, but what about you?"

"Make amends? By stealing my dog?"

"Instead of jumping to conclusions, maybe you should trust her."

"Trust and Linx Colson don't go together."

"Then you'll never find what you're looking for." Tami crossed her arms. "And I pity you."

He whipped around and stomped off the porch all the way to his truck. So, the big secret was his beloved dog and not a baby or child.

In a way, that was a relief.

Or maybe not.

A woman who would hide a dog could hide more, couldn't she?

* * *

Dry lightning sizzled in the charged atmosphere and raised the hairs on Linx's arms. She wrestled the steering wheel of her SUV and lurched up the rutted drive to Grady's plot of land.

The air was heated and charged, and a heat wave lingered in the area. Even though clouds loomed above and lightning crackled, no moisture made its way down to the ground—perfect tinder for a wildfire.

Beside her, Cedar leaned out the passenger window, her ears erect and her nose quivering. Giving her back would be the second hardest thing Linx had ever done.

Tami had already called and told her Grady was on the warpath, and she couldn't put it off any longer. She had to make it up to Grady and face his wrath. It was what she deserved for keeping him from his beloved dog.

Linx's heart raced as she climbed an embankment and turned her wheels to park. Four years ago, shortly after she found Cedar, she'd swung by to see if by chance Grady was hiding out here. Her stomach had squeezed in on itself when she spied the charred landscape and the ruins of his cabin—their long-ago love nest.

Now, greenery had returned, and the plot was lush with grass and bushes. The building site was recently leveled, and a black tarp was anchored over the foundation by large rocks.

Stacks of logs were piled around the site, and a fifth-wheel trailer was parked under a large tree.

Linx swallowed and wet her lips as she and Cedar jumped from her Durango. Another bolt of lightning arced above them, and thunder boomed without rain. But Cedar didn't seem to be spooked. She ran around the building site, sniffing and bouncing excitedly. Following her nose, she went to the trailer parked under the tree, but Linx didn't think Grady was home since his truck was missing.

Lightning sliced across the sky, flashing over the treetops, and Linx shuddered as the rolling thunder crashed overhead a few seconds later. She held her palm up, praying for rain.

Every summer, dry thunderstorms all across the West ignited hundreds of forest fires, keeping fire crews busy and exhausted. If what she'd heard was correct, it was one such late season fire that had consumed Salem.

Linx picked her way around the property, secure in knowing Grady wasn't around. The cabin under construction was much larger than the tiny one-room cabin from before. This one spread out into two wings, and the logs stacked around were at least one foot in diameter.

She lifted part of the tarp and studied the raised stone foundation. She visualized the walls of the cabin, growing to surround what was left of the old fireplace, and once again, her memories took her back to the tiny one-room cabin of the past.

She had been young, stupid, and in love.

A truck door slammed, and Cedar leaped up barking. She scampered with her tail wagging toward Grady, acting as if her daddy had come home, and that nothing was out of the ordinary.

Linx watched Grady hug and kiss his dog. She froze where she was, letting the tarp slip from her fingers and stupidly hoping he hadn't seen her.

As soon as he let Cedar go, she raced back to Linx, acting as if she had something to show her.

"Woof! Wooooo!" Cedar howl-barked, her tongue lolling out with excitement.

When Linx didn't move, Cedar did that scampering move and made back toward Grady—clearly wanting to lead her to him.

If she could talk, she would be saying, *Mommy, Mommy, meet Daddy. He's come home finally. Mommy, why aren't you moving?*

Linx let her gaze rest on Grady, and she stood up straight from her crouching position. She'd done her duty. She'd brought his dog back officially, and it was time to leave. All she had to do was walk by him, get into her SUV, and never see him again.

The man was too arrogant to care for. Even though there was no sun out, he wore dark aviator glasses. He was probably watching her, but not acknowledging her.

Eff him. She didn't need his type, no matter how much chemistry sparked between them, and she darn well wasn't going to shed a tear for him.

Nope. All the tears were for Cedar, but Cedar would get used to not having her around. Cedar would go back to being Sasha, and the circle was complete.

She was through with being Grady's slut, a quick hookup, trading sex for affection. Been there, done that, and didn't even get the T-shirt.

Nope, now that she'd lost Cedar, he could lose something, too—her body in his bed. That ought to grind his gears.

"Hold it," Grady commanded.

Linx kept walking until a strong hand gripped her arm.

"Let go of me." She leveled a stern glare at him.

"I'm ready to hear you out."

"I've nothing to say to you." She twisted her arm from his grasp. "I'm sorry I kept your dog. She's yours now. Goodbye."

"Linx ..." Grady's thick voice burred, drawing a sizzle down her spine. "I might have been wrong about things."

"Oh, really?" She tossed her hair over her shoulder. "So, the infallible Grady admits that he might have a problem."

"Yeah, you." He ripped off his aviator sunglasses and those big brown eyes held her gaze, strong and intense, but surprisingly watery.

Linx swallowed, feeling herself waver. Mean and hateful, she could take and even counter. But the hint of regret and sorrow was something she'd never seen on Grady Hart—who was always entirely too sure of himself.

"Why am I the problem?" She set her lips in a firm line and flared her nostrils to show him she wasn't cowed by whatever false feeling he was throwing her way.

"Because you're hiding something from me, and it isn't your dog."

Now he wanted to know? For what? It wasn't as if he could fix anything. What was done was done, and the sooner she got away from Grady Hart, the better.

"Spit it out. What am I hiding?" She made her voice hard and cold.

Even though Tami thought it was time to tell, Linx wasn't going to give him an inch of hard-fought ground until he was ready to grovel at her feet and admit he'd been wrong.

Grady pursed his lips and swallowed hard. His Adam's apple bobbled, and he averted his gaze, blinking hard, wetting the tips of his lashes.

A surge of adrenaline lifted Linx's heart like the burners on a hot air balloon. He was actually unsure for once in his life.

"Well? What am I hiding?" she challenged him.

He opened his mouth as if to speak, then swallowed again. Shutting his mouth, his eyes wandered to her lips and it was over. The window of vulnerability shuttered as quickly as a summer shower blown away by the wind.

"Nothing. Nothing at all." His gaze turned lusty as he licked his lips. His sexy grin was back, and he tilted his head toward his trailer. "How about we talk in there?"

Linx raised her hand as if to slap the cheeky grin off his face, but she didn't strike him. "I'm no longer interested in what you have to offer. Goodbye, Grady. I've finally seen you for what you are. A selfish, self-centered, heartless jerk."

Lightning flashed, thunder boomed, and this time, the rain started to pour.

* * *

She'd called him a jerk!

Grady Hart was not a jerk. Never.

He prided himself on playing by the rules and treating everyone fairly. He was spectacular in bed, he gave into their fantasies, even said the right things to give them mind-blowing climaxes, but he'd never promised anyone a relationship or a future.

He was a rolling stone—they knew it and they all were okay with it because they were so eager to get in bed with him.

But count on women to renege and pull emotional blackmail.

Maybe she *had* been pregnant. Maybe it had even been his, although the dates were off. The case was closed. There was no baby, and it shouldn't matter what she did with it.

A woman's choice. Right?

That was assuming it wasn't a false scare with nothing coming of it. Which was what she'd told him.

He didn't need answers out of nothing.

Jerk indeed. If she told him it was nothing, then why was he a jerk for not believing her?

He could barely close his mouth at the audacity of Miss Linx Colson calling him a jerk as she stalked off in the rain toward her SUV.

She cut a sight to make men drool. A swaying ass over mile-long legs, lush enough curves over slender muscles, and hair that draped like a silk curtain over his face while she rode on top of him.

She was also strong and challenging, and the fact that she called him a jerk was like throwing a red cape in front of a raging bull.

"Sasha!" he called as his dog jogged after Linx.

The dog looked back, but didn't break a stride.

"Sasha!" he called again, then threw up his hands. He wasn't going to lose his pride by going after the dog. That meant dealing with the likes of a woman who'd called him a jerk.

Turning his back, he made his way to his trailer to get out of the rain. It was a perfectly good place to brood and curse his fate.

Of all the women in the world, why was he tied into knots by one he didn't even like?

He heard a barking whine and turned for one last look.

"Stay!" Linx commanded Sasha. The dog sat on the wet ground, ten feet from the SUV as Linx got into the driver's seat.

"Wooo ... woof!" Sasha whined again, wagging her tail. She was clearly an obedient dog, and she was waiting for Linx to give her the "all clear" command, signaling it was okay for her to approach the vehicle.

Instead, Linx turned on the ignition and backed out of the parking spot. The dog still sat, her ears upright and eyes fixated on Linx, waiting for a treat or praise.

The SUV made a three-point turn and barreled its way down the steep driveway.

"Woof. Woof." Sasha barked, at first not believing Linx wouldn't return.

Grady's heart broke when the dog looked back and forth, as if realizing she'd been abandoned. Her ears sagged down, and she laid down on the same spot, resting her snout over her paws.

The steady rain wet her coat, but she didn't move from the spot Linx had ordered her to stay.

"Sasha." Grady rushed to her. "It's okay, Sasha. Come here. It's okay."

The dog quivered on her haunches and gave him the saddest look he'd ever seen. Her tail was tucked between her legs and she lowered her head, making a low whine.

"It's okay, baby. I'll take care of you." He bent down and lowered himself to the ground. "You're home now. Everything's going to be okay."

Except nothing was okay, and the ache inside of him mirrored Sasha's distress.

They'd both been abandoned and forsaken by the fiery and hot-tempered Linx Colson—the "Short Fuse" who had a bad temper, but a very good heart, especially for dogs.

Chapter Seventeen

The next morning, Grady put Sasha in his truck and drove down to town. As they got closer to the town square, Sasha's ears perked up and she leaned eagerly out the window, as if she thought he was taking her home.

"Sorry, girl, I can't take you by the rescue center," Grady said. "I'm not allowed on the premises."

Sasha's brows wrinkled with a worried look and her tail drooped. Somehow his dog reflected the dull ache in his chest at the cold way Linx had left them.

No fire.

Only ice.

As if the spark that always surged between them had gone out. She wanted nothing more from him—not even a fight.

"I know you want to go see your mommy, but now's not a good time. Tell you what, let's go visit Aunt Cait and Uncle Brian. They'll love you to pieces." Grady tried to sound upbeat.

His sister was still gung-ho about locating her wedding and memorabilia business in the middle of this nowhere town, and now that Brian was part of the fire department, she was even more eager to put down roots before their baby was born.

The bed and breakfast was an old, rambling house which had definitely seen better days. While the paint wasn't exactly peeling off, the exterior had that worn, tired look and the white had faded to a dull gray—the evidence of soot fallout from nearby fires.

Cait opened the door with a big smile which quickly morphed to a furrowed brow as she spotted Sasha. "Why do you have Linx's dog?"

Grady let Sasha step into the room first, then closed the door behind him. "Cait, Brian, meet Sasha, *my* dog."

"Your dog?" Brian set his electronic tablet down and leaned forward, beckoning Sasha to greet him. "What's the story here?"

"Remember when my cabin burned down way back?" Grady swiped a hand through his thick hair. "Apparently, Sasha got away from the fire and somehow, Linx Colson found her."

"Wow, and all this time you thought she was dead?" Cait petted the dog. "I can't believe I didn't recognize her."

"She was only a puppy when I brought her home that one time," Grady said. "But yes, she was here all along. Apparently, Linx held onto her and never told me."

"Whoa, wait. Rewind." Cait raised her hand. "Maybe she didn't know it was your dog. She's got so many dogs in the center."

"Oh, she knew all right." Grady couldn't keep the anger from his voice. "Remember she made a big deal about how her dog hated me, so I couldn't go to the center? All of it was a smokescreen to keep me away from my dog."

"Why would she do that?" Brian asked. "She's always trying to help people find their dogs. Works really hard at locating owners before letting a dog get adopted."

"She's got something personal against me." Grady's fists clenched and the rock in his chest pressed against his heart.

Dammit. Why was he so affected by her? Why couldn't he write her off and let it go. He got his dog back, and there were plenty of other women who could rock his socks off—if that were all he wanted.

"I don't get it." Cait still wanted to defend her friend. "How did Linx know Cedar was Sasha? Did you post a lost dog notice?"

"She used to visit the cabin seven years ago when Sasha was there." Grady stomped around the room, punching the air with his fists. "I had no idea she'd hate me so much that she'd steal my dog."

"Wait a big fat minute." Cait stabbed an index finger his direction. "You lied to us. You said you didn't know Linx Colson. Pretended you were strangers. What did you do to her to make her hate you?"

"I dumped her." Grady's words blazed from his lips. "Dumped her when she wouldn't take no for an answer."

"Wow. Just wow." Cait backed to the sofa and collapsed as if losing all her muscle tone. "Are you saying she's a crazy stalker-type? You dump her and she takes your dog?"

"I'm starting to believe so." Grady crossed his arms, his face as stiff as a mask.

"She's the reason you're done with women?"

"Yes, done. Finished. No more."

"Then why are you still flirting with her? Verbal sparring? Checking each other out and pretending you're interested in hooking up?"

Grady's heart dropped like a heavy stone into a deep well. His cover had been blown. Cait would leave no leaf unturned until she figured out exactly what was going on between him and Linx.

The cogs seemed to be turning in Cait's mind as she counted her fingers and moved her lips. When she looked up at Grady, her face was pale. "Seven years ago, you were an instructor for the Forest Service. Linx was a rookie. She told me she'd jumped one season. But after that, she quit."

"Did she tell you why she quit?"

"Said she lost interest and decided to work with dogs." Cait shrugged. "I take it there was something else?"

"Maybe."

"You slept with her, didn't you?" Cait nailed him with her sharp green eyes. "You were an instructor, and you weren't supposed to fraternize with the rookies. She could have had you fired."

"Well, I wasn't fired. She quit instead."

"Do you think she was pregnant?" Cait's mind worked at warp speed.

"She doesn't have any children. I, uh, don't think that's her problem."

Cait's face twisted as if she were checking off clues at a mystery dinner. "She quit firefighting abruptly. She pretends she didn't know you when we met. Her family wants to run you out of town, or at least her big, overprotective older brother does. She kept your dog."

"Yeah, she kept my dog, but what does that have to do with whether she was pregnant or not?" A flutter in his heart jittered down to his gut, but he wasn't worried. She'd assured him there was no kid. It had been a false alarm, or a blatant ploy to force him to marry her.

"She might have kept your dog to have a piece of you close to her." Cait blinked, her eyes now watery. "Or maybe she wanted revenge, or at least your attention. I'm not blind. I sense a lot of angst and tension between you two."

"Yeah, well, it's all one-sided. I'm the innocent victim here." Grady patted his thigh at Sasha, beckoning her to come with him. "I've got to be going. Just thought I'd let you meet Sasha and let you know what a snake Linx Colson is. Are you sure you two want to settle here? Her family owns the entire town."

"It's a charming town, full of potential," Cait said. "Millions of people drive by on Interstate 80 on their way to Tahoe and Reno for their quickie weddings without realizing if they took a little more time, they'd have something more unique."

"I wish you lots of luck then, but I have a feeling the Colsons like this place quiet and backward the way it is." Grady headed for the door. "I'm wondering if someone in her family set fire to Mom and Dad's place as a warning."

"You mean they want us to stay away?" Brian asked, setting down his tablet. "Is that what you're implying?"

Grady shrugged. "I heard around town that people are calling you two carpetbaggers. Seems Tami has a big mouth about how much money you have to invest in this town."

"But, Grady, your cabin burned down, too." Cait idly rubbed Sasha's mane. "What if they're trying to run you out of town? You're the one who has the entire Colson family up in arms—about their sister, Linx."

"Let's talk about that fire way back," Brian said. "Did they ever figure out who started it? Seems to me Linx is suspect number one."

"Linx wouldn't do something like that," Grady said, his hackles rising. "She wouldn't have endangered Sasha."

"She could have saved Sasha before lighting up the place," Brian said. "Fatal attraction meets dog lover. Just saying."

"But Linx fought fires," Cait said. "She told me once it was her first love, before taking care of dogs."

"Someone's burning down houses around here." Brian picked up the tablet he was reading and woke it. "Did you see the news? Up north?"

"No, I've been working on my cabin," Grady said. "More fires?"

"Yep, near Redstone Base Camp."

"Redstone." Grady grabbed the tablet and scanned the article. Redstone was one of the smokejumping camps he worked out of. It was a few hours north of Colson's Corner.

"Right. In the last month, a bunch of men have had their houses burn down, even the fire chief's."

"You mean, Chief Montgomery?" Grady read the article. "Did they catch who's doing it?"

"Not yet," Brian said. "Guys go out on a jump and they're busy fighting a forest fire, then come home to an ash heap."

"Sounds like someone has something against firefighters." Grady blew out a breath. "Or maybe it's coincidental?"

"I heard people mention a curse." Cait jumped in, her inquisitive eyes sharp. "The lady selling the Victorian we're interested in says a woman died on a jump up there and they never found her body."

"Bunch of baloney," Brian said, rolling his eyes. "Anyway, I'm wondering if the arson at Mom and Dad's cabin has something to do with what's going on up at Redstone. If someone's targeting firefighters, then our family is one big bull's eye."

"You think they blame us for not stopping the fire earlier?"

Brian crossed his arms and stared at him, nodding. "Maybe. Lots of people lost their homes."

"Some people aren't rational." Cait put her hand over her belly, as if comforting her baby. "You never know what goes through people's minds when they're under stress."

"That fire was wicked." Grady sighed, putting his hands in his pockets. "Torched up out of nowhere and had wings."

"Maybe their insurance claim got denied, or maybe it's a coincidence, which I don't believe." Brian picked up his note pad. "Tim Olson's trailer goes up in flames. Maybe he'd left a burner on, maybe he didn't. Then Duane Washington's place goes kaboom. He claims he had a leaking propane tank. Then it's the chief's house. Luckily his wife was out of town, or maybe the perp was considerate and didn't want to hurt her."

"I don't know what to say," Grady squirmed underneath Brian's focused glare. "I haven't been up that way since last season."

"Yeah, well, thought you ought to know," Brian said. "Right now, we have no leads. Todd's been questioning the transients at the campground, and of course, no one saw anything."

"You know? I have a thought." Cait snapped her fingers. "Whoever burned down Mom and Dad's place must have been watching us. They saw us go out for a walk and then started the fire. It means they didn't want to kill anyone. Same way they didn't want Sasha to die."

"A compassionate arsonist," Brian huffed, hooking a raised eyebrow at Grady. "How considerate."

"Linx has an alibi." The words jumped from Grady's throat. "She was with her family."

"Yeah, her family." Brian scratched his beard and nodded. "The same ones who want to run you out of town."

Cold sweat prickled Grady's brow and he shook his head like a terrier shaking a rat. "No way did Linx have anything to do with this. Linx hates fire. She calls it the red dragon and she fights it with everything she has. No one works the fire line harder than Linx Colson. She's brave and tough, and she'll fight to her last breath."

"She's fascinating," Cait sighed loudly. "And you're totally and completely in love with her."

* * *

The cabin felt empty without Cedar, but Linx didn't have time to mope. Gold Rush Week was coming up and she needed to spruce up the center and get ready for the adoption auction in the town square.

They wouldn't have live dogs up for auction, especially at a Fourth of July event with all of the noise and children popping firecrackers. Instead, the dogs would be safe in the barn inside their kennels. Instead, the auctioneer would hold up a picture of the dog, and people could look them over on their cell phones before placing a bid.

Potential adopters would need to come to the center to get pre-qualified and oriented, as well as have an opportunity to visit the dogs they were interested in.

Which was why Linx stood on the porch with her brows furrowed and hands on her hips staring at her mother's deadly creation.

A skull with a railroad spike through the eye socket and a hand with a wire heart in its palm was not exactly the kind of artwork for dog lovers.

"What are you going to do with that?" Tami asked while watering the potted plants.

"Move it to my dad's ranch," Linx said. "I don't want to hurt her feelings, but this thing's going to scare people away."

"Jessie doesn't seem scared," Tami said as Mrs. Patterson and Jessie sauntered up the walkway.

"Miss Linx! Is that for Halloween?" Jessie pointed to the rusted skull.

Mrs. Patterson's eyes widened and she fanned herself. "That's certainly unique. Is there a message?"

"Linx's mother is an artist," Tami explained. "She's very creative."

"I'll say. Jessie, don't climb on it." Jean guided Jessie away from what she no doubt thought of as Satanic influences. "Bye, Jessie, and listen to Miss Linx."

"I will." Jessie waved to her mother. "I want to play with the puppy."

"Great, because I need you to help me feed Ginger," Linx said. "Her eyes are open and she's pulling herself around."

"She's so cute." Jessie squealed at the side of the playpen. "I want a baby sister just like her. Look, she's crawling."

Linx picked the puppy up out of the playpen and handed her to Jessie. "Go sit on the sofa and I'll bring a bottle."

The little girl carefully walked with the puppy to the sofa, stepping over Cedar's doggy bed. She climbed on and then looked around, blinking. "Where's Cedar? Doesn't she want to help feed Ginger?"

"Cedar went home to be with her daddy," Linx said. She filled a bottle with warm puppy formula.

"Who's Cedar's daddy?" Jessie asked.

"He lost her a long time ago, and I kept Cedar safe. Now he's back, and she has to be with him." Linx shook the bottle and handed it to Jessie.

The little puppy squirmed and wiggled, nosing the bottle before latching onto the nipple.

Jessie giggled. "She's so hungry."

"Yes, she is." Linx sat next to Jessie and stroked the puppy's soft downy fur. Even the puppy missed Cedar, nosing around and sniffing for her.

Yes, Linx's heart was broken, but she had to carry on. There were so many dogs needing love, and once the dust settled after the adoption event, she'd adopt one of the guests who was left behind.

In the meantime, she had to hang up banners and put up educational materials for the visitors coming for Gold Rush week, maybe even set up an activity.

"Do you think Betsy went to live with someone else?" Jessie's expression turned serious.

"I think Betsy's out there waiting for us to find her," Linx said. "Want to go on a walk with me and look for her?"

"Okay. I wish we could find her right now. Can you wear your Wonder Woman cape?"

Linx was glad she only asked for the cape and not the costume. But then again, this was California, and the town's residents loved dressing up in costumes.

Footsteps sounded on the wooden porch and the screen door opened.

"Yoohoo, can I come in?" Cait Wonder peeked through the door. She stood at the threshold with a plate of steaming hot muffins.

"Sure, come on in." Linx opened the door.

Cait greeted Linx with a half-hug, then turned to Jessie. "Hello, are you Linx's little helper today?"

"I sure am. I'm Jessie Patterson."

"Nice to meet you." Cait glanced from Jessie to Linx and back. "I bet you're a big girl now. How old are you?"

"I'm five and a half." She took the bottle out of Ginger's mouth and put up five fingers.

Cait gave her a high five.

"Hi, Cait." Tami waved from the desk. "You brought us gifts?"

"I sure did." Cait waddled over to her. "Fresh from the oven. Mrs. Burris lets us use her kitchen. Isn't that sweet of her? Maybe instead of a wedding business, I should set up a bakery, or I can do both."

"Good idea," Tami exclaimed, taking a muffin. "By the way, are you up for a few showings today? There's a lovely Victorian that's come on the market."

Linx heaved a sigh of relief, thankful that Tami had distracted Cait from interrogating little Jessie.

Now that she and Grady were sworn enemies, a visit from Cait was like harboring a spy in their midst. What was Cait snooping around for?

Then again, there was no reason to keep the two retrievers from Grady. He was free to come and pick them up—from Tami.

Linx sent him a text message. *The adoption for Molly and Rex is approved. Tami will process the final paperwork.*

She might as well get used to having Grady in town. He was rebuilding his cabin. He got his dog back, and it was only a matter of time before he found himself a woman. He'd marry and have a family, and she would have to watch from the sidelines.

She would never make anyone a good wife, nor would she be a good mother.

She was too much like Minx, but unlike her mother, she wouldn't make the mistake of starting a family only to abandon them.

She was better than that.

Chapter Eighteen

He wasn't in love with Linx Colson.

He didn't do love—didn't believe in it.

Love always ended badly.

Like now.

Even though he got his dog back, she wasn't the same.

She followed him around all day like she was a prisoner out on a chain-gang. And now, she plodded into his cramped fifth-wheel trailer looking like a dejected and homeless stray.

"What's the matter?" Grady prodded Sasha, who lay on the floor of his trailer, her eyes wide open but resting her snout on her front paws. "I got steak for us. You want steak?"

The big dog wagged the tip of her tail and barely looked up at him. She'd been excited during their time in town, alert to her surroundings, but as soon as he headed up the mountain, her ears started to droop, and then her head. By the time they made the turn up his driveway, she was slumped on the bench seat.

She'd staggered from the truck and slunk to the trailer door, lapping listlessly at her water bowl. He'd tried throwing a tennis ball for her to fetch, but she only stared at it and then lay down on the floor with a resigned expression.

She obviously missed Linx.

Grady's gut clenched, and his heart beat hollow at the memory of the day Linx dropped Sasha off. She was cold and resigned, and she'd spoken sternly to Sasha, ordering her to stay behind.

She'd then driven away without looking back. There would be no more dog deliveries with motel room hookups for him—no more favors, no more fights, no more heat and spark.

The fire had died, and now, Grady was relegated to dealing with Tami for new adoptions.

Rejection hurt, and he wasn't used to being on the receiving end of it.

He bent over and rubbed the big dog's neck. "I'm sorry you had to leave your mommy. I didn't mean for you to get hurt."

What had felt like a victory was now fool's gold.

"I was mad at your mommy for so long," he said, scratching Sasha's ears. "But now, I've forgotten why I'm so angry. She hurt me, because she lied to me. When I found out she kept you, I blew a gasket."

The dog lifted herself to a sitting position and rested her head on his knee the way she used to do. It should have been comforting, it should have made him feel warm and complete, but not now—not when he missed Linx with every fiber of his being.

He'd spent so many years denying her, running from her, drowning in casual flings, and convincing himself that she'd lied—and she had, one version or the other, and now, it dawned on him that she had ended it.

She was telling him it no longer mattered whether she'd lied or not.

It no longer mattered whether she'd had a baby or not.

It no longer mattered what he thought about her.

She was done, and this time, it was final.

As final as her leaving her very heart—Sasha, or as she called her, Cedar.

Well hell, it damn well mattered to him whether he was in love with her or not. He was supposed to hate her, but if his heart hurt so much, and love caused pain, then what did Cait's words mean?

One thing was sure. Sasha loved Linx and Sasha was in pain.

He stroked the dog's silky mane and rubbed her behind the ears. "Do you prefer Sasha or Cedar?"

The dog's ears perked when he said, "Cedar."

"Is it Cedar? Is that who you are?"

A light came back into Cedar's eyes, and her head snapped up with an eager look.

"You want me to take you back to Linx, don't you?"

Cedar wagged the tip of her tail and leaped to her feet, shaking herself as if to go right away.

Maybe his dog was right. Maybe he, also, should go back to Linx and ask for another chance. Swallow his pride and bury the hatchet.

He was hurting as much as the dog, and if he was honest with himself, he hadn't exactly treated Linx fairly. True, he had no idea how a woman felt being pregnant and alone, and he'd always assumed they wanted to trap him, as if he were the big prize.

How wrong he was. He was no prize—just a has-been firefighter.

But he could still do something for her.

He could give Cedar back, and he could volunteer at the rescue center. He could be nicer to her, for a change, and then, maybe, he'd get over this big fat ache in his heart.

If he was in love, he was in trouble. It was going to hurt either way—with or without Linx, because the way his heart was, he could never fall out of it.

Damn his heart.

"Okay, let's take you back to your mommy." Grady hugged Sasha and let her lick his face. "I'm going to miss you. You were always my puppy. My little lost puppy."

So much like Linx, a lost puppy.

Now, where did that thought come from?

Cedar's worried, lost expression the moment Linx had left her was exactly the same as that crestfallen abandoned look Linx had given him when he told her their fairy tale was over.

She was nineteen and had her entire life in front of her, and he was twenty-two, at his physical peak. He couldn't settle down, even if it was with a fellow smokejumper, and have her tagging along to all the stations around the world.

Respect for women wasn't universal around the world, and the facilities were primitive in many of the outposts. Sometimes, they had to live off the land, hunting and fishing for food, and hike back to base, instead of being picked up by helicopters.

The men were gross and sexist, and he couldn't have protected her everywhere they went.

Besides, he wasn't the type to get tied down, especially so young. The excuses looped through his mind, sounding hollower and hollower.

He couldn't get past the fact that her dates were off. If she was pregnant, it wasn't his. Impossible since he was already halfway around the world at the estimated time of conception.

He'd plugged in all the possible dates at the online pregnancy calculator website, and there was no way, no how, he could have been the father.

But, then again, Salem also accused him of fathering her baby, and her range of dates was so wide that any number of guys could have done it.

Damn. Grady slapped his forehead. If Salem's baby were his, then her dying caused his baby to die too. Had what he'd told her before the jump caused her accident? Or was it worse—her suicide?

The weight over his shoulders pressed like sacks of lead pellets, suffocating him with gnawing regret.

It was time to stop sowing wild oats, and time to act like a responsible man—a Hart man who took responsibility seriously and never let anyone down.

A chilling thought drilled fangs of ice through him.

How many babies had he lost? Or had he caused to die? How many of those false pregnancy claims had been true? He should never have sown any wild oats, because each one was an individual—a little boy or girl—a tiny Hart—his flesh and blood—family.

"Let's go, Cedar." Grady sighed and opened the trailer door. Cedar jumped over the small steel steps with a spring in her trot.

When Grady opened the door of his truck, Cedar eagerly hopped in, happy that she was going back to Linx.

He got into the driver's seat and patted her. "We used to be so tight. Me and you. Found you behind my woodpile. You were just a tiny puppy. God knows how you survived the fire, but you did. I would have looked for you, but I was taken to the hospital. You must have had smoke inhalation, too. She took good care of you, didn't she?"

It was always easier to talk to his dog than to people. Dogs understood and they listened. But most of all, they simply accepted. And trusted.

Right now, Cedar's entire face had lifted from the gloom and despair earlier, and she was perky and looking forward to going back into town.

Okay, decision made. Going forward, Grady would do whatever it took to make things right for Linx. Whatever had happened in the past, he could let it go, if only she would give him another chance.

Grady's spirits lifted the closer he got to town. Linx would be so happy and relieved once he brought Cedar back. He might even put a smile on her face. Maybe he could start something with her. He sped through the town square, his heart beating seventy miles an hour.

A siren roared behind him and flashing red and blue lights pulled him over.

Crap. Linx's brother was not the man he wanted to see.

Todd Colson ambled up to the driver's side window with a ticket pad in his hand. "Where's the fire?"

"I'm bringing Linx's dog back to her."

Cedar barked and Todd frowned. "You shouldn't have taken her in the first place."

"Hey, she was mine, and you know it." Grady had had enough of Todd's gruff attitude. "I know your entire family is against me, but Linx hasn't told me the whole story. She's holding things back from me, like this dog, for example."

"You disrespected her." The sheriff scribbled in his ticket book. "You never treated her fairly."

"If I knew what all of you had against me, I could fix it. Why don't you spit it out?"

"It's not for me to say." Todd handed him the speeding citation. "You can pay at the jailhouse, but a word of advice. If you're not going to make it right for my sister, then I suggest you move out of here. I can't make you go, but I'm going to be on your ass like stink on a skunk."

"I have sisters, too," Grady said. "But I don't meddle with their sex lives."

Steam seemed to ooze from Todd's red face, but he grunted and ambled back to his patrol car.

That ought to give the overprotective brother something to stew over.

Chapter Nineteen

Linx peered out the window at the sound of Cedar's happy bark and the car door slamming. She blinked once, twice. A squeal squeezed through her throat, and she ran out the front door, and down the wooden steps.

"Cedar!"

Her dog scampered up the walkway and bounded to her, licking her face and panting with happiness.

"I missed you so much, girl. So much." She knelt and hugged and kissed the companion who'd been with her for four years. "Did your daddy bring you back for a visit?"

Grady's boot was in her line of vision, but her heart pounded with hesitation. He'd probably come by to pick up Molly and Rex—not to let her visit with Cedar at all, but to rub it in her face that she was now his dog.

"Aren't you going to say anything to me?" Grady asked, his voice low and husky.

Swallowing, she let her eyes travel up his fine legs, past his well-endowed crotch, the plane of his six-pack abdomen, his hard and hot chest, landing on his rugged handsome face.

He held out a hand and lifted her the rest of the way, his eyes intense and dark with passion.

Words escaped her as she met his hungry gaze. He drew her close, and there was nothing she could do but smash her lips against his.

She held on tight, opening herself to him and devouring him at the same time. She was helpless, throwing her hands around his neck. Her body pressed to his heat, and at the same time, she wanted so much more.

Her need, his desire, her want, his demand collided like the storm surge after a hurricane, breaching the walls of her resolve and swamping her with endless desire.

Closing her eyes, she felt the strength of his yearning, the potency of his vulnerability, and yes, the possibility of more—of love, maybe, and hope.

Had he come to her bringing peace offerings? Could he accept what she'd done? No matter how horrible?

Could they?

"Miss Linx," Jessie said, coming out the door. "Ginger made a mess on the floor."

Yikes!

Linx and Grady popped apart with such force she stumbled against the porch railing while he crashed into the metal skull, missing the spike by a few inches.

"Uh, Jessie, I'll clean it up," Linx muttered, turning away from Grady who naturally followed her and Cedar into the cabin.

Great. If she'd thought she had something to hide before, she now had an even bigger dilemma.

Grady was staring at Jessie as if he'd never seen her before.

"Are you Cedar's daddy?" Jessie asked.

Grady squatted down to her level and said, "Why I believe I am."

"I knew you'd bring her back. You're not divorced, are you?"

"Oh, no, I'm not divorced." Grady smiled at the little girl whose soulful brown eyes were a mirror image of his own. "Don't worry about Cedar. She'll have both her mommy and daddy loving her."

"I have a mommy and a daddy, too," Jessie said. "But my dog is lost. Her name is Betsy, and Miss Linx is going to use her superpowers to find her."

"I'll help Miss Linx find her. I promise." Grady turned on the charm, and from Jessie's animated expression, she was lapping it all up.

The screen door slapped, and Cedar jumped to her feet, panting a greeting as Jessie's mother stepped in.

"Did you have a good time?" she asked Jessie and waved to Linx and Grady.

"Mama!" Jessie said, hugging the woman's legs. "Cedar's daddy brought her back. Do you think he'll bring Betsy back, too?"

"I'm sure everyone here wants to find Betsy," Mrs. Patterson said. "Did you help Miss Linx take care of the puppy?"

"I did! And I drew a picture of me feeding Ginger." Jessie's double ponytails bounced as she skipped to the playpen where little Ginger was practicing her Army man crawl.

In a flurry of chatter, waving, and patting, Jessie bade everyone goodbye, and Linx was left alone with Grady and Cedar.

The jitters returned to her belly, and she wondered why Grady had come by.

Grady parked himself in front of her, invading her personal space. He gently tucked a strand of Linx's hair behind her ear. "Tonight, I want it to be me and you. We need to talk and really get to know each other."

"Where's all this coming from?" Linx's voice wobbled as the undeniable ember of hope smoldered behind her guarded heart. "Why are you being nice to me all of a sudden?"

"Why shouldn't I be nice to you?"

"You want something."

"I'm giving Cedar back to you. I want to spend time with you—like normal people, instead of fighting all the time."

"I do appreciate you bringing Cedar back, but what changed?"

Grady's lips pressed together tight, looking utterly miserable. "She thought you'd abandoned her. It broke my heart to see how down she was, slinking around. She doesn't understand what's going on between us. It's not fair for her to feel rejected."

"Grady ..." her voice sounded breathless. "I don't know what to say."

"Why don't we relax and chill, have a good time tonight?"

She held up a hand and backed away. "This isn't one of your twisted dog deliveries, is it? Because I'm not sleeping with you tonight, even though you brought Cedar back."

"I would never turn you down if that's what you want, but no, this isn't a sleepover. It's a peace offering." His fingers brushed over her cheek. "I brought steak. If it's okay with you, let's have a date night."

"Date night?" The concept had never crossed Linx's mind.

She didn't date, and now that she thought about it, he'd never taken her out on a date, ever.

They'd had after-sex snacks and before-sex drinks, and weekends spent in bed, but she'd never spent time with Grady when sex was off the table or off the bed.

"Okay. No funny business." Linx grabbed at the remnants of her self-respect. "I told you earlier I'm not sleeping with you."

"If you sleep with me, it'll be because I deserve you. Right now, I'm in the doghouse." He grazed her lips with a kiss. "Prepare to be wowed."

"You're still so arrogant, Doghouse Grady," she chuckled. "Thanks for bringing Cedar back."

He gave her lips another almost chaste peck, and she kissed him back, tangling her arms around him. For the first time since she'd known Grady, she felt playful and carefree.

For tonight only, she'd pretend her other secret didn't hang over their heads. She'd enjoy the evening as if she were on a first date with an attractive prospect. She'd let herself imagine he'd forgive her and maybe even cherish her.

Pulling back from the kiss, she whispered, "Let me go upstairs and get ready for our date. I'll want flowers, candlelight, and the whole experience."

Chapter Twenty

Linx dabbed perfume behind her ears and over her pulse points and checked her reflection in her full-length mirror. Her dark-brown hair flowed effortlessly over her bare shoulders, and bright red lipstick accentuated her exotic looking face, so much like her mother.

The ghostly outline of the avant-garde wedding dress designed by Grady's sister faded like an old photograph compared to the vibrant colors she'd dazzle Grady with on this very first of all dates—a stretchy black miniskirt with a bold red rose pattern over knee-high black leather boots and bare thighs.

It felt strange to be up in her loft getting dressed while Grady manned her kitchen with Cedar at his feet.

Now that they were both present and accounted for, Cedar perked up and was back to her happy self. She pranced around her home and wagged her tail whenever Grady looked at her, begging scratches and kisses.

Linx had never seen Cedar happier and more content.

She stood at the top of the stairs and watched Grady set the table, wearing a barbeque apron. His shirt sleeves were rolled up past his elbows, and he had a chef's thermometer tucked over one ear.

This.

Looked.

So much like home.

This.

Couldn't.

Be true.

Domestic and tranquil were not words belonging to her and Grady's story.

But still, she watched, mesmerized while love songs played on the stereo—another relic from her grandmother, complete with large speakers and a tuner in which she'd plugged an iPod. He'd found her secret playlist, the one she'd never admit to listening to—never dared to hope.

Grady set her rustic wooden table with a pair of candlesticks over a pinecone centerpiece. After lighting the candles, he took a platter and exited the back door, followed by Cedar.

An essential oil diffuser spilled scents of pine, cedar, and vanilla, mixing with the aroma of grilled steaks wafting through the kitchen window. A bowl of tossed salad sat on the kitchen counter along with two wine glasses and a bottle of red wine.

Slowly, Linx descended the stairs, hardly believing the warm, cozy cabin belonged to her. He'd spread her grandmother's wedding knot afghan on the lodge-pole couch, and arranged wildflowers in the vases on the end tables.

Ginger slept curled up with a hot water bottle in her playpen, and the curtains were drawn, the lights dimmed.

Grady Hart sure knew how to put on a date night. He'd even swept and cleaned the kitchen.

The screen door in back swung open, and the man who tied her heart up in knots came through with a platter. "I hope you still like your steaks medium-rare."

"You remembered." Her fingers fluttered over the silverware in the drawer. She'd use her grandmother's silver tonight. Thankfully, she'd had them polished for the Gold Rush Festival display. "This is all so special. Thanks."

He set the platter on the counter and leaned toward her. "See? I'm not such a bad guy."

"I never said you were." She set the table, her breath quickening. "Although I'm still a bad girl."

"I'm not sure I can forgive you for keeping Cedar," he said, grinding pepper over the steaks. "But I'd like to hear your reasons."

"I'm evil."

"So am I." He set the plates on the table and put the salad bowl between them. "That's why I can't forgive you, even though I'm going to let you have Cedar."

"You'll come visit, won't you?"

"Yeah, maybe we should have joint custody. Shall we kiss on that?" He stood in front of her, too close, raking her with his scorching gaze.

Linx wet her lips, but turned away from him. "I don't think it's a good idea to be kissing and touching."

"But we're evil, so we'll always do the bad idea." He feathered his sturdy fingers through her hair. "Since I'm going to be staying in the vicinity, and my sister's going to join the Chamber of Commerce, and possibly live in that haunted house Tami showed her, I want to start over with you. Wipe the slate clean. Will you let me volunteer here?"

"You want to volunteer?"

"Heard you couldn't afford to pay, so I reckon it's free labor you're looking for." He feathered his fingers through her hair, tilting her face toward his.

"Sure, burying the hatchet is good. I don't want us at each other's throats."

"Oh, I don't know about that." He raised an eyebrow and smirked. "I'll draw blood for make-up sex."

"There's nothing for us to make up for." She speared him with narrowed eyes. "Since you won't forgive me."

He patted her behind. "You didn't think I'd go soft on you, did you?"

Oh, no, he was never soft, ever. Not that she'd complain. She didn't need forgiveness, not after what she'd done. Any forgiveness now would be wasted on her when he discovered what else she'd kept from him.

For now, she'd enjoy date night and steak—maybe a little dancing and a little touching.

As for accepting him as a volunteer? It made sense, and it was only fair for her to let him take Cedar out on walks.

She was, after all, his dog.

"I'll expect you to stay long and hard, whenever I'm around." She inhaled the mouth-watering aroma of grilled steak and aroused male. Opening her mouth, she let herself enjoy one more hungry kiss before they'd attack the steaks.

* * *

Grady dimmed the lights and pulled the antique cane chair back for his date. Time slowed as he admired her beauty, the way she swept her hair back, the smile she graced him with, and the soft voice of thanks.

He couldn't help leaning down and feathering his lips over the column of her neck. Her sultry scent and the indrawn breath sizzling through her lips stirred the want deep in his gut.

She turned her head and rubbed her face against his. Her gaze studied him, taking all of him, open and vulnerable. Was this his wildcat, or had he never seen this side of her—feminine, comforting, and accepting?

Taking her hand, he pulled her from the table. The steaks would be stone-cold by the time he was done with her, but it no longer mattered.

Gazing into the dark pools of her eyes, he touched her, lightly, exploring the contours of her face, slowly, gently, as she, too, touched him—truly touched, considering, getting acquainted.

Below their feet, Cedar lay on a braided rug over the heart-pine floor, watching them as they swayed to "Once in a Lifetime Love." This was the way it should have been—all those years ago. He needed her and he needed her love—or her brand of love, however she expressed it.

He shouldn't have run. Only cowards ran, and even though it had never made any sense back then, now, surrounded by her perfume, her touch, her warm breath, inside her home, with her dog at his feet—time stood still.

He never believed in love, didn't trust it, and ran from the slightest whiff of love. But love had a way of worming its way, like the puppy found behind the woodpile, or the newborn cradled in a father's arms.

And love had a way of growing and consuming and crowding out hate, turning bitter and lonely men like Connor into smitten husbands and doting fathers. Taking each of his sisters from selfish and entitled girls and changing them into beautiful, glowing women whose eyes reflected love at the sight of their men. They touched and comforted, they considered and cared. Their serene faces while growing babies in their wombs were polar opposites to the frantic anguish on the faces of women with unwanted pregnancies.

He didn't know how long he drank in the sight of Linx, or the feel of her in his arms, or the way their bodies moved. But the candles burned out and the steaks grew cold. The sun set and the cabin grew dark, but he didn't want to let her go.

Not now, and not ever.

And as he kissed her, he knew that whether he loved her or hated her, the pain would never leave. He might as well love her and risk the tragic ending, rather than an aborted beginning.

Chapter Twenty-One

Grady poked around the ruins of his parents' cabin early Saturday morning. He wasn't sure what he was looking for, since he wasn't a fire investigator.

The fire hadn't been an accident. If it was directed at him, he needed to get to the bottom of it before Cait or any other member of his family got hurt.

He hadn't said anything to Brian, but every man whose house was set on fire had slept with Salem Pryde: Tim, Duane, Jake, Chief, himself. Of course, the list of men sleeping with her was longer, including Paul and another half a dozen guys at the base camp.

He circled what was once the porch and stared at the spot where the front door used to be.

Someone had left a cross made of railroad spikes. The ground had been brushed clean of ashes, and the longer side of the cross was pounded into a charred log.

This had to be a message from one deranged person, but who was it aimed at?

Last Christmas, Cait had been kidnapped by an ex-boyfriend, and Brian had gotten on the wrong side of a powerful senator who found out he'd had an affair with his deceased wife.

What other enemies did his family have?

Grady took a picture with his cell phone camera and texted it to Brian. *You cleared the area, right? Someone nailed a cross to one of the wooden beams. Call the sheriff and have him take it for evidence.*

He was about to get into his pickup truck when something rustled in the dry brush behind him.

Grady snapped to attention, narrowing his eyes.

A gray dog with floppy ears and matted fur sniffed the air and watched him.

"Betsy." Grady recognized her from the posters. "Come here."

The dog skittered away when he went toward it. Her head lowered, and she tucked her tail between her legs, shivering.

Grady got down on his haunches and put his hand out. "You must be hungry. Come here, sweetie."

The tip of the dog's tail wagged, but she was still leery.

Reaching into his truck, Grady found a wrapped rawhide bone he'd bought for Cedar. It wasn't much, but hopefully, it would get the lost dog to trust him. She would be hungry, since she'd been lost quite a while.

He called Linx and told her he'd found Betsy at the site of his parents' cabin.

"That's great. Jessie's with me right now," Linx said. "We're on our way."

* * *

Grady kept watch over Betsy as she tentatively approached him and took the rawhide bone. He looked away from the dog, appearing disinterested, and waited for Linx to drive up.

Their date night had been both special and sweet. After the candles burned down and the playlist looped, he and Linx had eaten cold steak and drank warm wine. They'd held hands and taken a walk with Cedar through the dusky woods.

The trail took them up by the creek and Cedar led the way, her ears upright. She scampered from rock to rock, looking back to make sure she hadn't left them behind.

After the walk, he'd bade her goodnight instead of going back into the cabin for a nightcap. They'd kissed under the moonlight, and when he drove away, he spied her shadow up in the loft window waving to him.

He wasn't sure if he preferred her so subdued, but knowing Linx with her short fuse, she was sure to fire up again without a moment's notice.

Somehow, that thought got his juices flowing.

Linx's SUV drove up the gravel driveway, raising a trail of dust. Betsy slunk to the back of the burned cabin, but Grady wasn't too worried.

"Betsy!" Jessie jumped out of the SUV even before it had fully parked. "Betsy!"

Woof! Woof! The dog bounded toward the little girl whose eyes popped wide along with her mouth.

Squealing with happiness, she ran at the dog and fell in a heap over her, hugging and trading kisses.

The love and affection passing between the dog and child made Grady's heart swell and his throat lump up. It had been a long time since he'd had a dog who loved him so unconditionally.

Linx joined in the lovefest. She knelt down to hug both the dog and the girl who wiggled and bounced, full of excitement. The entire picture was sweet to the bone, and Linx laughed as the girl whispered in her ear.

Both of them sported similar expressions as the dog licked them, their eyes closed with pure enjoyment and identical closemouthed smiles, head tilted slightly up.

Grady's entire body jolted as if someone had kicked his behind.

Could this child be his? And hers?

They looked almost like twins, although years apart, and there was genuine affection between them.

But no, he'd met the middle-aged woman who was Jessie's mother. She must have had her late in life.

Or not at all?

Again, questions raised in his head.

He took a picture of Linx and Jessie, catching their identical smiles, and texted it to Cait without a message.

A jumble of emotions swamped him as he watched the woman who had him twisted up inside and out, and the sweet little girl whose dark-brown hair and eyes and olive-colored tan resembled Linx more than Mrs. Patterson's washed out gray eyes and translucently pale skin.

Linx noticed him staring. Turning, she stood and came to him, all smiles. "How'd you find Betsy? You don't know how nervous Jessie was on the drive up. She kept worrying that Betsy would run away or that you'd mistaken some other dog, so we came right away without waiting for her mother."

"I knew it was Betsy as soon as I saw her. I gave her a rawhide chew toy to keep her nearby." Grady dotted a kiss on Linx's cheek. "I have to show you something."

While Jessie played with Betsy, Grady led Linx to the metal cross erected over the burnt logs of the cabin. "Kind of reminds me of that sculpture your mother left on your porch."

Linx's lips pursed tight, but she shook her head. "That's a simple cross made of railroad spikes. Anyone could have placed it there. My mother always uses more than one medium. Metal, pieces of bone, rock chips, even dirt and sometimes feathers and bits of skin. This is beneath her. It has no imagination."

"Sounds gruesome." He gave her a pat on the behind. "And you sound proud of your mother."

She averted her gaze and shrugged, but didn't answer him.

"Miss Linx," Jessie said, dragging Betsy by the collar. "Mommy said Betsy's lost forever and I can get a puppy. Will she still give me a puppy?"

"We'll have to ask her." Linx's face relaxed, smiling. She ruffled the little girl's head. "Let's go find your mommy. Did you thank Grady for finding your dog?"

"Yes!" Jessie turned those big, brown eyes on him, blinking sweetly. "Thank you, Superman!"

"Superman?" Grady grinned, glancing at Linx.

"Yes, you're Wonder Woman's boyfriend." Jessie tugged Linx's hand but faced Grady. "And you found Betsy."

"I think Betsy found me." Grady chuckled. "Will she let me pet her now?"

Somehow the sound of him being Linx's boyfriend not only didn't bother him, but made him feel warm and gooey inside.

"Sure," Jessie said. "Betsy, meet Superman. Superman, meet Betsy. Betsy, say thank you and shake."

Betsy raised her paw for Grady, and even though he felt silly, he shook her paw and smiled at Jessie.

The thought that she could be his daughter was too painful for him to acknowledge, because it would mean Linx had told him one big whopping lie.

That she'd never been pregnant.

Even worse, she'd betrayed him by giving his baby away.

But as warped as Linx was, she would never do something this heinous, would she?

Grady took a deep breath and watched Linx, Jessie, and Betsy get into Linx's SUV and drive off.

He was overreacting, overwrought due to the rash of suspicious fires. Many people had dark hair and eyes, especially in California.

Sheesh. At the rate he was going, every child he saw would trigger his paternal instincts. He needed to focus on the arson investigation, and the only way to find out if the fires were connected was to go to the source and retrace the arsonist's steps.

* * *

"The gig is up." Tami blew her way into the dog rescue office and flung her large kente cloth purse on the sofa.

Linx looked up from giving Ginger a bath in the kitchen sink. "What happened? What gig?"

Tami marched toward her with her hands on her hips. "Grady, that's what. Tell me what's going on."

"Nothing's going on between me and him." Linx wrapped a fluffy towel around little Ginger and dried her. "We had a date night, and that was it. He brought Cedar back, and we've buried the hatchet."

"That's not what concerns me." Tami opened the refrigerator and grabbed a can of soda. "It's Cait. She showed me a picture Grady texted her of you and Jessie."

"Where? What picture?" Linx's pulse ratcheted up a few notches. "I haven't taken any pictures with her."

"Grady took a picture of you two hugging Betsy yesterday," Tami said. "He texted it to Cait. You two look like twins."

"So? What did Cait say? She can't prove anything."

"She didn't say anything. She showed me the picture and watched my face."

"Oh, crap. Did you give me away?"

"Of course, I didn't, but I'm sure she suspects. You better fess up to Grady and come clean."

Linx held Ginger close to her chest and paced around the kitchen table, her heart throbbing wildly.

"I'm finally getting along with him. I can see us being friends, and maybe develop into something normal. I know I have to tell him, but he's only going to hate me again. He hasn't forgiven me for stealing Cedar."

"Oh, posh. Any man will forgive any woman if you have him in the right position." Tami waved her hand dismissively. "I'll tell you how to do it. Invite him over for a bottle of wine."

"Won't work. We already shared a bottle of wine and nothing happened." Linx swallowed the frustration bottled up inside of her. "He insisted on taking Cedar for a walk. After we returned, he kissed me goodnight outside and left me high and dry. Of course, I'd taken sex off the table, but I thought he'd at least try."

"Did you flash a boob? That should work. Or start stripping. That'll get his attention."

Linx cuddled Ginger and put her in the playpen while she mixed her formula. "Yeah, but we don't talk much when we're in the throes of passion."

"Then tell him while he's still basking in the afterglow." Tami poked her upper arm. "Look at you. You're wound up as tight as a virgin in a chastity belt, and you need to get good and laid."

Linx rolled her eyes. "You're tempting me, but I don't think a good lay is going to fix what's wrong between me and Grady."

"It might not, but since you stopped giving him favors, he's been as grouchy as a grizzly wearing a beehive on his tail." Tami swatted Linx's behind. "Get going. I don't want to see you back until you're wearing that delicious 'I just got laid grin.'"

"Right, it'll be more like my 'I just got laid and dumped' crying face."

"At least you got laid first. Yep, I'd definitely get off first and answer questions later. It's about time you two had a heart-to-heart talk anyway. And if you don't, I'll reserve the right to tell Grady for you."

Linx narrowed her eyes, feeling smoke seep from her nostrils. "If you do, I'll never say a good word to my brother for you."

"You'll thank me, girlfriend." Tami grinned. "Besides, a bad word might get me further with that squarepants."

"Fine, I'll put out feelers with Todd for you."

"You do that," Tami clapped both hands on Linx's shoulders. "It's about time he stops letting me off with a warning. I mean, he needs to get me good and arrested so I can flash him a boob or two."

"I'll work on it. Promise. My brother can be pretty dense when it comes to women."

"No denser than you when it comes to men." Tami pitched the empty can of soda into the wastebasket. "Text him now and ask him to come over. Don't make him hear it from Cait."

"Did you spill?" Linx grabbed her friend by the hand.

"No, but you know how my face gives everything away." Tami's lips twisted downward and she blinked. "I'm sorry."

Chapter Twenty-Two

Linx couldn't put it off any longer. This thing with Jessie ate away at her, and tore her heart to pieces. She texted Grady a simple message.

I have a huge secret and you're not going to like it. Meet me at my place.

There was no ignoring such a message, and sure enough, he texted back. *Coming over.*

Date night had been a new beginning, and tonight would be the dreaded end.

The fact that Grady didn't ask her what the secret was about meant he had an inkling.

Swallowing the bile that surged from her gut, she brushed her teeth and took a quick shower. She wasn't going to flash him a boob or use sex to soften the blow.

There would be no makeup. No perfume. No sexy dress. No bare thighs.

She would face his wrath head on and endure the aftermath, whatever it was.

Cedar alerted her that Grady was at the door, so she hurriedly pulled a Dickies work shirt over her camisole and patted her damp hair down.

Slipping her feet into flip-flops, she shuffled down the stairs and threw open the door.

Grady stood there, his face foreboding and grim, his eyebrows clenched and his jaw tight.

"What's this big secret you're keeping from me?"

Instead of answering, she took his hand.

It was stiff and unresponsive, but at least he didn't twist out of her grasp.

"Come upstairs and let me show you."

His mouth twisted to one side, and he narrowed his eyes, but he didn't resist.

Gingerly, she led him up to her room up on the loft—her most private sanctuary.

"Have a seat." She patted her futon and opened the drawer on her nightstand.

He stood at the doorway, looking around her room, his eyes suspicious. "I don't know what game you're playing, but I'm tired of it. Tell me what you did to my baby."

Boom. She bent over, crumpling as if he'd punched her in the gut. Her hand shaking, she dug through the top drawer, setting aside her gun and Bible until she found what she was looking for.

Two of her most precious photos.

She handed him the first picture, and he raised an eyebrow. "Why are you showing me this?"

It was a picture taken of them back in her training days. In it, she and Grady sat on the grass at the town square. She was wearing a white tank top and black jeans with holes across both knees and he was holding her, happy, as if they had forever in front of them.

It was right before he told her he was going away, and asked her not to wait for him.

"I want you to remember us that day. When you asked me to meet you in the park, on that field of wildflowers, I thought you were about to propose to me. I thought you were offering me forever. Instead ..."

"I broke your heart," he finished for her.

"No, my heart is too hard to break." Even now, she didn't want to give him the satisfaction. "You rejected me, but you know what? It made me tougher and stronger."

He flapped the picture in front of her. "Were you pregnant at the time?"

She nodded. "But I didn't know it."

"Where's the baby now?"

Linx unveiled the second picture. It was Jessie within a few hours of birth. Her eyes were closed and her tiny fists were clenched tight.

Grady drew in a thick breath. "Who is this?"

"Your daughter, Jessie."

"You gave her away? How could you? You never told me." Grady's words lanced through Linx's heart as she clutched his shirt and collapsed onto her futon. Her pulse thudded behind both ears, and she gasped for breath.

"You didn't want anything to do with me. What else could I do?" Linx averted her gaze, unable to withstand the way Grady's narrowed eyes drilled into her soul. "You said I lied."

"Dates, Linx. Tell me the dates."

"She was born in July."

"Was she early?"

"Full term. I thought she was early, but she was actually late. So late, she almost died." Linx turned her face into her pillow as Cedar came up behind her and nudged her, trying to comfort her.

It no longer mattered what Grady thought about her. Nothing mattered other than Jessie. She'd given her a better life with normal parents—the kind who went to church and read her bedtime stories. A father who coached softball and a mother who doted on her, celebrating every birthday with a party and showered her with love, pretty dresses, cookies, dance lessons, and toys.

"I, I don't know what to say." Grady laid down next to her. "Why did you wait so long to contact me?"

"I didn't know if I was still pregnant." Linx wiped her eyes. "I had bleeding. I thought I wasn't pregnant, so I counted from the wrong date. I didn't know until she was born that she was full term."

"You didn't get prenatal care?" Grady swept her hair aside, his voice kinder.

"I didn't want anyone to know."

"You didn't tell your family?"

"Not at the time." She didn't have a mother who cared, and Tami was off in college. She was a nineteen-year-old—she was in denial, wishing it would go away.

"Only Salem knew, and she said if I had a miscarriage, then no one needed to know. But then the baby kept growing."

"Salem was with you?"

"Yes, she was the only one who knew. I didn't even tell my family I was back. They thought I was smokejumping with you. Salem got all my groceries and I basically hid from everyone."

"And you tried to contact me?"

"Yes, I texted and tried calling—left messages. You didn't answer." Linx turned her face away from the concern, years too late, written on Grady's face.

"When was this?"

"December, around Christmas when Salem said you were back in San Francisco."

Grady blinked, jolting and stiffening at the same time. "I didn't come home that Christmas. I was in Australia. Why would Salem know where I was?"

"She said she kept in touch with you. She gave me your phone number, and I called, but you never answered. I texted and texted, left you messages."

"I never heard from you until March." Grady's voice was tight. "Why so late."

Blood drained from her head as horror flooded her heart. "I never called or texted you in March. I gave up by then."

"No, I definitely got text messages from you, accusing me of knocking you up and threatening me with a lawsuit. You were texting me so much, I had to change my phone number. You even blackmailed me, said if I didn't pay for your pregnancy costs, you'd accuse me of sexual harassment. I even called you and told you to back off."

"It wasn't me you called." Linx clawed at Grady and pounded on his chest. "I would never blackmail you. Never. All I wanted was you to let me know what to do with the baby. You have to believe me."

His stare was hard and steady, and a vein twitched on his forehead. "No wonder you didn't say anything when I yelled at you."

Linx held his gaze, unflinching. Her pulse quaked as she shuddered with anger. "Believe me, if I heard from you before Jessie was born, I would have screamed at you to come back. Instead, I got a text message telling me you denied everything and to get rid of the baby."

"I would never say something like that." He snarled as if he were falsely accused.

"Yes, you would. Right before Jessie was born, you sent me a nasty letter. You accused me of lying. You said the baby wasn't yours and you never, ever wanted to hear from me again. So ... I ... gave her ... away ... to give her a better life."

"My lawyer told me to send you written notice. I was going to countersue you for defamation." Grady slapped his palms onto the futon, startling Cedar who jumped and squared off against him. "It's because the dates were all wrong."

"I didn't know the baby was coming in July," Linx wailed. "I was hiding in the mountains—in your cabin. My water broke and I didn't know what to do. If Salem hadn't come to bring my groceries that day, both Jessie and I would have died. Please don't hate me."

"I don't hate you." Grady wrapped her into his arms and cradled her. "I'm pissed at myself. I should have come to check it out. I shouldn't have stayed away. I've a feeling the text messages you sent went to Salem, and then she texted me the blackmail threats. She must have sent the text telling you to get rid of it. God knows, I would never ask you to do that. No wonder she was so smug the entire time she was on the fire crew, like she knew something."

"I thought she was my friend. I saved her life that day when she got hurt. I thought she cared about me." Linx wasn't sure why she was babbling, except she was numb and aching at the same time. "I blew it. I really blew it."

"No, I did. I should have come home when I got those messages. I should have called you."

"You did, once, after Jessie was born, and you sounded so suspicious and pissed. At that point, I didn't care anymore, so I told you nothing happened. I thought I'd never see you again, that it wouldn't matter."

"Because I'd been such an ass." Grady knocked his forehead against hers. Tears sprinkled on his eyelashes as he gazed into her eyes. "Now what? Can we get her back?"

"I don't know. You've met her. Isn't she wonderful? Isn't she precious?"

"She's adorable, and I'm so glad she got Betsy back. She's such a determined kid, so much like you." Grady wiped his eyes and smiled at the same time. "What do we do now? Will her mother let us talk to her?"

"Her mother doesn't know you're the father," Linx said.

"But she's mine, you're sure?" He lifted an eyebrow and swallowed. "I've always been so careful with birth control."

"We got blasted drunk after that last fire ..." Linx's voice was little more than a whisper. "The one where the fire rolled over us and we had to hide under the fire shelter."

"I wasn't sure you made it." Grady's voice softened and that old familiar look, the one that melted her heart, reflected on his rugged face.

"I thought I'd die if you didn't make it." Linx moved closer, her eyes locked to his, then closed them when he pressed his lips over hers.

He kissed her, softly and slowly, his hands and fingers stroking her, comforting her, and she let her tears mingle with his. All she'd ever wanted was him to acknowledge her, to believe her, and most of all, to trust her.

He tasted different, sweeter, and more tender—like he was baring his soul with the whisper of a kiss. And she didn't want it to end, this peaceful, soothing, blissful state of receiving comfort.

She came up for air and gazed into his eyes. "I'm so sorry. So sorry I didn't tell you."

"I'm the one who's sorry." He feathered his rough fingers down the side of her cheek. "I should have believed you."

"If you had believed me, would things have been different? Would you have come back?"

"Yes. I would never have left you alone and pregnant. I should have known those weren't your texts. I'm still kicking myself. I don't know if I can live with this. I hate myself so much." Grady's face scrunched, and he sat up with his elbows over his knees. He pinched the bridge of his nose and drew in a shuddering breath. "I don't know if I can go on, knowing how I screwed up."

"We both screwed up." Linx wrapped her arms around him, resting her head on his shoulder. The man was broken about this. It was too much to take in all at once. Ironically, this was exactly what she'd wanted—him to hurt as much as she had been hurting.

But all of this hadn't been his fault. It had all come down to Salem intercepting their messages and twisting them around for her own enjoyment.

And now, Salem was dead, and there were rumors she was pregnant with Grady's baby.

"One more question," Linx said, knowing it would bug her if she didn't ask. "Was Salem pregnant by you when she died?"

Grady rose to his feet and paced around her tiny loft, then knocked his head against the wall.

Linx waited. A pit grew in her belly as the silence dragged on. Did it really matter? Salem was dead now and so was the baby she was carrying.

Grady cursed under his breath. "You deserve to know everything about me. I owe that to you, and if you choose to have nothing to do with me, it's what I deserve."

"The baby was yours?"

"It could have been." Grady's voice was a deadpan. "She sort of went through the crew."

"What did you whisper to her before her last jump?" Linx put a hand on Grady's back and leaned against him, wanting to comfort him.

"That Paul had gotten her a ring, and that she'd better be sure whose baby she was carrying. I wanted her to stop lying. She picked Paul because he's loaded, but he's my buddy, and I didn't want him to be hurt."

"You had sex with your buddy's girlfriend?"

"No, it happened before she hooked up with Paul. Then I tried to stay away, but she kept throwing herself at me. Hounding me, wanting to make me fight for her. You know how it is in the fire camp. It's no excuse, and I shouldn't have gotten involved with her."

"I'm sorry." Linx hung her head. "I don't know what to say."

"Me either. We both effed up, and I'm going to fix it." He ran his fingers through his thick hair and left.

"What are you going to do?" Linx trailed after him as he jogged down the stairs.

"What do you think?"

***

"What do you usually do when you eff up?" Linx answered his question with a question.

He ran. Or he hid and withdrew.

But that cowardly behavior was what had brought on this disaster in the first place.

"I fix it," Grady declared, hoping his voice was firm enough. "I undo the damage, which means I want Jessie back."

"I don't think you should do anything about it." Linx stepped back and studied him as if he were a sick puppy. "Jessie has a home, a very happy one. Her father teaches high school and is the town pastor. Her mother's a homemaker and the church pianist. They love her to pieces."

Grady's jaw tightened and a whirlwind stirred inside him. The more he thought about it, the more he wanted to explode. "I never gave consent for the adoption."

"You weren't in the picture."

"Because you didn't try hard enough to contact me and you lied to me." He turned away from her. "Isn't this more important than your hurt feelings?"

"You wanted nothing to do with me." Her eyes blazed and she clenched her fists. "You told me to leave you alone."

"You didn't have to take it literally. If it's this important, you should have sent me proof. Or told me before the adoption was final. They have a grace period when you can change your mind." His head throbbed as his pulse thundered behind his ears. "I'm sorry for being a jerk, but I can't just stand here and let those two strangers, no matter how good they are, raise my kid."

"You're the stranger as far as Jessie is concerned."

"Thanks to you." He strode toward the door. He had to put some distance between them or he'd say something hurtful. Seemed like she'd already taken the Pattersons' side. No loyalty or concern for him—as usual.

"Where are you going?" Linx followed him "You can't just go barging into Jessie's life."

He whirled around and glared at her. "I screwed up, but that doesn't mean I have to accept this. All these years, you got to see Jessie grow up, got to be her friend, and I got nothing. Why did you wait so long to fess up?"

"I wanted to tell you, but I was afraid you'd break up with me."

"What's there to break up?" He rolled his eyes and shook his head with frustration. "Last night, when I trusted you, you could have come clean and said something. Instead, you acted like the worst thing you ever did was steal my dog."

"I didn't want to ruin the mood." Linx stopped in front of him, horning into his personal space. "But now I see you were playing a game with me. You're right. We don't have anything worth breaking up. Certainly not the "I hate you" sex. It's sick. All of it. Go ahead and walk away. Now you know everything."

He winced at the "I hate you" sex part. But then, he'd been determined to hurt her, too, for what he'd believed were her lies and blackmail threats.

"Right, now I know." He sneered at her. "Are there any other surprises you have for me?"

"No. It's all out now."

"How about when you stayed at my cabin—without my permission, I might add."

"You'd given me a key, and you were away." She tilted her head and curled her lip. "I needed a place to stay, and I was carrying your baby. I felt I was justified."

"Maybe." He ground his teeth as the knot in his stomach grew. "Did you also feel justified in burning my cabin down?"

"You think I burned it down?" Linx's eyebrows shot up and she jabbed a finger at him. "See what I mean? You always think the worst of me. You think I'm evil, don't you?"

"I'm asking you a question. Just like you asked me about Salem and her baby." Grady's head throbbed with a splitting headache, but he couldn't let her denials derail him. "Answer it without all the hysterics. Did you burn down my cabin?"

"No. I would never burn it down or hurt Cedar."

Despite his rage, relief swarmed over him. Of course, he didn't believe she would have done such a heinous thing as to hurt a dog.

"Right, I believe you," he finally admitted.

"Then why did you accuse me?" She threw up her hands and made an exasperated noise.

"Just clearing the decks. Anything else before I leave?"

"You're leaving?" Her voice stuttered, but she quickly regained control. "Nothing else. We're even. I effed with you and you effed with me. We're both psychopaths and we don't even deserve each other."

"Right, so this is goodbye." He gave her a mock salute.

"Pretty much." Linx pursed her lips so tight, her jaw wrinkled. "Thanks for leaving Cedar with me."

The dog, who had been slinking around during their altercation, perked up and wagged her tail, looking at Grady with an unsure expression.

"You're a good girl." He patted her, soothing the worry off her face. "The best."

He opened the door, and Linx didn't stop him.

His feet felt like they were mired in wet concrete, and his heart was crushed under a steamroller.

He was the lonely man, a rolling stone, stripped bare and clean—no moss and no entanglements.

Except he had a daughter, and he was going to fight for her with all he had.

Chapter Twenty-Three

Grady needed a drink. He wasn't the type to hang out at bars or drown his sorrow with Johnny Walker, but what happened today beat the crap out of him.

He was a damn dad. That was the biggee.

He'd never wanted to be a dad. Hated being tied down. Didn't need to make his mark on the world or have someone carry on his genes or legacy.

He had a huge family, willing and eager to do the breeding—fill the world with Harts.

But now that he was a dad. Hot damn! He rather liked the feeling.

Especially with a little girl.

The sweetest, cutest, little spitfire—Jessie. She'd insisted her dog would come back to her, and she wasn't taking no for an answer.

When she was reunited with Betsy, the happiness and relief glowing on that little face had Grady's heart humming in harmony.

He and Linx sure made a perfect child.

Except she belonged to someone else. She had adoptive parents, a family, and a home that didn't include him.

A boulder of pain crushed him as he strode through the swinging wooden slat doors of the Sixty Miners Saloon.

"Look what the dust storm blew in." Paul leaned on his elbows over the counter. "What are you having?"

"Whiskey on the rocks."

"That bad, huh?" Paul jiggled a ball of ice into a rocks glass and poured some no-name bourbon over it. "Heard you put out a fire at your place."

"Kind of hard not to when I was the first one on the scene." Grady knocked the amber liquid back, burning his throat as the heat spread down his gullet. "Makes me miss smokejumping."

"Like I said, don't let me hold you." Paul's eyebrows lowered into a dark scowl.

Grady glanced at the bleak surroundings around the mostly empty bar. "This place isn't hopping. Why are you hiding here?"

"You know why." Paul's eyebrows lowered. "This was the last place Salem called home. She rented a room right up there."

He pointed to the ceiling. Like a lot of old-fashioned buildings, living quarters sat above the business.

"So you bought all of it, and you feel at peace? Like her spirit's resting here?"

"Sort of."

"She's gone. You know that."

"Thanks to you." Paul's voice roughened. "You jumped and you made it. Why didn't she?"

"Freak change in the wind," Grady said. "The fire makes its own weather."

"Whatever you said to her got her confused." Paul slammed a fist on the counter. "Why won't you tell me?"

"It doesn't matter anymore," Grady said.

"Matters to me. You know, closure and all that. Were you sleeping with her? I mean, like you say, it doesn't matter now, does it?"

"I never touched her after she hooked up with you." Grady took a deep swallow of the whiskey, emptying it. He slapped the rocks glass on the counter. "Another one."

"She was pregnant." Paul whipped up another rocks glass and filled it. "Was it yours?"

"Unlikely."

"That's what she said you'd say." Paul's left eye twitched as he glared at him.

"She told you?"

"No, she didn't. She said you would deny it, just like you denied every other woman you knocked up."

"You should check her dates. When was the baby due? Or when did she say it was due?"

"She couldn't tell without an ultrasound," Paul said. "She died before she could get one."

"How do we know she was pregnant?"

"Why would she lie? Especially with all the guys who could have been the father." Paul scratched his few days' growth of beard.

"Drama? Stirring up trouble in the team?" Grady shrugged. "Salem struck me as being an attention hog."

"I was going to marry her no matter whose baby she had." Paul pursed his lips and drummed the counter with his fingers. "But my parents froze all my assets. They wanted to wait for a positive paternity test."

"Might have been wise to know. You know, for health reasons." Grady finished the whiskey. "I'm going up to Redstone tomorrow to check out those suspicious fires. Some psychopath is running around burning down firefighters' houses."

"Thought all the causes were natural," Paul said. "Dry lightning strikes, stuff like that. Media thinks there's a curse."

"Right, but whoever started the fire at my parents' cabin did it on purpose. Investigators found evidence of an accelerant, and since I was on it shortly after it started, it didn't burn everything down." Grady kept his eyes focused on Paul, detecting a slight flinch, before he pulled his face into an impassive mask.

"Your fire's unrelated, obviously." Paul grabbed a rocks glass and started polishing it. "I'm thinking it's the

Colsons. Kind of convenient for them when one brother's the sheriff, another one's the fire chief, their uncle's the mayor, and the judge is married to their aunt."

Grady made a noncommittal sound and put down a couple of bills to pay for his drinks. "Except the guys who lost their houses all slept with Salem. Strange coincidence, isn't it?"

"Go to hell," Paul grumbled and turned away from Grady.

* * *

Tami rushed over to the Mountain Dog Rescue Center with a tub of cherry moose track ice cream. She hugged Linx tightly. "Is he gone? Did you tell him?"

"Yes, he didn't take it well. I mean, at first, he was understanding, or maybe just shocked, but after he thought about it, he got angry."

"That's expected." Tami hustled to the kitchen and took out two bowls. "You want chocolate sauce?"

"Yes, with whipped cream and a cherry on top." Linx moaned, holding her throbbing head in both hands.

"That bad, huh?" Tami blew a tendril of her blond hair from her face and dug into the ice cream.

"He's pissed off that I didn't tell him. He's hurt. Crushed. All the things I wanted him to feel for hurting and crushing me."

"And?"

"I feel like crap." Linx cradled her bowl of ice cream and sank onto the sofa. "It's like I got my revenge and now it's hurting me more than him."

Tami sat down next to her. "He's not as bad as you made him out to be. He has a heart."

"I know, and I've hurt him again. I keep hurting him, and now that he knows Jessie's his daughter ..."

"Is he going to leave them alone?"

"I don't think so. He says he wants to fix it, then we got into a fight." Linx twirled the chocolate sauce into the ice cream and licked her spoon.

Ginger woke up and squealed from the playpen, obviously hungry—or maybe she heard Tami and wanted cuddles.

Linx set her ice cream down and picked the puppy up from the playpen.

"I'll warm up a bottle," Tami said, surprising Linx and getting up. "You should see the website. People are signing up in droves to adopt her. We ought to put up a webcam on her. They did that with the baby otter and tons of people watched."

"That's an idea," Linx said. "Maybe I should get security cameras, too. Then I'll catch my mom when she dumps off her latest creations."

Or snag an arsonist.

Linx snuggled with the puppy while Cedar rested her head on her knee. Now that Tami was here, everything would be okay.

Okay, for her. But what about Grady?

She had a family to support her. She had friends. This was her hometown, and most of all, she had contact with Jessie.

But Grady? He was locked out in the cold.

It wasn't fair.

And she'd done this to him.

Tami returned with the bottle. "Why don't I take care of this little sweetie and you go find Grady. I know you're not done with him."

"This time, we're done." Linx blinked as the tears pooled from her eyes. "I got the idea when he left that it was our final goodbye."

"What about Jessie?"

"What about her? She's the pastor's daughter. He's not going to get the adoption overturned."

"He's not going to leave this town either." Tami pursed her lips. "I've gotten to know Grady, and he doesn't seem like the type of man who would leave his flesh and blood. For all that rolling stone bluster, he's really close to his family. He has a twin sister."

"I know, but he feels disenchanted by the big family scene. Just like me." Linx held the bottle for the puppy who suckled greedily. "He told me he doesn't feel like he fits in. His twin sister's a fashion designer and the apple of his parents' eyes. His big brother's a fireman and a natural born leader. His baby sister's sweet as pie and his baby brother's the family clown. As for Cait, well, you know how organized and efficient she is. How does a dyslexic kid who was always getting into trouble compare?"

"Wow, you know that much about him? I thought he barely spoke." Tami picked up her bowl of ice cream.

"Only when he's drunk." Linx let out a chuckle. "That's when the filter flies from his lips."

Among other things.

"How many of these drunken bitch sessions have you had?" Tami gave her a side-eyed smirk. "Or were you two too busy making little Linxes?"

"Always with protection, well, with one or two slip-ups." Linx grinned sheepishly.

"What if he's had other slipups and all those women he knocked up were real?" Tami scratched the side of her head. "Maybe this rolling stone has left a trail of moss."

"Ewwee. That sounds gross when you put it like that." Linx couldn't help laughing.

"Think Salem's baby was his?" Tami recovered from the laughter first.

"Maybe, but it doesn't much matter now. It's kind of sad, isn't it?" Linx sobered up as the puppy finished the bottle.

"What's sad?"

"That of all the pregnancy scares, no one had his baby except for me."

"Heard you almost lost it, too." Tami had been at college when all of this went down.

"Thankfully, Salem found me on the floor with my water broken."

"She saved your baby's life."

"Yes, and I saved hers by carrying her out of the fire when she got impaled by that firebrand." Linx's shoulders slumped as the weight of Salem's death pressed on her. "After Jessie was born, she stopped calling and coming by. I never figured out why she broke away from me."

"Some friendships were meant to end." Tami gave Linx a hug. "I know it hurts when someone you thought was a friend fades away."

"We never had any words, no arguments or upset. And then, she died." A sob caught Linx's breath, and she put her face down on Ginger and let the tears roll. "She was a piece of work, but I still miss her."

Linx told Tami everything about the intercepted text messages, the fake phone number Salem had given her, claiming it was Grady's, and the fake messages she sent between them.

"Why, that bitch! Er, sorry, witch!" Tami clapped a hand over her mouth. "I'm thinking she wasn't exactly a good friend. Maybe she was only keeping an eye on you because you had Grady's baby."

"Why would she care either way?" Linx felt her heart contract and expand, pulsing and aching. "All she cared about was smokejumping and getting on the fire crew."

"So she could sleep with Grady, that's why," Tami exclaimed. "Once she had you two safely broken up, and the baby given away, and you out of firefighting, she went back and jumped what, three or four seasons?"

Linx could only nod mutely.

If Grady had known about Jessie, things would have been different, and he might not have slept with so many women. He might have become a responsible father.

And pigs might be able to fly.

But still, Grady Hart wasn't an ogre.

She'd seen him speaking to Jessie, reassuring her that he'd find her dog, and then later, when Grady did find Betsy, she'd noticed how attached Jessie got to him.

She should have made sure Grady knew, because then, the blissful picture in her dreams, the one where Jessie held both their hands as they strolled down a country lane, chasing butterflies and picking flowers, would have been real and true.

"I should have trusted Grady over Salem." Linx bowed her head.

"You know, it's not too late," Tami, the eternal optimist, said.

"I hope you're right, but somehow, I think you're wrong."

Chapter Twenty-Four

"Miss Jessie, don't you look pretty today," Tami exclaimed the next morning at the diner where she and Linx met up for breakfast.

Linx looked back over her shoulder. "Wow, Miss America, here she comes."

Jessie wore a little girl's version of a Wonder Woman costume: a red cape, blue skirt with white stars, a golden headband and belt, and a red top with a big 'W' patch.

She made puny muscles and smiled at her mother, Jean. "When I grow up, I'm going to be Wonder Woman just like Miss Linx."

"Jean, please, sit with us," Tami said, patting the bench seat of the booth.

"Oh, I don't want to interrupt whatever you two are discussing," the pastor's wife said. "Jessie is ever so grateful you found her dog."

"Actually, I didn't find her," Linx clarified. "Grady Hart found Betsy. Is she doing okay now?"

"She's fine. Lost a bit of weight, and we had to take her to grooming to remove all the stuck-on burrs and dirt."

"That's good to hear." Linx made room for them. "Please join us for breakfast."

"Can we? Please?" Jessie asked, bouncing up and down so that her cape fluttered. "Miss Linx said me and Betsy can march in the dog parade."

"Is that right?" The pastor's wife smiled and swept her flowing skirt to sit. "Will she be a bother?"

"Not at all. We'd love to have her and Betsy in the parade," Linx said. "Everyone who has a dog can march under our banner."

The Annual Fourth of July celebration started with a parade around the town square, before the festivities that included the pet rescue auction and a town fair.

"Can you march with me?" Jessie slid into the booth next to Linx and tugged her sleeve. "Can you also be a Wonder Woman?"

Linx hadn't even thought that far ahead, given all the Grady craziness. "Only if it's okay with your parents."

"She's in her superhero phase," Jean said. "But don't you Colson girls usually show your father's horses?"

"I'll let Joey and Vivi do the honors," Linx said. "We have a big push for adoptions going on at Mountain Dog. We're pretty overcrowded right now, and we're hoping Ginger will bring in a lot of donations."

"I want Ginger," Jessie said, tapping her mother's arm.

"No talking out of turn." Jean gave Jessie a stern look. "What do you say?"

"Sorry." Jessie clapped a hand over her mouth.

"As I was saying, you look lovely, Miss Jessie," Tami said, easing over any awkwardness. "I'll tell you what. If it's okay with Linx, you can help us with the auction on stage."

"Of course, it'll be okay," Linx said, peering at Mrs. Patterson. "As long as it's okay with your mother."

"What exactly will she do when she shows the dogs?" Jean asked. "I want to make sure it's safe for her."

"We wouldn't ask her to hold dogs or anything," Linx said. "Dogs tend to get too excited at these auctions, so we leave them in the kennel and show pictures of them. Only prequalified people can bid and we don't actually close any sale until they come to the center to take their dog home."

"In that case, it sounds harmless." Jean said, as Joey poured coffee for the grownups and placed a glass of milk in front of Jessie.

After everyone gave their usual orders, Jessie raised her hand. "Mama, remember you said I could get a puppy?"

"I did, sweetie, but only if we didn't find Betsy," Mrs. Patterson replied.

"Betsy's lonely. I bet she'll love to have a puppy to play with," Jessie said with the cute earnestness only little kids could muster.

"Betsy has you," Mrs. Patterson said firmly. "She'll never be lonely."

"Where do you think Betsy went when she ran away?" Tami was always good at conversation. "Do you think she lived in the forest?"

"She did! She lived deep in the woods in a fairy wagon." Jessie bounced in her seat. "Next time Betsy runs away, I'm going with her."

"Remember how worried and scared you were when Betsy ran off?" Linx asked Jessie, patting her back. "Your mommy and daddy will cry and cry and be worried and scared."

"I don't want Mama and Papa to cry." Jessie crossed her arms and looked at her mother.

"No, you don't." Linx stroked the girl's silky hair. "You and Betsy need to stay home so everyone can be happy."

"Okay." Jessie nodded. "But we'll be happier if we have a puppy or a baby brother or sister."

Linx glanced at Mrs. Patterson who pursed her lips and placed her napkin primly over her skirt.

Jessie didn't know that her adoptive mother was unable to have children, and she couldn't fault the little girl for being lonely.

"Tell you what," Linx said. "Next time you come to the center, you can teach Ginger to eat dog food."

"Can I?" Jessie raised her hand and beamed at her mother. "Please?"

"Sure, you may." Jean flashed her daughter an indulgent smile. "You can help Miss Linx as much as you want."

Even though Linx was glad for Mrs. Patterson's trust, her gut cringed at the thought of Grady taking it all away from her. But then again, if he actually won custody of Jessie, would he let her visit and spend time with Jessie?

"Mama, can I say grace?" Jessie raised her hand.

"Of course, darling."

Linx lowered her head and closed her eyes as little Jessie prayed.

"Father, bless our food and bless our home. Bless Miss Linx and all her puppies. Bless our town and bless everyone. Thank you for bringing Betsy back. Amen."

* * *

After breakfast, Linx dropped by the post office to mail off her bills. She hadn't heard head or tails from Grady, and he hadn't sent anyone to claim the dogs he had lined up for the veterans he was helping.

"There you are," a female voice called out to her after she dropped her letters in the mailbox. It was Cait, Grady's sister. "Last I heard, Grady had a date night with you. Have you seen him since? He hasn't returned any of my calls or text messages."

Linx put her hand over her forehead and shook her head. "I screwed up badly. He's hurt, and he's skipped town. I'm surprised he didn't say goodbye to you."

"What happened?" Cait clutched Linx's sleeve. "How did he get hurt? Is it physical or emotional?"

"It's emotional, and it's a long story." Linx blinked and averted her gaze. "I'm not sure I should be the one to tell you."

"If Grady's missing, how's he going to tell me?" Cait put on her elder sister tone. "I'm really worried about him."

"I'm sure he's okay," Linx reassured. "Probably working at his homesite. We can go up and check."

"Great. Let's go now." Cait threw her letters down the mail slot. "On the way, you better tell me what happened."

"I don't even know where to begin," Linx said, feeling a knot bury deep in her belly. "I really think Grady should be the one to tell you."

Cait screwed up her eyebrows and glared at Linx. "Okay, then tell me what's up with you. You don't look so happy. In fact, you look like your heart's broken. Did Grady do it? Did he hurt you? I told him not to fool around with you if he has no intention of ... Never mind."

"Grady and I hurt each other." Linx swallowed dry rocks in her throat. "We're the type of people no one should ever get involved with. The ones you keep away from anyone you care about."

"Why would you say that?" Cait's green eyes widened. "You're both strong and self-sufficient, but you have tender hearts inside. I mean, look how you care for the dogs, and Grady, well, he might be gruff, but he cares for his family."

"Right, except all we do is hurt each other. I feel like he's quicksand or something. I can't live with him, and I can't live without him. It hurts too much to be with him, but it hurts worse to let him go."

"Human quicksand, eh?" Cait quirked an eyebrow as she unlocked her car. "Are you sure it isn't love?"

"It's not love," Linx hastened to clarify. "Love shouldn't hurt like this."

"No, it shouldn't, but it does when you're not on the same page."

"We're never on the same page." Linx got into the passenger seat. "I'm sure he hates me right now. I really screwed up."

Cait started her engine and backed out of the parking spot. "Since you won't tell me what's wrong, you don't get to tease me with riddles. We're friends, aren't we?"

"Yes, we are." Linx glanced at the generous woman who always stopped by with treats and good cheer. "I suppose you'll get it out of Grady anyway."

"Darn tootin' right," Cait chirped. "You might as well spill. What did you do that was so bad to Grady other than keeping his dog?"

Linx swiped her face with both hands and blinked, her heart racing and pulse speeding. "I kept his daughter from him."

Errrrr! Cait slammed on the brakes and jerked to a stop. Linx braced herself for the rear-end slam, but fortunately there was no other car behind them.

"I knew it. That picture was a dead giveaway." Cait shrieked so high-pitched, it stung. "Why didn't you tell us? My family would have adopted her."

Great. Now she'd not only hurt Grady, but also Cait and the entire Hart family. The first grandchild for their parents was given away without them having had a chance to claim her.

There was nothing she could do for them than to admit the whole truth. They'd hate her and she'd lose Cait's friendship. But then, psychopaths like her didn't deserve the kind of love and acceptance normal people enjoyed.

"I gave her away for adoption." Linx's voice was as flat as steamrolled roadkill. "She's the pastor's daughter now."

"And you never told Grady?" Cait's voice was accusing. She pulled off the road and glared at her.

"I tried to tell him, but my messages were intercepted. When he finally called me, it was already a done deal, so I told him I was never pregnant." Linx stared out the side window. With a heaviness inside her chest, she relayed the entire story to Cait, about Salem, the missed messages, and all the years of hiding.

By the time they arrived at Grady's plot of land, everything was out in the open, and Cait now knew what an evil, black heart Linx had. It was exactly as her mother had predicted. No one who got close to her would survive unscathed. Even someone as big and bold and beautiful as Tami could one day fall victim to Linx and her horrible judgment. Maybe she should save everyone the trouble by running away and becoming a hermit.

"He's not here," Linx said, looking at the empty parking are. "His truck's not here."

"Maybe he's hiding in the trailer." Cait parked next to the fifth wheel.

Linx didn't think so, but fear prickled chilly icicles up her spine. He wouldn't be hiding in the trailer, but could he have hurt himself? Or worse?

Both women rushed out of the car and pounded on the trailer door, calling for Grady.

"He's not answering," Cait said with a worried look on her face.

"I hope he hasn't hurt himself." Linx's heart pounded like a bag of jagged rocks, and she jiggled the door handle. *Please, please, please, don't be too late.* She jimmied a credit card into the slot, popping the trailer door open.

"I'll reserve comment on where you acquired those skills," Cait said as they both peered into the darkness of the trailer's interior.

The trailer was empty, thankfully, and there was no note on the table. The closet was empty and his toothbrush was missing from the small bathroom.

"He's gone AWOL," Cait concluded. "He does that when he's upset. Disappears for months at a time. No calls, no mail. Nothing. I'll call my parents and let them know he's missing."

"I'm so sorry. It's all my fault." Linx hugged Cait. "I don't know what I'll do if anything bad happens to him."

She definitely couldn't live with herself.

If it wasn't for the fact that she needed to see Jessie grow up, she'd just as soon disappear, too.

"Maybe we'll never see Grady again." Cait burst into tears. "Imagine having a child and not being able to acknowledge her. The agony must be overwhelming."

While Cait carried on, Linx spotted Grady's cell phone on a bench inside the trailer and she slipped it into her pocket.

Grady didn't want to be contacted. Smartphones left a trail of clues—GPS locations, websites he'd visited, trips he took, even where he had parked his car. By dumping it, he was truly free from the electronic tether.

Linx closed her eyes and whispered to herself, "I'm going to find you, Grady Hart, no matter where you are."

Chapter Twenty-Five

Sweat chafed under Grady's collar as he picked his way through the fire-damaged area up near Redstone where Salem had been blown off-course.

The charred ground was still visible under clumps of baby trees and bushes sprouting between the burnt trunks of their parents. Twisted metal of fence posts and storage sheds littered the barren landscape. Blackened boulders jutted from a thin coat of wild grass. With the summer heat hitting high temperatures, the grass dried into straw, creating a fire hazard.

Grady checked his GPS and trail map. The drop area was right around the bend in the hill, a relatively flat area with a rocky exposure. It hadn't been a comfortable place to land, but it was visible from the air. Everyone on his jump squad, except for Salem, had made the landing successfully.

He hiked to the location, now covered with dry grass, and pointed his compass due west at the nest of black tree trunks, looking more like telephone poles than trees.

How could Salem have missed so badly?

Using his topographical map and compass, he marked the location where they'd searched for her. The entire team had fanned out, spiraled around the area, but found no trace of her: no bones, no metal clips or rings from her parachute or jumpsuit, no melted helmet, nothing.

No wonder Paul had a hard time accepting her death. Without a body, all they had was a memorial service, where he'd shown the mourners the diamond ring he had for her and declared her his posthumous fiancée. It had been an emotionally wrenching service. Salem's Kids, Paul's charity to help street kids, was born from the donations and contributions of those who'd been touched by her story of having once been a runaway.

Grady stopped in front of a metal cross Paul put up at the base of a boulder in Salem's memory. It was made from twisted and jagged scraps of metal, rusted nails, coils of wire around bits of dry bone.

Despite Linx dismissing the cross at the Hart cabin as being similar, Grady couldn't mistake the fact that they were both crosses. If this one was in Salem's memory, whose memory was that one for?

He turned away from the memorial, his stomach boiling over with acid. There was no beauty in the sculpture—only the ugliness of death.

"Thought I saw you up drive up." The sound of footsteps crunched behind him, and Melvin Montgomery, their chief, lifted a hand to shake.

"Busy season," Grady stated, knowing how many wildfires burned out of control at the moment. "Sorry about Salem."

"She died doing what she loved." Melvin said, crossing his arms. He looked across the landscape, not meeting Grady's eyes. "She was good at it. Real good. Sometimes, I think her spirit's still hanging around these parts."

"There are worse places to hang around."

"Yep." Melvin kicked the dirt. "How's Paul doing?"

"Bought himself a bar. Doing okay. How about you?"

"Been busy with never-ending wildfires," the chief said. "We have over a hundred fires burning out of control covering two million acres all across the continent. Worse fire season ever."

"Heard about your house. Sorry about that. What's going on out here?"

The chief shrugged. "Lots of vegetation waiting to be burned. We need you back on the fire line."

"I promised Paul I'd stay out this season. Salem was my jump partner." Grady hung his head.

"It's not your fault." Melvin clamped an arm over Grady's shoulders. "You fight fires as long as I have, and you're going to lose someone. It never gets easier, but it's the circle of life. She didn't have family to mourn her, so we're it."

"Yes, we're her family." Grady's throat tightened at the thought of how close that remark came. The thought that her baby could have been his was too depressing to stomach.

"Come back to the camp for a visit," Melvin said. "The boys and girls would love to see you. Catch up with you. Everyone misses you."

Like family.

Family never left anyone behind.

"Does it bother you that we never found her remains?" Grady scanned the ground, knowing that every inch had been thoroughly scoured, multiple times.

"We might have been mistaken on the direction she took," the chief said. "It might be over that ridge, or on the other side of the drop zone. We'll never know."

Grady looked at the map, wondering. He'd been the lead jumper, the guy responsible for scouting out the terrain and the direction of the moving fire. He had also jumped ahead of Salem, and was on his way to the drop zone.

"I have to find her." Grady's jaw tightened. "Maybe she did go a different direction, although it would have been tricky to maneuver around the wind."

"Salem's an expert at steering." Melvin rubbed his chin. "Which got me to thinking."

"Thinking what?"

Melvin leaned closer and lowered his voice. "Leslie thought she might have been suicidal."

Leslie was one of the mental health experts who traveled around the base camps.

"Why would she think that?" Grady wouldn't have pegged Salem as suicidal. That woman always looked like a fat cat with a canary in her mouth.

"You've heard the rumors." Melvin licked his lips, his eyes flickering over the landscape. "She'd been running around like crazy, trying to pinpoint the father of her baby. What she didn't know was that Paul was going to propose."

"She did know," Grady said. "I told her right before she jumped."

"Oh, well, then, that changes the whole situation," Melvin said, shaking his head slowly. "But knowing Salem, even if Paul stepped up, she would have still gotten her claws into whoever the baby's father turned out to be. I hate to speak ill of the dead, but Leslie thought Salem exhibited signs of being a psychopath. I should have taken her off the team when she started making threats."

"I've got to get going." A wave of sadness pressed down on Grady's chest, making it hard for him to catch his breath. "There's a reason for the no fraternizing rule, not that anyone paid any attention to it."

"Join us for dinner," Melvin said again, although not as emphatically as before.

"Thanks, but not tonight." Grady bade Melvin goodbye and headed in the opposite direction. Whether Salem was a psychopath or not, somebody out there was wreaking havoc with fire season. It could be Paul, most likely, or someone who had a crush on Salem, or maybe even one of the men she slept with who was jealous of the others.

Grady left Salem's strange monument behind and headed toward an area that had been upwind from their jump site.

The fire had consumed the entire ridge, but parts of the valley had been spared complete destruction because of a creek running through it. It had been hard work pumping water, but they had saved the few farms and ranches downstream.

What if Salem had landed there, instead of where they thought? It had been hard to see through the smoke. Hard to pinpoint any landmarks.

Taking long strides, he hiked down the ridge toward the valley, keeping his eyes open for a metallic glint that was out of place. Her bones, if any, would have been scattered by wildlife by now, and finding clasps or buckles now that the area was covered by grass would be almost impossible.

He might never know exactly what happened to her, and her lies had already cost him the two most important people in his life: Linx and Jessie.

Especially Linx.

That woman might have a hot temper, but she was good inside. In contrast, Salem was sweet and sugary on the outside but poison lurked in her heart.

There was no contest between Salem and Linx.

Linx had been betrayed, and her prickliness enabled Salem to pull the wool over both of their eyes.

Anyhow, Salem was dead, and he had to make it right with Linx—no matter how much it would hurt or cost him.

Hugging Linx was like hugging a cactus, but at the same time, he couldn't think of a pain more worth having.

She'd been forced into making a decision based on the information she had. She' also been a casualty of Salem's deviousness—betrayed by the very friend she thought had cared for her.

If he lost Linx now, it would give Salem the victory.

* * *

Having Grady's phone was like a persistent itch Linx wanted to scratch. She didn't want to snoop, but she couldn't help wondering about all the women he'd have in his contact list.

Unfortunately, she couldn't take a peek since his phone was locked.

About the only thing she could do was receive calls and glance at the first line of text messages, because the phone didn't require unlocking to pick up a call.

His family called and called and called. Cait, Jenna, Connor, Larry, Dale, Brian, Mom, Dad, Melisa, Rob, Nadine, as well as phone numbers without a contact name.

Linx didn't pick up any of the calls. After all, what could she say? That she'd stolen Grady's phone? Maybe this was what Salem had done. She'd gotten ahold of Grady's phone, unlocked it, and used it to intercept his messages. It wouldn't have been difficult, if Grady had ditched his phone before going overseas.

Since Tami was bossing the volunteers around, Linx had some free time, so she headed for the Sixty Miners Saloon.

Paul McCall was the link to both Grady and Salem. Maybe he would know where Grady had gone.

Midafternoon was too early to go to the bar, but she drove into town and parked in front of the old-fashioned saloon, complete with swinging wooden doors and weathered wood façade.

Most of the old-timers hung out at the diner, but every town had their barflies, and Linx quickly spotted the mayor, Chip Colson, and his buddies playing cards in the corner.

She zipped by them and climbed onto a barstool. She'd served on a few crews with Paul back when she was a hotshot firefighter, working on the ground, but he was in one season and out another, depending on whether he was rebelling against his parents or taking a job in one of their companies.

"Linx Colson." Paul wiped down the counter in front of her. "What can I get you?"

"Seltzer water and a twist of lime," she said. "And some information."

"Gonna cost you." He smirked as he grabbed a tall glass and filled it. "Let me guess, you want to know where Grady went."

"That'll be it."

"I told him to go to hell, and I reckon that's where he's heading."

"Back to the fire line?" Linx guessed. "Or that last fire up north."

"He went back to the burn scar near Redstone."

"Why would he do that?" Linx asked. "Reliving it, isn't he? I wonder if he dreams it, replaying it over and over in his mind."

"I wasn't there when it happened. I was in another crew," Paul said.

"I'm sorry." Linx took a sip of the seltzer water. "Very sorry."

"You were her friend back in the day."

"Yeah, we were friends. She used to live upstairs."

"I know. That's why I bought this place." Paul clasped his hands and pursed his lips.

Linx drank her water. Her knee jittered, and she felt awkward talking to Paul about Salem. Another customer approached the bar and Paul served him, then returned to stand in front of Linx.

"You done Grady wrong," he said in a low voice. "Real wrong."

"I know. That's why I have to find him."

"To say you're sorry?"

Linx squirmed under Paul's scrutiny. "A lot more than that."

She figured, he, being the town bartender, had already heard the gossip about both Cedar and Jessie.

"Then what do you want with him?" His tone was dead serious.

Linx stared over Paul's shoulder as if seeing a ghost. "I want him back. For better or worse. Whatever mistakes we made are in the past."

"That's one way of thinking about it," Paul said. "Except the past haunts the present. There's no way Grady can take back what he said to Salem right before she jumped to her death."

"How do you know it caused her death? Maybe he wished her good luck."

"He's still responsible." Paul punched a fist into his palm. "It's not right that he's walking around assuaging his guilt while my Salem is gone."

"I'm so sorry," Linx said again. "I know you set up Salem's Kids under her name. You have a good heart."

"Yeah, but what good does it do when the likes of Grady Hart get all the women. I hate to admit it to you, but I think Salem was carrying his baby and he offed her so he wouldn't have to take responsibility."

Paul's words slapped Linx like a splash of cold water. "That is so far-fetched as to be ridiculous. You want to know what Grady said?"

Anger surged inside her belly like the roaring of a red dragon. She didn't know why Grady put up with taking the blame, but the truth was, Grady didn't say anything to jeopardize Salem. Instead, he gave her a reason to live. He told her about the pending engagement.

"Whatever he told you is a lie." Paul all but growled.

"No, I believe him. Maybe it wasn't his business to tell her, but he told her you'd gotten a ring, and that she'd better figure out whose baby she was carrying because he didn't want you to get hurt."

Paul narrowed his eyes and snorted. "How was she going to do that? The baby wasn't even born."

"News flash. They can do prenatal paternity tests by drawing the mother's blood and isolating fetal DNA, then comparing it to a cheek swab of the prospective fathers. No need to touch the baby. It's not cheap, but hey, you're loaded and I bet you'd want to know."

"Damn." Paul slapped the bar counter. "Why didn't I know about this?"

A cloud of gloom draped over Linx's shoulder, pressing her spirits down. "I guess it no longer matters, now that she's gone."

"It matters to me. Grady wasn't the only likely father."

"I'm sorry." Linx put her hand on his. "Really sorry."

"Not your fault," he said, flinching. "Salem really admired you. Said you were her friend—the only one she had. I think she might have been a little jealous of you, though."

"Why? She's the smokejumper and I'm the dropout."

"Yeah, but she once admitted to me that Grady called her by your name when ... you know ..." Paul cleared his throat. "Guess I'm jealous of Grady."

"Don't be. Seriously." Linx blinked back her shock at what Paul had just spewed. How had she missed the obsession Salem had had with Grady?

Could it have pushed her off the deep end? Or had she always been a psychopath who only cared about herself?

"Yeah, you're right," Paul conceded. "What does it matter now? Dead is dead."

Chapter Twenty-Six

After leaving the chief and the site of Salem's memorial, Grady hiked down the ridge and circumvented the burn area. The charred remains of someone's home lay covered with dust and ashes—a relatively fresh burn site. Blackened garbage cans and the hulk of a wood burning stove stood testament to another destroyed life. Grady poked around the ruins and gaped at the twisted bars of a large bird cage. The ashes had blown away, but small bone chips and the remnants of the metal food and water bowls showed the demise of someone's beloved pet.

Bits and pieces of crime scene tape were scattered around the foundation, leading him to believe this had been arson.

A footstep startled Grady.

"Place has been picked clean." A man with a scraggly beard and dusty clothes leaned against what was left of the chimney.

"I'm not looking for anything," Grady said. "Any ideas of what happened here?"

"Some crazy person's burning down the houses of the firefighters," the man said.

"You mean the guys at the smokejump camp?"

"Yep. This was Jake Collins' place. Burned down three weeks ago."

"I know Jake," Grady said. "I was one of the smokejumpers. Who else lost a home?"

The man scratched the back of his neck. "You know the chief? His place burned down a month ago, and six weeks ago, it was Duane Washington's cabin. Before that, Tim Olson's trailer burned to the ground."

"The police catch anyone?"

"Nope," the man said. "I've a ranch on the other side of the creek, and we're setting up patrols to protect our property. Anyway, the fires seemed to have stopped. Fingers crossed."

"Do you have any ideas who's behind all this?"

The man shrugged. "Could be insurance fraud. Maybe money's tight and these guys want to cash out."

"Not the chief," Grady said. "He's owned his home since way back."

"Maybe it's bad luck, but I'm telling you strange things have been going on this summer."

"Like what?" The hair on the back of Grady's neck bristled.

"Stuff missing, pets getting lost." The rancher cracked his knuckles. "Someone cut the barbed wire at O'Hara's place and let his bull out. Another neighbor had his car burned in the middle of his driveway. Like I said, we're setting up a patrol around our property."

"Good idea," Grady said. "Summer brings out the gremlins and smoke demons."

"Tourists and vagrants." The man scratched his beard. "Anyway, whatever you're looking for, it isn't here. Investigators combed through everything looking for clues."

"Have they found anything that didn't belong?"

"No, but like I said, the place is picked clean. Someone's removing pieces of scrap metal and selling them to a bunch of rich hippies going to that Burning Man Festival out in the desert."

"They catch anyone?" Grady asked.

The man only shook his head. "Frankly, there are too many fires this year all over the west for anyone to keep track and pay attention to. That's why we're setting up our own patrols."

"Good thinking." Grady figured he'd hit a dead end. It was time to put Salem Pryde and her brand of chaos in the grave and head back to the two people who really mattered—Linx and Jessie.

If Salem's remains were out there somewhere, may she rest in peace.

* * *

A day went by, and another, but no one heard from Grady. His family had been by, and Linx had shown them Grady's homesite. They'd scoured it for clues and found nothing. Linx should have given them Grady's phone—that would have been the right thing to do, but somehow, she couldn't part from it.

Instead, she would pull it out like an addicting video game and stare at the text messages popping through the lock screen. She couldn't concentrate on her work, and papers piled up at her desk.

She hadn't told Tami or anyone about having Grady's phone. It was a secret pleasure for her, one that became a guilty obsession.

Grady's family texted numerous times a day, as well as a woman named Vanessa Ransom. From the frequency of her texts, she had to be someone who cared about him—maybe his real girlfriend.

Linx slapped her forehead and forced herself to put the phone down and go through her paperwork. She had no right to worry about him with other women. She and Grady weren't even friends, much less in any form of a relationship, and other than this one-sided connection or obsession she felt for him, there was nothing substantial to hold onto—other than Jessie.

She had a lot to do for the Gold Rush Festival, and she needed prepare the center for the horde of adoptions she hoped would follow the "picture pet" auction, but she couldn't focus on it. Not when she was so concerned about Grady.

She updated the website with the biographies and personalities of the dogs and entered completed adoption applications into the database. Her eyes itched to go back to Grady's phone, but she resisted.

Three more applications to process. They were veterans and one mentioned that he'd heard about an elderly bulldog needing love.

Linx linked the application to Bob the Bulldog's entry, and was about to update the stats showing someone was interested in the dog, when Grady's phone rang.

A picture of an attractive black woman, Vanessa Ransom, popped onto the screen. She had long silky hair, just the way Grady appreciated in a woman. She also looked happy and perky, with a big wide smile and eyes sparkling with good humor—the product of a happy life, most likely with a loving and caring mother.

Before Linx knew what she was doing, she swiped to answer. "Hello? Grady Hart's phone."

"Who's this?" The woman sounded surprised.

There was an unmistakable quaver in her voice that showed she might be more than a little bit interested in Grady and she wondered what another woman was doing answering his phone.

"I'm Linx Colson. Grady's not available right now."

She was evil, making it sound as if Grady were in the shower after a hot round of morning wake-up sex. But why not? The woman had been texting nonstop.

"Oh ..." Vanessa sounded disappointed. "Linx Colson."

"What can I do for you?" Linx turned the screw another notch. "Shall I tell him you called?"

"He hasn't returned any of my text messages, and now it might be too late," Vanessa said. "Maybe you can help me."

"Me? How?"

This was unexpected. Linx thought Vanessa would hang up now that she had confirmation Grady was seeing another woman.

"Grady got Sam from your rescue center, am I correct?" Vanessa asked.

"Uh, yes, has something happened to Sam?" Linx's attention shifted from one-upping this attractive woman friend of Grady's to concern about the dog.

"He bit a friend of the veteran Grady placed him with, and I need to return him. The friend agreed not to press charges. Grady was supposed to come fetch him. As I recall, your rescue organization will take back any animal who doesn't fit in after a trial period."

"Of course, we'll take him back." Linx blinked and pushed herself up from her desk, startling Cedar who wandered to the kitchen where Ginger was napping. "I'll pick him up from your place."

She might as well check out the competition. This Vanessa chick sounded reasonable and levelheaded. She hadn't even gone hysterical and demanded to know why Linx picked up Grady's phone.

"Actually, I'm on my way over," Vanessa said. "I have a few clients I'm visiting out your way, so I figure I might as well drop Sam off. Also, I'd like to pick up a few more dogs. Tami approved my application."

"Sure, I'm at the center. Which dogs?" Linx was thankful Tami had kept things going while she was having her multiple crises.

"It's in the email I sent you this morning," Vanessa said. "Can you tell Grady I'm on my way? I'm a little worried about him. I'm about twenty minutes from Colson's Corner."

"Sure, yes, of course," Linx said, not wanting to admit that she also hadn't heard from him. "One more thing. Call me on my direct line. It'll be easier that way."

They exchanged numbers and hung up.

Her heart pounding and hands sweaty, Linx went to the kitchen for a glass of water. Little Ginger lifted her head from the blanket she was on and pushed up on her hind legs, wagging the tip of her tail.

"Oh, you sweet little thing," Linx crooned. "You're trying to walk."

The puppy made a cute little squeal as she crawled unsteadily with Cedar encouraging her by nudging her onto her wobbly feet.

Linx quickly switched her camera phone to video mode to capture Ginger's first tentative little steps as the puppy pulled herself with her stronger front legs and tottered with collapsing hind legs across the room.

A warm gooey feeling spread through Linx's chest, and her heart swelled with pride. Her two dogs were going to be best sisters. She encouraged Cedar and praised her, then rubbed her fur with extra attention.

After recording the scenes, she published it to the website, then texted the video to Grady, even though he wouldn't receive it.

She added a message. *I can't thank you enough for letting me keep Cedar. I hope you'll forgive me for everything I did. You have a wonderful heart. Don't ever let anyone tell you you don't. I miss you, and I wish you would come back.*

The resulting chime on Grady's phone made her feel stupid, but somehow special at the same time. Someday, he'd retrieve his phone and see the video of Cedar and Ginger, and hopefully, it would let him know that she appreciated his sacrifice.

If only there was something she could do for him. Something more than sleeping with him—although that seemed to be all he wanted with her.

To her, sex was more than purely physical, maybe. She couldn't read Grady, and while he enjoyed sex with her, he could be enjoying it with others too, like this Vanessa Ransom woman who was a much better catch than her—a stable, sensible-sounding woman.

"I better get ready to meet Grady's girlfriend," Linx said to the dogs as she turned on her computer. A few clicks later, she was even more intimidated. Dr. Vanessa Ransom was a psychotherapist dealing with post traumatic stress disorder, abuse, and addiction recovery. And she was a certified dog trainer for therapy and service dogs.

She sounded like she'd be good for Grady. She could help him deal with his traumas and talk him down from the guilt he suffered from Salem's death.

In other words, Grady's perfect woman.

Linx had no standing to be jealous, especially if another woman was better for him. She should be happy for him and wish them well. Grady needed someone with a level head on her shoulders.

With a heavy heart, Linx straightened her desk and swept the wooden floor of the cabin as she waited for Vanessa.

The doorbell rang and for a moment, Linx wondered if it was Grady. When Cedar lowered her ears and gave a warning bark, she knew it was a stranger.

Standing at the door was Dr. Vanessa Ransom and Sam, the German shepherd pitbull mix.

"Come in, it's good to meet you." Linx forced a smile as Cedar lunged forward and sniffed Sam.

The two dogs greeted each other with wagging tails, and Vanessa stepped in with a worried look on her face. She glanced briefly around the small cabin. "It's good to meet you, too. Grady says you do a great job with socializing the dogs under your care."

"We get a lot of abused animals and those who've been foraging for themselves. We nurse them back to health and try to give them hope, although it's hard when there are so many," Linx said.

"What you're doing is a good thing." Vanessa touched her arm. "Grady and I hope to do the same for the veterans. So many are hurt and scarred from their experiences. A dog who's been through grief and abandonment connects better with some of our veterans—gives them something to relate to each other."

Linx moved away from the therapist's touch. "That's why Grady and I go over each dog's past, as much as we can glean, and assess their personalities, any challenges they may have, and special needs."

"Anyway, it's not like Grady to leave things hanging."

"Right. I'm surprised," Linx said, bending down to pick up Ginger. "Please, sit down. Would you like to see some of the dogs Grady picked out for your clients?"

"Sure. Did you get our email about the husband and wife who want two retrievers?"

"Yes, we got their applications, but things are kind of hectic here." Linx swiped a loose strand of hair from her forehead.

Vanessa's smile was stiff. "What a cute puppy. I'm following her updates on your website. Is she starting to walk?"

"Barely, but yes, I just posted a video a few minutes ago."

"May I hold her?" Vanessa held out her hands.

"Sure," Linx said, even though it felt like letting another woman hold her baby—well, duh, she'd already done that, hadn't she?

Linx's mind flashed back to the day Jessie was born. She'd had to have a C-section because her water had broken and she wasn't making progress. As soon as the doctor pulled Jessie, all bloody and wet, from the slit in her abdomen, they'd wrapped her in a blanket and handed her to Mrs. Patterson.

Empty hadn't even begun to describe the hollowness in her heart.

"What a little sweetie you are," Vanessa said to Ginger. "You're putting Mountain Dog Rescue on the map."

"She's three weeks old," Linx added. "And Cedar's been playing mommy or at least big sister."

"Going to let her try solid food soon?"

"Yes, she's a real trooper." Linx's chest puffed with pride. "And to think someone abandoned her on a rainy day."

"I saw the pictures." Vanessa shuddered. "You've come a long way, baby."

Linx warmed up a bottle of formula for Ginger and gave it to Vanessa. "Want to feed her? I'll get you a towel."

"Oh, thanks." Vanessa's face spread with a genuine smile. "She's so adorable, I wish I could take her home. But I already have two dogs, and I live in an apartment in the city."

"I sometimes fantasize about keeping her, too," Linx admitted.

"But you have this wonderful dog." Vanessa sat down on the sofa next to Cedar who made room for her. "Grady says she used to be his dog."

Wow. Grady shared a lot with this woman.

Sheesh! More than he shared with his sister, Cait.

"I found her after a forest fire," Linx said. "She needed looking after."

Vanessa only nodded, her gaze fixed on the puppy as she fed her the puppy formula.

Linx sat on the other side of Cedar and ruffled her fur, and Sam plodded to her side, begging for attention. She scratched his ears and let him rest his head on her knee. "You're a good dog, but you can't be biting people."

"He was provoked," Vanessa said. "The man admitted he was jealous of Sam. It's not a good situation."

"Did Sam belong to his wife?"

"No, the woman wasn't even his girlfriend, and I gather Sam felt protective of her. She was making progress too, but this guy, who's also a veteran, wanted to be her protection. At the end, she chose the guy over Sam."

"Oh well, buddy boy." Linx ran her hand down Sam's back. "I know a man who's quiet and strong just like you."

"So do I," Vanessa said. "When you hear from him, will you let me know?"

So, they were on the exact same wavelength.

"Sure, I will." Linx wasn't going to admit to Vanessa that she also wondered when she'd hear from him.

Vanessa finished feeding Ginger and set her down on the floor. The puppy stumbled along like a drunk. She was so cute.

Both Vanessa and Linx took videos of the little drunk's weaving movements, her belly so full it was distended almost to the floor, and her tail upright and wagging.

They oohed and aahed over the sweet thing, and laughed at her attempts at howling. Cedar nudged and licked her while Sam basically ignored her. He jumped out of her way and quirked one eyebrow at Cedar as if to say, "keep your baby away from me."

"Such a typical male," Linx said, cracking up at Sam.

"Yep, that dog is Grady through and through," Vanessa said. "Can I take a look around at the other dogs on Grady's list?"

"Sure, let me put Ginger back in her playpen."

After securing Ginger, Linx and Vanessa went out the back door, followed by Sam and Cedar.

The dogs in the kennel let out volleys of excited barks. There were also a few who'd lost all spark of hope that they'd be adopted, so they stayed quiet.

Linx led the way out back to the kennels. "We have an elderly bulldog, two retrievers, a chow chow who's the sweetest young lady, a basset hound mother, and well, take your pick."

"Shhh …" Vanessa held her finger to her lips. "I'd like to observe the dogs first and let them get used to me."

Linx took a step back, no longer in realtor-mode, as she watched the therapist and dog trainer size up the animals. She went quietly from pen to pen.

After she made a round, she lingered at the pen holding the female chow chow, a black-haired dog with a mane like a lion's. The dog's tongue lolled in the heat and she peered at them through her furry, wrinkled face.

"How old is she?"

"A little more than two years old," Linx replied. "She'll make a wonderful guard dog and companion. Her name's Aurora and she was surrendered by a woman who was going into a nursing home—an Army nurse from the Vietnam War. Couldn't take her dog and had no relatives to help out."

"Oh, poor thing, so her former owner is a soldier?"

"Yes, that's right."

"Let me spend some time with her and see if she's suitable for my client who suffers from PTSD and night frights," Vanessa said. She turned to Linx and added, "I do believe a dog would be good for Grady, even though he's too macho to admit it."

"Are you saying I should give Cedar back?" Linx felt her heart race as her throat tightened.

"You know what you need to do." Vanessa gave her a close-mouthed smile. "Don't give up on him, okay?"

"I'm not, I mean, no, I won't give up." Linx swallowed as her heart expanded and contracted thickly in her chest. "I want to make him happy. Truly happy."

And loved. To the best of her ability.

Chapter Twenty-Seven

Linx closed up the Rescue Center after Vanessa departed with the two retrievers and Aurora, the black chow. Poor Bob had been passed over again. Vanessa wanted to take him, but because he was so elderly, she felt it would be another source of grief when he passed on.

Linx gave the bulldog a hearty neck scratch and patted him. "Someone will fall in love with you. You're such a good dog."

The rest of the dogs had been fed, and they were quieting down as the shadows lengthened into the cool, summer evening.

She opened Sam's pen. "Come on, boy. We're going to take a trip."

After checking that Cedar was comfortable inside the cabin, Linx snapped a leash onto Sam's collar and put him in the passenger compartment of her Durango.

Grady's family had been all over the town looking for him, but after talking to Paul, they decided he might have headed back to Redstone to join a fire crew.

Off they flew, probably on a wild goose chase, every single one of them, including his two pregnant sisters. Grady used to tell Linx how his family smothered him, and that the reason he went incognito was so he could come and go as he pleased, without worrying the people he loved.

He'd spent years training them to stop obsessing about him or bothering him. He claimed he didn't need anyone to care.

But Linx knew Grady better than anyone.

He was like her—embracing loneliness instead of admitting his need for companionship.

That was why he turned to dogs—until he lost Sasha and turned bitter toward any sort of attachment.

Once, long ago, there was a Grady who watched the eagles soar on a mountain peak, who climbed tall trees and sat up in the branches, looking at the clouds above. A Grady who splashed with her in a hidden swimming hole. Who explored caves and lay on a grassy meadow tracing stars.

He never spoke much, but surrounded by sweet nature, he was happy and content, and she had shared it with him, in those rare moments they'd been able to get away from the fire training camp.

Linx turned the truck up the unmarked road, putting it in four-wheel-drive. The landscape was surprisingly lush with charred stumps surrounded by the pale green shoots of new trees. Vines wrapped fingers around the spidery outlines of the dead, but the giant sequoias stood tall and alive, survivors of centuries of wildfires.

Sam hung his head out the window, sniffing and observing the hillside. He was a quiet dog, pensive, and he didn't require much attention or affection.

She had no idea if Grady was back, but it didn't matter. She'd take Sam up there and let him get acclimatized, and she could also use a walk to clear her head. Besides, she was curious to see the progress he made for the new cabin.

Smoke from a campfire drifted up in the wind—oily with charcoal and charred meat. Her heart quickened at the thought that he could be back. She hung the final turn and spotted his truck.

Sam let out a grunt as his nose worked overtime and his body shuddered with excitement.

"Looks like we're in time for dinner." Linx cut the engine and opened the door. "One guess as to who's at the camp stove."

So she was stalking him, invading his privacy, and he would be within his rights to throw her off his property. But she'd brought a gift, a peace offering, and hopefully, he would be open to her presence, despite the hurtful words they had said in parting.

She closed the door as silently as she could and walked light-footed with Sam up to the clearing.

Grady looked up from the ruins of his old cabin. He'd made a fire inside the stack of bricks over what had been the fireplace.

Linx rolled up Sam's leash tighter to keep the dog at her side and stood on the flagstones where the door used to be.

Grady took the steak off the grill and wiped his hands on his jeans jacket.

Linx waited.

Maybe he'd pretend she wasn't present and go on with his dinner. If he was surprised, he sure didn't show it.

Taking a knife, he cut the steak in half. The blood glistened from the piece of meat and beside her, Sam licked his chops.

Okay, so he'd acknowledged the dog, but not her.

Turning back to the remnants of the stove, he put on fire mitts and removed a covered cast iron Dutch oven from the fire. The smell of pork and baked beans wafted over the ruins of the cabin as he lifted the lid and stirred the contents.

Linx watched him, but she made no move. She wasn't going to enter his cabin uninvited. Maybe she should let go of the leash and let Sam go to Grady.

Then she'd leave man and dog alone.

Standing there watching him ignore her cut her like a knife. Her heart still bled, and every bone in her body ached to go to him. She needed to know she still meant something to him—needed to feel his arms around her, needed his lips on hers.

Needed what he couldn't give her.

Bending down, she unclipped Sam from the leash and rubbed his neck. "Goodbye, boy. Be good to him."

Sam needed no other encouragement. He padded across the dirt and pebbles toward Grady.

Linx turned around and walked away.

It was over. The hurt of losing Jessie was too much for him. She understood.

If the roles had been reversed, she'd fight like a mama bear to get her cub back. And she'd hate him forever for giving her away.

She opened the door of the SUV and whirled around when Grady put his hand over hers.

"You're not staying for dinner?" he asked, his voice gruff.

His eyes were rimmed with red, and he looked like he hadn't slept for days.

"Where did you go? You had all of us worried."

He shrugged and looked back at the camp stove. "Let's eat. How'd you end up with Sam?"

"Vanessa dropped him off. She's worried about you, too."

"Look, I'm not a man any woman should be worried about." Grady put a hand on the small of Linx's back and guided her back to the ruins of the cabin. "Tell Nessa, I'm sorry I left her clients in a lurch."

And he even had a nickname for her, although she did seem more like a Nessa than a Vanessa.

"She seems like a nice woman," Linx said, swallowing a spike of jealousy. "Very kind-hearted and understanding."

"She is." Grady bent down and rubbed the dog's neck. "I totally blanked out about going to fetch him. He's not a bad dog."

"No, not at all." Linx watched as Grady set out two plates on a pile of wood and divided the steak between them. He served the baked beans and put a fork and knife beside each plate.

"Want to eat out here or in the trailer?" he asked. "Trailer's a little cramped but we can sit."

"Let's stay out here," she replied. "I love the way it cools down in the evening."

He cut a piece of steak and threw it at Sam. "How'd you know I was back?"

"I didn't. I just came up here to check. Your family came up here to look for you, too."

"They don't know about Jessie," Grady said, then gestured to her steak. "Go ahead. Dig in."

"You haven't told Cait." It was more a statement than a question, since Linx had already spilled the beans to Cait. By now, the entire Hart clan would be up in arms, speculating about the little girl. They could even be stalking her at church where her father pastored.

"Why hurt everyone?" Grady shrugged as he chewed on a piece of steak. "It's not like I have custody of her."

"Sorry." Linx sawed at her half of the steak. "I thought you were leaving and not coming back. I'm glad you're back."

"My daughter's here. And you."

Her heartbeat accelerated at his acknowledgment of Jessie and her. Could it mean he was softening toward her? After the unspeakable thing she'd done?

"Where did you go these past few days?" Linx hazarded a glance at Grady's solemn face.

His lips turned down. "I went to Redstone to look for Salem's body. I can't get over the feeling she deliberately turned her chute into the fire."

"She committed suicide?" Linx gasped and coughed.

"No. I took a closer look at the terrain, visualized the way it looked with the smoke and burning trees, and the drop area where we landed. Thing is, I might have gotten the directions reversed. The plane turned around several times during the jump."

"Are you saying she's alive?"

"They never found her body."

"The area was burned to the ground, wasn't it?"

"The place I thought she landed," Grady said. He pursed his lips and shook his head. "Met Chief Montgomery on the trail."

"How's he doing? Fire season must be busy," Linx said.

"It's a crazy season. They've had a rash of suspicious fires. Chief Montgomery's house, Jake, Duane, Tim's trailer all went up in flames three to six weeks back."

"That's a heck of a coincidence."

Grady tugged his collar and nodded. "Especially since they all slept with Salem."

"Wow." Linx dropped her fork and reached for Grady across the woodpile. "That explains your parents' cabin being set on fire. Is Paul in danger?"

"Paul bought the saloon about three weeks back. The fires stopped up there and started here, or at least one fire did. Coincidence?"

"You mean he might have set the fires?"

Grady shrugged and chewed on his steak. "What would be his motive?"

"Revenge, especially if he blames you guys for Salem's death." A chill wiggled its way down Linx's spine, and she glanced at Grady's trailer. "Is it safe for you to spend the night here?"

"Now that you brought me a dog, yes. Plus, I'm packing a pistol."

"No, you're staying with me." Linx rubbed his arm. "You can still come up here and work on the cabin, but I don't want you attacked."

Grady rolled his eyes and twisted a corner of his mouth, looking halfway amused. "A man stands his ground. He doesn't run and hide, especially behind a woman."

"We have to report this to the police," Linx argued. "I'll ask Todd."

"To do what? Run a patrol every so often? Heck, your brother would rather I leave town."

"Not if he knew that Salem intercepted all of our messages. My family thinks you dumped me and denied the baby." Linx moved her hand down Grady's arm and held his hand. "Come to dinner with my family tomorrow night and I'll explain."

"It won't change what you did." He gave her hand a squeeze.

"I know, but it'll change the way they think about you. It's important to me."

Since they were both standing in front of the woodpile, he leaned toward her. "Why do you care?"

Linx felt the earth tilt on its axis, and her heart beat on overdrive. Why did she care? Was this crazy off-balanced feeling something more than sexual desire?

After all, if she only wanted to get laid, why would it matter if her family hated him?

"You're Jessie's father. I don't want them to think he's a jerk."

"You didn't mind that before." His voice deepened and he closed in, his expression softening.

"I do now. I feel everything differently, knowing Salem cut the lines of communication."

"We can't blame her for everything. She was only the catalyst. I still should have followed up."

"Is that why you went to Redstone? To see if Salem somehow survived and had her baby?"

He nodded solemnly. "I didn't find her."

"If Salem's still alive, do you think she had her baby?"

Grady nodded slowly. "She would have had it end of May, if she's still alive."

"Wouldn't she have contacted Paul? Or asked for paternity tests?"

"Could have decided it wasn't Paul's and put it up for adoption."

"I'm sorry." Linx stroked Grady's arm to comfort him. "You can't let all these what ifs paralyze you. All we know is there's no body, and someone's setting fire to the houses of the guys she slept with."

"I wish I'd never touched what she offered." Grady's voice was laced with regret. "That's not how I feel about you."

"Oh ..."

What could she say? She hated even being compared to any other woman.

He drew her into his arms and held her so close she could hear and feel that big heart of his beating. What was he trying to tell her?

"I'm having a hard time deciding what to do about Jessie." He finally broke the silence. "I want to be her father. It's my right, because I never gave consent."

Linx squeezed her eyes shut as she shuddered with emotion. She, also, had fantasized about taking Jessie home with her, raising her alone and somehow, miraculously becoming a better mother than her own.

"I should have never given her away." The words choked out. "I could have made it as a single mom. Many women do it."

Grady's body tensed and he pushed back. "You were young and confused. It was a good decision at the time. You didn't know I'd be back."

"Are you saying I would have been a horrible mother?" Linx whipped her glare at him, not understanding why she felt so defensive.

"No. Not at all." His dark-brown eyes pierced through her. "I've seen you with Ginger. You had no support system, and if Salem were your only friend at the time, I'm sure she told you to give it away."

"I wanted to keep her, but with my grandmother passing away a month before Jessie was born, no one knew what to do. My father least of all. He'd done the single parent route and it was rough, even with my grandmother around. I wish I hadn't been so weak." She bit her knuckles as a surge of tears wet her eyes. "I wish I'd stuck to my guns and been braver."

"I'm going to consult a lawyer and see what we can do." He gripped her tightly. "If you're okay with it."

"I ... I want her back, all the time, but what about her? She doesn't know we're her parents."

"Right, but living a lie is never a good solution." Grady fixed her with a solemn stare. "I want to be her father, whether you want to be her mother or not. I never gave up my rights."

"My sister's a lawyer," Linx said. "We can get a free consult from her."

"Sure, guess I will be meeting your family then." He kissed the top of her head and tucked a tendril of hair behind her ear. "We both have a lifetime of regrets, but while I was looking over the burn scar, I realized something."

"What?"

"Wildflowers, shrubs, grasses springing up around the dead trees. New hope."

Linx peeked at Grady's face, wondering if this was the same surly grouch she'd known these last few months. He seemed strangely at peace.

"Knowing Jessie's mine." He swallowed as he cupped her cheek. "Knowing she's got a home here means I have a home here, too. I want to watch her grow up. I want to teach her how to fly a kite, hit a softball, ride a horse, and be here for her."

"I want the same."

If only he'd said these beautiful words seven years ago. Linx leaned up to Grady, her insides melting, and he met her halfway with the most tender, sweetest kiss she'd ever tasted from him.

Her emotions bloomed. She let her lips tangle with his, inhaling his masculine breath, the heat of his body, and gently caressing the two-day growth of beard on his strong jaw.

This was the Grady she'd wished for, the strong, silent type with the big heart. Maybe it'd taken the shock of having a daughter to bring him out of his shell, but whatever it was, her heart ached while a delectable movie played in her mind.

Jessie, Grady, and her, the three of them holding hands as they hiked to the top of the mountain, watching eagles soar and letting the breeze of hope wash over their upturned faces.

Chapter Twenty-Eight

Grady tilted Linx's head to the side, deepening the kiss. His emotions soared and plunged whenever he was in her orbit, and his body ignited on contact—plain and simple.

This wild and wonderful woman was the mother of his child—his flesh and blood. Even though he was the black sheep of his family, the one who acted as if family ties didn't matter, he was still a Hart, through and through, and despite it all, they loved him and he loved them.

Which was why he needed to call them and let them know he was back. He'd lost his cell phone, and he had a gloriously hot woman in his arms—one who'd said she didn't want to sleep with him anymore, but was now kissing him with everything she had.

Catching his breath, he broke the kiss—barely, and whispered, "You okay with this?"

He felt, rather than saw, her nod. Her breathing was hot and heavy as she captured his lips, tugging ruthlessly on his lower lip, then plunging her tongue deep into his mouth.

He'd checked for consent, and she hadn't put a stop to it, so it was all systems go.

Once, he'd almost fallen in love with this spitfire, and his immaturity and Salem's treachery had screwed everything up—turned him into a bitter, resentful male, distrustful and detached.

That was then, and this was now.

Being a father was serious business, and getting this woman to be truly his wasn't going to be easy.

Heck, nothing about Linx Colson was easy.

Which was just the way he liked her.

"Trailer or truck?" he muttered in between devouring her lips.

"Trailer." She moaned urgently as she ran her hands down his chest. "Is this going to be different? Are we?"

"Yes." He gazed into her warm brown eyes, darkened with emotion. "It's completely different. I want this. Want you. Only you."

"Grady ..." She spoke his name like a prayer. "From now on, I'm not taking the back seat. If this isn't real, I don't want any of it."

"My thoughts exactly. I've lost so much. No more regrets." He lifted her, and her long legs wrapped themselves around his waist.

They crashed through the small trailer door, disengaged enough to crawl up into the loft above the fifth wheel and smashed themselves onto the thin mattress.

He'd never been able to control the explosive heat between them, and from the way she writhed and moaned as she wiggled out of her clothing, neither could she.

She unbuttoned his shirt and he ripped it off, then shrugged out of his T-shirt. Her gaze fixed on him, hopeful but sharp. She wasn't a baby doll, innocent and naïve. The suspicion was still there, masked behind lust and desire.

Smoothing a strand of hair from her forehead, he kissed her gently, then rested himself face to face, needing to reassure her.

"I'm taking my stand here, with you. I'm not ever leaving unless you want me to go. You got it?"

She nodded, yet the doubtful expression still marred her furrowed brow. "I want to believe you. But are you sticking with me because you want Jessie back? If we can't get Jessie back, will you leave?"

"No. I won't leave you."

Her lips quivered and she touched his cheek. "What if Salem has your child? What if she's alive and you find out she has your child? Would you leave me for her?"

"No, but would you still want me? I've screwed up my life by playing around. I don't know what I was thinking. Thought I could shirk responsibility, be the opposite of my family, run away and be free—all that crap."

"You're like me." She palmed his jaw, stroking his beard fuzz. "Scared to commit. Better to be free and lonely than get hurt."

"Yeah, exactly right." He kissed her hand. "Except we both managed to get hurt anyway. I figure if we can't stay away from each other, then we might as well stop hurting each other."

"Sounds sensible, but can we really keep this up? This niceness? This togetherness? What happens if we can't get Jessie back? Will you blame me?"

He ran his hand up and down her bare back and held her close, pressing her belly against his jeans. "I'll blame myself for letting you go."

"What happens if we make each other miserable? We fight and curse? We're like oil and water. We're not like Jenna and Larry or Connor and Nadine."

"No, we're not. We're like two cats hissing and spitting, clawing and scratching, but if we fight, we'll make it up with love." He gulped, unable to keep a silly grin from his face. He'd just mentioned the one word he'd never wanted to associate with any woman.

Love wasn't an emotion he yearned for, but rather one he feared. It was dangerous, suffocating, and made him feel like a trapped animal.

"Are we capable of love?" Her brow wrinkled, as she, too, had her doubts. "Or is it sex?"

He let his gaze run down her beautiful body. "If it were only sex, why are we talking about love?"

"We don't know what it is without the sex." She grasped his hand and held it, her fingers twined with his.

"It doesn't have to be either or." He brought her hand to his lips and kissed her knuckles. "Shall we learn it together? Learn how to make love?"

"I've been making love since the very first time." Her eyes narrowed with a mischievous and naughty glint. "But I'll take great sex anytime."

With a hearty purr, she launched herself at him, claiming his mouth and kissing him like a possessed woman.

"I want this to last, this lovemaking," he muttered, gasping and shying away from her touch. "Want to feel you against me, skin to skin, closer than any two people can get."

"Then what are you waiting for?" She touched him, shooting tingles throughout his body.

He stifled a long moan as lust and love rushed through his veins, cascading into his heart. "Tonight's about you, my wildcat. When I'm done with you, which will be never, you'll know beyond a shadow of a doubt that you have my heart."

She moved her hand to his hard abdomen and up his chest while smoothing his hair with her other one. Gazing into his eyes, she said, "You've always had mine, but even now, I'm afraid to admit it. Will having your heart hurt?"

"If I hurt you, I hurt me. I think we've established that already."

She nodded, biting her lip. "It's like we're stuck together. I can't live without you, but I can't see us not hurting each other."

"Then we're just going to have to make it hurt so good." He nipped her lower lip and rolled her hair around his hand, pulling her back so that her eyes dilated with hot passion.

"Oh, yeah." She sighed and grasped his face. "Hurt me so bad, Grady. Hurt me until I scream your name."

* * *

Dark, unspoken passion drilled into Linx, turning her blood into rivers of fire. She whimpered when Grady drew her lips to his.

He kissed her thoroughly and with more heart than she'd ever tasted, and this time, instead of fighting him, scratching, biting, and challenging him, she let him make love to her, slowly and patiently building the embers of her need into a mighty, all-consuming climax.

She hadn't expected him to take her over the edge so easily, not so close to the hot and cold internal combustion of the first one.

"I love you." She surprised herself with the words that had been percolating at the edge of her heart. It didn't even matter if he didn't say them back to her—not now when she felt his love so intensely.

His eyes dilated, softening into an expression of adoration and hardening at the same time with wicked lust. "Oh, baby, love is just the start. I'm staking my claim now and forever."

Heck, a Grady in love was a clear and present danger, a minefield, but one she'd gladly step into, time and time again. Was she nuts? But oh, she couldn't help it, not when everything she'd secretly wanted was offered to her in such a delectable and hunky package.

She floated down through the afterglow of loving with the burr of his deep voice purring her name, "Linx, Linx, my sweet girl, my heart."

* * *

Grady closed his eyes, hugging and spooning his woman as her breathing quieted down, easing from the heights of pleasure he'd brought her to.

He was proud of himself, and yet, he braced himself for her push and shove. Would she regret the pleasure and her loss of control? Would she back off, afraid to let that glimmer into her heart stay open?

She'd uttered those words, and he wanted to believe she'd meant them. But at the same time, she'd hurt him—sometimes deliberately—sought her revenge for him hurting her.

Could she go back to that as easily as a woman putting on a bra?

He rested his head on the thin pillow and gazed at the closeness of the trailer roof. Here, on this tiny bed, he and Linx were pressed as close together as two people could get.

Gentle moonlight dappled though the curtains of his trailer, and the soft, satisfied purr of Linx's breathing rained balm on his wounds.

It was strangely peaceful and intimate.

He moved a tendril of her dark-brown hair that had curled onto her face. She looked so innocent, lying there with her eyes closed and her mouth partially open.

She shifted in her sleep and took in a deeper breath through her nose and her eyelids fluttered as if she were dreaming.

Were they sweet dreams or nasty nightmares?

He watched as her face scrunched and she whipped her head back and forth. Her eyes snapped open and she stared straight up, and then moved her gaze to his.

"What's wrong?" he asked.

"I have to go." She sat up so quickly she bumped her head on the roof above them. "I left Ginger and Cedar. We have to call your family. I stole your cell phone and I snooped on you and Vanessa. I'm a horrible, horrible human being."

"Whoa, wait, where's this coming from?" Her words jolted him from the intoxicated languor her body had left him in.

She groped in the pocket of her discarded jeans and handed him his phone. Covering her face with her hands, she shuddered. "I'm a bad person. I gave your baby away. How can I ever forget that? I don't deserve your heart, Grady Hart. I have to leave. Have to leave."

"If you need to get back to the center, I'm going with you." He kissed the back of her neck, nuzzling her with his face. "You're all I have and all I want."

He reached down and traced her C-section scar, now that he knew what it was. "You gave her life. It could have been worse."

Her shoulders heaved and she shook her head. "This isn't going to last. You're going to hate me again. I don't know how to be a mother. I don't know how to love anyone. I'm the last person you should have in your life. I have an evil heart. I'm tainted with poison. I ruin everything I touch."

"Not true." He refused to let her flail out of his arms. "I'm also the black sheep. I break hearts. I screw up people's lives. I'm the bad twin, always getting into trouble. I'm the dark heart of my family. I ruin what I touch."

"Then we'll never be happy together."

"And we'll never be happy apart. Stick with me, Linx, and trust me."

"I want to, but we have to get Jessie back. It's my fault if we don't." Her body wracked with agony and she turned away from him, curling up into a fetal position.

Chapter Twenty-Nine

Linx spent a sleepless night tossing and turning on her futon. By now, Grady had already called his family, and they were all on their way back.

He probably regretted joining forces with her, or maybe it had all been a lie, his usual modus operandi of saying and promising sweet things in bed to enhance the experience, and then disappearing without a trace.

Damn, was she stupid.

She rolled off her bed, disturbing Cedar who groaned and shook herself before settling back onto her vacated pillow.

Picking up little Ginger, she took her downstairs.

"You're so adorable." Linx kissed the sweet little fluff ball who licked her with a tiny tongue, wiggling all over.

The online bidding to adopt Ginger had gone over two thousand bucks, and the center needed the money. It was going to be excruciatingly hard to let her go when the time came.

Linx flashed back to the weeks and months after she let Jessie go. The adoption counselor hadn't encouraged her to see Jessie or speak to the adoptive parents, but since Jessie was the pastor's daughter and everyone in the congregation got to see her, Linx had gone to church and tortured herself every Sunday until she'd had an emotional breakdown, crying nonstop for an entire week.

It had been too much, too soon, so she and Salem had joined a ground crew far up in Alaska. Fighting fires and living in the hell of grief and regret beat burning in her biggest mistake every Sunday.

By the time fire season was over, Linx came back to the property she inherited and threw herself into rescuing dogs and reuniting them with their owners.

She stayed away from Jessie and from church until two years ago when the pastor and his wife visited her and invited her back into Jessie's life.

They were so kind and accommodating, letting her babysit and be her big sister. She'd kept her part of the bargain—promising never to talk about her relationship to Jessie.

She'd respected their wishes and their plans to tell Jessie when she turned eighteen and had agreed that it was best for the little girl to grow up loved and pampered by her adoptive parents.

And now, Grady made plans to upset the entire applecart. If he won, would she be a part of Jessie's life? Or was he using her to get early access? To make friends with Jessie before he dropped the sledgehammer?

If he lost, she'd lose her friendship with the Pattersons and risk Jessie's future hatred of her for hurting her family.

A pinching headache constricted like an iron band around Linx's temple and she groaned, squatting to the floor as she encouraged Ginger to relieve herself on the newspaper.

Talk about a no-win situation.

By the time Linx opened the center, she was fortified by coffee and breakfast, but feeling no better.

Tami sashayed through the door with her eyebrows raised. "Where were you last night?"

"I delivered another dog to Grady." Linx figured it would all come out anyway.

"Oh ... do tell. Was it a happy ending dog delivery?"

By now, nothing about Grady could make her blush. She'd been around the block so many times with him that she'd worn permanent grooves in the pavement.

"It was nice," she muttered, unable to suppress a warm smile from tickling her cheeks.

"Good. That's progress." Tami beamed at her as if she were a particularly bright student. "So, no ugly words were exchanged. He's cool with you snooping through his things, bringing his family up to his private place? Don't think I didn't know about you holding onto his phone."

Linx's face heated, and the tension returned to her neck and throat. "He wants to get Jessie back."

"Wow! I didn't know he wanted to take responsibility." Tami set her bag down and turned on her computer. "What's he going to do? Be a single dad?"

Linx took a seat at her desk. "I think he wants to raise her with me."

"You sound scared."

"Yeah, I am." She wiped her hair back from her forehead. "I don't know if I'm a good enough mom."

"You won't know if you don't try." Tami's eyes were large and sympathetic. "Besides, I've a feeling you'll be the very best mom a girl could want."

Linx forced a smile. "You have to say that because you're my bestie."

"Guilty." Tami blinked. "The question is, do you want to be her mother? Better think fast because Jessie's coming to spend the day with the puppy."

"Don't say anything to her." Linx took a deep breath, but couldn't dislodge the tightness clamping around her chest. "I want her, but it would be a betrayal to the Pattersons. I signed long ago."

"Yeah, but Grady never signed."

Tami's words hung in the air until midmorning, when Jessie and her mother showed up at the center. The little girl wore denim overalls and a pair of cowgirl boots and a straw hat with a red bandana, and she greeted Linx with a tight hug.

"Can I take Ginger for a walk?" she asked, bouncing up and down with a wide smile on her face.

"She's a little young for a walk," Linx said. "But she's getting stronger every day. Would you like to brush her?"

"Yes! I love her!" Jessie shouted. "My birthday's coming up, and I want a puppy, pretty please?"

Mrs. Patterson cleared her throat and cupped a hand around one side of her mouth. "Have you seen how high the price is for Ginger?"

"The highest bidder may not get the puppy," Linx said. "We have to qualify the owner, check references, and make a call."

"I hate for her to be disappointed," Jean said, bending down to her daughter. "Mommy will be back later. You listen to everything Miss Linx and Miss Tami say. This puppy already has a special boy or girl."

"Awww ..." Jessie's face drooped. "But she's so cute."

"Yes, she is. But you're here to learn how to take care of a puppy. You already have Betsy. You wouldn't want to take this puppy away from her special boy or girl, would you?"

"No, they'll be so sad." Jessie shook her head resolutely. "I don't want anyone to take Betsy away from me."

Linx swallowed and bit her lip as turmoil churned in her belly. How would Jessie feel if she and Grady took her away from the only parents she knew?

"Bye, now, and be good." Mrs. Patterson gave Jessie a hug and rose.

"I will!" Jessie jumped up and down. "Bye, Mom!"

Linx had Jessie feed Ginger from the bottle, then brush her fur, and change her papers.

Jessie played ball with the puppy, rolling it around and letting Ginger chase it with her tottering little steps, and she handfed Ginger soft puppy food.

"You're real good with dogs," Linx praised Jessie when she cuddled the puppy and put her down for a nap. "Let's go out back and visit the other guests."

"I love dogs, and I want to be just like you when I grow up." Jessie hooked her thumbs around her overall straps and sauntered through the kitchen to the back door.

Linx showed her the kennels and the storeroom where they filled the food and water bowls. Together, they swept and hosed off the runs, and fed the dogs. Linx taught Jessie how to approach strange dogs and not to assume a dog was friendly. She understood the importance of giving a dog a friendly and safe distance and not patting it on the head or raising a hand.

Jessie was a quick learner, and soon, she understood doggy body language and posture, whether a dog was fearful or curious, and how to speak to them.

Linx's chest filled with pride as she walked around the compound with her little shadow, her "mini-me" following her around, chitchatting nonstop.

She didn't want to lose any of this, but at the same time, her greedy heart yearned for more. She wanted to be the one who tucked this sweet child in at night, wanted to be the one she ran to for comfort, wanted to read her stories, to take her hiking, horseback riding, and be the one in the delivery room with her when she birthed her first baby.

"Come, let me show you the system of gates we open to get the dogs to their exercise yard," Linx said, taking Jessie's little hand. "I move them in between the zones by shutting this gate first, then opening this one, and shutting the one behind it."

True, it was like the way they moved prisoners, but it helped her gather the dogs in an orderly fashion.

"Can I go into the yard and play with them?" Jessie asked.

Linx shook her head. "Not right now. Some of them are new, so I have to watch how they behave. But later on, we can take the old bulldog, Bob, out for a walk. He's slow but very lovable."

"Yay! I always take Betsy out for a walk. Do you think Bob wants Betsy for a friend?"

"Maybe." Linx bent down and gave Jessie a hug, unable to help kissing her. "You're my best little helper. Want to help me open the gates?"

Jessie headed for the first gate as Linx unlatched it. She motioned to Jessie to push a button to open the wheeled gate nearest the barn. Cedar followed close behind, but her ears perked and she pranced toward the front gate, barking and panting excitedly.

Car doors slammed, and a horde of footsteps and voices advanced up the gravel path with Grady leading the way.

It was the entire Hart family.

"Are you saying that's your dog?" Grady's father pointed to Cedar who whined and turned circles, eager to get to Grady.

"She was," Grady said, then turned to wave at Linx. "But Linx saved her from a forest fire, and since I was out of the country, she took care of her for me."

That was certainly a nice way of putting it.

Giving Grady an appreciative smile, Linx opened the gate and Cedar charged forward, leaping all over him.

If the Harts resented Linx for keeping Cedar or the even worse crime of giving Jessie away, they didn't show it.

Cait waddled up to Linx and hugged her warmly. "I'm so glad you're talking to my brother again."

Jenna, Grady's twin, gave her an air kiss. "My brother needs someone like you."

His two brothers, Connor and Dale, shook her hand and complimented her on the dog center.

Everyone had something nice to say to her, shouting over the chorus of barks and yips. They surrounded Linx with questions and invitations to lunch, dinner, and getting together. Even more unbelievably, they seemed genuinely happy to see her, acting like she was someone special.

"Would you like something to drink? Tea or orange juice?" Linx to the kitchen door. "Or a tour?"

"We'd like to see the dogs," Cait said. "I'm still looking for one big and strong enough to handle these backwoods."

"I might want one too," Melisa agreed. "A small one who won't scare my birds."

"I'll need a few dogs for the teen center," Dale said to Linx. "Did Grady tell you I'm volunteering at Salem's Kids?"

"Great, follow me to the barn," Linx said. "We're going to let the dogs out for exercise and that'll give you a chance to look at them."

As the Harts headed for the barn, Jessie came running out, waving her hands. "I opened all of the gates and let the dogs out! Wanna see?"

"On no!" someone shouted. "She opened the front gate, too."

"Woof, woof, woof, woof."

Linx's hands flew up as a tidal wave of dogs made a run for the front gate and freedom.

Two things happened at the same time. The male Harts, Grady, Connor, Dale, and their father chased the dogs, and the female Harts, Cait, Jenna, Nadine, Melisa, and their mother gasped and gaped at Jessie.

"Sorry." Jessie shrank behind Linx's legs. She peered shyly at the female Harts who clasped their hands and bit their lips.

"It's okay," Linx reassured the little girl. "All those guys are firemen and they'll round up the dogs in no time."

Melisa was the first to stop staring. She got on her knees and said, "What's your name, sweetie? I'm Mrs. Reed and I teach kindergarten."

"I'm Jessie and I'm five and a half." Jessie put up five fingers. "My birthday's July Fourth just like Uncle Sam's and I'm going to be six."

"Born on the Fourth of July, that's awesome," Melisa said. "Do you like fireworks?"

Jessie nodded enthusiastically. "I like to wear red, white and blue, and when I grow up, I'm going to be Wonder Woman just like Miss Linx."

Grady's mother bent over and held out her hand to shake. "Miss Jessie, I bet you're a real good helper here."

"I'm good with dogs," Jessie said. "But not so good with gates. Do you want to see Miss Linx's puppy?"

"Sure," all the female Harts squealed. "We love puppies. Lead the way."

As soon as Jessie turned her back, everyone cast meaningful looks at Linx. By now, the entire family knew her and Grady's secret, but they were considerate enough not to say anything in front of the little girl.

Melisa and Jenna ohhed and ahhed over the puppy, distracting Jessie as Cait and Mrs. Hart hung back, obviously wanting to pump Linx for information.

"She's adorable," Cait whispered.

"My stars." Mrs. Hart fluttered her hand. "She looks just like Grady. Whatever are we going to do?"

Linx swallowed hard as a weight pressed her shoulders down. She'd forfeited her parental rights.

"There's nothing I can do." She blinked back tears. "I wish I'd known all of you back then."

"Oh, Linx, I wish you did, too." Cait tugged her into a hug. "We don't blame you. None of us."

"You were so young and all alone," Mrs. Hart said. "If anyone's to blame, it's my son."

"No, he was duped. It's a long story, but his cell phone was intercepted and our communications were altered by a person I thought was a friend." Linx bit her knuckles, overwhelmed at the kindness pouring from Cait and her mother.

"Whatever happens, we have to handle this with care," Mrs. Hart said. "But Linx, darling, you are one of us now. Heart comes first before anything else."

"Grady loves you," Cait pronounced confidently. "He's real sorry and admits he's had his head up his ass for too long."

"I don't know what to say," Linx blubbered. "Not a day goes by that I don't regret what I did."

"At least you gave her life," Mrs. Hart said, patting her arm. "You gave her a chance. These days, that's special and commendable."

"I wanted her to have a better life. I wanted her to have everything: a complete family, love, stability. I wish I'd tried harder."

"Miss Linx," Jessie shouted from inside the cabin. "We're taking a picture with me and Ginger, and I want you to be in it. Please?"

God help her. Being so close to Jessie, holding her in her lap along with the puppy, watching her chat with the family she didn't know, shredded Linx's already wounded heart.

No doubt, the Harts would treasure the pictures taken today, and Linx couldn't help wondering what Mrs. Patterson would think if she knew they'd been visiting with Grady's family—especially after Grady sued for custody.

Chapter Thirty

"Oh boy, you're in for it," Todd said to Linx when he stopped by to pick up Tami for lunch. After Linx gave Todd a nudge, he'd agreed to be friendly with Tami, but only as a little sister. Whatever, the guy was clueless, and he was about to get hit full force by Hurricane Tami. Good luck to him.

"You're really in for it," Todd repeated when Linx didn't respond. "And what are you smirking about?"

"Oh, nothing, but what exactly am I in for?" Linx had just sent Jessie home with her mother. Fortunately, the Hart clan had retired to Joe's Diner minutes before Mrs. Patterson arrived to pick up Jessie. They were staying for the festival and had taken every room in the Over Easy Bed & Breakfast, leading Tami to declare the need for a hotel in town.

"Dad invited Grady's entire family to dinner tonight." Todd lifted an eyebrow to watch for her reaction.

"Oh, no!" Linx flapped her hands uselessly. "I wanted to introduce Grady first and explain what had happened without his family milling around."

"Everyone knows by now," Tami said, sidling up to Todd. "It's the talk of the town."

"Do the Pattersons know?" Linx was horrified that they might stop Jessie's visits to the center, but at the same time, she wasn't sure what exactly it was that everyone knew.

"Look at you, all guilty." Tami guffawed and hooked her hand around Todd's arm. "Everyone knows you've got a new guy, but no, we would never let on about that other matter. Have a little faith in us."

"I want what's best for Jessie," Linx said. "Only I don't know what that is. I fantasize about the life we could have had. Me, Jessie, and Grady, but I don't think we would have been as good for her as the Pattersons."

"Don't shortchange yourself." Tami slipped her hand down Todd's arm and grasped his hand. "You and Grady will make great parents. Look at how you take care of Ginger."

"A dog is not a baby." Linx huffed while perversely enjoying the way her brother was frozen stiff. "Anyway, I asked Becca to drive up from Sacramento so she can give Grady some advice."

Todd withdrew his hand and punched a fist into his beefy palm. "That's great. Looks like the family powwow is all set."

It was going to be explosive all right.

"I need to go speak to Dad separately," Linx said. "I can't spring this on him in one go, especially if Grady's family is going to be there. I trust you'll let Chad, Vivi, Joey, Scott, and Becca know about how Salem got in between Grady and I?"

"You bet," Tami said, leaning up against Todd. "They need to know Grady isn't all bad. Now that we know he's Jessie's father, we need to do what we can to help, and Salem makes a perfect villain."

"She was my friend, though." Linx heaved a sigh. "Guess I'm not good at reading people."

"Are you saying I'll betray you, too?" Tami rolled her eyes.

"No, but I feel like I'm betraying the Pattersons." Linx pinched the bridge of her nose. "Becca's going to give Grady advice on taking Jessie away from them, and I'm fantasizing about me being Jessie's mom for real. What kind of person does that make me?"

"A normal one." Tami slid by Todd, making sure to brush against him, and reached to hug Linx. "You and Grady made mistakes like everyone else, but I think you learned from them already."

"I want Jessie back so bad, but I gave my word." Linx's throat tightened. "I'm not sure Grady can get her back, and then he'll be mad at me forever."

"We'll cross that bridge when we get to it," Todd said. "You go talk to Dad and let him in on what's going on, and Becca will take care of the legal side of things."

"Everything will work out. You'll see." Tami slung her purse over her shoulder and batted her eyelashes at Todd. "You listen to your big brother. He knows best."

Yuck. Linx wasn't sure if she could stomach Tami's blatant flirting, but at the same time, if it made Todd sweat bullets, the entertainment might be worth it.

* * *

Grady found himself sitting between his parents at Joe's Diner where his family took up half of the tables.

"You've made a fine mess," his father said. "Why didn't you look her up once she told you she was pregnant?"

"Or had us look into it," his mother said, fanning herself with the menu. "She's such a sweet girl."

Grady did a double take and ran his fingers through his hair. No one who knew Linx Colson would ever describe her as sweet.

"Look, our lines got crossed, okay?" he grumbled, wishing he were at the other table with his younger siblings.

"Linx is partially at fault, too," Cait said, wrinkling her nose. "She played games with Grady when we met her last Christmas."

"If she really cared, she would have contacted us. We would have helped her." Connor put his arm around his wife possessively. "That baby was a Hart."

"She also kept his dog," Brian added. "What kind of woman does that?"

"A fragile woman who's insecure. Her mother hates her and said she was the worst kid." Grady's fist tightened over his knee. "She left them because she couldn't stand Linx."

"Oh, my stars," Grady's mother exclaimed. "Then we must love her even more. The poor child."

"You're not upset she gave away your first grandchild?" Connor tugged his wife even closer as she held their daughter, Amelia, the first official Hart grandchild.

"Mistakes were made by everyone," Father said. "Question now is what do we do about it?"

"I want what's best for Jessie," Grady said. "She should be with her real parents."

His mother glanced at his father and then at Cait who tightened her lips in a frown.

"Some might say the Pattersons are her real parents," Nadine, Connor's wife, said in a soft voice. "They're the only ones she knows."

"I was never given a chance to know her." Anger rolled through Grady's gut.

"That's not the Pattersons' fault," Nadine said. "They took Jessie when no one wanted her."

Nadine was an artist, and the product of an affair between her father, who was married to another woman, and her mother, who was the side piece, and she had a sensitive soul.

She had a point, although the sooner Jessie knew the truth, the more time she would have to adjust to it.

Grady swallowed a lump in his throat and blinked. "I don't want to hurt Jessie or the Pattersons, but I have my rights."

"It comes down to Linx signing away her parental rights." Connor's voice boomed a little too loud, and several other patrons turned toward them.

Everyone in the small town knew who they were, and Grady cringed when he recognized two of the rescue center volunteers and their parents.

"Let's not discuss this here," Grady said. "Linx asked her lawyer sister to dinner tonight, and we can get advice from her."

"I looked up the law on the internet," Cait chimed in, always eager to upstage her siblings. "You might be out of luck because you didn't claim your paternity before the adoption was finalized."

"How could I when I had no clue?" Grady slapped the menu onto the table.

Cait shrugged. "That's all I know from the website."

"I looked also," Grady grumbled. "They said the father had to be notified. Linx never notified me, and the courts never tried to track me down, because she said the father was unknown."

"Then you have a case," his father said. "The court didn't do their due diligence."

"Still, it's been almost six years." Mother wrung her hands, always the worrywart. "They might ask why you didn't come back once Jessie was born and take a paternity test."

"Because Linx told me she was never pregnant. That she didn't have a baby." Grady threw up his hands and growled. "How was I supposed to know that scar on her abdomen was a C-section scar? I thought she had her appendix taken out or something."

The entire diner went silent, and Grady wished he could sink into a big hole. His family knew how to push his buttons, and they discussed things to death. It was no wonder he wanted to leave and never come back.

"I hope you won't hate Linx if you can't get custody." Cait had the knack for saying the exact wrong thing. "I think she really wants to work it out with you."

"Sure, because she has a snowflake's chance in hell of getting custody of Jessie except through me." Grady shoved himself from the table. "I need some air."

* * *

Linx leaned with her father against the white three-rail fence of the horse corral. He squinted in the sun at the trainers exercising his show horses and nodded as Linx told him about Grady and their big misunderstanding.

"The worst part of it was that I lied to him when he finally contacted me." She kept her eyes on her favorite mare—a fiery chestnut named Reina. "Why do I do stupid things like that?"

"You were running." Her father chewed on his words, letting each one come out in a slow drawl. "Running from the truth."

"There's no excuse." Linx hefted a sigh. "I'm simply a bad person. I got pissed at him for not caring, so I lied."

"Suspect you were hurt. Like your mom was hurt."

Linx's stomach clenched and the air left her lungs. "Hurt? What could she possibly be hurt about? She left because of me, because you stuck up for me and that stupid red dress."

Her father pressed his hand on her shoulder. He still stared at the horses. "Wasn't because of that. She wanted to love you, but it hurt, so she left—easier that way. Just like you gave Jessie away and lied to Grady. Easier to pretend it never happened."

"No, that wasn't the reason. I'm nothing like her." Linx's heart roiled with fury. "I would never leave my family. My children. Seven of us. I gave Jessie away because I wanted a better life for her, not because I was hurt."

"You lied to Grady because it was easier to send him away."

"He wouldn't have believed me." Linx swallowed back a sob. "He thought the worst of me, that I'm a liar, have a bad temper, an evil and black heart."

Her father turned his flinty eyes on her. "After Jessie was born, you could have had the court order a paternity test."

"I know, but I just wanted it over and done with. What if he can't get Jessie back?" She covered her face as tears leaked from between her fingers. "He'll never forgive me."

"Maybe he already has," her father mumbled. "I've forgiven your mother."

"For leaving all of us? But that's you, Dad. You're loving and kind-hearted. You're a saint."

"Not a saint." Her father rubbed her back and pulled her into an embrace. "Just a man who understands why she left."

"Why?" Linx leaned against her father's solid warmth. "Why did she leave? Was it me? Did she hate me so much?"

"She saw herself in you, but no, she didn't hate you."

"She left because of me, didn't she?" Linx's heart pounded with a heavy dread. "It was me and my bad temper. I told her I hated her. It was my fault."

"Not your fault." Father's voice was gruff.

"Then why did she leave? I don't understand."

"It's not my secret to tell. You'll have to ask her." He kissed the top of her head, and pinched her cheek gently.

"I can't ask her if I can't find her." Linx could barely get the words out between her sobs. Except her mother had made contact—sort of.

"She doesn't much like talking. She needs her space—like a wild horse. Can't pen her in."

Dark rage boiled deep in Linx's gut, and she clenched her fists at the excuses her father gave, as if he cared more about her mother than his seven children.

"I still hate her. Unless you tell me her secret, I will always hate her."

"Remember that woman who drowned all her kids?" Father took off his Stetson and picked at the rim. "Perhaps running away saved your life. Maybe it was the best thing she could have done for you."

"She wanted to kill me?" Linx staggered, grabbing onto the rail fence.

"She needed help, and she refused to get it." He held Linx up and led her from the corral. "Despite it all, I believe she loved all of you."

"Even me?"

"Even you." His deep cowboy voice sounded so reassuring, and he'd never lied to her.

"Am I nuts also? Do I need help?" Linx hardly dared to raise her eyes.

"You need help accepting what you did. I never used to cotton to those psychotherapist mumbo jumbo, but after your mother left, Gran invited one to the ranch to stay with us. She helped you guys, too."

"I don't remember going to any therapist," Linx muttered, shaking her head.

"The nanny who helped with the babies, Miss Sharon was a licensed child psychologist. All of you were hurting. You're still hurting, more than the others. You were always the wild one."

"Whatever happened to her?" Linx walked alongside her father back into the ranch house. "She was like a ray of sunshine, always happy and playing games with us."

"She got married and moved away, but unfortunately, her husband died earlier this year. When Todd told me you were seeing Grady on the sly, and how you loved and hated him at the same time, I wrote to her and asked her to come for a visit. Will you let her help you?"

"I'm not lying on a couch." Linx stopped in front of the front door. "And I hate talking about myself."

"Then talk about Grady and Jessie." Father opened the door and they stepped into the house. "Or Cedar or Ginger. Or what makes you happy."

Sharon looked up from the couch where she was working on her laptop, and a smile crinkled her eyes.

She was older than Linx remembered, but it had been twenty years since she helped out around the ranch.

Linx rushed to the woman who'd helped Father and Gran and threw her arms around her.

"Linx, you're more beautiful than your father described." Sharon gave her a warm, tight hug and leaned back, beaming at her. "And so tall."

"Dad brought you here for me?" Linx's heart was flooded with warmth, and she turned to her father, throwing her arms around him. "Thank you, Dad. I'm so tired of hurting. So tired of fighting. Of running, and of hating."

Chapter Thirty-One

Grady's heart pounded, and his lungs burned as he went running up and down the hilly roads outside of Colson's Corner. He needed to stay in shape if he were ever to go back to smokejumping or even plain old firefighting.

True, his traveling days were over if he got custody of Jessie, but he was tired of sitting around at essentially a desk job matching dogs to veterans—not a good way to stay in shape.

Grady sprinted up the hills and jogged down, doing interval training, mile after mile, until he found himself outside of Linx's place.

He hadn't spoken to her or texted her after they'd made love the night before, because as soon as he'd told his family where he was, they had swarmed into town and surrounded him.

It turned out Linx had told Cait about Jessie and him being her father, and there was nothing he could do but answer questions until his tongue went numb.

He spotted Linx's Durango parked in the carport. Next to it was another car, which looked like Jessie's mother's minivan.

Grady's heart galloped as he approached the center. Maybe he shouldn't meet Jessie's adoptive parents until he saw them in court.

He was about to turn around when Linx opened the front door and waved him in, probably alerted by the barking dogs in the back.

"Missed you." Bending toward her, he kissed her cheek and acted like she was his girlfriend.

Her eyes twinkled, and she darted him a fluttery look. "How'd you ditch your family?"

Cedar and Betsy greeted him with wagging tails and sniffing, so Grady gave both dogs a neck rub before answering.

"I ran out on them at the diner. Monday morning quarterbacking's what they do best." He tipped his head toward Mrs. Patterson who was brushing tangles and twigs from Jessie's hair.

"Grady!" Jessie said, brightening up. "Mom, that's Superman, and he found my dog."

Grady couldn't help the grin creeping onto his face as he gave Jessie's shoulder a pat. He'd become a character in her make-believe world, which meant she remembered him.

Mrs. Patterson looked indulgently at Jessie and extended her hand. "I think we met before. I'm Jean Patterson. We're so grateful you found Betsy."

"Grady Hart." He shook Jean's hand. "Glad I could help."

"It's a good thing you found her," Mrs. Patterson said. "Jessie didn't want another dog. Only Betsy would do."

"But Mom, I do want another dog!" Jessie beamed, blinking cutely. "Now that Betsy's back, she wants a friend so she won't be lonely."

A smile teased over Linx's lips as she ruffled Jessie's head. "Are you going to be in the Fourth of July parade?"

Good tactic. Changing subjects. Seemed Linx already knew some of the tricks mothers used.

"I'm going to ride on a real fire truck." Jessie bounced up and down. "Can I sit with you, Superman? Miss Linx says you're a fireman, too."

"I'll have to check with whoever's in charge here," Grady said, hating to disappoint his daughter, but loving that he was asked. "Is Betsy going to ride with you?"

"Yep, I get a fire helmet, and she gets to be fire dog. I won the prize for the entire town." Jessie stood straight and tall. "But I still want to be in the dog parade and wear my Wonder Woman costume."

"You want to do everything, don't you?" Linx gave the little girl an affectionate hug. "You're a little ball of energy."

"I get to turn the wheel and ring the bell, and Betsy gets to look out the window." Jessie's eyes were wide. "But I also want to walk the dogs and ride horses, too."

"You can't do everything in one year," Mrs. Patterson said. "I think riding in the fire truck and doing the show and tell at the dog rescue auction will be lots of fun."

"Only if Superman gets to drive it and let me turn the wheel." Jessie put her hand in Grady's, melting his heart on the spot.

"I'm sure there are real Colson Corner firefighters who will drive the fire truck," Grady said, not wanting to usurp anyone's authority, but wishing like heck he could sign up to drive.

"Actually, it's an antique fire truck, not the real rig," Jean cut in. "Your brother-in-law, Brian Wonder, has one he offered for the parade. My husband and I would have gone with Jessie, but he's going to be street preaching and I'm passing out tracts. There are a lot of visitors up for the Gold Country Festival, and that means a lot of souls to save."

Good. The Pattersons were such wonderful servants of God that they were sacrificing time with their supposed daughter. He could use this against them, if needed, and it gave him a chance to get to know his daughter.

Grady gave the little hand a light squeeze. "Well, then, if it's my brother-in-law's fire truck, then sure, I'd be honored to drive Miss Jessie around."

"Yay!" Jessie cheered. "Can you wear your Superman cape?"

Grady didn't have a Superman costume, but whatever Jessie wanted, she was going to get. "If it's what people do here."

"We all wear costumes for the Fourth of July parade," Mrs. Patterson explained. "This little one wants to be Wonder Woman because Miss Linx is always Wonder Woman."

"Really?" He squinted at Linx, picturing her with a cape, low-cut tank and short shorts.

Linx shrugged sheepishly. "It's a town tradition, and I can see how you'd think we're weird."

"Not any weirder than some of our Hart family traditions." Grady couldn't help grinning at Jessie's pleased expression. "You sure you're not pulling my leg?"

"Honest John," Mrs. Patterson said. "My husband and I are old-time settlers, but Jessie doesn't want to wear Little House on the Prairie dresses."

Grady couldn't argue with that either. There was a clear choice between a superhero and an old-fashioned fuddy-duddy.

"Then we're all set." Grady let go of Jessie's hand and waved goodbye. "Just don't bring any kryptonite."

* * *

"You're seriously going to wear a costume?" Linx couldn't help smirking at Grady after Jessie and her mother left the center. "You hate costumes, and I hate to break it to you, but Superman wears tights."

"Ugh." Grady rubbed the back of his neck. "I'm only doing it for Jessie."

"It's going to be epic. Grady Hart in tights." Linx pinched his jeans and pretended to snap it back. Even though she kept her voice light, she couldn't help the heavy feeling lying deep in her gut.

Grady Hart wasn't a man to banter and joke. He, too, must be feeling the strain of knowing about Jessie, but pretending she was a mere acquaintance.

"Don't forget, I'm a man in a cape. That has to count for something." He cupped her cheek and brought his lips close to hers.

"But I also have a cape and superpowers." Linx narrowed her eyes and puckered her lips. He definitely wasn't ready to deal head-on with her guilt, and flirting and kissing was his way of relieving tension.

She could go with that. For now.

Turning his head, he captured her lips. Sparkles and sizzles traversed her body as she clasped onto him and let herself meld into the urgency of the moment.

All morning, he'd been stuck within his family, broody and angry, and she'd wanted to go up to him and comfort him. He clearly didn't fit in with the gregarious Harts, being a loner and a guy who craved silence.

She understood that, because she understood him.

While it was wonderful to be loved and cared for, it was also stifling and suffocating to have so many people worrying and offering their opinions.

Whatever happened between him and her and Jessie was something only the two of them could face.

Even good listeners like Sharon could be tiresome, because Linx really didn't want to rehash everything and gaze at her navel. She couldn't believe Sharon had been an undercover child psychologist, and she wondered why Dad had brought her back—after she was widowed.

Could it be he was interested in her?

Hadn't she been a good friend of Minx's?

Linx let those thoughts drop as Grady backed her up against the doorframe and deepened the kiss. His manly scent, the sweat dampening his shoulders, and the salty tang of his tongue made her greedy with want and desire.

Who needed to talk when an inferno raged deep in her belly? And from the state of his body, she knew he needed to release steam and tension, too.

Except so much more was between them now—and it wasn't just sex. They had to be responsible parents, the type of people who could offer stability and security to a vulnerable child.

Linx broke the kiss and ran a finger over Grady's chin. "Last night was awesome, but I need to know. Are we a team now? Is everything going to be okay?"

"If you're worried about me running away from Jessie, don't be. That little girl is mine, and I intend to be everything she'd want in a dad." Grady's eyes blazed with both determination and a softness she'd never seen before. "I also intend to make everything right for you, too."

Linx swallowed hard, her heart both fluttering with worry and expanding with hope. Was he only with her because he thought he had a good chance of getting custody of Jessie? What if the courts turned against them because of her lies? Could he forgive her if they lost Jessie forever?

"I want this to work, too. Let's put the past behind us." Linx feathered her fingers over the back of Grady's neck. "Let's start over with a clean slate."

"Not too clean." He grinned and looped one arm under her legs, sweeping her off her feet. Kissing her fervently, he carted her up the stairs to her loft and slammed the door shut, leaving Cedar and any other curious dogs outside. "I know we have a lot of work to do, but it was pure torture being surrounded by my family and having to keep my hands off of you."

"Do you mean it? This isn't just about Jessie, is it?" Linx knew her eyebrows were furrowed, and she wished she could trust him fully. "I mean, us playing house."

He caressed her cheek. "It's about time I took responsibility. Settle down. Be a man, and that starts with you. I'm not the type to say gooey words, but I think you know how I feel."

Actually, she wasn't sure, and she would have loved to hear gooey words, but only if they were real. Tension skittered through her belly with the feeling that she was about to get everything she'd every wished for—a man to love and a family of her own.

Except fate had taught her not to count her puppies too early. She tempered herself, knowing that despite Grady saying he wasn't good with gooey words, he seemed to say them all the same when in the throes of lovemaking and then forget all about them when confronted with reality.

She nodded and drew his body down over hers and closed her eyes. This was as good as it was going to get. Who was she, an evil-hearted and spiteful girl, to believe she deserved the traditional white knight and happily ever after?

It would be boring, eventually, and it was so not her style. She and Grady were doomed to fight and make up, to love and hate, and to struggle for the few mountain peaks and the fleeting, but oh, so explosive climaxes, made more intense by the valleys of soul-destroying grief.

When Grady's lips and tongue crashed over her, breaching her boundaries, Linx gave herself over to the only pleasure she'd ever know—the fight for a passion too desperate to abandon.

Chapter Thirty-Two

Grady drove with Sam to the Colson ranch. It was located on a country road at the entrance to a large valley wedged between the mountain tops of the Sierra Nevada range.

He passed under the traditional wooden entrance of the ranch, consisting of two vertical logs and a horizontal one across the top with the word "Colson" burned in.

Large, metallic sculptures, similar to the one on Linx's porch, lined the way—monsters, horses, gargoyles, and other odd pieces welded together in a disturbing fashion.

Grady gaped at one that looked like half the face of a woman with shiny metal tears trailing down one side, and jagged cuts and wild zigzag hair on the other.

A twisted and torn heart was perched precariously in a bone-dry ribcage of a cow, with a rusted railroad spike drilled through it.

Grady narrowed his eyes at the railroad spikes. What if Linx's mother was mixed up with the fires? Hadn't that man mentioned scrap metal disappearing from the burn sites and sold to artists?

Also, who else could have left the crude cross at his parents' cabin?

They could call it art all they wanted, but to Grady these heaps were no more than tortured trash.

These were not the kinds of artwork that soothed and expressed peaceful emotions—the way his sister-in-law Nadine's artwork conveyed, but the product of a strange and demented mind.

After passing the grove of grotesque sculptures, Grady drove by a pasture holding horses and an empty training corral and parked on the circular driveway in front of the ranch house.

Linx and Cedar had made it there before him, but barely, judging from the tinkling sound her SUV's engine gave as it cooled.

Grady let himself and Sam through the gate, and the dog took off across the field when he saw Cedar running around with another dog he didn't recognize.

Linx welcomed him at the door with a kiss. She led him inside, introducing him to the few siblings he hadn't gotten to know—mainly, Scott, the fireman and Vivi from the general store.

Grady waved to Todd, Chad, and his cousin Kevin, and Joey from the diner. He could sense the tension in the room and the awkwardness of making small talk with people who barely tolerated him, and he wished his family were gathered around as a buffer.

Fortunately, the news that Salem had caused a rift between Linx and him during her pregnancy seemed to have diminished the hostility from the Colsons, and Linx's father welcomed him with open arms.

"So, you're the man who knocked up my baby girl." Joe Colson gripped Grady's hand with his big, beefy one. "Guess I'm too late with the shotgun, but welcome to the family. I know you'll do the right thing."

"Thanks for the confidence," Grady said, not sure at all what Linx's father meant. Did he want him to retroactively marry his daughter? That way, once he gained custody of Jessie, Linx would also be able to be the mother.

The Colson brothers gathered around—all big men, sizing him up.

"You here to stay or going back to smokejumping?" Scott asked.

"I'm staying around," Grady said. "Might stick to ground crew work."

"Good, we can always use more hands," Scott said.

"Think you'll get your kid back?" another brother, Chad, asked.

"Hope so."

An awkward silence descended on the gathering, as no one had much to say. Instead, they looked at him and he glanced away from them.

Grady sighed with relief when he heard car doors closing outside and a horde of footsteps coming toward the entrance. His family was here.

His parents stepped through the door first, followed by all his siblings and some of their spouses.

Grady's family milled around Linx's brothers and sister, with Cait remaking their connections from the past Christmas when they helped with rescuing her from a kidnapper.

Even though they insulated him from the Colsons, it soon got too loud and stifling for him, the way everyone carried on about family and looking after each other.

They couldn't help giving him concerned looks and wondered out loud where the lawyer was.

Grady hated being the problem child, singled out for this gathering of the clans, as everyone either gave him a thumbs up or whispered their well wishes—as if he'd gotten a cancer diagnosis or was told he had months to live.

The truth was, his family didn't think he could do anything right without them and all their opinions.

Grady backed away from the commotion and spotted Linx at the opposite side of the great room, standing under a portrait of a strikingly beautiful brunette—probably her mother.

The woman had long, dark brown hair and a wild, free-spirited glaze in her eyes. She wore beads in her hair and masses of silver jewelry.

Grady could picture her living in a gypsy wagon, never settling in one place, telling fortunes and causing havoc in people's lives.

He stepped toward the grand piano and studied the family pictures crowded on top of the dusty lid. Across the room, Linx studied him, so he kept his expression neutral.

The wedding picture was old and faded, showing a young cowboy, Joe Colson, with his hippie bride complete with ribbons in her hair, dressed in a flowing multi-colored gown. They looked happy enough, even though he was steady as a rock and she was wrapped around him like slivers of running water.

Then, the children started to appear, and the pictures were still happy. Grady counted the children until he reached the one where Linx was the baby.

Gasping, he stepped back. In each of the previous pictures, Linx's mother held the baby, the father held the next oldest, and the older ones gathered around.

The one with Linx was different.

Joe held the tiny infant in his arms, but his smile was strained, while Linx's mother hugged Chad, the next oldest. Her body language was partially turned away from the infant who had her fists clenched, eyes wide and haunted, and looking like an alien.

Had Linx been adopted?

He glanced up at her and she gave him a scowl, crossing her arms.

He started toward her, but the door opened and a stern, serious-looking woman in a gray suit stalked in. She lowered her eyeglasses and peered at him for a brief second before heading toward Linx and embracing her.

It was Becca, of course, and her first words to Linx were, "Let me guess, he's the one casing the room from behind the grand piano."

The women peered at him again, so he turned away from them right as Cait rushed toward Becca.

While the women went on about Cait's pregnancy, Grady sidled up to Linx.

"Are we going to get time with her?" he whispered, tugging her aside.

Linx put a finger over his lips. "Let's get Becca alone after dinner for the consult."

"I don't think any of us can eat a crumb until we know. I can't believe your dad invited my entire family."

"He didn't know about me asking Becca to come until it was too late. He saw them at the diner. I'm sorry."

"Don't be." He squeezed her shoulder. "I liked you better when you were never sorry for anything."

Linx jutted out her lip. "You're right. No sense wallowing when we have to get on with our lives."

"That's my Linx." He kissed her lightly and grabbed her elbow. "Now, go separate Becca from the herd so we can meet somewhere private."

Linx pushed her way to her sister's side, but a middle-aged woman stepped from the kitchen banging a pot, cutting her off.

"Time for dinner," she shouted. "We have a buffet set up on the farmhouse table and barbecue out back."

"Wait!" Cait held up her hand. "We need to know Grady's chances."

Count on Cait to put business and bossiness first before food. Good for her. He needed answers, and God help him if the case were a lost cause.

"We want to consult with Becca in private," Linx shouted above Cait's demands. "You guys go out back and get started."

His family looked reluctant to leave, even though the rest of the Colson clan made gestures, inviting them to follow.

Becca put her hands around her mouth like a megaphone. "Everyone, please go ahead and eat while I talk to Grady and Linx. As you know, nothing is clear-cut, black or white. I cannot let you know what will happen in court. I can only advise Grady and Linx on their chances."

Their chances?

Did she mean this wasn't a sure thing? Why, he was never informed. He'd never signed away his rights.

He rushed after Linx and Becca as they headed to what looked like the den. Becca's expression was grim, and Linx looked fearful. He put his hand on the small of her back, trying to reassure her.

He was pretty sure his lack of signature giving up his rights would hold up in court. Everything he read told adoptive parents to get the birth father's written and signed consent.

They shut the door to the den and remained standing.

"Thanks for coming," Grady said to Becca. "Just give it to us straight."

The lawyer nodded and flicked back a stray strand of her curly auburn hair which had escaped her bun.

She fixed her gaze on her sister instead of Grady, as if about to lecture her. "I did some investigating on the court order given by Judge Stephens terminating the 'unknown' father's paternity rights. It seems to have been railroaded through the system, and the judge did not verify the proof that you did everything you could to find Jessie's father."

"That's good, isn't it?" Grady stepped forward. "That proves I didn't have a chance to give consent."

Becca held up her hand. "Yes and no. It's positive for you, Grady, but in order to proceed, all the blame for this falls on Linx. She committed perjury and lied to the judge, saying she didn't know who the father could be. She testified she was drunk at the time and implied she was sexually abused by an unknown assailant."

What the heck? Linx had completely erased him from the picture, or was it more sinister?

"You were raped?" Grady's jaw dropped as Linx's face whitened.

"I never said I was raped." She staggered back, and he steadied her. "I just said I had no clue who I had sex with."

"In other words, you lied, and that's a crime." Becca's voice was accusing.

"What does this mean for me?" Grady asked. "I'm the innocent victim here."

"You might have a case," Becca said, "but it's based on Linx's perjury and the judge being too lenient and not insisting she pursue this unknown assailant."

"Crap!" He stalked across the room and threw up his hands. "Can't we keep Linx out of it? Just say I got suspicious when I saw Linx and Jessie together, and I had a nagging feeling something had happened that night."

"You're admitting to allegedly sleeping with a drunk woman who was unable to give consent?" Becca drilled him, stabbing a finger at him.

"Sure. I'll do anything to get Jessie back," Grady said. "The statute of limitations is past, isn't it?"

"Sorry, the Governor signed a bill last year ending California's ten-year statute of limitations because of the Bill Cosby case."

"But Linx won't press charges, will she?" Grady asked, darting his glance from Becca to Linx.

"The prosecutor can still file." Becca gave a chopping motion with her hand. "You two are still within the ten years, bill or no bill."

Grady gasped, not catching his breath. This was worse than he'd imagined. Linx premeditated giving that baby away and cutting him out of her life.

Maybe he'd been too soft on her recently, believing her apologies and letting his feelings bubble to the surface.

Maybe it was better to lock up feelings and emotions and deal only with logic and reason.

"It's all based on my lie!" Linx threw her hands up. "I can't let Grady take the hit when I lied. I'll stand trial for perjury. I'll go to jail. Anything, so Grady can have his rights reinstated."

"Oh, sissy, why did you perjure yourself?" Becca's eyebrows drooped as she wrapped her arms around Linx.

Linx sank to the floor, covering her face, and dragged her sister down onto the carpet, still holding onto her. "Because Grady abandoned me, and I wanted to erase everything. Make it all go away and give Jessie a better life. Plus, the Pattersons were willing to let me stay in Jessie's life. They only started the church here because of me and Jessie. They could have gone anywhere. I didn't want Jessie to ever be abandoned by anyone."

"You picked the Pattersons because they would be her perfect parents." Becca's voice was gentle as she rubbed Linx's back.

Sobs broke from Linx's gasping breath. "Our mother left because of me. And I carry the curse of running away. I'm the most like her, the most unstable. I didn't want Jessie to be hurt the way I was."

The baggage Linx was carrying was far heavier than he'd suspected. That and the haunted look in that baby's eyes—as if she'd known she wasn't wanted and loved—had Grady's heart splitting wide open just like the twisted sculpture left on her porch.

"Why are we trying to take her away from the Pattersons?" Becca asked.

Why indeed? Grady scratched his head, knowing he would hate doing the right thing. He wanted his daughter, but was it already too late?

"I want Grady to have his rights, so he won't hate me forever." Linx couldn't stand to look either her sister or Grady in the eye.

"Linx, I don't—" Grady grabbed her arm, lifting her from the floor. "I mean, it's not fair, but ..."

If she were doing this for him—to make up for hurting him, it was unnecessary. She'd just validated that she truly loved him, and that he could trust her, but she still didn't believe he wouldn't hurt or abandon her—or as she put it, hate her.

"Don't lie to me." A blaze of fire shot through Linx's dark-brown eyes and she shoved herself from him. "Don't stand there and tell me it doesn't matter. I screwed up your life, and I deserve to take the hit."

He couldn't let her go down because of this. She'd been a vulnerable young woman—just like she'd been a vulnerable baby, a small child abandoned by her mother. But still, he wanted his daughter and he wanted her—maybe more.

"Wait, what are our options?" Grady turned to Becca. "Is there any other way? I want to be in Jessie's life. I want to be her father."

"You will be. You deserve to be," Linx screamed, pulling her own hair and shaking her head wildly. "Just not with me. I cheated you out of it and I'll go down. Perjury, jail, a record. You'll all be better off without me."

He reached out to grab her, but Becca blocked him as Linx tore from the den, slamming the door behind her. "Let her go. She needs to be alone. As for you, I'm going to order a paternity test before we do anything else."

"You mean, the child might not even be mine?" Grady's entire chest caved in and he staggered, holding himself against the wood-paneled wall.

Chapter Thirty-Three

"Why do I need a paternity test?" Grady's jaw clenched as he heard Linx exit the house and zoom off in her SUV.

"A precaution. I'm sure she believes the child is yours," Becca said. "But if what she says is true, that she did get drunk and had sex with unknown parties, then we have to be sure. Besides, there's no chance a judge would hear your case without a positive paternity test."

"Okay. How do we get the test done?" Grady's heart galloped unsteadily. "Are you going to inform the Pattersons about my claim?"

"It will have to be a court order," Becca said. "I have to present reasonable evidence, based on Linx's testimony that she now believes you are Jessie's father. Obviously, we can't have people ordering paternity tests on random children."

"Can't I make a claim based on my sexual relationship with Linx approximately nine months before Jessie's birth?" Grady wiped his sweaty hands on his jeans. "I don't want Linx charged with perjury."

"They probably won't charge her," Becca said. "But it's something Pastor Patterson can use against her. No two ways about it. Linx is going to take the hit."

"You're her sister. Can't you shield her?"

Becca shook her head. "I have to follow the law, but I can refuse to take your case—conflict of interest."

"Fair enough." Grady heaved his shoulders, blowing out his frustration. "So, I find an attorney and ask for a paternity test. If it's positive, then what?"

"I might be defending my sister if it comes down to your attorney suing Linx for defrauding you. That would be the tactic he'd take. He would also go after Judge Stephens for not following up on finding the father. Also, since there was no father listed, your paternity rights were never officially terminated. The entire adoption could be overturned—if you want to pursue it. On the other hand, the Pattersons' attorney could dig up dirt about your attitude toward Linx, calling her a liar, denying the possible child was yours, and not making an effort to determine if she actually had a baby or not—letting almost six years go by. It'll be ugly."

"Ugly." Grady shook his head as a soggy weight settled over his shoulders. Ugly would hurt everyone, especially Jessie. "Thanks for the advice. What do I owe you for the consult?"

"No charge." Becca leveled her hazel-colored eyes on him. "But if you eff with my sister, I'm coming after you. My sister made mistakes. Lots of them. But you weren't around to help her. You saw the pictures on the piano, didn't you?"

Grady huffed as he walked toward the collection of family portraits. "Your mother seemed detached from Linx. She wouldn't even hold her. Why is that?"

"My mother had issues, and unfortunately, she picked on Linx. I think she suffered a breakdown. She watched too many horror movies and dabbled with the occult. She believed Linx was the devil's child."

"But why Linx? Why not Joey or Vivi?" Grady fumed at the unfairness of it all.

"I don't know the answer to that," Becca said. "Maybe there's no reason. Or some chemical imbalance causing her to reject Linx. She wasn't exactly a normal mother to the rest of us—acted more like an aunt."

Grady walked by the piano and stared at the picture of Linx as a baby, held by her father. Even at that age, she looked tense and lost, as if she already knew she wasn't wanted.

"All I did was make things worse for her when I rejected her." The realization slammed him like a firestorm flashing through a blind canyon. "My issues are nothing like hers. My parents smothered me to death, and I reacted to her clinging by shoving her away."

"Her issues are not yours unless you want them to be," Becca said, narrowing her eyes. "If you're stringing her along because you think being with her will help you win custody of your daughter, I'm telling you it won't. You're better off being the aggrieved party without her."

"What are you saying?" Grady felt his heart hammering to escape his chest. "That I'm only with Linx because of Jessie?"

"I want to know why you're hanging around her. If you're using her to get to know Jessie, then I'm going to hang you high. My sister doesn't need you to lead her around like a donkey with a nose ring."

"I didn't come here looking for Jessie—not initially. I didn't even know about her. I suspected Linx might have lied, but I thought she'd had an abortion."

"So you came looking for answers." Becca crossed her arms. "You'll get them with the paternity test. Then what?"

"I don't know." Grady headed to the front door. "I need to find Linx. I need to make it right with her, and then we'll figure out where to go from here."

"I love my sister." Becca pointed a finger at him. "There's not a Colson on this ranch who doesn't love Linx. We're only tolerating your presence because Tami and Todd told us about Salem getting in between your messages, but you, Grady Hart, are not off probation. You hurt my sister, and we'll run you out of this town. You can take your hotshot smokejumping ways back to Montana, Idaho or even better, Siberia."

"I won't hurt her." Grady swallowed a thick lump in his throat. "Because I love her."

He turned quickly and opened the front door.

"Hold it." Becca's bark was like a command. "You don't get to throw words like that around when you're dealing with my sister unless you mean them."

Grady swallowed rocks all the way down his throat. "It's not easy for me to admit it, but I need Linx like I need oxygen—with or without Jessie. She's my first priority, and I'm worried she might have run off for good."

"She goes off to sulk, but because of Jessie, she'll never leave Colson's Corner." Becca put a hand on his arm. "If you're so worried, I can tell you where to find her. My mother used to have an artist's cabin past the cow pasture. It's near the creek so you'll see a grove of trees. Linx hides there when she's hurt. We pretend we don't know where she is, but we keep it stocked with canned food, and after a few days, she always comes back."

Maybe this time was different. This time, she might never come back—because of Jessie and him.

"Show me where the cabin is," Grady said.

Becca walked with him partway to his truck and pointed toward a green patch past the fields of hay.

"Thank you." Grady clasped her hand. "For trusting me. Whether I get Jessie back or not, Linx and I are on the same team."

* * *

Linx sped toward the interstate with Cedar in the passenger seat. She had to get out of the state of California before Grady and Becca informed the court that she'd committed perjury.

Stopping at a convenience store, she hit the ATM machine and withdrew her limit of cash for the day. Then she called Vanessa Ransom. She needed someone to take care of her dogs, and Nessa had contacts with other dog rescue centers.

"Hello? Dr. Ransom speaking." Nessa answered her phone.

"It's Linx Colson. I need someone to take over my rescue center, and you mentioned you were a dog trainer."

"I am a dog trainer, but what's going on with your rescue center?" Nessa asked.

"I need to leave the state. Short notice. Do you know anyone who could take over? Any other centers needing space to expand?"

"I, uh, don't get why you're leaving."

"I'm a fugitive from the law. Please don't tell anyone I called, but I have to leave California. I can't leave the dogs without anyone to care for them. I have volunteers, but I need a center director to take over."

"Grady's family is out there," Nessa said. "Have you asked them?"

"I can't let Grady know where I'm going. He's going to sue me for fraud. I shouldn't be calling you, but I don't know anyone else to turn to who won't turn me in."

"How do you know I won't turn you in?" Nessa asked.

"I want you to be my therapist. Client confidentiality," Linx replied. "You told me that I could call you. I need your help."

"Then come to my office and we can talk."

"I can't do that." Linx hung up the phone and started up her Durango. Less than an hour later, she entered Nevada and headed north toward Montana where the forest service had a large firefighting base camp.

* * *

Grady hiked the last mile down the creek to the abandoned artist's cabin Becca described. The trail in front of him looked undisturbed, and Sam, who walked at his side, didn't seem to be excited about tracking Cedar—the closest dog he had for a girlfriend. Not that they got it on, since both had been fixed, but they enjoyed playing together.

Grady stopped when he spotted the tiny cabin. It was little larger than a storage shed and the roof was covered with pine needles.

"Cedar?" he called half-heartedly. "Linx?"

The place looked deserted, but he hadn't come so far to not take a look. Maybe Linx's mother left tools behind, or unfinished work. Or this was the place she used to assemble her horrid metal sculptures.

Sam sniffed the trail and picked up speed as they approached the cabin. He definitely picked up something interesting, although it could be a squirrel.

Someone had been by, and it could have been Linx. He rushed to the door. It was unlocked and opened easily.

He turned on the light and peered into the dimly lit space. An old easel was stacked along one wall and pieces of scrap metal lay in a heap in the back.

Grady swept aside cobwebs and stepped through the door. Sam sniffed the corners of the cabin and appeared disinterested.

"Think she sent me on a wild goose chase." Grady rubbed Sam's neck. "Nothing to see here."

He examined the artist's sink which was bone dry, and kicked the mattress lying on the floor. A tangle of metal was piled behind the easel. The windows were so dirty no one could see out or in, and from the tiny droppings in the corner, the only residents appeared to be mice.

There was, however, a sour smell, as if vagrants had sought shelter inside. But who would pass through this remote ranch out in the middle of nowhere?

Grady walked by a covered trash container right outside the doorway. He opened it and recoiled at the sight of charred bones among a pile of ashes.

Human or animal?

Salem Pryde?

But no, it couldn't be. No one had found her remains. These could be a rack of ribs for all he knew.

He let the lid slam over the trash container, then using his sleeve, he wiped his prints off the handle.

"This is stupid. Probably a barbecue dinner. Someone had a picnic here," he muttered to himself as Sam sniffed the container. "Come on, let's go. Linx isn't here."

He dragged Sam's collar and walked as fast as he could away from the artist's cabin. Maybe he was creeped out by the bones, or it was the dank breeze wrapping itself around him, but Grady's spine tingled as if someone were watching him.

As they stepped back onto the trail, Sam emitted a low growl, raising his hackles. Grady stumbled and stubbed his toe.

His jaw dropped and his heart pounded. He'd tripped over a row of rusted railroad spikes welded together in the shape of crosses.

Chapter Thirty-Four

On the way back to town, Grady texted Linx, *Whatever's bothering you. We can fix it.*

He didn't expect a reply, and he didn't get one.

If Linx's mother wanted attention, wouldn't Linx's cabin and the dog rescue center be targeted next? What better time than when the entire clan was gathered at the ranch?

Grady raced back to Colson's Corner in record speed. As he approached Mountain Dog Rescue, he saw dogs running loose up and down the road and scattering into the forest.

What happened? Had the arsonist set the dogs free before torching the place?

Grady slammed the door of his truck and ran toward the building, followed by Sam.

The front gates were wide open.

"Linx!" he shouted. "Linx, where are you?"

Not only were the gates wide open, the cabin door was unlocked. Grady rushed in, but no one was there.

Grady called Linx's cell phone. After four rings, it went to voice mail.

He left a message. "I'm at the rescue center. The front door was unlocked and the gates are open. Dogs are outside. Ginger and Cedar are missing. Did you take them both?"

He hung up and scanned the empty cabin. There were no signs of anyone pouring gasoline. The weird sculpture still stood on the porch. Sam sniffed around, not scenting anything that raised his hackles.

Whoever it was had been interrupted by him showing up, and they could be watching to see when he'd leave.

Grady went upstairs and checked the loft. The expensive designer wedding dress Linx purchased from Jenna was still on the form, and her clothes, along with her favorite boots and cowgirl hat, were in the closet.

He opened the nightstand drawer and found the two photographs Linx had shown him. She wouldn't have left town without them, would she?

Her gun, the one he'd noticed was sitting on top of her Bible, was missing. But then again, she had a concealed carry permit, and she probably took it with her in case the arsonist came around.

Perhaps she had only gone somewhere to unwind. She certainly had a lot to think about, given what Becca said about the perjury charges she was facing if he decided to go through with the paternity and custody issue.

Grady checked his phone and opened the photos that had been taken earlier in the morning. Little Jessie and Linx with the puppy. They wore identical grins and matching dimples. Their dark brown gypsy eyes crinkled with mischief, and the love they had for each other was palpable.

Would he destroy all of this?

But heck. She was his daughter—or was she?

He had a right to know.

And then what?

Of course, if she was family, he should take care of her, raise her and nurture her. It wasn't fair to slough off his own child on another couple.

But where would Linx fit in?

Grady walked out the back door to check on the dogs who'd stayed behind and see if he could get the rest back into their pens.

Old Bob the bulldog wagged his tail, barely lifting his head for a pat. It was a shame such an adorable animal would be left to languish because people preferred younger pets. At least he hadn't flown the coop.

Grady opened the box for the gate controls and sectioned off the play yard where several dogs had congregated, making sure they couldn't join the escapees outside the compound.

Walking toward the front gate, he spotted a red bandana snagged onto the chain-link fence.

Grady couldn't remember if Jessie had been wearing it or not when she came to visit the second time, but he should contact someone to let them know she'd left it.

He herded the dogs that were still hanging around back into the pen and went into the cabin to look for the volunteer list.

A text message chimed and the phone rang at the same time.

Grady picked it up. It was Nessa.

"Nessa?" He wondered if he'd forgotten an appointment he had with her. "What's up?"

"Have you heard from Linx?"

"No, has anything happened?" His throat tightened and worry thumped in his chest. "She's not at the rescue center. Is she okay?"

"I don't know, but she called me asking me to take over the rescue center. It sounded strange, like she was going away and not coming back."

"Not coming back?" Grady's breath hitched. "I'm at the center and someone's opened all the gates. Half of the dogs are missing and I'm about to call my brothers over to help me find the dogs. Linx's SUV isn't here and neither are Cedar and Ginger."

"She tried to invoke client confidentiality, but the more I thought about it, the more worried I got," Nessa said. "She said she was a fugitive from the law. Has she done anything?"

"Nothing other than a lie she told years ago. It's not like her brother's going to arrest her or anything."

"Anyway, thought I should let you know. She wants someone to take care of the dogs. I'm on my way from San Francisco, but it'll take me a couple of hours to get there. Sounds like you have a mess on your hands."

"Yeah, thanks. I better go round up the cavalry." Grady thanked Nessa and hung up, as text messages and missed calls flooded his phone.

It was his family, probably berating him for bailing out on the dinner with Linx's family.

But then again, couldn't Becca smooth it over with them? He wasn't exactly in the mood for socializing after the bombshell she dropped about Linx's lies and the possibility he wasn't Jessie's father after all.

Grady typed a message to Dale. *Need you, Connor, and Brian over at Mountain Dog asap. Gate's wide open. Dogs are missing.*

A siren cut off as a police cruiser tumbled up the gravel driveway.

Well, that was fast. He certainly couldn't complain about the response time. They showed up before he'd even called.

Grady ran toward the police car, waving at Todd as he stepped out of the car.

"The dogs are missing. We need to get them rounded up and put back in the barn."

The sheriff pulled a gun. "Stop right there."

What the hell?

Was he being blamed for Linx's disappearing act?

Slowly, Grady raised both hands and gaped at the sheriff. "Someone let the dogs out, but there's no sign of burglary."

"What are you doing here?" Todd's eyes narrowed over Grady. "I need to take you to the station to account for your movements."

"I came over from your father's ranch." Grady couldn't believe he was being given the third degree. "You were there."

"You left well over an hour ago." He put his gun down and gestured to his deputy. "Secure the area and call in the search party."

"Linx isn't here. I already checked," Grady said. "She took off."

"We know that," Todd said as a minivan pulled onto the driveway and Pastor and Mrs. Patterson tumbled out. "It's Jessica Patterson. She's missing."

"Jessie? Missing?" Grady jumped and felt like his insides were turned out. "What happened? Where?"

"She disappeared from church," Pastor Patterson said. "We had a festival to kick off God and Country Week. When it was over, Jessie was nowhere to be found. We questioned the other children, and they claim Jessie was talking about getting a puppy."

"Someone must have taken her from the church property with promises of a puppy." Mrs. Patterson wrung her hands and wiped a tear. "Have you seen her?"

"No, neither Jessie or the puppy are here," Grady said. "But her red bandana is caught on the chain-link fence."

More cars screeched around the corner and bounced onto the rutted dirt lane leading to the barn. It was his family joined by the Colsons.

Todd circled his hands around his lips and yelled, "Stay back. This is a crime scene. Nobody move. Jessica Patterson is missing."

Shock and consternation fell over everyone's face. Becca ran toward him and grabbed Grady, shaking him. "What did you do? Why couldn't you wait for the paternity test?"

"Just because Jessie's your daughter doesn't mean you can take her," Chad stepped forward.

"I didn't do anything. I came here to check on Linx." Grady held his hands up.

"Then Linx must have taken her." Cait sidestepped the sheriff and stood in front of Grady, as if she would protect him. "She left the ranch even before Grady did."

"What's going on here?" Pastor Patterson's booming voice knocked everyone back. "If you two did anything to hurt my daughter, I'll ..."

He cocked his fist and slammed it into Grady. "Arrest him. He kidnapped my daughter."

Bedlam broke loose and everyone shouted to be heard, as Todd snapped the handcuffs over Grady's wrists and shoved him into the patrol car.

Chapter Thirty-Five

Linx couldn't believe the text message she received from Grady promising to work things out with her. She glanced at the voice mail icon and missed call from him, but her heart couldn't take it to hear his voice, pleading for her to return.

Once he found out he was unable to gain custody of Jessie, he would regret everything about her. His only chance was for her to leave and admit her guilt. That way, he could work out a deal with the Pattersons.

Perhaps they would feel sorry for him that he'd been cheated out of having a say on the adoption.

Or maybe the court would side with him, and Grady and Jessie would live happily ever after—as long as Linx wasn't around to screw things up.

So much like her batshit crazy mother.

She had to make a clean break—no looking back. Grady deserved to have a home in Colson's Corner with his daughter. Eventually, he'd find another woman—one who wasn't nuts—to settle down with. He could take over the Mountain Dog Rescue Center, and she was sure her father would let Jessie have her horse.

They would live a good life, one they deserved, while Linx would disappear into the fire lines, fighting forest fires until the flames finally caught up to her, like they did for Salem, and she would simply disappear without a trace.

She should shut off her phone, but text messages came in fast and furious like popcorn over a hot campfire.

Cedar nuzzled her thigh and whined, wondering why they hadn't moved from the parking area.

"I need to see if Nessa will agree to take care of the rest of the dogs," Linx said. "Sorry you'll never see them again, especially little Ginger."

The tip of Cedar's tail wagged, and Linx rubbed her furry neck, knowing that she'd selfishly kept Cedar from Grady.

She scanned the messages and swallowed as she realized she'd never see her siblings and father again. They were all texting her, including Grady's sister, Cait, pleading with her to come back.

One message flashed at her like a hot branding iron on bare skin. *Call me, my daughter. I can help.*

From Minx.

Why was she texting her now, of all times?

A while ago, Becca had tracked their mother down, using her attorney skills, and had called her for Christmas. Linx hadn't wanted to say 'hi' and had run away to the artist's shed to hide out for the rest of the day.

When she'd returned, none of her siblings mentioned the phone call, and Becca had taken her phone and added Mom to the address book.

Linx had immediately changed "Mom" to "Minx" and debated deleting the number.

But every night for the next two weeks, she had instead pulled out the phone and stared at the number—never ginning up the courage to call.

Why should she?

Minx hated her.

What would she say to her?

Tips on how to elude the law?

Linx swallowed hard and closed her eyes. She should call Minx and let her know exactly how bad she was and how she'd turned out just like her.

Before she could change her mind, she hit the green call button and waited breathlessly as a woman answered.

"Hello?"

"It's Linx."

"Ah, Linx, I knew you'd call." The woman's voice was scratchy, as if she'd been chain smoking since the day she left.

"Why did you ask me to call?" Linx said. "Why now?"

"Wanted to help."

"Because I screwed up my life? I'm on the run—just like you. Are you proud of me? Happy?"

"You finally stopped pretending to be a Colson." Minx chuckled and then coughed.

"What's that supposed to mean?"

"The Colsons are goody-two-shoes. The whole lot of them. The kind of people who won the West. Brave, courageous, honest, hard-working, and do-gooders. I always knew you couldn't keep it up. What did you do now? Kill someone?"

"I, uh, no, of course not." Linx's voice trailed off. What had she expected from her mother? Apologies? Compassion? Maybe even a little motherly concern?

"Then what? Broken heart? You still chasing after that smokejumper?"

"How do you know?" Linx's body tensed, causing Cedar to jump.

"I know a lot of things, and I've been waiting for you to call."

"You have? Since when?"

"Since you refused to wish me a Merry Christmas. Now why would that be? Are you afraid of looking in the mirror? Afraid to see your ugly self?"

"I can't be as ugly as you." Linx spat, her voice deep and tight.

"Don't be so sure. I know what you're capable of, and you're no better than me. You're worse."

"At least I don't hate my own daughter."

"Who says I hate you? Has your dad been lying to you?" Minx's raspy voice scratched like fingernails on a chalkboard.

"I don't know why I called you," Linx choked on the lump in her throat, "but I'm not going to give you the satisfaction of turning out just like you."

"Oh, but it's too late. You already have. No one will ever trust you. No one will ever believe in you. You're nuts, and your heart is black just like mine. I know you stole that man's dog, and I know you stole his kid."

Linx ended the call and turned off her cell phone.

She wanted to smash it, but all the pictures she took of Jessie were on the device. Instead, she turned her SUV due north. She would pay her dues and seek redemption on the fire lines—burn her sins and herself into white ash.

Maybe that was what Salem had done to atone for her wrongdoings.

Hellfire raged all through the northwest, Canada, and Alaska, burning millions of acres and scorching the entire earth. If she could do nothing right or bring happiness to nobody, she could at least consume herself in the fiery inferno, purify her soul and redeem her pitiful self.

* * *

"You're wasting your time with me," Grady said to Todd in the interrogation room. He was flanked by the deputy who took notes, and his temporary attorney, Becca Colson. "I've given you a timeline of my whereabouts, and I did not go near the church."

"The pastor said there were a lot of tourists and visitors at the barbecue they held, and you could have easily gotten mixed up with them and lured Jessie away with promises of the puppy," Todd said.

"Objection," Becca said. "My client has told you everything he knows. You have no evidence he had anything to do with the child's disappearance."

"Other than your words, Counselor." Todd glared at his sister. "Your first words were something to the effect that he should have waited for the paternity test."

"I misspoke." Becca rolled her eyes.

"Look, I don't know what game you two are playing," Grady said. "But there's a little girl missing, and you're wasting time playing cop and lawyer. If I'm not being charged, I demand you let me go."

"He has a point," Becca said. "Linx is also missing."

"Right, I have an APB out for her and her vehicle," Todd said. "But Linx wasn't the one cleaning up the scene of the crime."

"If I were cleaning up, why did I leave Jessie's bandana on the fence?" Grady slapped his palms on the table and pushed himself back. "I'm out of here. You have something against me personally. I can't help that, but right now, we need to find Jessie and Linx. Maybe they're both in danger."

Todd groaned and palmed his forehead. "What do you think happened?"

"I don't know," Grady said. "But every minute is critical. What if Linx came back to the center and the kidnapper held her at gunpoint and made her drive off with Jessie and Ginger? Her gun is missing from her nightstand."

"Why didn't you tell me?" Todd barked, snapping to his feet.

"You were too busy arresting me to listen to me." Grady stood up to him. "Am I free to leave? I want to start the search, if you don't mind."

"We have men searching already. We're interviewing witnesses and we've put out an Amber alert." Todd huffed. "And yes, you're free to leave."

"Thanks," Grady said. "Did you send any men to the pastor's house to see if Betsy's missing?"

"Who's Betsy?" Todd asked.

"Jessie's older dog. She'd gotten lost earlier this month and I found her wandering around my parents' property after it was burned down."

"We'll check," Todd said. "Although I don't see the point. If the kidnapper nabbed her from church, he'd be stupid to go back and get the other dog."

"So, let me get this straight," Becca said. "You think the kidnapper broke into the center, took the missing puppy, and then went to the church and lured Jessie into his or her car?"

"That's the most likely scenario, now that you spell it out," Todd said, then turned to his deputy. "Any other ideas?"

"I know she's your sister," the deputy drawled. "But she could have come back to the center, taken the puppy, then opened the gates to make it seem as if there'd been a burglary, then lured Jessie into her car. It makes sense since Jessie knows and trusts her."

"Linx would never do that," Grady said hotly. "Unless the kidnapper forced her. No, she wouldn't even do it at gunpoint. She'd take the shot and tell Jessie to run."

The deputy shrugged. "Like I said, you won't like my scenario, but I think it's the most likely. Something caused your sister to crack. I don't know what it is, but the entire town knows she's Jessie's biological mom. We think the pastor's too naïve and kind-hearted to let Jessie get so close to Linx."

"My sister would never hurt that little girl," Todd said.

"Linx is not that underhanded," Becca argued. "She's friends with the Pattersons."

"Like I said, I don't know what kind of stress she's been under," the deputy said. "But you might want me to lead the investigation if you can't be objective."

"Hell no!" Todd stormed. "I'm a lawman and I'll follow the trail wherever it leads. Let's get out there and find my sister."

"She could be in grave danger," Grady warned. "Let's not pin this on her without proof. Jessie must be so scared right now. Scared and lonely. We have to find her and bring her back to her parents, and we have to work together."

Chapter Thirty-Six

While Todd and his men zoomed off with their sirens blaring to check out a lead, Grady rounded up his family at the diner to organize the search.

The atmosphere was tense as they walked in. Conversation stopped and the locals eyed them with suspicion.

Pastor Patterson and his wife sat in a booth, surrounded by a circle of church members who alternately prayed and comforted them.

Grady took a deep breath and sliced through the crowd toward them. He held out his hand and said, "Grady Hart. I'm here to help you find your daughter."

"Is it true?" Pastor Patterson said. "You're Jessie's biological father and you're suing us for custody of Jessie?"

The crowd drew in a collective breath, and an uneasy hush fell across the entire diner.

"I'm here to help find Jessie." Grady kept his hand extended. "Right now, there's a scared little girl out there, lonely and lost. I don't want to think about the monster who has his hands on her."

"We must keep praying," Mrs. Patterson blubbered, fanning herself. "Ask God to put a hedge of protection around our little Jessie."

"Mark Patterson." The pastor reluctantly shook Grady's hand. "You haven't answered my question. Are you Jessie's biological father?"

"I might be," Grady said. "But right now, we need to find her. What I want to know is where Betsy is. Is she at home or at the church, or is she also missing?"

"Betsy!" Mrs. Patterson clapped a hand on her chest. "Why, Jessie brought her to church and she was playing with the other dogs. Mark, we plumb forgot about her. Maybe she's still back at the church."

"She's not there," one of the praying church members said. "The police already came through and searched the property. Everyone took their dogs, and I thought you guys took Betsy home already."

"Damn!" Grady said. "If the dogs were there, it means they trust or know the kidnapper. Otherwise, how could he or she have pulled it off?"

"Right, I'm sure Betsy would have barked up a storm," Pastor Patterson said. "What do we do now?"

"We organize search parties," Grady said. "Let's divide the town into sectors. We go door-to-door asking residents if they saw either Jessie, Betsy, or little Ginger. We have pictures of Ginger from the website and also Betsy from when she was lost."

"Let's do it." The pastor stood and put on his suit jacket. "Everyone keep praying, but I'm going with Mr. Hart."

Grady and the pastor quickly organized his family and the congregation. Everyone was equipped with pictures of Jessie, Linx, Betsy, Cedar, and little Ginger. The pastor had ready-made maps he used for soul-winning and he passed them out to the team.

After adding their cell phone numbers to a group chat, the civilian search party spread out from the diner and headed to their assigned sector. Grady fetched Sam from Dale, who had, along with Connor and Brian, recovered all of the missing dogs by luring them with beef jerky.

"Where are we going to search?" Mark asked Grady. "I checked with the neighbors and they haven't seen Betsy either."

"I'm going to the campground and find out if anyone has seen Betsy."

"Shouldn't we look for Jessie instead of Betsy?" The pastor looked perplexed.

"The police are all looking for Jessie, but I have a hunch." Grady opened the door of his pickup and Sam jumped in. "I may be wrong, but Linx told me once that Jessie said she wanted to live with Betsy in a fairy wagon deep in the woods."

Grady started the truck and drove to the Kingman Camping Area.

They fanned out, asking campers if they'd seen Jessie, Betsy, and Ginger, but the police had already been there, and no one claimed to have seen the three of them.

"It's no use," Mark said. "I doubt the kidnapper would have taken them here with so many witnesses."

"I wish Linx had told me more," Grady said. It was getting dark, so he flicked on his flashlight. "I must be missing something."

"You think Jessie followed Betsy to a hiding place? But what about the missing puppy and the bandana on the fence?"

"That could have been left there from before, when Jessie opened all of the gates," Grady said. "But you have a point. Who opened the gates and let the dogs out, and who took the puppy?"

"Linx must have." Mark's jaw stiffened and he grabbed Grady too hard, whirling him around. "We trusted her with Jessie. Never thought she'd hurt her."

"She wouldn't." Grady pulled out his cell phone and called Linx. This time, it rolled straight to voice mail. "Dang, she's turned off her phone."

"We're not going to get anything done here," the pastor said. "I'm going to check in with the police to see if they have anything. The kidnapper could be miles away by now."

"Or right under our noses," Grady said. "I keep feeling the dogs have something to do with it."

Beside him, Sam grunted and huffed as he put his nose to the ground and sniffed.

* * *

Miles rolled by as Linx drove through the Nevada desert. The sky had darkened into dusk, and the ghostly hills on the horizon barely dented the big, black sky above.

Tears rolled down her face as the cruel words of her mother taunted her. How could she hate her so much?

From the sound of it, she also hated the Colsons—including her dad, calling them goody-two-shoes. She never imagined her mother could store up all that spite.

The Colsons were the original settlers in town and the most prominent residents. Her uncle was the mayor, and her grandfather had even been a congressman. Her family also toiled the land, built the towns, fought the fires, and operated the businesses.

She had always been proud of her family. But Mean Minx said she wasn't one of them—that she was pretending to be a Colson. What had she meant?

Linx's breath stilled inside her, hardly daring to stir as a new thought took root. Suppose she, Linx, wasn't a real Colson. Then who was she? And where had she come from?

Her heartbeat stuttered as a deer leaped across the road. She slammed on the brakes and swerved, narrowly avoiding the animal.

How did her mother know about Grady and the dog unless she'd been spying on her? Or maybe one of her siblings spoke to her and told her everything?

Or, maybe she was the one who burned down the cabin and left the railroad spike cross to taunt her. But why hurt Grady when it was she her mother hated?

Duh, of course. Minx must have figured out that Linx loved Grady.

Cedar whined and Linx realized she hadn't fed the dog or taken her on a bathroom break. It would be miles before another exit, so she pulled to the side of the road and led Cedar onto barren landscape.

"Sorry, girl. I need to find food, too. Kind of skipped dinner." She stared up at the rising moon and the distant stars while large semis whooshed by.

Linx leaned against her SUV as a wave of exhaustion and fatigue pressed down on her. Her mother's words washed over her. *No one will ever trust you. No one will ever believe in you.*

"No one will ever love me," Linx spoke the omen aloud. "Because I turned out just like you."

Cedar finished her business and rubbed her nose against Linx's hand.

"You're kind of stuck with me, aren't you?" Linx bent down and let her lick her face. "I wonder how Ginger's doing. I hope Nessa found someone to feed her. Crap. I am just like Minx. I abandoned all my dogs except for you."

Worry hovered at the edge of her mind. Poor little Ginger could be starving and crying for food, and here she was with another hungry dog out in the middle of the desert.

Meanwhile, if her mother was lurking around her cabin, she could be planning her next step to hurt those Linx loved: Ginger, the dogs, Jessie, and of course, Grady.

Cedar nosed her and nudged her, licking her hand, and a fury of anger boiled inside her gut.

She wasn't going to be like her mother.

She was a Colson like her father.

A hard-working, honest, loyal, and brave frontier-woman. She had a heritage—a proud one, and she was just as courageous as the strong women who tamed the wilderness.

And most of all, she was not Mean Minx.

She would face her problems head on and stand her ground. Like red, white, and blue, her colors didn't run.

She had to go back.

Linx turned on her phone and it chimed continuously with a stream of messages. Her eyes zeroed in on Grady's.

If he needed her to testify that she had lied to the court, she would. She would pay for her mistakes, but she would never, ever run again.

Her phone rang and she answered it.

"Linx!" Grady's voice snapped her from her stupor. "Is Jessie with you? We're all looking for her."

"Wait, what? Jessie?" Every nerve ending pinched and fired at the same time. "What happened?"

"She's missing. We can't find her. I'm with her dad, searching the campgrounds. Didn't you say something about her and Betsy running away together?" Grady's voice tumbled, out almost incoherent.

"You mean she ran away?" Linx's heart jolted against her ribcage. "Did you call the police?"

"The police are looking for her. Ginger's also missing. Did you go to the center after leaving your father's house?"

"No, I'm in Nevada. What's this about Jessie? It's getting dark," Linx wailed. "I have to come back and help find her."

"You said something about Jessie and castles in the mountain, caves or something?"

"She talks about fairy wagons," Linx said. "Gypsy wagons with stars and moons. She has a great imagination, but it's all a fantasy world. She doesn't know any real gypsies."

"But she likes to wander off," Grady said.

"She knows her way around town and usually pops in at the center," Linx said. "But not this late. What if it's worse? What if someone kidnapped her?"

"That's what we're afraid of," Grady said. "You have to come back."

In the background, she heard other male voices.

"Mark wants to talk to you," Grady said. "I'll hand you over."

"Okay." Linx waited, her pulse surging in every artery until Mark got on the line. "Mark? What happened to Jessie? I'm really worried."

"You don't have her? Is she in the back of your SUV? Anywhere?"

"I didn't see her, but I can check," Linx said. "Cedar's with me. She would have alerted."

Linx opened her tailgate and peered inside. There was no sign of anyone.

"No one here. I'm really getting worried."

"Did Jessie ever tell you where the fairy wagons are?" Mark asked.

"No, but it's a make-believe world. She tells me stories and we add to it together."

"Humor me," Mark said. "Where does she say these wagons are?"

"In the deep, dark woods, so far away that no one can find the way. She has a nice fairy godmother who gives her sweet cookies. Her hair looks like spider legs, and she wears a dress made of colorful ribbons. I thought it was her imagination." Linx's voice trailed off. "What if it's one of the transient people who hang out at the campground?"

"That's what we're afraid of," Pastor Mark said. "I'll pass this information to your brother."

"I have to get back and help find her."

"If you think of something, let us know," Mark said. "By the way, I need to ask you something. Jean and I are very upset you didn't tell us."

"Tell you what?"

"Is Grady Hart Jessie's biological father?" The pastor sounded stern and accusing. "How come you told us you didn't know who he was? How could you have let us adopt Jessie without consent of the father?"

"I'm sorry. I lied, but I'll make up for it. I'll do anything you want," Linx pleaded, her heart wrung out and dry. "But please, don't take it out on Grady. He deserves to know the truth, and he'll be wonderful with Jessie. You can ban me for the rest of my life, but don't take her away from Grady. Don't."

"We can talk about this later. After we find Jessie."

Chapter Thirty-Seven

Linx jumped back in her Durango and did an illegal move. She pulled onto the road and swerved across the grassy divider, zooming back the way she came.

This couldn't be happening. Jessie. How could she be missing? Where had she gone? Who could have taken her?

More importantly, where would they hide her? Was there an evil person living in the campground they didn't know about?

What if it were her mother?

Where would she hide?

Certainly not at a campground—that was for sure. It was too public and she would encounter too many people. She hated people. After all, that was why she left her huge family, wasn't it?

Think. Think. Think.

A while later, Linx tore up the backroads, taking a shortcut to her father's large spread of land. The wilderness had reclaimed portions of the former farm, and there was plenty of pastures and fields lying fallow.

She pulled open a rusty gate and bounced over the old rutted roads, passing storage sheds, broken down barns, and the ramshackle cabins where farm and ranch hands had lived in centuries past.

The road ended in an overgrown paddock, so Linx hiked the rest of the way with Cedar trotting at her side. She swung a steady arc with her flashlight, looking for a campsite.

Cedar bounded ahead and stopped in front of a fence post, sniffing it with interest. Had another dog been by to mark his territory?

Linx arced the light from the fence post to the rocky area in front of an abandoned shed. Her flashlight flickered. A damp wind whistled, wrapping around her while the sounds of the night, chirping and croaking, added to her uneasiness.

She stumbled on a rock and landed on her rump. When she brought up her hand, she smelled soot and ashes.

A campfire, and one that had been recently used.

Linx shone the dimming flashlight around and spotted tire ruts.

Someone, whether it was her mother or another vagrant, had been camping on the backlot of her father's ranch.

She crept toward an abandoned storage shed and tripped over something round and metallic. In the dying light of her flashlight, she saw an acetylene tank—the type used for welding.

The flashlight went dark, and Cedar emitted a low growl. Linx froze, waiting for her eyes to adjust to the dark. Someone or something could be hidden in the storage shed.

An owl hooted and a soft flutter of wings whooshed by her as she pried open the rusted hasp. Beside her, Cedar was tense, her head down in a guarded position.

Linx pulled back the creaky door, hoping against hope she wasn't too late and at the same time afraid of what she might find.

She woke up the phone and flashed its light inside the shed. Gasping and jumping out of her skin, she clapped a hand over her mouth.

Bones. White, bleached bones hung from the rafters, some were tangled up with wires, and other pieces stuck through twisted pieces of metal. A large welded cross stood against the wall, ornamented with dry bones held in place with barbed wire.

Linx's first instinct was to turn tail and run, but she had to be brave. If Jessie were somehow hidden here, she would never be able to forgive herself if she didn't find her.

Taking a deep breath, she stepped into the shed, forcing herself to look at each hideous sculpture.

* * *

"There's an artist's cabin on the property," Grady said to Pastor Mark as they got into his truck with Sam. "Linx's sister said she went there to hide when she was little."

"But we're looking for Jessie, not Linx," Mark said. He glanced at his cell phone. "We're coming up empty everywhere we look."

"Tell me more about Jessie. Is she always disappearing like Linx used to?" Grady asked.

"I wouldn't call it disappearing," the pastor said. "She likes to wander around the town. We know everyone and didn't believe we needed to keep her confined the way parents in the city do. Everyone knows everyone, and Jessie likes visiting people she knows."

"Except there are tourists and outsiders at the campgrounds." Grady's jaw tightened. "How could you let a five-year-old wander around by herself?"

"Don't start." The pastor huffed. "As I said, this is a very safe place. We go door-knocking at all the houses in town, and everyone knows Jessie. We look out for each other here."

"Except no one knows where Jessie is," Grady said. He checked the group message. "Tell me about this fairy godmother Linx says she talks about."

"She's never told us about any of her imaginary friends," Mark said. "Anyway, we're wasting our time. Let me call the sheriff and see what he's come up with."

"You do that, and I'll call Linx." Grady told his phone to call Linx.

"Anything?" she asked as soon as she picked up.

"No, nothing. We've gone over the entire campground. How about you? Where are you?"

"I found a storage shed full of bones and twisted metal. I'm really scared."

"Where?"

"Eastern side of the creek where the ranch hands used to live, but she's not there. I found a recent campfire."

"Wait, you say bones? What kind of bones?" Grady's scalp prickled with chills.

"Bones used as artwork. I don't know what kind."

"You stay safe," Grady said. "I saw burned bones, and I tripped over crosses made from railroad spikes at the artist's cabin. You know where that is?"

"Sure, it's down the creek from here. Want to meet me there?"

"You know what I think, don't you?"

"Yes, my mother might be involved. I'm really scared," Linx said. "What if she's taking revenge on us?"

Mark tapped Grady. "Hey, shouldn't we tell the sheriff?"

"Linx, you stay put. We're on our way." To Mark, he said. "She's headed to the artist's cabin, and yes, we should let Todd know."

Mark spoke to Todd and nodded. "He knows where it is. He says to meet him at the gate."

"Linx, don't go anywhere. We're on our way," Grady said.

Mark tapped his shoulder. "Ask her about the fairy godmother."

"Jessie says she has a fairy godmother and a gypsy wagon," Grady said to Linx. "Do you think it could be your mother?"

"That's what I'm afraid of. Should I call her? I don't want to tip her off."

"Wait, you can call her? The police might be able to lock in on her if you talk to her." Grady motioned for Mark to listen in. "Go ahead, Linx, call your mother and talk to her as long as you can."

"Sure, I will," Linx agreed. "I'll keep her on the line as long as it takes to trace her."

Mark relayed the information to Todd, as Grady sped the truck down the steep, winding road, racing his heart around the turns.

Please, please, please don't let them be too late.

Chapter Thirty-Eight

Every minute counted and Linx needed to find Jessie. There was nothing in the shed, but a bunch of dried bones and twisted metal, and waiting around for Grady and Todd would cost precious time.

Nope, she'd investigate all of the other hiding places she used to visit while running away as a kid. Meanwhile, she'd call her mother and keep her on the line. Posing as a fairy was exactly the type of crazy thing Mean Minx would do—but it was still hard to believe she would hurt a little girl.

Then again, she'd hurt her own daughter that Christmas day when she flew into a rage over the red dress.

Linx swallowed the unwelcome memories and concentrated on navigating her SUV through the dark and rutted field.

Even though the going was rough, she put her phone on speaker and called Minx.

"It's you again," her mother said without preamble.

"Yes, it is," Linx said.

"What do you want?"

"Where are you?" Linx forced out the next word. "Mom?"

The rough voice cackled on the other end. "Too late to be calling me Mom, isn't it?"

"Stop playing games," Linx said. "I want to see you. It's important."

"Why would you want to see me? You never wanted to speak to me before."

"I miss you and want to know all about you." Linx strained to hear if there was any background noise—anything that would give her an idea of whether Jessie and Ginger were with her.

"You finally decided to miss me. What happened, you out of money?" Minx mocked.

"Tell me about your travels. Where do you hang out when you're not in California?"

"You're awfully nosy." Minx coughed. "Don't you have a fire to fight? Oh, I forgot, you quit. Always were a quitter."

"I had a good reason to quit," Linx said. She jerked the wheel as a tree branch swatted her windshield.

"Ah yes, you couldn't even get a man to marry you while pregnant. But then, you didn't try hard enough."

Typical. All Minx ever did was hurl insults and bile. But it had toughened her, and Linx didn't mind hitting her back.

"At least I didn't walk out on my kid," she spat. "I gave her to responsible people."

"They're so responsible they let her wander around unsupervised." The dry voice cackled. "While they're busy saving souls. Honestly, you had a good thing going, but you blew it, as usual."

"What good thing? I was young, pregnant, with no role model on how to be a mother, thanks to you."

"You were stupid. You could have held onto your baby and used her for leverage." The rough, smoker's voice huffed while coughing. "But I've fixed things for you."

"Fixed things? How?"

"Meet me at Grady's trailer, and I'll show you."

Linx's heart pounded full of rocks. Grady's trailer? Why would she lurk over there?

Was she a distraction from the search for Jessie or did she know something? What to do, what to do?

Keep her on the line, but what if this were a wild goose chase? Why would her mother have anything to do with Jessie?

"Sure, what are you doing there?" she challenged Minx. "I don't think Grady's there. What do you mean fixed things for me?"

"You and Grady. You're made for each other, except you did something really stupid. You gave his baby to those Bible thumpers."

"So?" Linx's stomach crunched into her spinal cord. These were only words. They'd long ago lost their ability to hurt her. She had to keep her mother talking, no matter what. "They were a good and stable family. They could give her a better life."

"Except Grady never gave consent. He'll grow to hate you."

"Maybe he will, but what's it to you? How do you know all this? Who've you been talking to?"

The reply was another long bout of coughing and chuckling.

"I can fix everything for you and give you everything you want. How's that for motherly love?"

"I don't need your kind of love. Tell me what you did. Is it Jessie? Did you kidnap her?" Linx finally navigated off her father's land and turned her SUV up the grade toward Grady's cabin.

"I fixed your biggest regret. That's what mothers do. All you have to do is receive my gift."

"No, Minx, don't tell me you did this. Please, let her go. Don't hurt her. Don't."

"It's a big surprise, you'll see."

"I don't like surprises, Mom," Linx said, needing to keep the conversation going. "Not after you ruined that red dress I got for Christmas. After that, no more surprises."

"Okay, no surprises, you just show up at Grady's trailer and it's all yours."

"If you've hurt Jessie, I'll never forgive you. Ever."

"Nuh, uh, uh. No getting the surprise out of me," her mother admonished. "I've got to be going. See you soon."

"Wait, don't hang up." Linx gritted her teeth as a plume of sweat dampened her forehead. "Mom, I just want to talk to you. I want to get to know you."

"You don't need to know anything about me."

"Who's my father?" The words slipped from her mouth. "You said I wasn't really a Colson."

"I was playing with you, girl." The older woman cackled. "Just joking with you."

"It's not funny."

"Ha, ha, ha. How far away are you from Grady's place?"

"I don't know, Mom. I'm coming from the ranch where I found your collection of bones and spikes. Whose bones are they? Animal or human?"

"What does your dark and evil heart tell you?"

"Whatever your dark and evil heart says," Linx replied. She marveled at how calm she was, but she needed to keep Minx on the line. Unfortunately, keeping her on the line also meant she couldn't call Todd, unless she could somehow put her on hold without her knowing, and she could three-way conference him in. "Mom, tell me a bedtime story, will you? A long one, so I can concentrate on driving without falling asleep. I can't wait for your surprise."

"Have I told you the one about the Black Widow and The Firestarter?" Minx cleared her throat. "Guaranteed nightmares."

"Oh, goodie," Linx encouraged.

"Yes, goodie," Minx said. "You always liked fire. You played with matches. You burned noodles on the gas fire. You even blackened my steak knives. Oh, but you were a real firebug."

"Yes, Mom, I was, so tell me about the Firestarter and the Black Widow."

"It was your favorite."

Once her mother started the story, she put her on hold quickly and called Todd. "I've got Mom on the line. She says she has a surprise for me at Grady's plot of land. She says she's going to fix my biggest mistake. I think she has Jessie and she's holding her there. I'm staying on the line so you can track her."

"Good, let me call the phone company and see if they can get a GPS location for her. Don't go to Grady's place, no matter what. She could be dangerous."

"But, if Jessie's there."

"I'll send a squad car, you don't know if she's luring you into a trap. My guys have been up there already and the area was clear. Now, patch me into the three-way and I'll mute my phone so she can't hear me."

"Good idea, ready?"

"Go ahead."

Linx waited one second and patched Todd's call into a three-way conference.

"Linx, where were you? I just got to the good part," Minx said.

"Sorry, I got lost and had to check my GPS. Took a wrong turn off Dad's property."

"It's dark out there. Clouds hiding the moon. Now pay attention, the fire's about to start. She wants to fry the Black Widow, not knowing she's her mother."

"Oh ..." Linx said to keep her going. "Really?"

"Yes, so pay attention." Once again, her mother's voice droned, rough and crackly, but also dark and spooky, as she continued the very odd tale.

Linx concentrated on driving, almost missing a turn, but fortunately, her obsession with Grady meant she could get to his place blindfolded. Moments later, she pulled her SUV up the steep incline of his driveway, scattering gravel as Cedar jumped up and craned her head out the window.

Smoke and an orange glow reared their ugly faces as she turned into the clearing.

The logs assembled around the cabin were on fire.

"Mom, get out of the fire!" Linx jumped from the SUV as Cedar rushed toward the trailer.

The fire jumped and sparked from log pile to pile, and the grass caught fire near the trailer.

Cedar lunged against the trailer door, barking like she sensed someone was inside. Linx sprinted after her, but the door was locked. She jiggled it desperately.

Why wasn't it opening? She'd wiggled it open before with a credit card.

"Anyone in there?" Linx pounded on the door. "Mom, get the hell out of there. Open up. Open up."

A child's piercing scream shrieked on the other side.

"Jessie, open the door," Linx shouted.

But the child kept screaming and screaming. In between the screams, a puppy howled and little claws scratched at the bottom of the door.

Either Jessie couldn't reach the door, or she was tied up, or frightened out of her wits. If Minx was there, she wasn't answering.

Linx tried the lock again, then realized it was shiny new. Grady had replaced it after she'd broken in last time!

Crap. What now?

Linx turned as Cedar yelped, disappearing through the flames toward the creek. Hopefully she'd get to safety, but Linx couldn't worry about her. She had to get back to her car and get a credit card to jimmy the lock.

Heat seared behind her, and as she turned toward the Durango, a wall of flames blocked her way.

"Grady!" she shouted. "You better have your stash."

Linx always kept her firefighting tools: her axe, shovel, Pulaski, and even a chain saw close by her cabin. Every wilderness firefighter did that—one set in the truck and another right outside the living quarters.

She pulled at the storage compartments outside the trailer. No firefighter locked up firefighting tools. Ever.

The outside hatch opened and Linx grabbed a shovel. She had to throw dirt on the advancing fire before it reached the trailer.

Coughing from the smoke, she hit the ground with the shovel, throwing up as much dirt as she could. Unfortunately, the ground was hard and she wasn't making progress fast enough. The fire licked around toward the back of the trailer where it was parked against a screen of bushes.

"Not a good spot, Grady."

Grabbing a flame retardant jacket, she slapped it over the grass, putting out one hotspot only to have another one flare up. If the fire spread to the bushes and trees, it would surround the trailer.

She could use the chainsaw and level the bushes, then dig a trench and create a firebreak, but she was one person and she didn't have time.

The smoke was already thick and her eyes stung. She couldn't catch her breath, and her throat was raw with coughing, so she put on the flame retardant jacket to cover herself.

There was no time to put out the fire. Only time to get the girl out. She had to break the lock.

She was going in.

The Pulaski was the ultimate wilderness firefighting tool. It had an axe head on one side and a sickle-shaped mattock on the other side, useful for prying and digging.

"Stand back," she yelled, although she was sure the puppy wouldn't understand.

Swinging the axe side, she chopped at the door, keeping her blows high and away from any little bodies on the other side. Once she cracked the door, she turned the tool to the mattock side and wedged the digging edge into the crack.

She ripped the door out and a little ball of fur wiggled into her arms.

"Jessie, Jessie!" Linx screamed as she felt inside the dark trailer.

The puppy squealed and barked, then wiggled into the trailer, leading the way.

Linx stumbled toward the bed over the fifth wheel and climbed into the loft.

A limp body, still warm, lay still on the mattress.

"Jessie!" Linx scooped the girl over her shoulder with one arm and picked up the fur ball with the other. She tucked Ginger into her jacket and zipped it, then stepped from the trailer into a mountain of fire towering over her, snapping, cracking and popping up the pine tree above her.

They were about to be overrun.

Chapter Thirty-Nine

"They're headed to your piece of land," Pastor Mark shouted as he got off the phone with Todd. "He says Linx got in touch with her mother who hinted that Jessie is there, that she solved her biggest regret."

"On it." Grady did a U-turn in the middle of a hairpin turn. He swerved and wrestled with the steering wheel and the truck tilted onto the soft shoulder overlooking the side of a sheer cliff.

Pastor Mark lunged to the left, smashing into his body and throwing Sam across his lap, and the truck righted itself. As soon as the wheels touched solid road, Grady gunned the engine and made for his plot of land.

"Can we patch Todd in? Keep him on the line?" Grady asked.

"Sure, let me try. I shouldn't have hung up," Mark said, fiddling with his phone. "Will we have a signal up there?"

"Thank God, yes," Grady said. "They just finished the tower a month ago."

He'd been pissed off at the time, knowing that a new tower meant more people moving into the hills, but progress was inevitable, and now he was thanking God for the signal.

"I have to take a shortcut. Be ready for a rough ride," Grady said, as he put his truck in four-wheel-drive and crashed through a set of wooden gates guarding the backside of his property.

It would take too long for him to wind around the mountain to the front, and hopefully, he could follow the creek up and climb the steep grade to the pad where the trailer was parked.

"Got patched in," Mark said. "I muted our mic, so she can't hear us. Todd's going to be silent, too."

"Who's that freaky woman?" Grady's eardrums prickled at the scratchy tone. "She sounds familiar, sort of."

"You know Linx's mother?"

Grady shook his head. "No, but the accent, that spooky, clipped way of speaking ... Never mind. I'm hearing things. Why's she telling Linx about a Black Widow?"

Every so often, he heard Linx make random comments designed to keep the other woman talking. His heart swelled at how brave she was, and how much abuse she was taking to keep the witch on the line.

A car door slammed and the last words from Linx were, "Mom, get out of the fire," followed by excited barking.

"Fire?" Pastor Mark barked. "There's a fire up there!"

"Here, take my phone and call the fire department." Grady opened the glove box.

The roar of a crackling wildfire could be heard over the speaker, followed by cackling laughter.

"Fooled you," Minx said gleefully. "I'm not in the fire, girl. I'm not even your mother. Fooled you good."

"Who is that?" Mark shouted. "I'm turning on the speaker and talking to her."

"No, don't," Grady said. "We need her to incriminate herself. Let her gloat."

The laughter continued, but since Linx wasn't answering back, there was a really good chance Minx would hang up.

Mark lowered his head and prayed. "Heavenly Father, protect our Jessie and Linx. Put your hand on them and keep them safe, and don't let this deranged woman get away. Keep Jessie and Linx under your tender and merciful wings, and be a tower of strength against our enemies. Let the authorities catch this woman and bring her to justice. And please, don't let anyone get hurt tonight. In Jesus' name, amen."

Grady splashed through the creek and caught sight of an animal. He swerved, narrowly avoiding it, but the animal jumped and threw itself against his door.

He braked hard and Sam started barking. Grady stared at the muzzle pressed against the window.

"Cedar," he shouted, opening the door.

The large dog had a panicked look in her eyes, and instead of jumping into the cab, she tore away down the creek.

"Oh, God, oh, God," Grady prayed. "Let Linx and Jessie be okay. Let Linx be okay."

He shifted to low gear to get the truck out of the muck and lumbered up the banks of the shallow creek. Up ahead, the hot orange glow of a raging fire blocked his way. He got as close as he could to the fire before cutting the engine.

"Help me get this pump into the water," Grady said to Mark. "Then stay back here with the dogs."

"If my little girl's in there, I'm not staying back," Mark said.

"We don't know if she's there, we just know there's a fire and Linx is there," Grady shouted as he opened the tailgate and uncovered his portable pump.

"Tell me what to do," Mark said, helping him drag the pump into position.

"Okay," Grady said. "Stay here and man the pump. Make sure the intake hose is covered with water."

Grady attached the discharge hose and unrolled it as far as it could go.

"Fire her up!" he shouted, and the pastor pulled the line to turn on the gasoline-powered water pump.

The fuel around his cabin site had burned itself out—all the logs he'd gathered and the building materials had fed the flames, but now, the fire raged in the vicinity of his trailer.

He couldn't see clearly through the smoke, as he charged up the hill from the creek, stretching the hose to the max.

The pine tree above the trailer snapped with fire, and a shower of flames fell onto the trailer, engulfing it. Grady aimed the water at the trailer as fire hissed and popped.

He tried to douse the trailer, but couldn't keep a steady stream. The creek wasn't deep enough and Mark wasn't able to hold the intake hose low to grab enough water.

Grady swept what water he had on the trailer, but the fire was too strong and his hose ran dry, sputtering little more than a garden hose. The fire had burned through the hose, and since he didn't have a team to cover the hose line with sand, he was out of luck.

The fire-fueled wind whipped over the trailer and consumed bushes and trees around it, throwing embers and sparks. Flashes of light blinded Grady, and he lost sight of the trailer as the pine tree exploded overhead.

Through the eerie light and thick smoke, his eyes burned. He couldn't stop staring as the metal on his trailer twisted and crumpled. The fire found new fuel as it consumed the trees and bushes surrounding the trailer. With a wicked roar, it sprang up to the night sky as it overran the entire trailer and headed down the hill toward the driveway.

* * *

Blinded by thick smoke, Linx scrambled for the thin aluminum-covered fire shelter every wildland firefighter had for emergency situations. They were one-man cocoons that lay low on the forest floor and provided last ditch protection.

Grady had one, and fortunately, she had pulled it clear of the trailer when she found his tools.

The ground underneath the pine tree was littered with flammable needles and would bake them alive. But they had no time to find the perfect area.

Stumbling blindly away from the fire, she crashed through a row of dry bushes toward the driveway. The flames were gaining on her and Jessie was in a panicked state, hyperventilating in the smoke.

She stumbled down an embankment into a sandy area and set Jessie, who was mewing and crying, onto the ground with Ginger. "Hold the puppy. Head down and don't look up," she snapped sternly as she pulled off the protective covering and grabbed the two tabs.

Coughing from the smoke, she shook out the shelter to its full-length tube shape and covered Jessie with her body, tucking all three of them in before looping her arms around the hold down straps.

"Breathe into the dirt and don't look up. No matter what." She knew she was squishing Jessie, but it didn't matter. The closer to the ground the better. Even inside a shelter, she could still get smoke inhalation. She had to get down as low as possible, especially if the fire burned through the protective layer.

Jessie snuffled and cried, "I want my mommy. I want my mommy."

The roar of the flames crashed over them, and heat rose inside the shelter. Linx's hands blistered as she held onto the straps, fighting the wind that ripped at the shelter.

Please God. Please God. Linx prayed, not knowing what to say. The shelter was supposed to be good for an hour, but at the same time, nothing was truly invulnerable to the fire. Tears rolled down her eyes as she thought about the members of her crew who'd died when a fire overtook them.

She sucked in dirt from the ground, keeping herself frozen as the fire surged over them. She was going to die. She was going to die with her precious daughter. How long should she stay in here? Slowly shaking and baking to a crisp.

Pressing Jessie down, she could be suffocating her, but she couldn't let her take a breath of the hot air that would immediately sear her lungs. As for the puppy, she was probably smothered, as there was not a sound or a squeak.

Flame front after flame front hit them, gusting and ripping at the shelter. The noise was deafening, whooshing over and around them. Pinecones popped and trees snapped as debris tumbled over the shelter, thrown and tossed by the fierce and unrelenting firestorm.

She buried her face into the sandy dirt until she thought she'd pass out. Her sweat ran dry as heat baked and fried around them, and the fire roared over them like a steamrolling freight train. She lost track of time, her arms and hands frozen in place, tight to hold down what was left of the sweltering shelter.

"I love you, Jessie," she muttered into the dirt. "I love you like a mother. Like a real mother. I love you."

The little girl sniffled. "Mommy, Daddy, Mommy, Daddy, Betsy."

"Grady, Jessie, Grady, Jessie, Grady," Linx whispered, losing hold of her mind. Pain covered her entire being, and she couldn't tell where the fire ended and where she began. All she knew was she had to protect Jessie. Had to cover her. Couldn't let her go. "Jessie, Jessie, live, Jessie, live. Live. Live. Live for your mommy and daddy and Betsy."

Chapter Forty

Sirens cut through the roar of the fire, and horns blared as a pumper truck groaned its way up the driveway.

Grady burst through the fiery bushes and shouted, "The trailer burned down. We can't find Linx and Jessie."

He knew he was delirious, but it didn't stop him from grabbing an ax. He would starve this fire if it was the last thing he did.

A tanker truck scrambled up the hill, and Connor, Brian, and Larry flung themselves out. They grabbed fire gear from the storage compartments as the Colson's Corner crew connected the hoses.

"We've a pump down by the creek, but the water stopped," Grady shouted.

"Got it. Let us put out the fire," the chief commanded. "You guys search for survivors."

"Flashlights," Mark shouted. "Give us flashlights."

The firefighters held the flames at bay with water, while Grady and his brothers dug a fire line, keeping the fire from spreading down the hill.

The burned ground was hot, and Grady felt the heat blistering the soles of his feet, but he ran toward the remains of his trailer.

"Linx! Linx! Can you hear me?" he shouted. "Linx!"

"We don't even know if she's here," Mark put a hand on his shoulder. "I just got a call from Todd, he's got a lock on her mom, and it isn't here."

"But Cedar's here. Linx's Durango's right over there."

"Her mother might have taken them hostage and set the fire as a distraction," Mark said, dragging Grady back to the clearing where the fire engines were assembled. "Todd said he'll have more intel when he moves in. They've surrounded the van with a SWAT team. Let's get going."

"Get out of my way. I'm standing my ground here." Grady charged the fire line and chopped at the trees, trying to deprive them of fuel. Meanwhile, the pumps cranked up and fed a steady stream of water at the remaining flames. Little by little, they beat back the fire until it was reduced to steaming embers.

"The fire's out," the fire chief said. "If you want to help with mop up, be my guest. There's nothing here but that burned out trailer. If they're here, it'll take us some time to open it up after it cools down."

"They're not there," Mark said. "God promised to protect them. Let's go back to town and wait for the sheriff."

"You go ahead," Grady said, stiffening every muscle in his body. "I'll stay here to mop up and keep searching."

"You okay?" Dale put a hand on his shoulder. "You know Linx is a tough one. She's probably hiking down the hill right now."

"No, Cedar was still here." Grady yanked his gaze around, looking for the two dogs. He'd lost track of Sam, too. "She would never leave without her."

"Animals are afraid of fire," Dale said. "The dogs are probably hiding somewhere. Maybe with Linx."

"Then I'll find her, if that's the last thing I do." Grady grabbed a flashlight. "Give me a canteen of water and a first aid kit."

"Sure, take some boots and gear," the firefighters offered.

Grady changed out of his singed clothes, noticing for the first time how he was almost naked. He slipped his blistered feet into the boots and donned the protective pants and jacket. They gave him a helmet with a searchlight attached and packed supplies into a backpack.

"I'm staying with you," Dale said, putting on a jacket and grabbing the first aid kit.

"Thanks, bro," Grady said.

"We're staying, too," Connor, Larry, and Brian said. "We can take over the cleanup and if she's here, we'll find her."

The rest of the vehicles pulled away and Grady and his brothers and brothers-in-law spread out, each with a beacon of light, looking over the piles of smoldering wood and rising steam.

"Linx! Linx!" Grady shouted until his throat was raw. He followed the ridge to the remains of his trailer and focused his beam on a shovel blade.

She had to have been here. That shovel didn't pop up from nowhere. At the back of the trailer, he found the metal tip of a Pulaski. The door was hanging off the hinges, allowing Grady to shine his light.

"Linx? Linx!" The metal was still too hot to touch.

He went back to the Pulaski and shovel.

If Linx were fighting the fire, she definitely would not have stayed inside the trailer. She knew how dangerous it would be to be high up off the ground when a fire overshot her position. One of the chiefs had died when he tried to shelter himself in the cab of his fire truck.

However, if she'd gotten into his supplies, she could have found the fire shelter.

Grady pointed the beam of the flashlight at his storage bin. It had been opened.

His heart drove him forward as he scanned the ground for a lower depression away from the pine trees and their flammable needles.

A ledge of rocks led down to a hollow where he had planned on building a carport. He'd cleared the bushes and laid down a bed of sand, but hadn't gotten around to putting in asphalt.

Grady slid down from the rock face and almost fell onto a blackened tarp—a burnt fire shelter that was charred to a crisp.

"Linx!" he screamed and pulled at the shelter with his gloved hands. It was still hot to the touch and he dreaded what he'd find.

A woman's body lay face down, still holding tight to the straps. She could be dead already, with rigor mortis setting in, and she wasn't letting go of the hold-down straps.

Grady ripped what was left of the shelter from her and wrapped his arms around her, moving her from the ground. "Linx, say something. Say something, Linx. Tell me I'm an ass. Tell me to get lost, but say something."

"Mommy, Daddy, Linx, Grady, Mommy, Daddy, Ginger, Betsy," a small voice was muffled underneath Linx's stiff, but still hot body.

"Woooo!" another small voice howled and sneezed.

Grady moved Linx aside and looked straight into the eyes of Jessie.

"I want my mommy and daddy," the little girl cried as tiny paws scrabbled out from her side and a little dog barked, her voice raw and dry.

"Oh, Jessie, you're safe." Grady hugged her tight. "You're safe, and your mommy and daddy are coming right now."

"But what about Miss Linx?" Jessie rolled over and shook Linx's body. "Miss Linx is also my mommy. I asked God and He says it's true. God won't let my mommy die, will He?"

"No, He won't." Tears rolled down Grady's face as he cradled Linx's blistered face, shaking her. "Wake up. Wake up, my love. God knows I love you."

She sputtered and coughed, then gasped. Her arms clenched tight as if still holding onto the straps of the fire shelter. "Is Jessie okay? Is Jessie going to live?"

"Yes, Jessie's okay, but you don't look so good," Grady said. He fumbled with the canteen to get water into her cracked and raw lips.

"I'm dead, aren't I? I burned to death so Jessie can live." Her eyes rolled back and she passed out, relaxing her hold on him.

* * *

If she died, she most certainly had gone to Hell.

Linx was stuck in a forever loop of fire. Her body was ablaze and every nerve ending stabbed her with excruciating pain. She was trapped in the fire shelter, fighting to keep it over her and Jessie, while voices in her head told her to let go. To let it all fly away and run, run, run.

She flung the shelter from her shoulders and stood up, leaving Jessie and the puppy. Raising her arms, she took a hot breath and sprinted down the hill, her skin melting. Pain chased her, and a whoosh of white heat seared into her lungs, burning her from the inside out while evil, orange sparks charred her to the core of her bones.

"Jesus, save me, please," she gasped as fiery tongues scraped her skin off and set her blood boiling. "I'm a sinner, but save me, please. I believe you. I trust you."

But it was too late.

Why hadn't she listened to Pastor Mark? Why hadn't she gone forward to have her sins washed away? Why had she held back while Miss Jean had pleaded with her to receive Christ as her Saviour? Why?

Because she still held evil in her heart. Evil and vengeance against Grady Hart.

She didn't deserve Heaven, and now, she was doomed to forever in Hell.

"Jesus, please, give me a chance," Linx screamed. "God, forgive me. Give me another chance."

There was no answer. Only the throbbing pulse of fire stinging and consuming her, and yet, somehow, not killing her. Pain, pain, all around her, forever and ever, like the Bible had promised.

There would be no second chance, no matter how hard she prayed. There was no redemption from doing good works, no free pass because she'd saved Jessie.

She'd died in her sins, and not even the tears bathing her face could cool the everlasting agony.

"God, forgive Grady, please, save him before it's too late. Forgive me, too, even though I'm too late. I didn't know what I was doing. I. Didn't. Know. What. I. Was. Doing."

"She's coming out of the anesthesia," a disembodied voice hovered above her. "Put her in the recovery room, but require all visitors to wear gowns. One visitor at a time."

"Yes, doctor," a female voice said. "Her fiancé's going to be very happy. He hasn't left the hospital."

"It's going to be a long road for her," the first voice said. "But at least she has family, unlike the other one."

"Right, they should lock her up and throw away the key," the female said.

Linx didn't know up from down as she lay on a bed of nails, with pain prickling from her every pore.

"Juh ..., Jess ..., siee," she mumbled, her heart rate jumpy. All she remembered was the fire and Jessie.

A while later, a nurse told her she was in the recovery room and that she had a visitor.

"Linx, it's me, Grady," a rough, male voice cleared his throat. "Can you hear me?"

"Juh ..." Nothing came out of her dried throat, and everything hurt when she moved her mouth.

"Here, have a sip of water." A straw appeared at her lips, and she sucked in as cool, refreshing liquid soothed her insides.

"Where's Jessie?" she croaked, surprised at how raw her voice sounded.

"She's safe, thanks to you," Grady said. "Jessie and Ginger are fine. No burns, minor smoke inhalation. It's a miracle, but you protected them."

"No burns at all?" She struggled to turn her head, but pain shot through her entire back.

"None, whatsoever. Not even first degree. Pastor and Mrs. Patterson are so grateful. You're truly Jessie's Wonder Woman." His voice came from somewhere above her.

"Is she here?" She wondered why all she saw was the white clouds below her. "I can't see anything."

"You're lying on your stomach," Grady explained. "Your entire back is covered with burns, second and third degree. The backs of your legs and your feet were also burned badly and need grafts. I'm right here. I can't touch your skin. Infection risk, but here's my hand."

He put his gloved hand below her face so she could see him. She tried to reach for it, but her arms were encased in bandages.

"I'm burned, right? Real bad? I thought I died," Linx muttered, a little disappointed she hadn't been transferred to Heaven—although now that she thought about it, Heaven would be much better than a bunch of white pads and a friendly voice.

"Then I would have wished to die with you," Grady said. "I never realized how much I loved you until I almost lost you."

"That close, huh?" She felt her face crack in a painful smirk. "I had to almost die for you to say it and mean it."

He cleared his throat. "I've always meant it before, but pretended I didn't. Too scared to admit it."

"Same here." Linx tried to take his hand, but hers was wrapped up like a mummy's. "Forgive me, Grady."

"I forgive you, even though you didn't do anything wrong."

"Oh, I did a lot to hurt you, starting with Cedar and then Jessie." Linx closed her eyes, exhausted by even the effort to speak.

"I hurt you, too." Grady's voice was raspy. "I didn't believe you, and I ran from my responsibilities. I had no right to play with your heart. I was a jerk."

"You weren't. I understand you and forgive you," Linx barely breathed. "Will we make it? For real?"

"Yes. We have our whole lives ahead of us," Grady said. "I wish I could kiss you, but I'll have to wait."

"Yes, please, and Grady? I forgive you everything, but please ask God to forgive you before it's too late."

He leaned close and she could feel his breath. "I already have, when I sat by your bedside and prayed for you. I asked Jesus to save both me and you."

"I did, too. Thank you, God." Linx nodded despite the pain radiating from her burns. Her eyelids were heavy and she wasn't sure if Grady had left her side.

Jessie and Ginger were safe and well. God had forgiven her and let them live. She could relax as the fiery pain receded and she drifted into a cool and soothing beachside cabana, lulled by the smooth sounds of a slow rolling surf.

Chapter Forty-One

Gentle hands changed her bandages, and soft voices hovered above her, but Linx's mind was full of cotton, not fully understanding. The pain ebbed and flowed, growing stronger at times and then receding like the tide.

She was alive, but no one told her what had happened to Minx. Had she been arrested? Or had she escaped? What if she'd been burned to death? The nurses mentioned someone else who hadn't been as lucky.

Could Minx be dead?

The next time Grady visited, Linx asked him about Minx.

"She's actually outside waiting for you," Grady replied. "Shall I ask her to come in?"

"But, why isn't she in jail?"

"I'll let her tell you herself," Grady said.

Linx closed her eyes and waited for Grady's footsteps to depart. Why should she see Mean Minx before she saw her father and her brothers and sisters? Maybe the sheriff had a special deal with her to let her apologize before locking her up for good.

Moments later, the door opened and someone approached her bed. Linx tried to turn her head to the side to get a better look, but her head was held suspended and all she could see was the white pillow. She was braced in some sort of face down support foam to keep pressure off her burned back.

"Nurse?" she asked. "Can you help me turn my head so I can see?"

"Of course," the nurse answered. "We're trying to keep as much pressure off of your backside as possible."

The nurse adjusted the pillow and turned her head to the side as a gowned figure sat down on the chair next to her. She wore a face mask, but her eyes were sharp and sultry at the same time.

"Your father called me, and I came as soon as I could," she said, her voice soft and airy—not at all the rough and gravelly voice of the woman on the phone.

"Wait, why aren't you in jail for kidnapping? How did you get Jessie into the trailer? Why am I talking to you? You tried to kill her and the puppy."

Her mother spread her gloved hand. "I guess Grady didn't tell you. It wasn't me you spoke to on the phone. I was traveling through Nevada when I got the news."

"Wasn't you?" Linx's voice was hoarse and strained. She tried to lift herself, but pain screamed through her bandages. "You told me that story about the Black Widow and the Firestarter. You said I had an evil heart like yours. You—"

"You told all of this to your friend, Salem," Minx explained. "When Todd found her in the van, she was still talking on the phone, gloating about how she was going to get you arrested for kidnapping Jessie and setting fire to the trailer. She wanted to ruin yours and Grady's lives because she believed you two ruined hers."

"Salem Pryde? But she'd dead, isn't she?"

"Apparently not," her mother patted her bandaged hand. "Although she's burned badly. Once she realized she was surrounded, she doused gasoline all over her van and lit it up. Of course, your brother had no idea Jessie and the puppy weren't being held hostage, so they rushed in and rescued her. It turns out Jessie's old dog was tied up to a tree outside the van, and they were able to save her."

"Why did she do it? She had everything going for her. Paul, does he know?"

"Todd says she wanted to speak to Grady. It turns out she was pregnant, but lost the baby."

"Whose baby?" Linx tried to lift her head, and all her skin chafed with pain.

"It no longer matters," Minx said. "She doesn't know, and this kind of stuff only comes between you if you let it."

"Like it did for you and Dad?" Linx had so many questions. "Salem says I'm a fake Colson. Where would she have gotten that information? Is Dad my father?"

"Salem spoke to other people, pretending to be me. She told everyone I was a chain smoker, and since I'd been away so long, they believed her. Perhaps she spoke to your father and he talked about it ..." Minx trailed off.

"Really?" Warning prickles stabbed the back of Linx's burned skin. "You must be lying. Dad would know your voice anywhere."

"How dare you call me a liar?" Her mother's voice lowered from the saccharine sweetness she'd exhibited earlier. "I had an alibi. You can't pin this on me."

"Salem, or you, claim I'm not a Colson," Linx persisted. "So tell me, who is my father?"

"Your father is Joe Colson," Minx said. "Salem was stirring the pot."

"And you know this how?" Linx jerked her face and narrowed her eyes, despite the pain, staring straight into her mother's eyes—the ones that mirrored hers.

"Why are you so distrustful?" Minx stood. "I came to see you because Joe asked me to. Now, don't get any ideas that we'll ever be mother-daughter."

"Do you hate me because of my real father?"

"I don't hate you." She bent over so close, Linx thought she'd kiss her through the face mask. Instead, she whispered, "I left because I would only have abused you."

"Then I forgive you, and we can start over."

"No. I am old, and I can't change. I'll leave a sculpture for you next Christmas." She kissed the air between them. "Goodbye."

* * *

"How's she doing?" Mark and Jean Patterson asked Grady when he entered the hospital cafeteria for breakfast.

"Much better." Grady picked up a plate of sausage and eggs from the grill. "She's in a lot of pain, but able to stay awake for longer periods. Her mother came by to see her."

"That's good, isn't it?" Jean asked, wringing her hands. "I can't believe Salem impersonated Linx's mother."

"Shouldn't the voices have been different?" the pastor asked.

"Maybe, although Salem was good at impersonating people." Jean put a small dish of Jello on her tray, topping it with fresh blueberries. "I should have been suspicious when she did the Easter skit and played the part of so many of Jesus's disciples, each with a different voice."

"Was Salem the fairy godmother Jessie spoke about?" Grady's eyebrows shot up and a chill slithered up his spine.

"The police have a child psychologist working with Jessie to figure it out, but as far as we know, Salem was a sweet member of our congregation and she did a lot of babysitting," the pastor said. "All the children and parents loved her and no one can believe she did this."

"What if Linx's mother framed her?" Jean collected two cartons of chocolate milk, putting one on the pastor's tray.

Grady scratched his head. "She has an alibi. The police checked it out. The person Linx was speaking to on the phone was Salem."

"True," Jean agreed. "I guess we have to be more careful who we allow to work in the church nursery."

"I'm putting together a new policy," Pastor Mark said. "New members cannot work in the nursery and we must have two adults present at any given time. One must be a member for more than five years."

"Sounds wonderful," Jean said.

They paid for their meals and found a small round table.

"We'd like to speak to you and Linx together, if possible," Pastor Mark said after saying grace.

"Yes, we are ever so grateful for the two of you saving Jessie's life," Jean added.

"Linx did all of it," Grady said. "Both of us would give our lives for her."

"We know you would," Pastor Mark said. He shook salt and pepper over his eggs and dug in, avoiding Grady's gaze.

"Yes," Jean replied, but she looked worried.

They ate in awkward silence, as Grady wondered how he should proceed. On the one hand, Becca had assured him that a judge would hear the case once he had a positive paternity test, but the grace period for the adoption had expired long ago.

It wasn't fair, and even though he'd forgiven Linx, it still burned that he'd essentially had no say on who would raise his daughter.

That moment when he thought he'd lost both Linx and Jessie was seared in his soul. He'd never experienced such raw fear, such paralyzing terror, and then the utter blessedness of sweet relief when he found Jessie and the puppy alive and unharmed under Linx's protective body.

She'd taken the brunt, protected them with her back on fire, and she'd kept the fire shelter over them tightly, despite the pain raging over her every nerve.

Linx had fought to keep Jessie alive. She'd done the heavy lifting, and now Grady had to do his part—take the pain in his heart to let Jessie thrive emotionally.

Grady swallowed the tasteless toast and cleared his throat. He caught the pastor's gaze and said, "I know you're worried that I'm going to fight Jessie's adoption. I never had a say in it, and it wasn't fair what Linx did to me."

Both Mark and Jean froze, eyes wide and fearful.

"I know how you feel," Grady continued, "because at that moment when I thought Jessie had been burned to death, my entire heart and soul caved in."

"You don't have to explain," Jean's voice squeaked. "We all love her and want what's best for her."

"Yes, that's what I want," Grady said. "And I have to follow my heart on this. In my family, we have a motto, 'heart comes first.' Even though logically, I should fight for my right as Jessie's father, I know in my heart it would hurt her. It would hurt all of us."

"What are you telling us?" Mark asked.

"I'm not going to pursue custody. I love Jessie and all I want is for her to heal after this ordeal. I want her to be loved and cherished, not fought over like a piece of meat." Grady dropped his gaze to the table.

If heart really came first, why did doing the right thing slice his heart into tiny pieces?

Chapter Forty-Two

Fourth of July descended on the tiny town of Colson's Corner, and Grady's family also descended on the burn unit to celebrate the holiday with him and Linx.

Grady looked up from the waiting room couch as his twin sister, Jenna, and his brother-in-law Larry entered with a tray of food and coffee.

The results of the paternity test had come back the day before, and Grady couldn't wait to share the results with Linx.

"Oh, Grady." Jenna gave him a tight, warm hug. "You need to come home and sleep in a real bed."

"Hey, man, we didn't mean to kick you out of our place," Larry said. "You and Linx will always have a home with us."

"Get out of here." Grady pushed his sister back, winking. "I'm not a homeless bum. Don't act like you had anything to do with this."

"Maybe not this immediate disaster," Jenna said. "But we all should have been friendlier to Linx. How is she doing?"

"She's in a lot of pain, and she's already had a few surgeries to repair the skin on her feet and legs." That area had taken the brunt, since fire shelters were deployed so that the feet pointed toward the advancing flames.

"Can she come out of her room?"

"Her back and buttocks are still painful, so she can't sit in a wheelchair, but she can turn over on the air mattress for short periods of time," Grady said.

"Great, then we can have a party." Jenna jiggled his arm. "It's Jessie's birthday, and the Pattersons agreed to have it in the hospital if Linx is up for it. As for you, you need to get a proper shower and shave for your daughter's sixth birthday."

Grady gulped down the eggs and toast, then washed it down with a cup of coffee. "First, let me speak to Linx. Then I'll go with you, but I'm not going to the festivities tonight."

"What about the puppy auction?" Larry asked. "Ginger's bid is up to seven thousand dollars."

"I can't afford that kind of money." Grady shrugged, rubbing his couple day's growth of beard. "As much as I know Jessie wants her, the price went even higher after all the news went out on how the puppy survived a fire. Jessie will get over it."

"Hey, it's okay." Jenna hugged him. "She has more than a lot of kids, including two sets of parents."

"Right. Let me tell Linx the good news. Thanks for breakfast." Grady looked Jenna in the eye. "Tell everyone not to worry about me and Linx, will you?"

"Okay, sure. I have faith in you," Jenna said. "And her. She may be fiery, but she has a good heart."

"A real good heart." He placed his hand over his heart.

"Yep, heart comes first," Jenna said. "And Linx Colson has one of the best."

After Jenna and Larry took off, Grady washed his hands and combed his hair, then stepped into Linx's room.

She was lying on her side, but sat up when he entered. The bandages were still layered over her hands and feet, but she was smiling. Despite the burns on her face, and her lack of eyebrows and singed hair, she was still the most beautiful sight in his eyes.

He kissed her over her bandages, being careful not to touch her injured skin. "How'd you sleep?"

"Okay, but are the dogs safe?"

"Yes, they're back at the rescue center. Nessa's helping Tami with the festival and auction. You don't have a thing to worry about."

"That's good. I sure do miss Cedar and Ginger."

"How about me?" He quirked a grin at her. "You don't miss me?"

"Jealous, much?" She winked and scrunched her nose. "You know I can't get enough of you, but really, you need to go home and shower. Have you even left the hospital?"

"When you leave, I'll leave."

"Great. I can leave tomorrow," she said. "The doctor says I'm healing well."

"What about the skin grafts? We have to make sure they don't get infected."

"Right, I'll need help changing my bandages, but I've got plenty of sisters."

"You have me." He brushed a patch of hair across a bald spot over her ear.

"I look hideous. It's bad enough that you're seeing me now." She grimaced. "It'll take months for my skin to heal, and my hair to grow back."

"You're not going to stop me from seeing you." He pulled up a chair. "I'm not going back to firefighting. I've decided to stay with Dogs for Vets, and if you'll have me, I'll work out of your office and live in your cabin while I rebuild."

"But, wait, you never told me why you took a break in the first place. Was it Salem? Were you waiting for her baby to be born?"

He pressed his lips tightly. "No, I believed her to be dead, but I promised Paul I would stay out as long as he did."

"How's he doing now that he found out Salem was still alive?"

"Shocked, but he's going back to the fire lines, although not back to Redstone." He didn't want to tell her that Salem was in dire condition and barely hanging onto life.

"And the baby? Is he Paul's son?" Linx's voice broke into a hushed croak.

"No. It—"

Linx's eyes widened and she reached for him. "We'll get through it, Grady. It's my choice to accept your son into my life."

"Wait, she lost the baby," Grady quickly added. "As far as we can figure out, she made crosses for each of the men she suspected. Todd found more crosses at the artist's cabin. She'd been squatting there, and she took Jessie there in her fairy wagon. She kept Betsy there, too, but Betsy got away when she set fire to my parents' place."

"It was all about revenge?" Linx's eyes popped wide.

"She's not talking, so we won't know until she does. They've taken her to a prison burn unit, but Paul says he's got a lawyer who's going to use the mental health defense."

"I hope she gets the help she needs." Linx swallowed a lump in her throat. "Why did she hate us so much?"

"She was jealous that you actually had my child." Grady's shoulders slumped. "Or at least that was Paul's theory. This isn't going to drive a wedge between us, is it?"

"Not as long as we communicate. Will you promise me we'll always communicate? First priority?" she asked, her face so earnest and open, especially without her doubting eyebrows.

"I promise." He trained his gaze on her, beaming as much love and reassurance as he could. "Let's decide that we will always communicate in person. No text messages and emails. We will always be sure who we're talking to."

"Right, I agree. Always face to face or voice to voice." Linx blinked at him, her eyes full of emotion. "How stupid I was to be fooled by Salem."

"Hey, it wasn't just you."

"True. What I don't get is why she was so hateful? Why hadn't she been honest with Paul, and gone back to him once she lost the baby?"

"He said he'd told her his parents were freezing all his accounts until the baby was proved to be his," Grady said. "When I told her he was going to propose, if only she'd figure out who the father was, it likely pushed her over the edge, and she purposely steered her chute into the fire."

"She was always good at pinpointing a landing place."

"Right. She found a way into the black, where the fire had moved on. In the heavy smoke, none of us could tell where she'd landed. From there, she disappeared, but was able to rob Paul's accounts. He's so fricking rich, he didn't notice until months later when he bounced a check."

Linx swallowed and shook her head. "I feel bad for the whole situation. I'm sorry if you lost your baby, if it was yours."

"The good news is that Jessie is mine." His face broke into a smile. "We got the results, and the Pattersons already know."

"I never had a doubt." What was left of her eyebrows furrowed. "I never slept with anyone else, and the only drunken sex I had was with you."

"I knew she was mine, too," Grady said. "But Becca said we needed the test for her to proceed."

"Are you going to tear Jessie away from her parents? You should have heard her crying for her mommy and daddy." Linx's eyes watered. "I held her, thinking we would both die, and I told her to live for her mommy and daddy. I told her I loved her, but that she had to go back to them."

"I'm not going to fight them." Grady grasped Linx's bandaged hand. "I needed to know for sure. There's no way I could rip her away from them, no matter how much I love her."

"Me either. I never knew I could love someone so much." A tear trailed from the corner of her eye.

"Same here." Grady swallowed, touching his chest. "She's truly our little angel—the best of both of us."

"Yes, God really blessed us, didn't He?"

"And he blessed me with you. I love you, Linx Colson." Grady air kissed Linx, but she leaned forward and their lips met, tender and full of love, comfort, and hope for a blessed future.

"And this black heart of mine loves you, too, Grady Hart."

* * *

"Happy birthday to me. Happy birthday to me," Jessie danced around Linx's wheelchair. The staff had agreed to let Jessie have her birthday party in one of their conference rooms.

Both Linx and Grady's large families crowded around, clapping and singing as Jessie got hugs from everyone.

"Miss Linx, I got to sit in a fire truck," Jessie bragged. "On Fourth of July. My birthday."

"Did you wave at everyone?" Linx asked, her chest filling with pride at how quickly her daughter had bounced back from the terror of the fire, with the help of Miss Sharon. Of course, she would continue therapy for a while, to make sure no lingering effects haunted her.

"Yes, and I'm a real fire sur-vi-vor." She made muscles with both arms as she enunciated each syllable. "All because of Wonder Woman."

"You are a survivor," Linx said, "because you're smart and you're not going to let any strangers trick you, right?"

Mrs. Patterson had pulled Linx aside and told her that Salem Pryde, under an assumed name, had joined the church a few months ago. She'd seemed harmless and volunteered in the nursery, gaining the trust of all the church members and of course, Jessie, who'd talked her ear off about the tiny puppy Linx rescued at the shelter.

On that fateful Saturday, Salem had spied Jessie opening the gates and letting out the dogs, then again when Jessie came back that afternoon, whining to her mother about wishing Ginger could be hers. She'd simply waited until everyone was gone, broke into the center easily through an open window, stole Ginger, and let the rest of the dogs out.

She was going to frame Linx for the kidnapping and murder, so she texted Becca, having already fooled her into thinking that phone number belonged to Minx and told her that she missed Linx. Becca had then texted her Linx's phone number. Easy peasy.

Salem knew it was the optimum time to strike. She could kill two birds with one firebrand—burn up Grady's place and frame Linx.

It was mincemeat pie for her to show up at the church with the puppy under her skirt and lure Jessie into her fairy wagon, the old VW van she had which was covered with moons and stars.

Linx shuddered at how diabolical Salem turned out to be, and what a close call they all had by not communicating face to face, but relying on text messages.

"I won't talk to any grownups unless Mommy and Daddy say it's okay." Jessie stood straight and tall, proud of herself. "And I promise I won't run away to join the circus or play with fairies."

Despite her bandages, Linx reached out and hugged Jessie to her chest. "Did you walk in the dog parade? I want to hear all about it."

"I did!" Jessie squealed. "I took Ginger on her first walk. She kept tripping over her leash and then biting it."

"She wanted to hold onto her side of the leash," Linx said. "I bet you did great. How about holding the dog pictures?"

"I held every picture up high and all the dogs got lots of money." Jessie clapped her hands. "Ginger got the most money. Ten thousand dollars."

"Wow!" everyone in the room exclaimed.

"The other dogs did well, too," Grady said. "Nessa is back at the center sorting everything out. If you're checked out tomorrow, I'm sure you'll meet a lot of the new owners. Even Bob got adopted."

"Really? Who?"

Linx's father raised his hand. "Bob's just my style. Grumpy but lovable."

"Oh, Dad!" Linx reached for a hug. "I'm so happy for him. He's really a wonderful dog. You'll love him."

"I already do." Her father smiled.

"What about the basset hound mother?" Linx asked. "I feel bad for her, since all of her puppies got adopted."

"She has a new family, too." Grady beamed at Cait. "Now, both of my sisters have basset hounds, a male one and a female one."

"I can't wait for the puppies," Dale exclaimed, wiggling his eyebrows.

"Did you say puppies?" Jessie skipped over. "Who has puppies?"

Linx's father picked Jessie up and put her on his lap. "Are we ready for your birthday presents?"

"Yay, and then we have cake!" Jessie flapped her hands. "I get red, white, and blue because I was born on the Fourth of July."

Everyone gathered around as Jessie picked from a pile of gifts and posed for pictures with each person. Linx marveled at how quickly the little girl took to all of her new aunties and uncles, as well as two new grandpas and one new grandma.

"We'd better hurry if we want to see the fireworks," Pastor Patterson said, while Mrs. Patterson carried in a sheet cake complete with miniature flags and the stars and stripes.

"I wish we'd had time to give Jessie a present," Linx whispered to Grady, as she sat with her head on his shoulder.

"Being godparents means we'll have plenty of chances to spoil her."

"Yes, we will." Linx pressed a kiss onto his lips. "And plenty of chances to be together as a family."

She'd never truly appreciated her large family until now. In the past, she'd felt stifled and suffocated, but this past week, both her and Grady's families had been full of comfort and hope—knowing there was always someone to help and many someones who cared.

The conference room door swung open and Paul stepped in. He was wearing a Santa Claus costume and held a squirmy sack over his shoulder.

"Is that the only costume you could come up with?" Grady laughed and clapped his friend on the shoulder.

"Hey, all the miner and sheriff costumes are gone," Paul said. "But, ho, ho, ho, I'm delivering Jessie's birthday present from you and Linx."

"Santa!" Jessie skipped over to Paul and twirled around, showing her cape and muscles. "You're early."

"Ho, ho, ho, and a very merry birthday to you." Paul opened the sack and extracted the wriggly red-haired puppy. "From your godparents, Mr. Grady and Miss Linx, to their little sweet angel."

"Grady, you didn't!" Linx exclaimed, clapping a hand over her mouth as she stared at feisty little Ginger.

"I didn't." Grady's eyes popped wide. "She was too expensive, remember?"

"I love her." Jessie squealed as she took the puppy she had survived the fire with from Paul. "Thank you, Santa, and thank you, godparents! God bless us every one."

Grady and Linx embraced Jessie and Ginger, and then both families and the Pattersons piled in for a giant group hug.

"Wooahh!" Little Ginger howled from the center of all the loving arms. She was most definitely the summer love puppy who brought many hearts together.

~ The End ~

Thank you for reading Linx and Grady's story. I hope you enjoyed it. Dale and Nessa are next in a fun-loving romance with Nessa's two mutts, Randi and Ronni. Please turn the page to read an excerpt from *Dog Days of Love*.

Dog Days of Love, Have a Hart #7

USA Today Bestselling Author
RACHELLE AYALA

Dog Days of Love
Have A Hart Romance

Can a woman looking for Mr. Perfect settle for a happy-go-lucky Mr. Wrong?

Vanessa Ransom has high standards and she's on the hunt for the perfect man. With limited time for a social life, she hires college dropout Dale Hart to walk her dogs and clean her house. Just for kicks, she decides to motivate him to succeed, only to find herself falling in love with him.

Can Dale show Vanessa that love doesn't come with a perfect report card or will Vanessa refuse to settle for Dale until he gets his act together?

Chapter One

Vanessa Ransom couldn't afford to sweat.

Not while stumbling after her two dogs through Golden Gate Park wearing a stiff business suit and a pair of power pumps.

The hot summer sun beat overhead, and waves of heat shimmered over the sweltering city streets—an unusually hot day for San Francisco.

Her two darling mutts, Randi and Ronni, circled around her legs, looking for that perfect place to potty. They sniffed every bush and fence post, tails wagging and tongues lolling, but they wouldn't settle down and do their business.

Vanessa, or Nessa, as she was known to her friends checked the time on her phone. She had a job interview clear across the city and she was running late.

Randi, a black and white rat terrier sheltie mix, pulled on her leash, lunging at a little boy bouncing a ball. Meanwhile, Ronni, a shepherd terrier mix with soft brown hair laid down on the grass and put her head down.

"Come on, you two. Any bush will do."

If only her dogs would hurry up. She had a job interview clear across town and she didn't want to be late.

"Woof, woof," Randi barked at a floating Frisbee, her upright ears alert and tail wagging.

Snap. Ronni leaped and snagged the Frisbee, as a man jogged up with his hand outstretched.

"Good dog." He patted Ronni, and she dropped the Frisbee at his feet.

Randi barked and nudged her way between them, hopping up on her hind legs for the Frisbee.

"Mind if I play with them?" the man asked. His light-brown eyes twinkled as he took her in, from her perfectly pressed hair to her starched blouse, understated silver jewelry, gray suit and skirt, and black leather pumps.

He was younger than her, tall, handsome, and white.

"I'm actually crunched for time," Nessa said, waving her cell phone. "Taking them out for a bathroom break before I head across town for an important interview."

"Best of luck, then," the man said. He threw his Frisbee, and it soared high in the air currents across the lawn.

She couldn't help her gaze from following its arc. It floated free and easy, like the man with his tousled curls and lazy grin.

He waved at Nessa before stretching out his long legs and chased after the Frisbee. What kind of weirdo played Frisbee by himself while hoping to pick up other people's dogs?

Randi barked and pulled against her leash, while Ronni gave Nessa an imploring look.

"Come on, you two," Nessa tugged at their leashes. "I'm sorry we can't play today. How about a trip to Fort Funston this weekend?"

Both dogs stared longingly at the man and his Frisbee, and Nessa couldn't help checking out the guy's physique. Tall, but not lanky, the man was well built but not bulky. He wore board shorts, a Warriors jersey, and sneakers without socks, and he was most likely unemployed.

Sure enough, he picked up his Frisbee and waved it at a Dalmatian who jumped up and down, eager to play. He had better luck, because the Dalmatian's owner, an Asian woman, laughed and unclipped its leash.

Score one for the white guy, Nessa thought. Not that she cared. Her mother had a short list of criteria for her as far as men were concerned, and even though race was not mentioned, gainful employment was at the top of the list.

A text message chimed, and Nessa groaned.

It was from the recruiting firm. *Are you able to come earlier? The managing director has a conflict. Half hour okay?*

Yes, I'll be there. Nessa texted back.

The sun broiled overhead, and sweat popped over Nessa's forehead. California was stuck under a state-wide heat wave, with highs, even in San Francisco, topping a hundred degrees.

Without another glance at Frisbee Man, Nessa commanded her dogs to heel. She marched toward the park exit at a rapid pace despite the sweat soaking through her suit.

She had no room in her life for carefree bums. That was one privilege she couldn't indulge in, no matter how hot the package.

* * *

Dale Hart let his brother's Dalmatian, Cinder, sniff at the Frisbee before flinging it high into the sky.

With a sharp bark, Cinder raced after the spinning disc. Dalmatians were one of the fastest breeds of dogs and extremely focused.

"You throw it too high, and it'll get stuck in a tree," his sister-in-law, Nadine, commented with her eyes glued to her phone.

A year ago, she'd been the one stuck in a tree with her kitty, Greyheart, when his eldest brother, Connor, had rescued her.

Of course, height wasn't his aim—it was distance.

The pretty, but businesslike black woman was Dr. Vanessa Ransom, Ph.D. in Psychology, and an acquaintance of his other brother, Grady, who ran Dogs for Vets, a charity matching veterans to therapy dogs.

Vanessa was an intern with the Veteran's Administration and a certified dog trainer who spent all her time on other people's dogs, but barely let her own mutts out to play. She could be seen racing across the park three times a day, plastic bags in one hand and phone in the other. As soon as both dogs relieved themselves, it would be game over for them and back to her apartment across from the fire station.

"You keep staring at her, and your eyes are going to combust," Nadine said, coming up to his side. "Excellent aim."

The wind lifted the Frisbee high, and then, because Vanessa was downhill from them, its descent was prolonged, drawing the attention of both of Vanessa's dogs.

The hyperactive black and white rat terrier mix yelped sharply and jumped for the Frisbee, while the more laid-back brown shepherd mix circled Vanessa's legs, barking encouragement.

Not to be outdone, Cinder leaped, flying magnificently through the air, her jaw wide open, her entire attention zeroed in on the yellow disc, her athletic and streamlined body a blur of spots and white.

Bam!

A tangle of brown, black, white and spotted fur spun like a funnel cloud touching down. Vanessa's arms windmilled, her phone went flying along with the plastic poop bags. The dogs' leashes wrapped around her legs and down she went, while Cinder and the rat terrier played tug-of-war with the Frisbee.

Dale sprinted down the hill. He edged out a man on a bicycle who laid his bike down to help. Swooping down on his prey, he lifted her up high.

"Are you okay?"

Rip! Her skirt tore, exposing her black laced panties and stockings. Dale's eyes caught fire as he struggled to avert them from her slim and shapely thighs.

Vanessa screamed, "Let me down. You're stepping on my clothes."

"Oops." Dale dropped her, a little too fast, and she turned her ankle, lurching backward.

By reflex, he yanked her sleeve, but she slipped from the suit jacket, popping the buttons, and landed on her brown dog, who gave a yelp of pain.

Cinder let go of the Frisbee and snagged Vanessa's fallen shoe. That dog had always had a women's shoe fetish, and quick as a whip, she raced away from the other two dogs to keep her prize.

By now, a crowd of people gathered around, and several punks pulled out their cameras to take videos.

Vanessa's hands flailed around, trying to pull up her torn skirt. Her brown dog leaped over her and licked her, tugging at her neat bun and smearing her makeup.

Her black and white terrier pounced on the suit jacket and shook it like a drowned rat, growling and pawing at it.

"I need my shoe back, and give me my jacket." Vanessa grabbed at her jacket, but the dog thought she was playing tug of war and dug in its heels.

"Miss, your phone's broken," Nadine said, picking up Vanessa's discarded phone.

"I need to get to my interview." She stared at her phone while trying to cover her abdomen and thighs with what remained of her skirt. "I need to get back to my apartment to change and call a taxi."

"I can help." Dale stripped off his tank top. "Here, put this on."

Instead of waiting for her to respond, he pulled the tank top over her arms and shoulders and picked her up. Thank goodness for oversized and overlong basketball jerseys.

"I still need my shoe," Vanessa cried. "And I'm going to be late."

"I've got this." Dale hefted her over his shoulder like a caveman with his bride and headed down the hill toward her apartment.

"But, my dogs are loose."

Dale whistled and picked up the Frisbee, and like the pied piper of old, he led a trail of dogs and bystanders across Martin Luther King Blvd and out the South Gate of the park.

"How do you know the way to my apartment?" Vanessa demanded, her legs flipping against his stomach as he walked.

"I see you at the ramen shop across from the station all the time."

"Stalker."

"No, rescuer. All my brothers are firefighters, but I prefer saving pretty women," Dale said. "Dale Hart, Chief Connor Hart's brother."

"Ah, now I know who you are. You're Grady's baby brother." Nessa wiggled and punched his back lightly with her fists. "And this is not a fireman carry."

"In that case." Dale shifted her horizontally across the back of his shoulders and stuck his arm between her legs, grabbing her front hand. "You asked for it."

This was turning out much better than he'd thought.

Vanessa was wearing his shirt.

He had a body part between her legs.

And he held her hand.

Dale grinned to himself until he felt the slap across his behind. "Let me down. I don't need rescuing."

Instead of obeying, he jogged across the street when the light turned green, bouncing her all over him, another one for the record books, as she made guttural, ah, ah, ah sounds—oh yeah, sweet music, that climaxed into a scream when he dropped her in front of her door.

"My keys! Where are they?"

[End of Excerpt, to read more, please look for *Dog Days of Love* at your favorite online bookstore.]

Many Thanks

This book would not have been possible without the diligent help and suggestions from my writing bestie, Chantel Rhondeau, who read it through twice. Many thanks also go to my beta reading team for pointing out things they liked and disliked. Thank you, Gina Griffin Johnson, Becky Brown, Barbara Cassata, Janine Waters, Charlene Burlison, Frances Hampton, Angi DeMonti, Patricia Rose, Audrey McGee Griffis, Sherelle Ellis, Jacqueline Driggers, Susan Delamare, Angelica Lichtnerova, Chantel Rhondeau, Reggaewoman, Becky Pelc, Carol Smith, Amber McCallister, Carol Smith, Yomari Suarez-Rivera, and Melissa Santoro.

Thanks also to my awesome proofreader, Kimberly Dawn, and Ella Gram did a final read through.

Special gratitude goes to Sherelle Ellis, who helped me get all of my details in a row. I really appreciate your dedication and kindness, as well as your sharp and logical mind.

Every book is a journey, and I invite readers to come along with Grady and Linx's story. My appreciation lies with you for reading and understanding these two characters.

Please let me know if you'd like to see more Hart Family stories, where Heart always comes first.

About the Author

Rachelle Ayala is a *USA Today* bestselling author of dramatic romantic suspense and humorous contemporary romances. Her heroines are feisty and her heroes big-hearted. She writes sweet and funny stories, and believes in the power of love and hope.

She is the winner of multiple awards:

Knowing Vera, 2015 Angie Ovation Award, Multicultural Romance

A Father for Christmas, 2015 Readers' Favorite Gold Award, Christian Romance

Christmas Stray, 2016 Readers' Favorite Gold Award, Christian Romance

A Pet for Christmas, 2016 Readers' Favorite Honorable Mention, Christian Romance

Playing for the Save, 2017 Readers' Favorite Gold Award, Realistic Fiction.

For updates and a surprise free book, sign up for Rachelle's newsletter at: http://smarturl.it/RachAyala

Check out her Reader's Guide at:
http://rachelleayala.me/reading-guide/

To chat and read new works in progress, join her Reader's Club at:
http://www.facebook.com/groups/ClubRachelleAyala/